The LAWS of

MENTAL MAGNETISM:

Your Personal Miracle Maker

JOHN TREADWELL

©1967 BY
PARKER PUBLISHING.

Re-published by Stax in agreement with Parker in 2024.

All rights reserved. No part of this publication may be reproduced, distributed, or transmitted in any form or by any means, including photocopying, recording, or other electronic or mechanical methods, without the prior written permission of the publisher, except in the case of brief quotations embodied in critical reviews and certain other noncommercial uses permitted by copyright law.

DEDICATION

This book is dedicated to the greater enjoyment of life for all people.

It emphasizes the existence of all the good things that make for a rich, happy, successful life. It high-lights the Magnetic Power of attraction which all people have within them, and it shows how this power can be used to attract the riches of life. It contains many practical methods for attracting health, wealth, and happiness.

May you, the reader, as the result of using your own Power of Mental Magnetism, attract and re-ceive an abundance of all of the good things that life has to offer you.

How the Miraculous Laws of Mental Magnetism Can Give You a Richer Life

This book will be of amazing benefit to you. It will show you how to use the magnetic forces of your own mind to attract all of the good things life has to offer you.

How many times have you desired to have something very special, and failed to receive it? There was a reason for this happening—you had not as yet learned how to use the Laws of Mental Magnetism effectively.

HOW THE LAWS OF MENTAL MAGNETISM CAN BENEFIT YOU

Every good thing that you can possibly desire already exists in a completed state for you to claim. You do not have to mold and fashion good health, for instance; good health, as you well know, does exist, for you, for everyone. So does self-confidence, courage, and the will to succeed. New opportunities, peace of mind, and happiness also already exist. You have the power to attract all of these good things to you. You also have the power to attract great fame and fortune. However, in order to do so you must first put the Laws of Mental Magnetism into action in order to draw to yourself what you desire to have.

HOW THE LAW OF MAGNETIC MENTAL ATTRACTION OPERATES

The three most important elements of Mental Magnetism are imagination, desire, and faith. You have used these attributes of your mind day in and day out, perhaps not knowing that they have made you what you are and have caused you to have what you have. However, when you know how to use them with *deliberate intention,* these faculties will attract everything needed to give you an abundance of health, wealth, happiness, and success. How? By your visualizing and making a vivid picture of what you desire to attract, thus making a deep impression of that picture upon your subconscious mind. You must also firmly believe that the magnetic power of your subconscious mind will draw to you exactly what you have visualized and cause you to receive that thing.

HOW THE LAWS OF MENTAL MAGNETISM CAN GIVE YOU A NEW LIFE

Regardless of what condition or circumstance you may now be in, you can start yourself in a new direction. You can attract and enjoy new vigor and health. You can attract and express dynamic courage. You can attract prosperity in great abundance. You can attract new friends and companions. You can attract and experience safety and protection at all times. You can, by using your talents effectively, gain great public acclaim. In other words, when you practice the Laws of Mental Magnetism conscientiously and with purposeful intent, all manner of miracles of successful living will happen to you.

NOW IS THE TIME TO ENJOY A RICHER LIFE

It is a fact that the past is gone forever. It is a fact that the present is the time of reality and what you are in the present will become your future. Many people have realized this truth and have used their imagination and faith to change their lives miraculously through the use of the Laws of Mental Magnetism. I have seen a total failure do this and become a millionaire. I knew one of the world's greatest inventors who became so by using his imagination and power of magnetic faith. I have seen all kinds of miracles happen to people who have practiced the Laws of Mental Magnetism. I have even had a broken shoulder of mine knit and heal completely by my own use of these Laws.

This book will show you how to adjust to or eliminate any problem you may have, and how to attract the beneficial opposite of that problem to you. Each and every day without fail follow the programs of the miracle-working Laws of Mental Magnetism set out in this book. Do so, and you will attract an abundance of all good things to you. Do so and you will experience a rich, happy, successful and enjoyable life.

CONTENTS

1. YOUR POWER OF MENTAL MAGNETISM: HOW IT CAN ENRICH YOUR LIFE 19

    Your Magnetic Power that Can Attract Great Riches • How to Discover Your Magnetic Power • How to Convince Yourself that Mental Magnetism Exists • The Laws of Mental Magnetism • How to Find a New Interest in Life • How John Ferris Turned His Hobby into a King-Sized Business • How I Attracted Great Success on the Stage • Why a Rich Full Life Is Important to You • How One Risked All to Gain Fame and Fortune • You Too Have Power to Make Your Dreams Come True • Mental Magnetism Reminders

2. HOW TO BREAK CAREER-CRIPPLING HABITS AND GAIN PERSONAL SELF-CONFIDENCE . . . 30

    How to Overcome Timidity and Gain Self-Confidence • How to Conquer Self-Pity • How to Change Laziness into Self-Confidence • How to Believe in Yourself and Your Power of Attraction • A Morning Exercise to Gain Self-Confidence • A Bed-time Exercise to Gain Self-Confidence • How Self-Confidence Increases Your Power of Mental Magnetism • How I Used Self-Confidence to Land a Well-Paying Job • Things to Avoid when Building Self-Confidence • How to Put Life and Feeling into Self-Confidence • Self-Confidence Reminders

3. HOW TO PLAN A RICH, NEW, DYNAMIC LIFE . 39

    How to Acquire Right Mental Attitudes • How to Change Your Personal Reflection • How to Rise Above Petty Annoyances • How to Develop Your Self-Importance • How to Make Your Personal Influence Felt by Others • How to Make Friends of Enemies • How One Man Attracted Good Fortune • How to Take Out a Shiny New Lease on

Contents

Life • How to Choose Things that Will Do You the Most Good • How to Make Your New Plan Come True • The Law of Repetition • New Life Plan Reminders

4. **HOW TO ATTRACT GOOD FORTUNE** 49

    The Great Law of Success • How a Movie Director Planned His Success • How I Made a Successful Sales Plan • How to Make a Realistic Plan for Success • Action Methods for Success of Your Plan • The Law of Persistence • How a Woman Attracted a Buyer for Her House • How a Total Failure Made a Rich Come-back • All Things Come into Being by Law • Good Fortune Reminders

5. **THE LAW OF DYNAMIC COURAGE** 59

    Why Courage Is Real and Fear Is False • Courage Is the Only Remedy for Fear • How Courage Gave a Man Great Victory • How a Woman Overcame Fear and Gained Courage • A Practical Method for Gaining Courage • A Walkie-Talkie Method for Gaining Courage • Do What You Fear and You Will Gain Courage • The Hum-A-Tune Method for Overcoming Fear • Imagination and Faith Will Make You Brave • How to Express Courage Every Day • A Poem that Will Inspire You with Courage • It Is Your Duty to Act with Courage • Reminders for Gaining Courage

6. **THE LAW OF RADIANT HEALTH** 68

    The Great Benefit of Health • Some Causes for Lack of Health • The Fountainhead of Health Within You • The Law of Constant Renewal • How to Attract New Health-Giving Power • A Method to Stimulate Good Health Conditions • Dynamic Affirmations for Gaining Health • The Healing Power of the Subconscious Mind • A Miraculous Example of Subconscious Mind Power • The Importance of Having a Will to Get Well • How to Develop a Healthy State of Mind • Afternoon Health March Exercise • Give Your Subconscious Mind an Order for Health • Laughter and

Contents

Merriment Stimulate Good Health • A Magical Mental Habit for Gaining Health • Radiant Good Health Reminders

7. HOW TO KEEP YOUNG IN MIND 78

Age Is Nothing but a Chronological Tick-Tock • Youth Is Primarily a State of Mind • Live in the Present to Stay Young • Too Young in Heart to Grow Old • An Amazing Example of the Spirit of Youth • A Secret for Becoming Younger Each Day • A Magical Technique for Keeping Young • A Daily Youth Renewal Practice • How to Become Young in Heart • Make Every Day a Youth-Conscious Day • How to Young-Line Your Figure • The Rich Rewards for Being Young in Mind • Reminders for Keeping Young in Mind

8. HOW TO GAIN A MAGNETIC PERSONALITY . . 87

Step One in Magnetic Self-Expression • Step Two in Magnetic Self-Expression • The Importance of Good Manners • The Value of Proper Attire • How to Make a Good First Impression • Put a Happy Ring in Your Voice • The Importance of Good Physical Posture • How to Become a Well-Liked Person • The Man with a "Stand Out" Personality • Some Personality Faults to Avoid • Seven-Day Personality Improvement Program • How to Check Your Personality Improvement • How to Put a Shine to Your Personality • Magnetic Personality Reminders

9. THE LAW OF UNLIMITED OPPORTUNITY . . . 96

Opportunity Springs from Imagination • What to Do When Confronted with Change • The Woman with Invincible Faith • How to Create a New Opportunity • How I Received an Amazing Opportunity • New Opportunity Door Openers • How a Gilded Chestnut Gave a Man a New Start • This Method Produced New Opportunity • The Magical Key for Gaining Employment • How an Actress Found Instant Work • How to Make the Right Decision • Make Each Day a Golden Opportunity Day • New Opportunity Reminders

Contents

10. **THE UNFAILING LAW OF PROSPERITY** 105

   The Reason Why Some People Are Poor • The Basic Principle of Prosperity • He Rose from Poverty and Prospered • How to Make a Money Goal • Give Meaningful Purpose and Action to Your Goal • Back up Your Goal with Magnetic Faith • This Man Is an Amazing Believer • His Twenty-Five Dollars Became a Fortune • Money Can Come to You in Many Ways • A Money-Attracting Technique • Use This Self-Convincer Method Daily • Giving Thanks Will Cause You to Prosper • Good Health and Prosperity to You • Law of Prosperity Reminders

11. **THE EVER-PRESENT LAW OF PROTECTION** . . 114

   Nothing Can Harm You but YOU • It Never Happened to Him Again • Wake up to Your Safety Factor • Safety Is a State of Mind • #1 Home Safety Method • #2 Auto Safety Method • #3 Air Safety Travel Method • How to Protect Your Loved Ones • How to Protect Your Valuables • Put Yourself "on Guard" Every Day • Safety Thoughts for Each Day • Ever-Ready Safety Reminders

12. **THE MAGNETIC LAW OF LOVE** 124

   What You Feel Love for, You Attract • A Mental Magnet in Action • Love Built Their Dream House • How Love Reunited Two Brothers • How to Attract Your Life Partner • The Healing Power of Love • A Miracle of True Love • Love Is the Motivating Power of Success • Let Love Make You Attractive • The Rich Rewards of Love • Law of Love Reminders

13. **THE MIRACLE-WORKING LAW OF FAITH** . . . 134

   A Dramatic Example of Dynamic Faith • How Faith Conquered a Suicide Impulse • I Believe! I Believe! I Believe! • The Faith of a Young Soldier • His Faith Put Him in High Office • He Quickly Received a Big Promotion • His Faith Survived Three

Contents

Wars • How Faith Attracts What You Look for • How to Use the Mental Attracter Chart • Miracle-Working Faith Reminders

14. THE CREATIVE LAW OF COSMIC MIND 146

You Are Greater than You Think • The World's Most Amazing Inventor • The Real World You Live in • Her Sudden Vision Became a Fabulous Reality • How Action Will Make a Dream Come True • Great Men Who Tuned in to Cosmic Mind • What You Concentrate upon You Attract • He Concentrated on Success and Became a Success • Practical Steps to a Richer Life • Practice and Action Attract Life's Riches • Law of Cosmic Mind Reminders

15. THE TRANQUILIZING LAW OF PEACE 156

How Serenity Increases Your Power of Attraction • People Are Creatures of Habit • He Was a Human Volcano in Action • This Man Has Great Peace of Mind • Nothing Can Bring You Peace but YOU • Their Home Is a Haven of Peace • Calm Down, There Is Nothing to Fear • How to Relax in Mind and Body • How to Control Your Emotions • Begin Each Day with a Peaceful Attitude • A Peaceful Walk Each Day Is Good Therapy • Some Peaceful Thoughts to Keep Worry Away • A Bedtime Treatment to Gain Peace • The Rich Rewards of Peace of Mind • Law of Tranquilizing Peace Reminders

16. THE EXHILARATING LAW OF HAPPINESS . . . 166

Why Some People Are Unhappy • Why Some People Are Happy • Sudden Good Fortune Gave Her Great Joy • She Exchanged Her Sorrow for Happiness • Music Will Put You in a Happy Mood • How One Woman Found Happiness • You Have a Decision to Make • Some Things That Will Give You Happiness • Three Magic Steps to Happiness • How to Make Every Day a Happy Day • The Rich Rewards of Happiness • Law of Happiness Reminders

17. HOW TO ATTRACT HAPPY HAPPENINGS . . . 176

All Good Things Exist for Your Benefit • I Have a Secret to Share with You • How to Attract a New World to Live in • How to Attract New Friends and Companions • How to Attract Things for Your Pleasure and Comfort • How to See Good Fortune Happening for Another • How to Attract Happy Happenings • What Happy Event Do You Want to Happen? • Law of Happy Happening Reminders

18. HOW TO ATTRACT PHENOMENAL PERSONAL SUCCESS 189

The Secret of Gaining Fame and Fortune • You Have the Power to Attract Success • The Magnetic Law of Mental Telesis • Making a Talent Goal for Outstanding Success • Determine to Play a Star Part in Life • Picture Yourself as Having Great Talent • Practice Will Give You High Voltage Confidence • Give Your Subconscious an Order for Success • How Your Talent Will Act as a Magnet for You • A Famous Star's Secret for Success • The Value of Stick-to-Itiveness • You Should Associate with Successful People • Grasp Every Opportunity to Express Your Talent • Think Success! Believe Success! Be Success! • The Rich Rewards of Mental Magnetism • Put Your Get-Up-and-Go Power into Action

19. QUICK MAGIC MAGNETIC REMINDERS FOR DAILY USE 200

Turn to this Ready Reference Guide at any time during the day or night for a quick boost in spirit. Make this Guide your constant companion. Do so and you will always have a bright outlook on life.

The LAWS of
MENTAL MAGNETISM:
Your Personal Miracle Maker

1

Your Power of Mental Magnetism: How It Can Enrich Your Life

It may surprise you, good friend, to learn that you possess thousands of times more Magnetic Power than does the most powerful man-made magnet. Sensational news! Yes. But even more surprising is the fact that how you have used the Magnetic Power of your *own* mind has caused you to become what you are, and have the things that you have.

However—and this is wonderful news!—during the past 100 years, Mind Scientists have discovered that the Magnetic Power within man can be controlled and directed towards changing man into a wonderful new being and make it possible for him to attract any or all of life's fabulous riches to himself.

My purpose is to show you how to CONTROL your own Power of Mental Magnetism, how to redirect this Power to constructive aims and purposes and, by so doing, cause a miraculous change for the better to take place in your life—making it possible for you to attract more of life's goodness and riches to yourself.

Your Magnetic Power that Can Attract Great Riches

Asleep within you is a gigantic Power capable of drawing to you any good thing you need. But, if you are not aware of this Power and do not use it for your benefit, it will remain dormant, like anything else which is not used. This tremendous Power is the spirit of your life. Use it often and wisely and it will attract to you all that is good. Use it unwisely and it will draw to you the very things you do not want.

How are you using your own Magnetic Power this moment? Are you using it to attract an abundance of health, wealth and happiness to yourself? Or are you using it wrongly to draw to you illness, poverty and unhappiness? You can answer these questions by taking stock of yourself and your present living conditions. If you are living a prosperous and satisfactory life you are using the Magnetic Power of your mind and spirit correctly. If not, this is a danger signal telling you to get busy and correct the mistakes you are making in the use of your own Magnetic Power. Then make it your duty to take CONTROL of this Power by directing it to the things you *do* want instead of the things you do not want. To help you do this I ask you to study the Laws of Mental Magnetism which will be explained to you in this chapter.

How to Discover Your Magnetic Power

Your own Magnetic Power is more a part of you than breathing. It is closer to you than your hands and feet. It is the Spirit of your life. The Spirit of your mind, yes, the Spirit of your heart and soul. Were it not for this mighty Spirit within you, you would not exist. This is the truth about you. You have a miraculous Power within you that can perform miracles for you once you become aware of it and use it wisely for your own personal benefit.

I ask you to get a small notebook and write down the following thoughts as an ever ready memory aid.

> **My own Magnetic Power is the Spirit of my life, mind, heart and soul, without which I could not exist. I will use this Power to *imagine, desire, feel, believe* and *realize* that which I desire to attract to me.**

Do this at once, for these are the most important elements of your Magnetic Power, and you will be shown how to develop them in the pages of this book.

How to Convince Yourself that Mental Magnetism Exists

One sure way to prove to yourself that Mental Magnetism does exist is to observe other people. Notice carefully how people are attracted to others with similar interests. Notice how men and women are attracted to each other and marry. Notice how a newborn infant attracts the love and joy of its parents and their friends. And, in another aspect, notice how the theatre, TV and radio performers attract your attention in order to entertain you. And, again, notice how a street-beggar will wear a pained expression and hold out his hand in order to attract your attention—and attract money from your wallet or purse to his hand. Yes, all people use their personal Power of Mental Magnetism to attract attention either to themselves or to the things they have to offer.

The Laws of Mental Magnetism

I have said the Magnetic Power of your mind has the power to attract. Now I shall explain how this great Power functions within you. You use it when you are mentally awake or active by being aware of who you are and what you are. You use it when you think, imagine something, desire something, feel something to be real, believe that you can attract to you the thing you most desire, and when you come to the realization that you can attract any good thing by consciously believing that you can.

However—and this is extremely important—the subconscious part of mind Power consists of pure, unconditioned life energy substance, the same creative material out of which thoughts are made into things. Thus the basic function of your own portion of subconscious mind Power is to receive the mental impressions you consciously impress upon it, and return them to you as conscious personal experiences. It also has the power to attract to you those things you imagine, desire and believe you will receive. So, you should be very careful about what you impress on your own subconscious mind, for it is at work within you 24 hours every day in the year to attract to you the things you have impressed on its amazing Magnetic Power.

I shall now pinpoint five steps you are to take in developing your Power of Mental Magnetism in order that you will know how to attract more of life's riches to you.

1. *Imagination.* The first thing you are to do is to imagine what it is you would like to attract into your life. This can be a finer place in which to live, a better job, more money, a new car, a marriage, or it can be good health, more strength and vitality, more wisdom and understanding, peace of mind, or anything else you can imagine which you feel would make your life more enjoyable. Then form a vivid mental picture of that thing in your conscious mind, and determine to attract it to you.

2. *Desire.* Having done the above, you are to desire that thing above anything else. Then develop an intense desire to possess it. Make it the most important desire you have ever had in your life; and make up your mind you can and will attract it to you.

3. *Feeling.* Next, become aware by feeling that the one thing you desire exists especially for you. Feel the joy it will give to you. This action on your part will give life and meaning to your desire. It will cause a magnetic connection to take place between you and the thing you desire to attract.

4. *Faith.* Now add all the faith you possess to the thing you desire. Believe it will be attracted to you, and that you positively WILL receive it. Know without one shadow of a doubt being in your mind, that you WILL receive it.

5. *Realization.* Finally, you must realize, and know for a certainty that the thing you imagined, desired, felt to be true, and believed in, is now firmly impressed on your subconscious

mind Power. Now, the Laws of Mental Magnetism take over, to cause your subconscious Power of mind to go to work, and attract to you the very thing you have consciously determined to attract to you.

As a simple example of what I have been saying, I ask you to imagine what a $100 bill looks like. If you do not know, ask a bank teller to allow you to look at one. Make a vivid mental picture of that bill in your mind. Think of all the good things that bill would buy for you. Next, have an intense desire to possess a $100 bill. Get the feeling that one exists especially for you. Now take a giant step further and believe that you will receive a $100 bill. Realize that this is the absolute truth. See yourself buying something good for yourself with it—and in some way or another a $100 bill will be attracted to you.

Conscientious practice by you of the five steps in developing your Power of Mental Magnetism can cause you to become a great scientist, a brilliant author, a successful business man or woman, an outstanding artist, a famous musician, singer, dancer, an efficient homemaker, or anything "great" you desire to become. This leaves the door of unlimited opportunity and progress in any field wide open to you. The decision is up to YOU whether to remain the rest of your life in the same old rut or to decide to make something really wonderful and outstanding of yourself. I say to you in all sincerity, my friend, you have the Power within you to create your own good fortune. Why not take opportunity by the hand this moment, and begin to attract your rightful share of life's abundant riches, by making proper use of the Laws of Mental Magnetism?

This simple explanation of the Laws of Mental Magnetism will be found throughout this book under the headings of The Laws of Health, Prosperity, Courage, Youthfulness, Happiness, Peace of Mind, The Law of Success, and so forth. I ask you to practice these Miracle-Making Laws. Make of each a Personal Miracle-Maker, ever ready at your conscious command to change your life for the better by attracting to you those wonderful and glorious true riches of life which are yours to enjoy freely by Divine Right!

How to Find a New Interest in Life

Everyone today wants something. There isn't a person in the world who doesn't want something good. This good could be health, courage, more money, peace of mind, love, joy, success, or greater recognition and renown. Yet few of us, indeed, know how to go about attracting any of these good things of life. The reason for this is that too many people are afraid of change, while others are too lazy to make an effort to do something new that would be to their benefit.

It is a fact that in order to really enjoy life, you must be keenly interested in something new; something that excites you and stimulates you; something that lifts you up in mind and spirit. What can you think of this moment that would give you a new interest in life? It could be an interest in art, music, literature, singing, a hobby, starting a new men's or women's club. Or it could be an interest that would make something really great and outstanding of yourself in your present occupation or field of endeavor. Whatever it is that really holds your interest and fascinates you, make that the new desire of your life, and use the five steps I have given you regarding the Laws of Mental Magnetism to turn that thing into a reality.

How John Ferris Turned His Hobby into a King-Sized Business

Mr. John W. Ferris, President of the Indiana Die Mould Company of Ft. Wayne, Indiana, whose father, grandfather, and several uncles were railroad locomotive engineers, used his spare time to make good-sized scale model trains. He began to have a longing to own his own private, full-sized Pullman car. Finally, the day did come when he was given the opportunity to purchase a private Pullman car which had been used as a campaign car by at least one United States President. This became a personal, or rather, a family hobby, since his wife, two daughters, his son, and their friends helped restore it—from steam-cleaning and sand-blasting to painting. He said, "We've made six trips in 'Capital Heights' since May, 1962, covering 20,000 miles in all."

Now for the big surprise! Mr. Ferris' story captured the interest of newspaper writers. Soon thereafter he appeared on the *I've Got A Secret* national TV program, and was seen and heard by millions of people. Business and club groups became interested in his unique story and asked permission to rent his private car for pleasure or convention trips. This caused Mr. Ferris to set up a new company called Private Railroad Cars, Inc., of which he became president. Today he owns several private railroad cars, and is organizing a travel department to rent luxury private sleeping and dining cars to groups of people who desire to travel anywhere in the U.S.A. on a special car rental basis, plus railway fares.

How to Make Your New Interest a Reality

When you have decided what it is you most desire to attract, you must do the following things three times a day for the next ten days:

Go to some quiet place where you can be alone, away from outer disturbance. Sit in an easy chair, close your eyes and completely relax. Let go of the world and its problems—your problems. Become peaceful in mind and body, focus your attention on becoming peaceful for a few moments. Now think of your new interest for a few moments. Imagine how happy it would make you were you to have it. Visualize it as being something very special. Make a vivid mental picture of it in your conscious mind. Now desire to own it and possess it. Feel it being attracted to you. Believe you will receive it and realize that it is now being delivered to you by the Magnetic Power of your subconscious Mind.

How I Attracted Great Success on the Stage

I speak with authority when I say my own use of the Laws of Mental Magnetism rewarded me handsomely. Some years ago I discovered that I possessed a powerful singing voice. While on a boat trip from Florida to New York, I was asked to sing at a ship's concert. I did, and was warmly applauded. Suddenly I began to imagine how it would feel to appear before a large audience in a theatre as a star performer. My desire to do just that grew by leaps and bounds, and somehow I believed I could do it.

Very soon thereafter I met a man in New York who introduced me to a producer who was casting a huge musical comedy, with a cast of 135 people. I was given a small part, but the show closed in Chicago, Illinois four weeks later. This did not deter me, however. It only intensified my desire to become a success on the stage. I secured a role as leading man in a travelling musical comedy and, in fact, appeared in important parts with several other companies. I played 75 weeks in summer stock with some of Broadway's most talented people, and then turned my attention to vaudeville. Once firmly entrenched in this unique form of entertainment, I met all of the "greats," and appeared in every vaudeville theatre in the United States and in Canada, and even on the stage of the famous Palace Theatre of New York.

Finally, my desire and faith led me to use my God-given talent as soloist with a 110-person symphony orchestra. I tell you, my friend, nothing is impossible once you know what it is you want to do, desire to do, and believe you can do. Why not get busy now and do the thing you have always wanted to do? You can if you will but turn on the full Power of your Mental Magnetism, and let it attract you to your rightful place in life.

Why a Rich Full Life Is Important to You

The primary reason why you should have a desire to live your life to the fullest is that you are a human being endowed with exceptional Power. For instance, imagine a cow grazing in a field and chewing on its cud. That cow lives by instinct alone and has only the ability to bring forth calves and milk. You, on the other hand, have been given the power of self-determination and free will to make of yourself anything you can think of, imagine, and desire to be.

By making something really great of yourself, you will not only reap the benefits of doing so, but you will stand out as an object lesson to other people who will look up to you and admire you for what you have been able to make of yourself. Your very presence in the midst of other people will inspire them to emulate you in like manner. Some, at least, are bound to say to themselves, "If he can do it, I can do it; and I'm going to make it my business to do it!"

So, I urge you, my friend, begin to make something really great of yourself, and you will be exceedingly glad that you did.

How One Man Risked All to Gain Fame and Fortune

Robert Manry, a copy editor for the *Cleveland Plain Dealer*, for years had been fascinated by stories of adventures at sea, and secretly desired to experience such an adventure. His only previous experience in sailing was in a sailboat on Lake Erie. He finally came to a decision to do something about his dream of sailing at sea, which can best be summed up in his own words: "There comes a time that one must decide of one's dreams either to risk everything to achieve them or sit for the rest of one's life in the backyard." *
What did Mr. Manry do? He rigged up a 13½ foot sailboat and started, alone, on a perilous 79-day journey from Falmouth, Massachusetts, across the Atlantic Ocean to Falmouth, England. He made that amazing trip successfully, to the amazement of millions of people the world over.

I have inspected this tiny sailboat, named "Tinkerbelle," and all I can say is that what Mr. Manry accomplished is nothing else but a miracle, after considering the fact that he was washed overboard several times during his voyage, but managed to swim back to his boat and complete his journey. As a consequence of his amazing adventure at sea, Mr. Manry is now world famous and is swamped with many offers that are bound to attract to him great good fortune.

You, Too, Have Power to Make Your Dreams Come True

What is it you have dreamed about doing? What is it you have dreamed about having? Let me tell you your dreams are but thoughts and images in your conscious mind, and they cannot come true until YOU do something practical to make them come true.

First, you must refuse to sit in the "backyard" the rest of your life. Next, you must be willing to risk all to make your dreams come

---

* Quoted, by permission of the publishers, from Robert Manry's *Tinkerbelle: The Story of the Atlantic Crossing*, Harper & Row, Publishers, Inc., 1966.

true. You must make up your mind, and decide you will make your dream come true. You must imagine it as being a reality. Desire to make it come true. Feel that it will come true. And believe that it will be attracted to you in its complete entirety. Then take the necessary human steps to make your dream a positive reality.

By developing your Power of Imagination you will be inspired to imagine things and ways of doing things that others have not imagined. By developing your Power of Desire, you will be impelled to desire an abundance of greater riches. By developing your Power to Feel, you discover how to always feel good. By developing your Power of Faith, you will always receive that which you believe you will receive. And when you realize these basic truths of life you will know how to attract any or all of life's rich abundance to you.

So, my friend, there is no time like the present to change yourself into a strong, powerful, magnetic person. There is no time like the present to attract to you those things that will give you greater comfort and joy. So get busy today and put into practice the Laws of Mental Magnetism, and create for yourself a rich, dynamic, sparkling, new life.

MENTAL MAGNETISM REMINDERS

1. What you now are, and the things you now have, are the result of your use of the Magnetic Power of your OWN mind.

2. When you learn how to CONTROL this Magnetic Power, you can expel the things you do not want in your life and attract those things you DO want.

3. Right use of your Power of Mind will attract to you health, wealth and happiness. Wrong use of your Power of Mind will draw to you illness, poverty and unhappiness.

4. Your Power of Mental Magnetism exists in your mind, heart, soul and spirit. It can attract to you all of the good things life has to offer you.

5. Observe people and you will be convinced that Mental Magnetism does exist.

6. Use your Power of Mental Magnetism to imagine something, desire something, feel something to be real, believe you can

attract what you desire, and realize that you can attract any good thing by consciously believing that you can.

7. Your Power of Mental Magnetism can cause you to become anything great you desire to become, or attract to you spiritual, physical or material riches.

8. You have been shown how to find a new interest in life and why it is so important to have an interest in something new.

9. How one man turned his hobby into a new king-sized business.

10. How the writer used a discovered talent, and used imagination, desire and faith to become a success on the stage.

11. Why a rich, full life is so important to you. Why your Power of self-determination and free will make it possible for you to become anything you can think of, imagine, and desire to be.

12. You have been told you have the Power to make your dreams come true, and have been given a method to make them come true. You know how to practice the Laws of Mental Magnetism and thus create for yourself a rich, dynamic, sparkling, new life.

How to Break Career-Crippling Habits and Gain Personal Self-Confidence

I must be very frank with you and tell you that, although you do have the power to attract any good thing, there are certain things you must do first in order to draw them to you. You must know exactly what it is that keeps you from making progress in your life.

Is it that you are timid about making a change in your life? Is it that you habitually feel sorry for yourself? Or is it laziness on your part to make the effort to do something worthwhile with yourself? Or perhaps it may be lack of faith in yourself to do something really great. Whether it be any one of these or some other mental habit, you must break such career-crippling beliefs immediately. You must jolt yourself and spark yourself into the main stream of life by believing in yourself and the great Power within you. To help you do this let me show you how to regain confidence in yourself and positive self-assurance.

How to Overcome Timidity and Gain Self-Importance

To obtain the true sense of your own importance, you must first dispel all doubts in your mind that you are anything else but an important person—not only to yourself but to others as well. You must convince yourself that you are an individual endowed with talents and capabilities that no one else has exactly as you have. In order to strengthen this new concept of yourself, go to a full-length mirror, or sit down at your dressing-table mirror, and take a good look at the image you see in that mirror. Don't just gaze at the clothes you are wearing or your special "hair-do," but make a general, over-all assessment of yourself. If it reflects back to you a picture of shyness and timidity, say to that image, "I am going to change you. I am going to make you a positive, enterprising and self-confident person. You are going to become a very important person." Keep up this practice every day for two weeks. Each time you look into your mirror thereafter you will be surprised to see what a change is taking place. Your new conception of yourself as an important person will become more and more evident to yourself.

How to Conquer Self-Pity

To feel sorry for yourself is the worst kind of self-condemnation. Such mental practice can give you nothing but a feeling of utter despair. It reveals complete lack of faith in yourself and tells the world that you are a useless and powerless person. To break this exceedingly bad mental habit requires that you realize what harm you are doing to yourself, that as long as you persist in so doing you will be held in your own self-imposed bondage. To free yourself, I suggest you write down on a small card the following thoughts, and affirm these thoughts to yourself every day:

> **This day I count my blessings**
> **This day I refuse to pity myself**
> **This day I am determined to use**
> **The magnetic power of my mind to**
> **Attract to me greater good.**

Memorize these thoughts and make it a daily practice to recall them at every free moment. And as you do this, you will take your mind away from the things you are lacking and will begin to stimulate your own Power of Mental Magnetism to attract to you your rightful "share of the good things" of life.

How to Change Laziness into Self-Confident Action

The feeling that you cannot do anything about improving yourself is produced by a belief in laziness. This mental habit of believing in indolence will entrench you in the worst kind of poverty if you do not break it quickly. You can do this through the Laws of Mental Magnetism—by learning to put these Laws into action. Begin by finding something interesting to do, and then put all your effort and energy into that thing to cause it to become a huge success. This one accomplishment on your part will give you a stimulus to do more, and soon your feeling of laziness will leave you and you will become a lively, self-activated person.

You will then have proven to yourself that by your own thoughts and action you do have the power to accomplish that which you make up your mind you will do. And, having done it once, you can do it again in any other activity which you desire to achieve.

How to Believe in Yourself and Your Power of Attraction

It is a fact that if you do not believe in yourself, no one else will. I spoke these very words to a prominent senator one day, and back came his booming reply, "I have never had any trouble on that score in all my life!"

Why should you believe in yourself? Because, if you do not believe in yourself, you cannot possibly believe in the Miracle-Working Power of your mind, and the great good it can do for you.

To strengthen your faith in yourself, I ask you to write down the following thoughts:

> **I believe in myself. I believe I can do anything I make up my mind to do. From this day forward I will believe I have Power to attract all things that will benefit me and be for my personal good.**

Memorize these thoughts until they become indelibly impressed on your subconscious mind, which will then go to work for you to cause you to have faith in yourself, and give you the Power to attract your own good.

A Morning Exercise to Gain Self-Confidence

As an aid to help you regain confidence in yourself, I ask you to do the following each morning for ten minutes on arising:

> **Sit in your easy chair, close your eyes and completely relax. Imagine yourself as a very important person for one minute; believe you are extremely important for another minute. Then make up your mind that this day you will act as a self-confident person wherever you may happen to be. Feel this to be the absolute truth about you, and sustain this feeling for several minutes. Then open your eyes, lift your head up high, and go forth fully convinced that you will enact the part of personal self-confidence throughout the entire day.**

A Bedtime Exercise to Gain Self-Confidence

As you retire each evening and lie in a position of rest upon your bed, I ask you to do the following mental exercise:

> **Close your eyes and completely relax. Then imagine that you have great confidence and trust in yourself. Visualize yourself being very brave and courageous. Make a mental picture of yourself as being confident and self-assured. Believe that you are exactly that. Then imagine yourself going through the next day feeling calm, poised, and master of all you survey. Desire this to happen to you and feel and believe it will. Then close your eyes and have a good night's rest.**
>
> **Keep up this practice every night just before you retire. Your subconscious mind will then take over while you sleep and will cause you to feel self-confident when you arise the next morning. That feeling will stay with you throughout the next day, and as you keep up this mental exercise, it will cause you to feel self-confident every day thereafter.**

Why Self-Confidence Increases Your Power of Magnetic Attraction

There is a very good reason why you should practice the methods I have given you to gain confidence in yourself. Remember, you always attract to you what you think and believe. All you have to do to prove this truth is to notice how chronic complainers always are to be found in the company of other complainers; how people who are in poverty associate with other people who are also lacking in the good things of life, and how people who have wealth associate with those who also have wealth.

These people we call the "haves" and the "have nots" of life. Those who have no confidence in themselves continue in their misery and want. Those who do have confidence and therefore understand the Laws of Mental Magnetism, draw to themselves great abundance of life's riches.

As you develop your power to believe in yourself, you will attract the attention of people who will recognize you as one who is capable of doing great things. Then, often by the word-of-mouth method, they will mention you to others as a real go-getter. This, in turn, will draw to you new opportunities for personal advancement and gain.

Self-confidence will make of you a more interesting and attractive person. People will be drawn to you because your magnetic presence will lift them up in mind and spirit. And, best of all, the more faith you have in yourself the more power you will possess to attract to you whatever good thing you have made up your mind to receive.

How I Used Self-Confidence to Land a Well-Paying Job

Soon after I left the stage, I had a desire to go into the business world, and did so. Since this was an entirely new field for me, I made up my mind I would attract a very good job. Not long after my decision, I received a phone call asking me to see a certain man who wanted a sales representative to cover the Middle West for his firm. Immediately upon receiving this message, I began practicing the confidence-building methods I have just given you. On the first appointment with this man, I convinced him I was the man he was

Break Career-Crippling Habits 35

looking for. After two additional conferences, I walked out of his office with a good-sized check in my hand as my first weekly advance on sales I had not yet even made. I soon proved myself to be a star salesman and profited financially as well.

If you are in need of employment, you can do the same by being confident in your belief that you will attract the kind of work that is right for you. So, when opportunity knocks, go forward with a firm, self-confident attitude and close the deal, just as I did.

Things to Avoid when Building Self-Confidence

Now that you have become involved in learning how to become a self-confident person, there are certain things you must do in order not to weaken your faith in yourself.

1. Keep the methods you have been given to practice in this book to yourself. Why? Because what you are doing is for your own personal benefit, and interference or discouraging opinions from family and friends often can cause you to lose faith in yourself and what you plan on doing with your life.

2. Under no circumstances should you become involved in idle gossip or in what other people may think of you. What you think of yourself as a new, self-assured person, is the most important thought to you. To counteract any adverse opinions you may hear regarding yourself, make it a habit to say to yourself: "I do not care what people may think about me as long as I don't think and believe it." Your thinking should be, "I am a self-confident person. That is the real truth about me."

3. Never allow yourself to be disturbed by other people's attitudes or actions toward you. To do so would distract you from your avowed purpose of becoming a self-confident, self-assured person. Pay no attention to disturbing news reports. See them as people's wrong use of the Power of Mental Magnetism. Your most important business in life is to make a better person of yourself, and you can only do this by first becoming a positive, self-confident, self-assured person.

4. Never look back in memory to the old image of yourself as a frustrated, inferior person. Such practice will bind you to

whatever unpleasantness you may have experienced in the past, and make it impossible for you to go forward into the new life you are now planning to enter. The past is gone forever. The only reality is the present, and what you make of yourself today will also become your future.

How to Put Life and Feeling into Self-Confidence

How many times have you been low in spirits when some thoughts of encouragement spoken by a friend lifted you up and made you feel good? Thoughts contain tremendous power when spoken for good or for ill. The reason for this is that encouraging thoughts lift one up in mind and spirit, and those that discourage depress one and let one down.

Now, I am going to give you some thoughts to say to yourself that will give you a lift in spirit and mind no matter where you may be, whether at home, in the office, or on the street. Should you ever feel low, quickly say to yourself, "I am a wonderful person. I am a very important person. Nothing can get me down for I have Power to lift myself up. I am a powerful, self-confident person. This is the truth about me."

As it is a known fact that thoughts become things and experiences, I am going to ask you to imagine yourself as an actor or an actress on the stage of a theatre, about to speak these words aloud to yourself just as you would in a stage play. I shall assume the role of your director and coach you in the proper rendition of your lines.

Read that first line to me. "I am a wonderful person."—Stop!— No, no, no! You have not put enough feeling into your thoughts. Now, speak them again and put strong feeling into them. Make them come to life as if you really feel and mean what you say. "*I am a wonderful person!*" .... That's great! Keep it that way. Now read the next line, please .... "I am a very important person." .... Great Caesar's Ghost, no! You do not feel or believe what you say! Try it again. Put feeling into your words.... "*I AM A VERY IMPORTANT PERSON!*" That's perfect. Now let's go on to the next line. "Nothing can get me down, for I have Power to lift myself up." No, no, a thousand times no! You do not sound as though nothing can get you down, nor do you believe that you have the power to lift yourself up! Now put real power and feeling into your words.... "NOTHING CAN GET ME DOWN, FOR I HAVE POWER TO LIFT MYSELF UP!" By George, you have it. I believe what you say. You have convinced me you do have amazing power.

Now the last line, please. "I am a powerful, self-confident person. This is the truth about me." Hold everything! Now read your line over again. This time put zest and feeling into your thoughts. Make them come alive! *"I am a powerful, self-confident person. This is the truth about me...."* Bravo! That was magnificent.

I suggest you take the thoughts I have given you in this imagined stage rehearsal and learn them by heart. Make them the new rule and law of your life. And recall to memory that the Bible says regarding man: "For as he thinketh in his heart so is he." [Prov. 27:7.] Which is another way of saying that you become like the thoughts you impress on the Power of your subconscious mind.

I urge you to practice the simple methods I have given you in this chapter to gain confidence in yourself. By so doing you will have broken those mental habits which have retarded your progress and kept you in a rut. In truth you do have the Power and ability to make of yourself what you will and have what you most desire. But you can only do this through the practice of the Laws of Mental Magnetism. As the most important person in your life is YOU, you will be doing yourself the greatest benefit by putting into practice the methods I have given you and thus become a new, dynamic, self-confident, powerful person: one who has power to attract life's greatest riches.

SELF-CONFIDENCE REMINDERS

1. The feeling of being timid is produced by lack of enterprise or self-confidence in oneself. This feeling can be changed to a self-confident feeling by having trust and faith in oneself.

2. Self-pity can be changed into self-praise by having confidence in oneself and one's ability to respect oneself and the great Power of one's mind.

3. Lack of faith in oneself causes a lack of self-confidence. Greater faith in oneself produces self-confidence.

4. Laziness is produced by a belief in indolence which leads to

poverty and want. Being busily creative and active attracts wealth in abundance.

5. You break any bad mental habit by realizing the harm it does to you and by replacing it with a good mental habit that will do you the most good.

6. By using the early morning and bedtime methods given you, you can so impress the Power of your subconscious Power of Mind that it will cause you to feel self-confident day after day.

7. You develop self-confidence by believing in yourself and the Magnetic Power of Attraction within you.

8. You have been given four things to avoid in order to increase your power of self-confidence—refuse to listen to discouraging opinions from family or friends; disregard what people think of you; ignore idle gossip and discouraging news reports; and never look back in memory to the old image of yourself.

9. You have been given a method for putting more life and feeling into your thoughts and beliefs, thus gaining self-confidence and self-assurance.

10. By practicing the Laws of Mental Magnetism you can become a new, self-confident, powerful person.

3

How to Plan a Rich, New, Dynamic Life

Now that you know how the Laws of Mental Magnetism operate, you should make a plan to live a greater and more enjoyable life. I tell you truthfully that in the Divine plan of life there are many good things that are lavishly prepared for you, including an abundance of health, happiness, peace of mind, yes, and material riches. But you must first claim these good things, and use the Laws of Mental Magnetism in order to attract them to you. Let me show you how to do this by using the following methods.

How to Acquire Right Mental Attitudes

As your present outlook regarding yourself and conditions are the effects of what you believe in your own mind, the first thing you are to do is to change your mental attitudes regarding yourself and your conditions. Why is this necessary? Because as long as you maintain a low opinion of yourself and fight your problems, you will continue to attract more problems.

I ask you now to assume the attitude that you are an all-powerful, dynamic person. I ask you to say to your problems, "You have no power over me. I now cast you out of my life forever." You must really believe these new mental attitudes, and must maintain them each and every day. Soon you will recognize a great new change for the better taking place in your life.

How to Change Your Personal Reflection

Once again, I ask you to look at yourself in your mirror. What you see there not only reflects your physical image; your facial expression reveals what you believe to be true of yourself.

If you do not like the image of the face you see in your mirror, you can change it and keep it changed by doing the following: Put a big smile on your face and see how wonderful it looks. Next, put a mean, angry look on your face and see how ugly and terrible you look. Note how easy it is to smile and how hard it is to look angry. Do you know it requires little or no effort to smile but that you must use at least 24 face and neck muscles to look angry? Well, it's true. So why not go to your mirror each morning when you arise, smile at that mirror for two minutes, and make up your mind to keep that smile on your face every day for the next 30 days? If you do, everyone you meet will reflect back to you your happy smile, and you face will express that happy smile each day as a result of this simple magic mirror treatment you have given to yourself.

How to Rise Above Petty Annoyances

Include in your plan a resolve never to allow anything petty to annoy you. Why? Because minor aggravations develop by force of habit into major ones which, in turn, will emotionally upset you. If you work in an office, be courteous to your fellow employees. If your boss or department head comes in with a grouch or becomes angry at times, realize that he or she is not feeling well or is worrying about some problem. Do not let his attitude affect you one iota, for to do so would cause you inner disturbance. Go about your business as usual and thus maintain your self-composure and calm.

Never argue with people. There are two ways to avoid an argument and maintain your own self-control. One way is to treat the other person with absolute silence. Say not a word to him or her in return. The second way is to agree with everything your adversary has to say to you. The latter method takes all of the "steam" out of his wrong method of persuasion, and leaves him with nothing to argue about. I tried this method on a certain chronic arguer, and after agreeing with him several times, he said to me, "What is the use of arguing with you? You agree with everything I say!"

If you should find yourself in the presence of a rude or spiteful person, never enter into conversation with him. Treat him with utter silence and refuse to allow him to impress you with his uncouth thoughts and actions. To do so would cause you to descend to his low level of life. Avoid association with impolite and evil-minded people as you would an evil plague. You will then inevitably rise above all of the petty annoyances the human race is heir to due to their lack of wisdom and understanding, and their ignorance of the Laws of Mental Magnetism.

How to Develop Your Self-Importance

You should develop an awareness of your own true value and self-importance. Why? Because God created you for a special purpose. Realize He gave you Power to have dominion over all things. You use this Power and dominion when you become master of yourself and when you become master of all your experiences, instead of allowing them to become your master.

The first thing to do in order to become your own master is to forget what is past and decide to live in the present. Then make up your mind you are going to become a new, dynamic person, a person of considerable self-importance and creative ability, not only to yourself but to other people as well.

To help yourself to do this, think how important George Washington, Thomas Edison, Enrico Caruso, the Wright brothers, Sir Winston Churchill, and others were to the world you now live in. What do you think made them so important? Original, constructive ideas which affected other people as well as themselves.

What important thing can you think of to achieve for yourself which would be of benefit to others? Put that thing down on a sheet of paper and then imagine that, through this accomplishment, you, too, are extremely important to this world you are now in. Visualize yourself as being as great as any man or woman who has ever lived. Desire to become a great person. Feel and believe that you are now a very important person. Sustain and maintain this new feeling you have of yourself, believe it to be true and your subconscious mind will cause you to become important to yourself and others.

How to Make Your Personal Influence Felt by Others

You may not know it, but most people are psychic. By this I mean they are sensitive to the thoughts and feelings of other people. They have the ability to feel the mental vibrations constantly being generated and broadcast from within you as well as from any other person.

For instance, you yourself may have been in the presence at one time or another of someone who gave vent to a violent outburst of anger. If you were, you know you felt the impact of that person's rage, and promptly removed yourself from his presence. At another time, perhaps, you have found yourself in the presence of a very peaceful person, and "enjoyed" the vibrations of peace and calm sent forth from his presence.

Now the more important you make yourself feel, the more your feeling of self-importance will be felt by others with whom you come in contact. When you do something constructive and unusual, your personal influence will be felt by others, who will desire to accomplish what you have achieved. People of prominence and influence will become attracted to you and will desire to include you in their circle of friends. New doors of opportunity will open to you and make it possible for you to enter into a wonderful life, both in a business and social way.

How to Make Friends of Enemies

Your personal attitudes towards people will either cause them to become your enemies or your friends. This is shocking but true. Therefore, as there is no place for enemies in your new plan, remember what Emerson so wisely said: "To have a friend, be a friend." Now, if you are convinced that someone is your enemy, you should make every effort to be friendly to that person. If he refuses to respond in like manner, release him from your life immediately. Determine that you will attract someone else to you who will become a very good friend.

A good way to make a friend of a foe is to have love in your heart for that foe. This may seem a bit difficult to do at first, but you must remember there is no hatred or bitterness in love. Love can conquer all seeming opposition to you. As you begin showering the one who dislikes you with love, your feeling of love will be subconsciously felt in the heart of your opponent. His attitude regarding you will then experience a change. He will then feel more loving and kindly toward you, and you will become friends.

I ask you to practice these methods for changing enemies into friends, and prove to yourself that this use of your Power of Mental Magnetism *does* work like a charm.

How One Man Attracted Good Fortune

Recently, while I was living at a Park Avenue hotel in New York City, one of the room-clerks, who had been a light-opera singer and a TV and radio personality, appeared to be greatly depressed. In order to lift up his spirits I gave him the basic principles of the Laws of Mental Magnetism. Shortly after he left that hotel. I did not see him again for several months until one evening he came into the hotel looking like an entirely new person and a very prosperous one. He told me the following story:

> Shortly after I quit work at the hotel, I went to a hospital for an operation. As I lay on my bed regaining strength, I thought of the things you had told me. I imagined that I would be completely restored to good health, desired to be, felt I would be, believed and realized I would be, and I was. While there, I thought of the great goodness of God and desired to be showered with the abundance of His riches. I imagined myself rich in mind, rich in health, rich in financial abundance. I felt this to be true, believed it to be true and realized this was the truth about me. Soon I was discharged from the hospital in excellent health. A short time later I received a notice informing me that I had been named in the will of a certain elderly lady who, with her husband, had been

one of my admirers when I played in light-opera. She had left an estate of ten million dollars, from which she had left me stocks, bonds, jewelry, and considerable money. I have just returned from a trip to Italy and have never felt so well or been so rich in all my life!

Be sure to include in your plan a desire to attract an abundance of health, wealth and happiness. Imagine you will receive these good things in great abundance. Desire to receive them. Create that sense of certainty that you will receive them. Realize you will receive them—and they will be attracted to you.

How to Take Out a Shiny New Lease on Life

If you are the head of a business concern and are dissatisfied with your office space and accommodations, you know you can find more expansive quarters elsewhere. The same holds true for you who are dissatisfied with the circumstances and conditions that now prevail in your lives. You must first make up your mind that you are going to move out of these conditions. Then get a sheet of paper and write down at the top of it: *"This Is My Shiny New Lease on Life."* Under this heading, list the following: "I am going to live a new life." "I am determined to attract new vitality and strength; new courage and self-confidence; better living conditions; more financial abundance; greater peace and harmony; new opportunities; and speedy progress toward a joyous and happy life." Then write on the list all of the other things you desire to attract into your life.

How to Choose Things that Will Do You Most Good

Now get another sheet of paper and write down the things you think will do you the most good. Be selective and write down the very best. Should you desire a promotion, write that down. If you want to become a leader in your profession, write that down. If a salary increase is what you want, put down the amount of increase that you desire. Should you desire to become a star salesman, a capable sales-manager, the president of a firm, a successful lawyer, a motion picture or TV star, or anything else—list that thing on your sheet of paper.

Be sure to include in your plan greater understanding and wisdom to enable you to get along better with other people. Then select the one thing you intend to make the most important desire of your life.

How to Make Your New Plan Come True

I now ask you to pay strict attention to the following method for making your plan a concrete reality. This method has been used by millions of people with great success. There is no reason why it will not work for you, too, if you will but put your heart and soul into this method.

1. After selecting your most important need, and in order to impress a mental image of that thing on your subconscious mind, I suggest you go alone to some quiet place and sit in an easy chair or lie down on a couch or bed.

2. Now completely relax. Still your conscious mind by dwelling on some peaceful scene, such as mentally seeing yourself seated beside a peaceful lake observing a beautiful white swan gliding upon the lake.

3. Now think of that important thing you intend to attract. Make a clear mental image of that thing in your mind. Think of it as having actual existence. Imagine the joy you would feel were you to actually have it.

4. Now develop a strong desire to possess that thing as your very own. Long to have it as you have never longed to have anything else in your life. Promise yourself you will attract it to you.

5. Now feel with all the feeling you can muster that the thing you have imagined and so earnestly desire is being attracted to you. Believe that it is, and know for a certainty that it positively will be attracted to you and that you will receive it.

6. Now develop your power of faith by standing firm in your conviction that you will receive your imagined desire.

7. Now realize that the work you have done in your conscious mind has made a deep mental impression on your subconscious Power of Mind. Realize that this action on your part has set the Laws of Mental Magnetism in motion to act in your behalf to attract to you what you believe you will receive. Then open your eyes and go about your business.

The Law of Repetition

One sure way to tell whether you have used this method correctly is to think about what you believe you will attract the following day. When you do, and there is any doubt about your desire coming true in your mind, this means that you do not believe that it will. If such is the case, you are to go back and practice this method again and again, until you have convinced yourself you will receive what you originally intended to attract. I must remind you that "practice makes perfect," and the more often you practice this method, that much sooner will you receive the thing you desire. Do this and you will have proved to yourself that the Laws of Mental Magnetism do work like magic.

Now I want to say that you live in a mental world. Whatever enters into your life is but the material expression of some belief in your own mind. For anything you need in your life—a healthy body, a satisfactory vocation, friends, opportunities, and, above all, peace of mind—you must furnish the mental image of the thing you want by thinking about it a great deal; by thinking clearly and with interest.

Now I am going to tell you why many people who pray for things often do not receive what they want. They do not think about what they want with intense interest. They do not make a clear mental picture of the thing they want in their conscious mind. They merely wish to receive. They simply hope to receive instead of believing with all their heart and soul that they *will* receive what they desire. Consequently, few of the good things of life ever come into the lives of such people.

On the other hand, you who now know that you have the Power to create for yourself a new, dynamic, rich life, can do so by using your imagination to think of the things you want, by making a mental picture of these things in your conscious mind, by impressing these thought images on the Power of your subconscious mind, and by believing with solid and unshakable faith that you positively will attract and receive that which you so ardently desire to receive.

Therefore I say to you, make out your claim for a sparkling new life. Make it your very own. Practice the Laws of Mental Magnetism and you will attract and express a very rich life.

NEW LIFE PLAN REMINDERS

1. In order to enter a new life, you must first change your mental attitudes about yourself and your present circumstances. As long as you maintain a low opinion of yourself you will continue to attract problems. You are to assume that you are now an all-powerful person. You are to refuse to give power to problems, and you do this by casting them out of your mind forever.

2. It takes no effort to smile. You use 24 face and neck muscles in order to look mad. Make a habit of looking at your mirror every morning—put a smile on your face and hold it for two minutes. Keep that smile on your face for 30 days. Everyone you meet will like your happy smile, and you will like it too.

3. You rise above petty annoyances by being courteous. You can win arguments by keeping silent, or by agreeing with your adversary quickly. When you treat rude and impolite people with silence, you rise above them and retain inner calm.

4. Desire to become a great person. Feel that you are now a very important person. Believe this to be true and your subconscious mind will see to it that you are important to yourself and others.

5. To have a friend is to be a friend. You can make a friend of a foe by loving your foe. The love you send forth to an enemy will be felt in the heart of your enemy. His attitude to you will then change and he will desire to be your friend.

6. Remember how the man in the hospital used the Laws of Mental Magnetism to gain health and attract good fortune. Include in your plan a desire to attract health, wealth and happiness, and make it your duty to attract them.

7. You have been told how to take out a shiny new lease on life, and what to attract into that new life.

8. Choose those things that will do you the most good, make a list of those things, and attain them in the way that I have described.

9. You have been given a method to make your new plan come true. You have been told how to make a clear mental picture of what you plan to attract, how to attract it, and how to make that thing come into your life as a realized fact.

10. You have been given the Law of Repetition to use whenever you have any doubt. It will strengthen your faith, speed up your Power of Mental Magnetism, and deliver to you that which you are determined to attract.

11. You have been told to make out a claim for a sparkling new life, and that by so doing, you, too, will attract and express a very rich life.

4

How to Attract Good Fortune

Some people believe a four-leaf clover will give them good fortune. Others believe that a rabbit's foot or a horseshoe will bring them good fortune. Such superstitious beliefs are nothing but myths. What these people do not know is that good fortune begins in one's mind as a desire for something good, and that it is attracted to them by faith. I ask you to pay strict attention to what is said in this chapter so you will know how to create and attract your own good fortune. Do this and practice the methods I shall give you. You will be amazed by all the good things you will be able to attract to you.

The Great Law of Success

Good fortune and success do not happen by chance; they are produced by the law of mind. But in order to become successful you must first have an idea of what it is you desire to accomplish and then do the necessary mental work to make it a success. This desire can be for success in business or anything else you can think of that will help you to prosper. This is the first step you must take in what you plan to achieve. This requires your giving your undivided attention to your particular aim and concentrating on it.

Next you are to work at achieving this aim and to keep working at it until it becomes a success. These are the simple rules of the Great Law of Success that have been used by all successful people:

1. Get the idea of what you want to accomplish.
2. Make a plan for the success of that thing.

Go into action by working at your plan until it becomes a success.

How a Movie Director Planned His Success

My friend, Wally Van, who is a well-known moving picture director with over 200 movies to his credit, said to me recently: "Whatever you plan doing, put your plan on paper, even if it is crude; then work at your plan to make it a success." One night this amazing man conceived a plan for a one-reel movie, put his plan on paper, and completed that picture in every detail the next day at the motion picture studio. Another time, while at home, he conceived a plan for a five-reel "Western," complete with cowboys, Indians, horses, and much gunplay. He put his plan on paper in three days, then cast it, directed it and produced it at the movie studio in another five and one-half days. During his career he has directed many very famous stars. His experience proves the importance of planning for success in life.

How I Made a Successful Sales Plan

One phase of my own experience proved the value of having a plan and putting that plan down on paper. On becoming national sales manager for a division of a large corporation, the first thing I did was to create a new line of merchandise. Then the president of that firm said to me, "Set up your sales plan for this year and give me a copy of it." First I got a large map of the United States and divided the states into territories. Then I went over several lists of buyers in each state and wrote down the potential amount of business to be expected from those buyers. Then I set down on paper an advertising budget and the volume of business this advertising was expected to produce. Next I wrote down how many salesmen I would hire and the salaries these men would receive. I then gave the president a copy of my sales plan, which he approved. Then I began my real work of concentrating the energies of myself and the salesmen on producing orders for our new line of merchandise. On going over the sales at the end of that year, I discovered our volume of sales was 30 per cent higher than I had originally anticipated it would be.

How to Make a Realistic Plan for Success

You are now living in a world of great abundance and in a world where nothing is impossible anymore. The fact is that all things are possible to achieve today, but you must know what it is you want to make of yourself, or what you want to attract into your life. To convince yourself that you, too, can become a success, start observing successful people. Observe healthy, happy, and joyous people to convince yourself that these qualities of mind and spirit do exist. These qualities are the direct result of such people having a desire to express these good aspects of life. I ask you to go over the list of desires, as I have previously suggested you do. Then think of what you really want to become and want to have in your life. Write this down on the form sheet provided, so you will have an ever-ready, realistic plan.

This form sheet is for things you desire.

YOUR PERSONAL DESIRE LIST

I DESIRE TO BECOME ....

....

....

....

....

....

....

....

THINGS I DESIRE ....
....
....
....
....
....
....

IMPORTANT: Now go over your list of desires carefully and select *one* that you want to have come true in your life. Later on you can select other desires, but for the present choose only *one*. Then write that desire down on the next page of this book as the *one* thing you intend to concentrate on and make come true.

This form sheet is for your principal desire.

THIS IS MY #1 DESIRE

....
....
....
....
....
....
....

WRITE DOWN ALL OF THE BENEFITS YOUR DESIRE WILL GIVE YOU

....
....
....
....
....
....
....
....
....
....

Action Methods for Success of Your Plan

1. Look intently at what you have written down on the previous page as your #1 desire once every day for the next 30 days for five minutes each day. Make a mental picture of that thing in your mind as having real existence. Then look at the benefits you have written down that your desire will give you and visualize them in your mind. This is an extremely important practice, not only to keep your attention focused on the thing you desire, but to mentally imprint a picture of that thing on your subconscious mind. Your subconscious mind will then go to work to attract all that is necessary to cause your desire to become a reality.

2. For ten minutes twice a day for 30 days, go to some quiet place alone, sit in a chair, close your eyes and completely relax. While in this quiet state of mind, think of what you desire. Visualize it as having real existence. Take hold of that mental picture and claim it as your very own. Take possession of it. Sustain the feeling that it is your own and that it will be expressed in your life. Know for a certainty it will be expressed and made manifest in your life.

3. Each evening before you go to sleep, close your eyes and think of your desire. Visualize it in your mind as a reality about to come true. Believe it to be a complete success. See yourself doing all of the things you would do as if it were a huge success. Silently say to yourself, "I thank God my desire is a manifest success in my life." Then close your eyes and go to sleep. Keep up this practice each evening for the next 30 days prior to your going to sleep. This lets your subconscious mind go to work while you sleep to attract all that is needed to make your desire a success.

4. Now we come to the most valuable mental exercise for attracting what you want. This is faith on your part to believe that you will receive what you desire. The Bible, our greatest authority on the power of faith, has this to say: "What things soever ye desire, when ye pray, *believe that ye receive them*, and ye shall have them." [Mark 12:24] This is simple enough language, telling you that when you believe you will receive the things you desire, you will receive them.

To help you develop your faith so that you *will* receive whatever it is you desire, I ask you to get an index card and write down the following article of faith to yourself:

> I firmly believe that I will receive (name your desire)
> ....
> ....
> ....
> ....
> This is my firm, faithful conviction.
> Sign your name ....
> Date ....

Carry this card at all times in your pocket, wallet or purse. Look at it often every day for 30 days. This action will increase your faith and cause you to receive whatever good thing you desire—*provided* you have kept your pledge of faith to yourself.

5. Next, you are to do whatever seems right and practical for you to do. When your intuition urges you to go see someone who can open a new door of opportunity to you, by all means do so. Be on the alert to receive offers for advancement. Expect to receive good news by phone, letter or telegram. Live in a mental state of constant expectation, ever ready to receive all manner of good gifts. Never refuse to accept whatever good comes your way. And above all, expect, that you will receive all of the benefits contained in your #1 desire.

6. As a means of making yourself receptive to the receiving of more and more of life's riches, I ask you to give thanks for all of the blessings you have already received. Such mental practice will not only make you a grateful person, but it will open up your heart and mind so that more of life's blessings will be attracted to you.

When you arise each morning, I ask you to say to yourself, "I am thankful for being alive this day. I am thankful for being healthy this day. I am thankful for all of the good things that will be attracted to me this day, and for all of the good things that I shall receive." Then, just before going to sleep every night, say to yourself silently, "I give thanks for all of the good things I have received this day, and all of the wonderful things I shall receive tomorrow."

7. Finally, I ask you to make a check after each day you have practiced the methods I have given you. Do this for the next 30 days.

I Have Practiced	Yes	No	I Have Practiced	Yes	No
1st day	___	___	16th day	___	___
2nd day	___	___	17th day	___	___
3rd day	___	___	18th day	___	___
4th day	___	___	19th day	___	___
5th day	___	___	20th day	___	___
6th day	___	___	21st day	___	___
7th day	___	___	22nd day	___	___
8th day	___	___	23rd day	___	___
9th day	___	___	24th day	___	___
10th day	___	___	25th day	___	___
11th day	___	___	26th day	___	___
12th day	___	___	27th day	___	___
13th day	___	___	28th day	___	___
14th day	___	___	29th day	___	___
15th day	___	___	30th day	___	___

If you have practiced the full 30 days practice on this sheet, it means you have kept your pledge of faith to yourself. Now write down on the following lines all of the good things you have received in this period of time.

....
....
....
....

The Law of Persistence

Success in whatever you plan doing requires constant perseverance and persistence. This is where people of little faith fail when they embark on a new project. They do not continue doing what they ought to do in order to make it a success. I tell you, my friend, you have now embarked on the most important undertaking of your life—that of becoming a new, dynamic person, with power to enjoy a richer life. And the only way by which you can become so is by using your imagination, by careful planning, and by having faith. So, I tell you to persist in using the power of your mind to the fullest in attaining what you desire. Then you will know for certain that *you* are the creator and originator of all of the good fortune and prosperity that you receive in life.

How a Woman Attracted a Buyer for Her House

After a lecture I gave in Chicago on "How to Attract Good Fortune," a woman came to me and said, "What can I do to attract a buyer for my house which I am unable to sell?" I told her to believe that she would attract a buyer who was just as eager to buy her house as she was to sell it. Then I gave her the 30-day practice plan which I have given to you, and she promised me she would use it.

This is what happened. Two weeks after practicing this plan, she was invited to a party at which she met a real estate broker. In conversation with him she mentioned she had a beautiful house for sale. He became interested. He paid her a visit the next day and was greatly impressed with her house. Several days later he phoned her and requested an appointment to show her house to a client. The client, too, was greatly impresssed with it and the following day made arrangements to buy it. You see, this woman believed in what I told her to do and faithfully practiced the methods I had given her. As a result, her belief that she could sell her house attracted the right person to buy it.

How a Total Failure Made a Rich Comeback

A friend of mine at one time in his life was a total failure in the business world. I often reminded him how proper use of his imagination and faith would make him successful and rich again.

He began to believe what I had said to him, and for several months thereafter, he imagined and believed that he would be the president of a large corporation. As a result of this practice he was offered a position with a large firm, and through his imaginative ability, creative intelligence and faith, finally became its president. Then he imagined himself as the head of a dozen large business concerns, and firmly believed he would be. Today, he actually is in control of 12 firms and is a self-made millionaire as well.

All Things Come into Being by Law

Now that you have been given methods for creating your own good fortune, I tell you that these methods can be used to attract anything good you desire. Why is this so? Because the reality of all things begin as ideas, whether they be for courage, strength, power, health, wealth, happiness, success or whatever else that is good. The ones I have mentioned are ideal realities, but to actualize them in your life you must use your imagination, then desire them, and then use your power of faith in order that they be expressed in your life.

This is the law by which all good things come into being. Therefore, I say to you, my friend, if you desire to become courageous, strong, powerful, healthy, wealthy, happy and successful, practice the Laws of Mental Magnetism which I have given you. You will become a dynamic expression of life's truest and most beneficial mental, spiritual and physical aspects.

GOOD FORTUNE REMINDERS

1. Good fortune begins in your mind as a desire for something good and is attracted to you by faith.
2. You must plan your own good fortune in order to receive it.
3. In order to become successful you must have an idea of what you plan to accomplish.
4. You must make a plan and stay with it until what you plan becomes a success.
5. You have been shown how a moving picture director planned his own success.
6. How I made a successful sales plan.
7. How to make a realistic plan for success.
8. How to make a pledge of faith to yourself; and how to develop your faith.

9. You have been given a 30-day form sheet to check your practice methods for achieving success.

10. You have been shown how persistence and perseverance assure success.

11. How a woman used the Laws of Mental Magnetism to attract a buyer for her house.

12. How a total failure made a wonderful comeback.

13. You have been shown how the realities of all things begin as ideas, and are brought into being by imagination, desire and faith. Through practice of the Laws of Mental Magnetism, you can become a dynamic expression of life's truest and most beneficial aspects.

5

The Law of Dynamic Courage

It is your birthright to express yourself as a healthy, happy, successful person for a very good reason. This reason is that you were created in the image and likeness of God, and as such, you should be expressing all of the good qualities of life and enjoying all of life's benefits. However, you cannot express your true inner self as long as you are fearful instead of courageous. This chapter will show you how to set yourself free from fear, making it possible for you to live a courageous, dynamic life.

Why Courage Is Real and Fear Is False

First of all, courage is a spiritual idea. When you desire it, believe in it, and receive it, you are fearless, dauntless, gallant, bold and brave. Fear, on the other hand, is a false, man-made idea, conceived in ignorance through a disbelief in the goodness of God. It is based on a belief in a non-existent power of evil which can do harm to people. Thus you can readily see which is the better of these two ideas to believe in, and why courage insures your living a happy and successful life.

Courage Is the Only Remedy for Fear

You can take tranquilizer pills to eliminate feelings of fear, but when their temporary effects wear off you will still feel fear. Why is this so? Because fear is produced in your mind by imagining that something has power to harm you and by believing that something can harm you. When this happens, your subconscious mind goes to work to cause you to have a feeling of fear.

In reverse order, when you realize that nothing has power to harm you, and when you imagine yourself as courageous and believe that you are courageous, your subconscious mind goes to work to cause you to feel boldly courageous.

How Courage Gave a Man Great Victory

I once dined with an explorer who was commissioned to explore a jungle inhabited by headhunters. This was a dangerous assignment but, being a man of great courage, he refused to be daunted. He saw this adventure as a challenge to be met and overcome. During our conversation he told me how he made a plan for the successful fulfillment of his mission. First, he wrote on paper several things he must do. The first was to find a semi-civilized native who could teach him a few words of the language spoken by the headhunters. He found such a native, who told him it was a habit of headhunters to fear that which they could not understand. This gave the explorer an idea of how to overcome them. After being instructed with enough of the headhunter language to get by, he conceived a plan of action.

Soon thereafter, supplied with a quantity of dynamite sticks, copper wire and automobile batteries, he and three guides, travelling by canoe, set up camp in the midst of the jungle. They immediately went to work to place dynamite around the roots of all the trees that surrounded their camp. Some days later, a fierce-looking tribe of headhunters appeared and the man's guides ran away in terror, leaving him alone to face death. With great courage he faced the tribe and spoke to them in their language. Taking a whistle from his pocket, he said, "You see whistle. I have great power. When I blow whistle you will see my power." Then he blew his whistle and pressed a button on a crude panel he had devised, which set off a charge of dynamite around the roots of a large tree. Instantly that tree was hurled high in the air. He repeated this action time and time again and tree after tree was blown high in the air. At the sight and sound of this strange phenomenon, the headhunters panicked with fear and scampered away, never again to return. The explorer was then free to explore the land, and he discovered a very valuable mineral deposit. He returned back home, safe and sound, and was paid handsomely for his discovery.

How a Woman Overcame Fear and Gained Courage

A few months ago I sat next to a woman in a restaurant and, getting into conversation, she mentioned she had been for many years a nurse in one of New York's largest hospitals. Then she remarked she was filled with fear and could not sleep at night. I replied, "I can give you something that will take away your fear, but you must put your heart into doing what I tell you to do." She promised me she would. Then, after explaining the meaning and the value of courage, I wrote on a sheet of paper the following thoughts. I told her to keep repeating them to herself over and over again for two weeks and to *believe* what she was saying to herself. Here are the thoughts:

I am strong, powerful and courageous. Nothing in life can harm me.

Three weeks later I met this woman again and she said to me, "The thoughts you gave me to say to myself worked like magic! All fear has left me and I have never felt so good in my life." Then she continued, "I have given these thoughts to many of my friends and told them to put them on a card and paste the card on their bedroom mirrors." Should you be in need of courage, write the thoughts I gave to this woman on a card and keep repeating them over and over to yourself for two weeks. Put your heart and soul into these words, and you, too, will gain great courage.

A Practical Method for Gaining Courage

It is a definite law of mind that the more you concentrate your mind on any good thought, the more you will attract to yourself the benefits which that thought represents. So when you make it your duty to think courageously as often as you find time to do so, this practice will become a mental habit of thinking. It is also a law of mind that when you declare to yourself that you are already that which you desire to be, this mental activity will cause you to become that which you desire to become—provided you believe the declaration you make to yourself. For example, the more often you say to yourself, "I am fearful," the more fearful you will become. Conversely, the more often you say to yourself, "I am courageous," the more courageous you will become.

I ask you to get yourself an index card and either write or type on it the courage-producing thoughts which I now give you. Carry this card in a pocket, wallet or purse so that you can look at these thoughts often, and concentrate on them to regain instant courage wherever you may be.

> **I am bold, fearless and brave;**
> **It is impossible for me to be afraid.**
> **I am courageous in mind:**
> **I am courageous in heart:**
> **I am courageous in spirit, too.**
> **This is the great truth about me.**
> **I am strong, powerful and courageous.**

I promise you, my friend, if you will practice this method daily all sense of fear will leave you.

The Walkie-Talkie Method for Gaining Courage

Another method which I have used often for gaining more courage is as follows. While walking about your house or apartment, say to yourself with every five steps you take, "*I feel very courageous today.*" Keep repeating these thoughts with every step thereafter. These thoughts will then be impressed on your subconscious mind by constant repetition. Soon you will begin to feel more and more courageous with each succeeding day.

The Law of Dynamic Courage

Should you be in the business world you can use this same method on your way to and from your work, and between business calls on your clients or customers. As you walk along a street, say to yourself over and over, "*I feel very courageous and brave today.*" You will be surprised what a lift to your spirit this simple technique will give you. Give it a try and prove to yourself that this method really does work.

Do What You Fear and You Will Gain Courage

The reason some people do not enjoy success is that they are fearful of doing that which they know they ought to do. Should this be the case with you, make a small list of the things you are afraid to do; then make up your mind you will go out and do them.

> *To conquer fear, do the things
> you fear to do.*—(Author Unknown)

While I was riding in a taxicab in the city of Chicago the driver of the cab remarked that he sang in a cafe each night but was always frightened when he sang and dared not look at his hardboiled audience. I told him his thinking was entirely wrong; that he should concentrate on putting his heart into every song he sang; that every person in his audience had a heart, and when he sang to their hearts instead of to their faces, they would respond with applause. Some weeks later I met this same driver and he said to me, "I followed your advice and I am not afraid of my audience any more. Now I sing my songs from my heart to the heart within each one of my audience and, oh, how they love what I sing!"

If you are asked to give a talk to a group of people and are afraid to do so, put your heart into your subject and forget what your audience looks like. I speak from experience, and guarantee that if you will do this you will not fear anyone who comes to hear you speak. Instead, the people whom you address yourself to will sense your own interest in your subject. Furthermore, they will know that you are honest and sincere, and after you have finished speaking many of them will come up to you and shower you with praise.

Should you fear riding in a plane, the only way to conquer this belief in your own fear is to take a trip in a plane. I met this challenge when at Sioux City, Iowa. One day I asked an airline ticket seller, "What is there to riding in a plane?" The young lady replied, "It's all in your mental attitude." I replied, "If that's all there is to it, give me a ticket to Omaha, Nebraska." Since that time I have travelled on every airline in the United States and enjoy travelling by air immensely.

Whatever it is you are afraid to do, go and do it. And, when you have overcome one thing that you fear, tackle another, until you have gained so much courage that you are not afraid of people, things, or circumstances.

The Hum-A-Tune Method for Overcoming Fear

In New York City I have noticed that a great many people who cannot speak English—those recently transplanted from other countries—hum a tune to themselves while walking, in order to quiet inner fears. This is an excellent method for regaining courage. So, wherever you may be each day, hum some happy tune to yourself and see how calm and peaceful you become.

Imagination and Faith Will Make You Brave

Another good way to gain courage is to sit down, close your eyes, and imagine that you are very brave. Mentally picture yourself as a strong, powerful, courageous person. See yourself meeting people and looking them straight in the eye. See yourself walking the earth as a king. Mentally hold this image of yourself for ten minutes each day. Believe it to be true and realize it is the new courageous *you.* Keep up this practice and you will become a new, dynamic, powerful person, not afraid of anything that exists on earth.

How to Express Courage Every Day

There is no time like the present to free yourself from fear and live life courageously. In fact, you should start today, for the Bible tells us, "God did not give us the spirit of fear, but of love, power, and the spirit of a sound mind." (II Tim. 1:7) Now, when you realize how limiting it is to believe in fear, and how liberating it is to believe in courage, which will make you strong, powerful and courageous, common sense alone should make you decide to express

The Law of Dynamic Courage

it in your life, so you can enjoy all of the wonderful benefits courage will give you.

To help you do this, I ask you to say to yourself repeatedly:

Fear is an impostor. It has no power. I am through with it forever. I believe in courage, and am determined to express courage this day and every day of my life.

Then make a promise to yourself that you will. Keep up this practice and soon you will become so courageous that it will be impossible for you to believe that anything has power to harm you. Then make it a habit to lift your head up high and go forth each day with courage in your mind and heart. Mentally picture yourself as a conquering hero or heroine, afraid of nothing, ever ready to conquer and subdue anything that dares to impede your progress into a more fruitful and dynamic life.

By all means include courage in your Desire List. Practice all of these methods I have given you for gaining courage. Make courage one of your pet projects. Work at your project every day. Do this and I promise you will be surprised by the new strength and energy you will receive, and by what a powerful, dynamic, courageous person you will become.

A Poem that Will Inspire You with Courage

It's All in a State of Mind

> If you think you are beaten, you are;
> If you think you dare not, you won't;
> If you'd like to win, but don't think you can,
> It's almost a cinch you won't.
>
> If you think you'll lose, you're lost;
> For out in the world you'll find
> Success begins with a fellow's will;
> It's all in a state of mind.
>
> For many a game is lost
> Ere even a play is run,
> And many a coward fails
> Ere even his work is begun.

> Think big and your deed will grow,
> Think small and you'll fall behind;
> Think that you can and you will,
> It's all in a state of mind.
>
> If you think you are out-classed, you are;
> You've got to think high to rise;
> You've got to be sure of yourself before
> You can ever win a prize.
>
> Life's battles don't always go
> To the stronger or faster man,
> But sooner or later, the man who wins
> Is the fellow who thinks he can.
>
> —Walter D. Wintle

It Is Your Duty to Act with Great Courage

In order to be true to yourself you have an obligation to be true to the great power God endowed you with when he created you. Why do you suppose He gave you such power? To use it intelligently so you could enjoy life to the fullest. He gave you a mind, and the power to imagine; the power to desire that which you need. He gave you the power to believe, and by so doing, attract to yourself any good thing you desire.

Now the best way to fulfill the obligations you have to yourself and the creative power within you, is to think and act with courage so that you can enjoy more and more of life's riches. I tell you, my friend, it is your duty this day to get busy by throwing off all shackles of fear, and putting on the breastplate of courage. March forward into life as a conquering hero. Make up your mind now that you *can* and you *will* live a strong, powerful, victorious life. Do this and you will live the life triumphant.

REMINDERS FOR GAINING DYNAMIC COURAGE

1. In order to live a victorious life you must have courage and a will to win.

2. Courage gives you power to venture into new fields of endeavor and stay with them until they become a success.

3. Courage is the only remedy for fear.
4. You have been shown what an explorer did to overcome fear and win a victory.
5. The method a woman used to conquer fear and gain courage.
6. You have been given a practical method to use for gaining courage.
7. You have been given the walkie-talkie method for gaining courage.
8. You have been urged to do what you fear to gain courage.
9. How the hum-a-tune method will give you courage.
10. How your imagination and faith will make you brave.
11. You have been shown how to express courage in your life every day.
12. You have been given a poem that will inspire you with courage.
13. It is your duty to act with courage so that you may live a triumphant life.

The Law of Radiant Health

Over the main entrance of a hospital in Louisville, Kentucky, there is a large stone upon which is engraved *Health Is Wealth*. How true this is. Health of mind and body is true wealth which makes it possible for you to enjoy the other rich benefits of life.

It is your right to have health and have it in abundance. Why is this so? Because health is a priceless attribute of life, which makes it possible for you to do great things and live richly beyond measure. Should you be lacking in this kind of wealth, there is something you can do to obtain it. This chapter will show you what to do to gain radiant health. Put the methods you are about to read about into practice and you will enjoy the many blessings good health has to offer you.

The Great Benefits of Health

Health means soundness of mind and body. It represents freedom from bodily pain or disease. It is that vigor of mind that causes you to have a feeling of complete well-being. When you are in good health it is a sign that your mind and body are in good condition and functioning properly. When you have health this means you are full of life and vitality. It means you are strong, powerful, high-spirited, and sparkle with life. It is then you have the incentive to do big things and the power of strength and endurance to win. Use health-power with wisdom and it will make of you an outstanding person, one who is literally "healthy, wealthy and wise."

Some Causes for Lack of Health

Although it is natural and normal for everyone to enjoy the benefits of good health, many people block the flow of the vital health energy of life from their minds and bodies by harmful mental practices. They consciously give their attention to worry, fear, hate, jealousy, envy, selfishness, greed, sorrow and discontent. This sort of mental practice immediately sets up an inner mental disturbance within their minds. As a result they become emotionally upset, and the discordant vibrations of their emotions have a destructive effect on both their minds and bodies.

Other causes for lack of health are: Resentment at the type of work one is doing; lack of sleep and overwork; and, of course, lack of restraint in eating and drinking. Then when symptoms of illness appear, people rush to their doctors to repair the damage they have done to themselves. However, when these mental blocks are dispelled from the mind through right thinking and believing, health will again flow into the mind and body.

The Fountainhead of Health Within You

The original source of all health is within you. It is the spirit of your life. This dynamic power is the same power that created you and endowed you with spirit and power. In truth the Fountainhead of life and health is the Spirit of God within you, a Power so mighty that He will give you new life, energy, strength and vitality at any time. But, like all other good qualities of life, you must first desire health and believe you will receive it in order that the health-giving power of life can flow freely into your mind and body.

The Law of Constant Renewal

You are living in a universe wherein all things are constantly being reinvigorated and renewed. This is the fundamental law of life. You see this law of renewal in action at springtime when nature unfolds its magnificent newness and beauty; you see it when a child is born, and when new architectural structures take form around you, and new inventions come into being for your greater comfort. And the wonder of it all is that you have this same Spirit of renewal within *you*. When you use this power rightly by recognizing it and believing in it, it will rejuvenate you with new health-giving power in every respect.

How to Attract New Health-Giving Power

Recently I met a businessman who looked so ill that I asked him what ailed him. He said, "I have the 'flu' and the medication I am taking has not helped me." I told him the source of all health is within him, but that he must claim health in order to receive it. At his request I wrote the following statement on a card and told him to repeat it over and over to himself and to believe what he was claiming for himself. Here it is: "I AM STRONG, POWERFUL AND HEALTHY NOW." The following day he said to me, "Your method is beginning to work. I feel much better." The next day he said, "That method really does work." The third day he said, "I feel more strong and powerful today." I did not see him again for two weeks, at which time he said to me, "I want to thank you for giving me that positive mental statement; it helped me greatly and I am now in excellent health." So, if you should ever be in need of good health, say to yourself repeatedly: "I AM STRONG, POWERFUL AND HEALTHY NOW." And *believe* that you actually are that which you are claiming to be. Keep up this practice and when you are restored to health you will know that this method works, for you have proven it to yourself.

A Method to Stimulate Good Health Condition

A simple method to harmonize both mind and body is to take a walk in the fresh air. During your walk inhale a deep breath of air and hold your breath while you walk seven steps. At the end of your seventh step, start to exhale the breath you are holding and exhale it slowly while you walk seven steps. Repeat this method while you walk two blocks. Breathe in, hold your breath while you walk seven steps, exhale the same breath slowly while you walk another seven steps. Keep it up and you will really feel good. The purpose of this simple exercise is to restore perfect rhythm between mind and body. It is a mind and body reconditioner, for when both mind and body are in harmony, the natural result is mental and physical good health.

Dynamic Affirmations for Gaining Health

A line in the Bible contains a method for gaining renewed strength and vitality. It reads as follows: *"Let the weak say I am strong."* [Joel 3:10] There is rare wisdom contained in this statement, for when one who is weak declares to himself "I am strong," this mental action on his part dispels from his mind his belief in weakness and, as a consequence, new strength and power will begin to flow into his mind and body.

Today, we know that when you make a positive statement to yourself, and believe that you are what you desire to be, this mental activity is impressed on your subconscious mind. Thus when you repeatedly affirm to yourself, "*I am strong and healthy*," your subconscious mind will automatically cause you to become strong and healthy.

I am now going to give you some powerful affirmations to say to yourself each day in the week to obtain good health. Practice them conscientiously every day and you will feel new strength flowing into every part of your being:

> SUNDAY: *The health energy of the universe is flowing through me now, and I am whole and well and strong.*
>
> MONDAY: *I keep my mind on good health today and, as I do, new strength and power are attracted to me.*
>
> TUESDAY: *Every part of my being vibrates with good health today.*

WEDNESDAY: *This day I express radiant good health in both mind and body.*

THURSDAY: *This day I am healthy in mind, healthy in spirit, and healthy in body.*

FRIDAY: *Health flows through me in a mighty stream today and I am completely renewed in every way.*

SATURDAY: *This day I express dynamic good health; this day I am strong, powerful and vigorous; this day I enjoy perfect health in mind and body; this day I shine and sparkle with radiant good health.*

I have used this method for gaining health and staying in health often and as a consequence I always enjoy good health. I urge you to practice this method likewise and prove to yourself it really does give you new health-giving power.

The Healing Power of the Subconscious Mind

Your subconscious mind is truly a miracle working power. This power is always at work renewing every organ, gland, cell and tissue in your body. And it has been said that your body, unknown to you, is completely renewed every eleven months regardless of your chronological calendar age. But if you refuse to cooperate with this power and deliberately attempt to destroy its constructive work through creating body tension by worry and fear, it is little wonder then why you lack the good health you are rightfully entitled to have and enjoy.

However, when you turn to your subconscious mind for healing and *believe* it will heal you, and when you turn to it for health and *believe* it will restore you to health, it *will* do so. For this miracle-working Power of the Spirit of Life within you can and will do all good things for you, provided you yourself *Desire* and *Believe* that it can and will.

A Miraculous Example of Subconscious Mind Power

I am a living example of the fact that the subconscious mind can perform a miracle of healing. One day the heel of one of my shoes caught on the curbstone of a New York City street. This action threw me to the pavement with enough force to break my left arm. I had an X ray taken of my left arm and shoulder, which revealed that a bone in my shoulder was broken. The doctor who examined the X ray picture suggested I go to a hospital and put my left arm and shoulder in traction. Being a person who firmly believes in what he is writing, I refused. Instead I went to my hotel room, closed my eyes, and affirmed to myself there would be no pain in my arm and shoulder and there never was. Then I mentally visualized the bones in my left shoulder as knitting together and quickly healing, and *believed* what I had visualized to be the absolute truth. In three weeks my shoulder was completely well again, and I never lost a single day at work. The doctor who attended me had said to me often when I met him socially, "I cannot understand the miracle that happened to you." I understand it, however, for I believe that the Laws of Mental Magnetism will work in any emergency, but I must believe in them wholeheartedly to cause them to work for my benefit.

The Importance of Having a Will to Get Well

Any good doctor knows that a will to get well is a very important factor in the recovery of a patient from illness back to good health. In discussing this subject with my secretary recently, she said, "What do you mean by a will to get well?" I replied that that which we call will power is a faculty of the mind by which one chooses or determines what one will desire for oneself. So when a person has a will to get well it means he has a desire to get well. And a desire to get well is the first step towards returning to good health. If you are lacking in good health, use your will power by desiring good health. Then make up your mind that you will be restored to good health by *believing* that you will be. Keep up this practice and good health will become your constant companion.

How to Develop a Healthy State of Mind

As both health and sickness have their origin in the mind through the processes of thinking and believing, and the real you is mind and spirit (your body being only a vehicle), the first thing to do in order to regain health is to develop a healthy state of mind. How are you to do this? By concentrating your thinking upon health and the vital force of the life power within you rather than upon ill health and discomfort. To help you become health conscious, here are some mental exercises to practice each day.

Each morning after you have awakened, sit in an easy chair, close your eyes and completely relax. For five minutes imagine you are completely immersed in an ocean of health-healing power. Feel a torrential stream of this health-giving water of life all around you. Open the mouth of your mind and drink freely of this true water of life, and as you do, feel its curative power flow through every part of your being, washing away all impurities from both mind and body. Imagine yourself as a being with new health, strength and vitality. Silently say to yourself, "*I am now an expression of perfect health.*" Then go about your business believing in health and expecting health to be made manifest in your life.

Afternoon Health March Exercise

Each day after luncheon take a short stroll for yourself and while so doing imagine yourself as a young soldier about to start on a short march. Lift your head up high, hold shoulders erect, and swing both of your arms back and forth as you march. Then march in a brisk rhythmic pace and count as you walk, one, two, three, four, one, two, three, four, one, two, three, four. Now, instead of counting, say to yourself, "I AM HEALTHY—I AM HEALTHY—I AM HEALTHY." Keep repeating these thoughts to yourself for two or three blocks, then go about your business. The purpose of this exercise is to keep your mind focused on health and to claim health for yourself. Then as you continue in this good health-minded habit, the health energy of the life power within you will circulate through every part of your being.

Give Your Subconscious Mind an Order for Health

Each night before going to sleep give your subconscious mind a definite order to give you an abundance of good health. Remember, it is your servant and will deliver to you what you desire. So just before dozing off speak to your subconscious mind by saying to it, "Subconscious Mind, I am now giving you an order for an abundance of good health. Pour good health into my mind and body while I sleep. Strengthen and revitalize me while I sleep. Awaken me in the morning full of life and vitality. Keep me strong and healthy every hour of the coming day."

Keep up these three exercises every day for the next 30 days and so prove to yourself that these methods will regain for you radiant good health.

Laughter and Merriment Stimulate Good Health

There is nothing as good as a hearty laugh to release tension from both mind and body. The Bible confirms this fact when it states, "A merry heart doeth good like a medicine." [Prov. 17:22] When you have a good laugh, you not only relax your mind, but every nerve, organ and body muscle are relaxed too, making it possible for the vital health-giving energy of life to flow freely through you.

Mr. Ole Johnson of the famous comedy team of Olson and Johnson knew this to be true. He once told my brother that when he and his partner played the Winter Garden Theatre in New York they would look through the peep-hole in the stage curtain before each performance and pick out the most tense appearing man or woman in the audience. Then as the show began to unfold they would go down into the audience and do all kinds of ridiculous things until they had the person they had spotted from the peep-hole in hysterical laughter.

Now, you have the power to laugh and the power to be merry; but you must make up your mind to laugh instead of concentrating your attention on depressing things. So, why not look at the bright side of life and observe the humorous things people do? Why not see a comedy theatre production that will give you a big laugh?

Why not tune into comedy programs on radio or TV? You can even laugh at yourself and thereby release tension in mind and body. You can make of each day a day of laughter, and by so doing enjoy a greater measure of radiant good health.

A Magical Mental Habit for Gaining Health

It is a custom, when you meet people whom you know, for them to ask you, "How do you feel today?" Now, instead of replying, "Terrible," or, "Not good," say, "*I feel wonderful! I feel marvelous!*" The psychology in making this statement is that the moment you begin to declare it, you have begun to develop a new mental attitude about yourself and, if you persist in affirming it every time you meet a friend or acquaintance, you actually will feel more wonderful and marvelous each day. I use this method every day and you would be surprised to know how good I always feel. Please try this method immediately and keep it up for a month or two, and I assure you that you, too, will always feel good.

I ask you to get a large sheet of writing paper and write at the top, "My Program for Gaining Good Health." Then go through this chapter and copy the methods for gaining good health. Promise yourself you will practice these methods without faltering for the next two months. Start doing this today—for the sooner you start, that much more easily will you attract radiant good health.

RADIANT GOOD HEALTH REMINDERS

1. It is your right to have an abundance of good health.
2. Good health is a sign that your mind and body are in good condition. Hence you have the ability to do big things and the power of endurance to win.
3. Lack of health is caused by harmful mental practices. However, when these mental blocks are removed from the mind, health will again flow into mind and body.
4. The Fountainhead of health is within you. This fountain is the spirit of your life. Use this power rightly and it will rejuvenate you in every respect.
5. How a businessman regained health by believing he was "strong, powerful and healthy now."

The Law of Radiant Health

6. You have been shown how to inhale and exhale when walking as a means to stimulate good health condition.

7. You have been given a one-week Dynamic Mental Affirmation program to practice to gain good health.

8. You have been shown that your subconscious has power to heal, provided you believe in its healing power.

9. How the power of the subconscious mind healed a broken shoulder.

10. Why a will to get well is a most important factor in restoring a person to health.

11. You have been shown how to develop a healthy state of mind.

12. You have been shown how to use your imagination and faith in the morning to regain health.

13. How a short afternoon health march will help you gain health.

14. You have been shown how to give your subconscious mind an order to give you radiant health.

15. Why a merry heart is so valuable in restoring one to good health.

16. You have been given a magical method to practice in order to enjoy the wonderful feeling of radiant health.

7

How to Keep Young in Mind

Ponce de Léon, the Spanish explorer, had a marvelous idea when he went looking for the fountain of youth in Florida. The only thing wrong with his plan was that he did not know that the true fountain of youth is within each and every person, including himself. As a consequence, his exploration became an amusing myth.

Another great myth is the myth of old age. This belief has done more to slow up personal unfoldment into a richer and more abundant life than any other negative idea, with the possible exception of a belief in fear.

The truth of the matter is, you have the Spirit of Eternal Youth within you, and when you understand the Law of Mental Renewal, and practice this law, you can become young in mind—yes, and in body, too. This chapter will explain how you can become young and remain young and by so doing enjoy more of life's manifold riches

Age Is Nothing but a Chronological Tick-Tock

That which we term age is actually a mechanical measurement of time, a human invention conceived by man for measuring the events and experiences related to the lives of people. As such it serves a useful purpose in the business world and in many other human activities. However, when you put a time limit on your capabilities and productivity, and begin to believe that you are growing older each day and will soon come to the end of the line as a creative individual, you are indulging in a very bad mental practice. I urge you to dispel this preposterous belief from your mind immediately. Why? Because you have the mighty Spirit of Youth within you to which you can turn at any moment and drink deeply from its overflowing well-spring of new life, vitality and power.

Youth Is Primarily a State of Mind

At this moment you are living in a particular state of mind which you yourself created. This mental state is a mirror reflecting back to you that which you think and believe. Now, as a belief in old age means to decline in life, and a belief in youthfulness means to be young, fresh and vigorous, it is easy to see which of these two states of mind will benefit you the most. Therefore I say to you, toss the belief in old age out of your mind at once and start believing in becoming younger each day. Make this a daily mental habit and soon you will live in a young state of mind which will upgrade your entire being.

You Must Live in the Present to Stay Young

You are living in one of the most fascinating eras human beings have ever experienced. Too many wonderful new things are happening each day to waste time living in the past. And you can gain nothing by rehashing old experiences which are now only memories of the so-called "good old days." There are no such things as "good old days," for you have the ability and the power to make each day a good new day, a day more wonderful than you have ever experienced in your life. So I tell you to "get with it," get into the mainstream of life by forgetting the past. Make up your mind you will make of yourself a young-minded person with power to forge ahead to a new prosperous, successful life.

He Is Too Young in Heart to Grow Old

I have a friend who has had several highly successful careers, yet he is too young in heart to grow old. He started out in life as a doctor. While in attendance at a theatre he was called upon to treat an acrobat who had had a bad fall in that theatre. Through this incident he became a physician to Al Jolson, Sir Harry Lauder, and many other theatrical greats. Then he became surgeon for the New York City Fire Department, and upon retiring became medical director for a large insurance company. Next he was asked to head a savings and loan association with assets of $1,500,000. Through his high vision, careful planning, integrity, and faith he and his associates have guided this institution to its present state of well being of $330 million in assets. I call him the Miracle Man of the Century because this young-in-heart man of 93 is at his bank every morning at 8:30 AM and puts in a very active day. This man is a living proof of what can be accomplished by believing in youth rather than old age.

An Amazing Example of the Spirit of Youth

It was my good fortune to know Joseph E. Howard, a young-in-spirit man who electrified audiences wherever he appeared both on stage and screen. The last time I met with Mr. Howard was at the Nicollet Hotel in Minneapolis, Minnesota, where he was starring and, after each performance, his audience arose and cheered him. I asked him, "Joe, how do you keep doing what you are doing at 85?" He replied, "God has his arm around my neck and He won't let me stop." To me this meant that Mr. Howard loved what he was doing and had no desire to cease giving enjoyment to people. *You, too, when you really love what you are doing and love to give of yourself to others will never grow old in spirit, for the love that you have for your work will forever keep you young in mind.*

A Secret for Becoming Younger Each Day

Recently, while at luncheon with a highly regarded doctor friend of mine, we discussed youth and old age. He remarked, "Worry is mankind's greatest curse. It makes people old and feeble." Then he continued, "Look at you, you never worry, and see how young and dynamic you are." I replied, "My dear doctor, I have a secret. I refuse to worry and refuse to believe in old age. Instead I *believe* that the spirit of life within me renews me with new vitality each day. I *believe* that each and every day I am becoming younger and younger." My doctor friend replied, "You are certainly a living example of what you believe in, for each time I see you, you look younger and more vital." I ask you to reread this portion of this chapter over again very carefully and write down on a sheet of paper both my doctor friend's statement and my reply to him. Use the gist of this conversation as your own method for remaining young and becoming more youthful each day.

A Magical Technique for Keeping Young

Some years ago a wonderful idea popped into my mind—a way of becoming more youthful and active each day. Don't laugh at what I am about to tell you, for this idea really does work. It suddenly occurred to me that instead of believing that I was a certain number of years old, I should believe, "*I am one breath old, a brand new being.*" I latched onto this idea with pleasure and relish, and made it my duty to experiment with this idea. From that day to this, I affirm this statement every day to myself, and the change that has taken place in my mind and body is simply fabulous. I am a brand new being in every respect. You, too, can use this technique by saying to yourself, "*I am one breath old, a brand new being.*" Hold this belief about yourself, and see what a magical change takes place within you and all of your affairs.

A Daily Youth Renewal Practice

As a self-help aid in acquiring more youthfulness of mind and the ability to enjoy more of life's goodness, I ask you to practice the following mental affirmations each day in the week. Remember, what you claim for yourself will become a fact in your life, provided you honestly and sincerely *believe* it will.

SUNDAY: *The spirit of youth within me now flows freely into my mind and body, making me younger in every way.*

MONDAY: *I am young in spirit this day and all the world to me is bright and gay.*

TUESDAY: *I feel much younger today than I have ever felt before in my life.*

WEDNESDAY: *Every moment of this day I am constantly being renewed by the youthful spirit of my life.*

THURSDAY: *I am young in mind, young in heart, young in body today.*

FRIDAY: *This day I am so full of youth and vitality I could sing and dance with joy.*

SATURDAY: *This day I express youth in my every thought and deed. This day I love youth for the blessings youth gives me.*

The purpose of this mental practice is to keep your mind focused on youth, and to affirm to yourself what you claim to be, youthful in mind, spirit and body. Persist in this practice and you *will* become exactly that.

How to Become Young in Heart

Much is being said today about this person or that, regardless of how many birthdays they have celebrated, being very young in heart. What does this statement imply? It means they are carefree, happy, jolly and contented, regardless of how many candles well-meaning friends put on their birthday cakes.

Now, to be young in heart means to be young in spirit, and to be young in spirit means to be young in mind. "How about being young in body?" you may ask. That is a good question and my answer to it is if you are truly young in heart your body will respond and take on newness of life, strength and vitality.

There are five dynamic key words that will cause you to become young in heart but, before I tell you what they are, I must repeat that which I have already said. "Your subconscious mind is the Spirit of life within you." In you it is the pure unconditioned energy of life power. You condition this power by consciously having a desire. Thus when you desire to be young in heart, it goes to work to cause you to become young in heart.

Therefore, you must first *desire* to be young in heart. Next you must claim that you *are* young in heart. The best way to do this is to sit quietly alone, with eyes closed and completely relaxed. Then speak these five dynamic key words to yourself in your silent meditation—"I AM YOUNG IN HEART." Mentally visualize yourself as being a young-hearted, dynamic, powerful person, full of life, energy and vitality. Hold this mental image of yourself in your mind for a full fifteen minutes. Then for five minutes feel new strength flowing into every part of your being. *Feeling* is the secret in this technique, so the next thing you are to do is to affirm, "I FEEL YOUNG IN HEART." Keep up this silent meditation practice every day and you will become young in heart and feel young in heart.

Make Every Day a Youth-Conscious Day

Each morning when you awaken and arise from your bed, stand on your feet and say to yourself, "This is going to be my youth-conscious day, a day in which I will be conscious of possessing renewed youth, strength and vitality." Then go before your mirror and take a good look at yourself. Put the sparkle of youth in your eyes. Put a youthful smile on your face. Then say to yourself, "I promise myself I will be young in spirit and mind today." Then go about your business. Practice this simple exercise every day and you will become more youthful looking each day.

How to Young-Line Your Figure

You not only have the right to be young in heart, you have the right to enjoy a youthful appearance as well. Why are some people, then, burdened with excess weight? There are various reasons, but the main one is that they eat too much food. What is the prime cause of this mental habit? Loneliness. To compensate for this state of mind, people resort to food, with the result that they become grossly overweight.

At one time, when I weighed 191 pounds, a friend of mine said to me, "Look at you; you are very much overweight!" Stung to the quick by his sudden remark, I made up my mind to do something about my figure. This is how I accomplished it. That night, as I lay on my bed, for one full hour I imagined I weighed 165 pounds. The next day while at breakfast I discovered I had no desire to eat my customary amount. Pondering this sudden reversal in my eating habits, it dawned on me that I had made up my mind to weigh 165 pounds. Each night thereafter I made it a habit to imagine that I actually did weigh 165 pounds. One month later I got on a scale and, lo and behold, my weight was exactly 158 pounds. When my friend met me again some time later, he remarked in surprise, "What have you been doing with yourself? I have never seen you looking younger and better in my life."

What I am saying is that the power of your mind can be a mighty factor in conquering a desire to eat too much food by replacing that desire with a desire for a youthful figure.

Here again is the method I have used for taking off excess weight. Each night before going to sleep imagine the exact number of pounds you desire to weigh, and make a firm mental impression upon your subconscious mind by repeatedly claiming that you are already the number of pounds you desire to be. Keep up this practice every night for three weeks. Do not be surprised when all of a sudden you do not have a desire to eat too much food. This is a sign that your nightly practice is beginning to work. Then when you have reached what you consider to be your proper weight, make up your mind you will at all times maintain your normal weight.

If you are a woman you know how important it is that you have an attractive figure. One way, in addition to the above method, is to imagine yourself as wearing a smaller size dress than you are now wearing. Let's say you are now wearing a size 18 dress. Mentally imagine yourself wearing, say, a size 12 in its place. Keep up this practice for a month and if you really believe you will wear a size 12 dress, you will be impelled to go out and buy one, put it on, and wear it as proof that this method really does work in Young-Lining your figure.

A third method for Young-Lining your figure—if your problem is the loneliness state of mind—is to make every effort to meet new friends and companions, particularly those who can inspire you with new thoughts and ideas. Feast your mind on the mental food these contacts give you and you will soon find your lonesome feeling leaving you and your desire to overeat will leave you, too. When it does, you will find yourself acquiring that Youth-Line figure.

The Rich Rewards for Being Young in Mind

The first reward for being young in mind is that you will conquer the insidious belief in old age, a belief that would cause you to cease making progress towards a richer and more enjoyable life. Next, you will begin to think up new, fresh ideas and ways and means of doing things to your benefit and profit. Your imagination will come alive and make it possible for you to become greater than you have ever been in your life. New strength and vitality will flow freely into every part of your being. You will have a new outlook on life and have a desire to accomplish wonderful new things.

You will be too busily engaged in doing worthwhile things to spend time on worry. Your purpose will be to evolve into a much finer person than you have ever been and to enjoy more of the rich blessings of life. Therefore I say to you, my friend, make it your sacred duty to reap all of the rich benefits of life by becoming young in spirit and in mind. Let your life shimmer and shine with glorious youthfulness by believing in the youthful nature of your own mind and spirit.

REMINDERS FOR KEEPING YOUNG IN MIND

1. The Spirit of Eternal Youth within you can and will constantly renew you in mind and body.
2. Age is only a chronological "tick-tock" for recording human events and experiences.
3. Youth is primarily a state of mind. To believe in old age means to decline in life. By believing in youth you can become younger each day.
4. You are living in the most fascinating era of human history.

In order to enjoy all of the new things that are taking place in the world you must live in the present.

5. You have been told how a young-in-heart man stays young and active at the young age of 93.

6. How a famous singer and actor thrilled audiences at the tender age of 85.

7. You have been told about the doctor who said, "Worry is mankind's greatest curse, and makes people old and feeble." My method for keeping young in mind.

8. You have been given a magical technique for becoming more youthful each day.

9. You have been given a Daily Youth Renewal practice to use each day for becoming youthful.

10. You have been given a method for becoming young in heart.

11. You have been shown what to do to make each day a youth-conscious day.

12. You have been given methods to Young-Line your figure and to become a more attractive person.

13. How keeping young in mind enables you to have a new outlook on life and have a desire to accomplish great things. The rich rewards you will receive by believing in the youthful nature of your own mind and spirit.

8

How to Gain a Magnetic Personality

As an individual you should radiate personal charm when in the presence of other people. But you may say, "How can I express something I do not possess?" That's just the point, you *can* develop a radiant personality by letting the real YOU express itself in and through you. As you do, people will take delight in the magnetic charm of your true inner self, and you will become a very much liked, popular person. This chapter will show you how to unleash the power of your mind towards gaining a magnetic personality and becoming the kind of person people greatly admire. Put the following methods into practice and you will know how to unfold the real magnetic YOU into a charming and dynamic presence—one that will be greatly admired.

Step One in Magnetic Self-Expression

Socrates, the Greek philosopher, knew and stated a rule for acquiring a radiant personality. He said, "Man, know thyself!" Now, to know yourself means to realize the fact that you are a very unique person endowed with certain talents; to know that no other person is exactly like you; to know that life expresses itself in people in a great variety of ways, and has chosen to express itself in you through the talents you have been given. To know yourself means to realize that you are a creative being with free will to use the power of your mind constructively for your own benefit and for whatever promotes the happiness of others. Not to use the power you have been given to its fullest potential is to be lacking in loyalty to your own true self.

Step Two in Magnetic Self-Expression

It was Shakespeare, no less, who gave us the basic rule in obtaining radiant magnetic self-expression. In one of his immortal plays we find the power-packed line:

> *To thine own self be true, and it must*
> *follow as the night the day, thou canst*
> *not then be false to any man.*

By realizing your genuine true worth as an individual, and putting your talents to work, you are being true to yourself. How are you to accomplish this? First, find out what your true talents are by discovering what types of things you can do most easily; i.e., by doing "what comes naturally" to you. By applying these talents and developing them, and becoming a success through them, you are being true to yourself. Not only, however, does this apply to your life's work, it applies to your dealings with other people. Treat people with honesty and with sincerity, and you will not be false to any man.

The Importance of Good Manners

Being true to yourself requires that you have respect for yourself as an individual and have respect for other people. It means being polite and friendly in your everyday contact with others who have the same right to live a good life as do you. You can do this by making of yourself an ambassador of good will wherever you may be. Do this and people will respect you. Do this and you will develop a charming, magnetic personality.

The Value of Proper Attire

At all times you should see to it that you are attired in attractive apparel which complements your personality. As you know, there are types of clothing best suited for a particular occasion. For instance, if you have a business appointment, it will aid you to make a good impression if you are attired in a neat business suit or dress. The same rule for appropriateness holds true when attending a social function, which naturally calls for "dress" clothes. Being always in the right attire for the occasion is an indication that you have respect for the people involved in that occasion. Thus, by showing this common courtesy to others, people will instinctively like and respect you in return.

How to Make a Good First Impression

1. On being introduced to a person for the first time, PUT A BIG SMILE ON YOUR FACE. Shake hands with that person and look him straight in the eyes. Let your mental attitude be that of sincere friendliness. Make your attitude cause the one to whom you have been introduced to feel the warmth of your friendly nature. Be quick to memorize the name of the person so you can address him or her by name later on.

2. Do not monopolize the conversation. Wait for the appropriate moment to ask the new acquaintance where he or she is from. Seek to discover a personal interest as a conversation piece. Show keen interest in the other person. Address that person by name once or twice and you will make a big impression on him, for it is a well known fact that the most important name to any person is his own.

3. As you take leave of the person to whom you have been introduced, *smile*, and let your magnetic personality sparkle like a brilliant diamond. Shake hands with that person, and put the feeling of genuine friendship into your handshake. Look the other one in the eyes and say, "It has been a real pleasure to meet you, Mr. . . . . . . (or Mrs. . . . . . .)." By acting in this manner you will have made a tremendous impression upon the other person, one that will be long remembered with great pleasure.

Put a Happy Ring in Your Voice

Your manner of speech is a very important factor in making a good impression upon another. You should at all times be careful of your choice of words. You should pronounce each word correctly and speak clearly so your listener can understand the meaning of what you are saying. Improper speech is a sure way to cause people to lose interest in you. It is a sign of an improper education. So when you speak, put life and meaning into what you say. Put a ring of happiness and enthusiasm into your vocal chords, and people will enjoy the resilient cheerfulness of your speaking voice. Do this and you will make a wonderful impression upon all the people you meet.

A good way to improve the quality and tone of your speaking voice is to stand in front of a mirror and practice saying good morning to yourself. Say good morning in a whisper and note how lifeless it sounds. Now say good morning as if you do not mean what you say and note how unattractive your voice sounds. Now say good morning by putting vitality and a cheerful ring in your voice and note how pleasing to the ear your voice sounds to you. You can use this same method by saying, "This is a wonderful day," or "I feel very dynamic today," or any other short sentence you can think of to use. I once was given this simple test when auditioning for a big speaking part and won out over many contestants. So, begin today to improve the quality of your speaking voice and you will be surprised how soon you will become a more articulate and impressive speaker.

The Importance of Good Physical Posture

How you conduct yourself in the presence of others is indicative of your state of mind. In this respect your physical posture has a lot to do with the kind of impression you make upon other people. You should never sit slumped over in a chair while someone is speaking to you. This shows disinterest and disrespect to the other person. Sit up straight and show interest in what the other person has to say. Assume the attitude of cordial good will.

When you walk, never walk with your head bowed down. This suggests that you are weighed down with unsolved problems. When you walk, walk with your head up, chin in, shoulders erect—like a West Point cadet. Walk with dignity and an air of self-importance. Remember that dignity denotes to others a sound, stable character. So lift your head up high and walk through life with a regal manner. Do this and people around you will take it for granted you are a person of importance.

How to Become a Well-Liked Person

The quickest way to have people like you is to have a sincere liking for people. This may be a bit difficult in some cases, but the rewards of such mental action are tremendous. Will Rogers, that great soul, knew this truth, for he said, "I never met a man I did not like." He was not only liked by people; millions of people loved him for being his true natural self, a man of great humor and magnetic personality. How can you develop a sincere liking for people? Very simply, by beginning to express a liking for one person, and then for another, and another, until this mental habit becomes an automatic habit of your mind. Do this and you will be amazed by the number of well-meaning people you will attract to you. They will not only like you in return but will have a desire to become one of your true loyal friends. I urge you to begin liking at least one person each day for the next 60 days. This practice will develop your personality and cause people to like you. And when people like you for the wonderful person you really are, this is a sure sign that you have gained a powerful magnetic personality.

Some Personality Faults to Avoid

1. Never allow the presence of an overbearing person to upset and disturb you. Quickly realize that that person's egotistical facial expression is a false mask used for the purpose of hiding an inferiority complex. Treat that person with courtesy and kindness, but never let him force you off your own magnetic beam of happiness and good cheer.

2. Cast out of your mind all feelings of inadequacy. Remember you were created for a *special purpose*, this purpose being to use your own individual talents to the fullest, and by so doing to make of yourself a big success.

3. Never allow yourself to become self-centered or to indulge in personal egoism. Be true to yourself at all times and in all places. Then people will recognize you as being honest and true.

4. Don't "tell the world" that you are developing a more magnetic personality. This is no one's business but your own. Let your charming manner of dynamic self-expression be your own personal press agent, for true magnetic self-expression will tell more about you than will 10,000 words.

Seven-Day Personality Improvement Program

I ask you to practice the following method for gaining a magnetic personality. I ask you to remember that which you do repeatedly becomes a habit. So, make it your duty to practice the following mental acts for seven full days and you will become a person with a new radiant personality.

1. Each morning after you are up and dressed, look in your mirror and SMILE. Then say to yourself: *I look wonderful today. This day I am going to act in a charming, magnetic manner.*

2. When you meet the first person you know, greet that person with a *happy sounding,* "Good morning" or "Hello." Put a ring of good cheer in your voice and keep it there all day.

3. *Be friendly and kind to all of the people you meet during the day and laugh and be merry and gay. Speak kindly when you meet and part.*

4. When you arrive home each evening, look into your mirror and say to yourself: *This has been a wonderful day, a day in which I have expressed myself in a charming and magnetic manner.*

Now, enter a check mark on the chart below for each day you have practiced this method.

	Sun.	Mon.	Tues.	Wed.	Thurs.	Fri.	Sat.
1.	—	—	—	—	—	—	—
2.	—	—	—	—	—	—	—
3.	—	—	—	—	—	—	—
4.	—	—	—	—	—	—	—

28 check marks, Excellent;   15, Passably Good;   10, Fair.

How to Check Your Personality Improvement

At the end of each day during the time you practiced the seven-day personality improvement method, I ask you to sit alone, close your eyes and visualize the faces of all the people you feel you have made a good impression on that day. Now imagine that the next time you meet with any of these people they will say to you, "My, but you look attractive today," or, "You sure are radiant today," or, "What a happy, cheerful person you are." This is what is known as hearing the good news about yourself. The more you desire to hear people speak well of you and believe that they will, so shall you hear complimentary remarks about yourself. This is an indication that your personality is improving.

You can use this method of silent meditation in connection with your relatives, friends and close associates. Imagine hearing every one of them, from time to time, coming up to you and saying, "What a wonderful change has come over you. You look marvelous today," or "What a dynamic person you are." Under no circumstances are you to consider their remarks as insincere flattery. Recognize them as the direct result of your having imagined and believed you would hear people telling you what a fine, attractive person you really are. This is a sure-fire method for checking up on your personality development and I urge you to practice it at the close of each day.

How to Put a Shine to Your Personality

You know by using polish and some effort you can put a shine on your shoes. The same rule applies to your personality. Apply the polish of refinement and good manners to your mind and it will cause your personality to shine and sparkle. Then, there is the high polish of radiant thought, which when impressed on your subconscious mind, and used with extra-strength faith, will make your personality shine like a brilliant diamond.

Here are some sparkling thoughts that I ask you to affirm to yourself. Say them over to yourself *each day*, sincerely believe in them, put faith and conviction in your voice, and your personality will take on a shine everyone will admire.

1. I am each day becoming more attractive in every way.
2. I am this day carefree, radiant, and gay.
3. I am friendly to everyone I meet today.
4. I am cheerful to all whom I greet today.
5. I will today hear people speak well about me.
6. I will today make a good impression wherever I may be.

Practice saying these dynamic affirmations to yourself every day and you will automatically begin to believe they are true. When this happens, and it will if you firmly believe that it will, you will have become a person with a "standout" personality. The aureola of your radiant presence will charm all who are fortunate to know you.

Now, go out into the world and practice what you have learned in this chapter. Make a good impression on people. Cause people to like and admire you as you have never been admired before. Spread good cheer and happiness wherever you go. Be an ambassador of love and good will. Then, when people tell you what a wonderful person you are, you will know that the Laws of Mental Magnetism are responsible for your having gained an attractive and magnetic personality.

MAGNETIC PERSONALITY REMINDERS

1. You should radiate personal charm in the presence of others. You can develop a radiant personality through mental practice.

2. The first step towards magnetic self-expression is to realize you are a very unique person with special talents.

3. You discover your true talents by discovering "what comes naturally" to you. You are true to yourself when you put your talents to work for you.

4. Having respect for yourself and others is a right step in personality development.

5. Being attired in appropriate clothing will cause others to like and respect you.

6. You can make a big impression when being introduced to another person by smiling, being friendly, and showing a keen interest in the other person.

7. When you put a happy-sounding ring in your speaking voice, and speak clearly so people can understand the meaning of what you say, you will make a good impression on people.

8. Your physical posture reveals your state of mind. When you walk, walk with assurance, like a West Point cadet. Correct posture denotes a sound, stable character.

9. The way to become popular is to develop a liking for people.

10. Never allow yourself to become self-centered or egotistical. This is a sure sign of an inferiority complex.

11. A sure way to develop a magnetic personality is to practice the Seven Day Personality Program. *Do it now*.

12. You can check your personality improvement by using your imagination and faith to hear people speak well of you.

13. You can put a shine to your personality by using the radiant thought method. Keep up this practice and you will shine like a brilliant star in whatever company you may happen to find yourself.

The Law of Unlimited Opportunity

Today there is a tremendous change taking place in the lives of people all over the world. Although *change is a fundamental law of life,* today the pace of that change is vastly accelerated. For this reason many people are bewildered and do not know how to adjust themselves to today's changing conditions. Change is always an opportunity to advance and make progress, and those who are flexible in mind welcome new experiences and new things which will enrich them and so create for them a more abundant life.

This chapter will show you how to use the Law of Unlimited Opportunity in the fast-changing world you are living in. Practice these methods and you will know how to cope with every new condition and rise still higher into a wonderful new world of your own making.

Opportunity Springs from Imagination

The generally accepted belief that "opportunity knocks only once" in each person's life is a totally false belief, conceived by someone who was not aware of the Laws of Mental Magnetism. All things in the world first had to be imagined. This is why those who are lacking in imagination are lacking in opportunity, and those who have great imagination always will create their own opportunity in abundance.

What to Do When Confronted with Change

Due to automation and other devices many people today discover that the work they have been doing no longer is needed. Others discover that they will have to move from the neighborhoods they have lived in all of their lives. Still more business people are finding themselves suddenly dislocated from their present activities. Such an occasion is not a time for panic and fright. It is an opportunity to use imagination, to visualize a wonderful new position, a new position with a larger income. It is time to see oneself living in finer and more luxurious living quarters. And if a person really *believes* that this will happen, it positively will.

The Woman with Invincible Faith

I met a woman writer from Hollywood, California who was sharing an apartment with a woman in New York City. This woman told the writer she would have to move within 24 hours because her husband was returning from the army. I made several suggestions to this writer as to some hotels she could move to. She replied, "No, I know the Laws of Mental Magnetism, I am going to stand pat on principle. Something very good will show up for me." This conversation took place at 11 PM the night before she had to move out of the place she was living. At noon the next day she visited a woman's club and mentioned her dilemma to a friend there. This friend said, "How fortunate it is you came here today. I know a woman who is looking for someone to live in her beautiful six-room apartment, rent free, while she is travelling in Europe for the next seven months."

A phone call was put through, and the Hollywood writer moved into the six-room apartment that afternoon. Frankly, I have never seen such unconquerable faith expressed at the zero hour as was expressed by this woman from California. Should you ever have to make a change in your living quarters, know that a wonderful new place to live in will show up. Believe that it will happen and it positively will happen.

How to Create a New Opportunity

The saying, "When an old door closes, a better one will open," is true. Why is it true? Because when an old activity which was once an opportunity comes to an end, you have the power to create a new opportunity in which you can more freely express your talents. How are you to do this? Mark well the following rules:

1. Think of the kind of work you really have a desire to do.
2. Make up your mind you are determined to do that kind of work.
3. Imagine that you are already doing that kind of work.
4. Do not settle for 10, 25, 50 or 75 per cent performance in that field.
5. Make up your mind that you will be the greatest ever to be engaged in that kind of work. If you are a businessman, decide to become a top flight businessman. If you are a private secretary, decide to become the world's greatest. Whatever it is you decide to become, decide to become the greatest that ever lived. This is what is called having "a high vision of yourself," a mental vision that will lead to fame and fortune.
6. Assume the attitude that YOU ARE the greatest person in your kind of work. This is not ego. It is the avowed intention on your part to dedicate yourself and your talents to the work you have chosen to do for the benefit of other people, including yourself.
7. You are to use the power of your faith as you have never before used it to know that you already are what you desire to be. Believe that you are the most successful person in your particular vocation. You must *know* that this is true and continue to *know* this is true.

How I Received an Amazing Opportunity

One time I had a burning desire to become a star performer. I went hither and yon looking for my big opportunity, without success. Then, out of the blue, a certain manager rushed up to me on a street and said, "Can you learn the leading part in my production and go on and play it within 70 hours?" This was a tremendous challenge, for the man I was to replace was an outstanding star in his own right. I answered, "Yes, give me the part and I will play it to perfection." At 12 o'clock that night I started to memorize this immense part and vowed I would not stop until I could speak it by heart 25 times. At noon the next day I really did know the part. That same evening I broke in the four songs in the part before an audience of soldiers at an army base. Then my big moment arrived. Without even a rehearsal with the cast of this play, the following day I went on stage in a theatre before a large audience and played the part letter-perfect. Immediately thereafter, I was signed up for the run of the play.

New Opportunity Door Openers

Suppose you are presently employed and are dissatisfied with the progress you are making. Should you resign? Not necessarily. You can create greater opportunity for progress by doing the following:

1. Think up new ideas that will benefit the firm you are with.
2. Put your heart into the work you are doing.
3. Give more efficient service.
4. Make up your mind to be the most valuable person in the firm you are with.
5. Imagine and believe you will be called to the front office and told by the head of your firm you have just been given a big promotion with a large increase in salary.
6. Believe this *will* happen, and you will have opened a wonderful new door of opportunity to make progress right where you are.

How a Gilded Chestnut Gave a Man a New Start

A woman once said to me, "My husband was a $25,000 a year hotel executive and resigned his position in a huff. Now he is a coffee shop manager making $60 a week. I wish you would speak to him and give him some faith so he can get himself out of the rut he is in." I spoke to this man to no avail. Then I decided to use psychology on him. Producing a gilded chestnut from my pocket that had been given to me by the gate keeper of Abraham Lincoln's Tomb at Springfield, Illinois, I said, "Within this shiny chestnut are the roots, trunk, branches and leaves of a mighty chestnut tree. This tiny chestnut can produce countless other chestnuts that will produce mighty trees. Within you is the mighty power of your mind. Within you is the power to imagine and believe. Use your power of imagination to mentally see yourself in a wonderful new job and believe you will receive it."

Imagine my surprise when a week later, as I walked into my hotel lobby, there sat this man in a chair. Excitedly, he rushed up to me and said, "I have been sitting in this hotel lobby eight hours in order to tell you the good news. I have just landed a very big executive position that pays me handsomely." Then, producing the chestnut I had given him, he looked at it fondly and said, "I shall never forget the lesson in faith this chestnut gave me as long as I live." Then he departed, a very happy man.

This Method Produced New Opportunity

Should you be the executive type and want to make a change, here is a method used by a middle-aged advertising woman recently, with great success. This woman defined a certain area in New York City where she desired to work. Then she went to a public library, procured a book listing all of the advertising agencies in that area, and jotted down the names of the heads of those agencies, together with their addresses. Then she had resumes of her background and ability typed and mailed to these executives. She received many favorable replies and accepted one that was just a block from the place where she lived. She imagined this would happen, and believed it would happen, and it did.

The Law of Unlimited Opportunity

You can do the same, by jotting down the names of all the firms whom you think could use your abilities and talents. Send a confidential letter to the president of each firm you have selected, and include a resume. Rent a post office box number and give it as your address. Then *believe* that you will receive many offers of employment, one of which is made to order for you. Believe this sincerely, and you will receive the kind of work you desire.

The Magical Key for Gaining Employment

You have in your possession the Golden Key of Opportunity. This key is the magical key of FAITH. This key will cause whatever you imagine and desire to become a positive reality. So if you are in need of employment, imagine what kind of employment you desire. Then use your magical pass of FAITH to open wide the door of the right opportunity for new employment for you.

To aid you in believing and proving to yourself that which I have said is true, I ask you to memorize the following affirmations of faith. Keep repeating them to yourself every day for the next 30 days until you know them by heart. The reason I ask you to do this is that only FAITH can create a new opportunity for you. Faith and opportunity literally mean the same thing.

1. *I firmly believe that I am now receiving the greatest opportunity of my life.*
2. *I believe I am receiving new opportunity in abundance.*
3. *I believe I am being divinely guided to my right place in life this day.*
4. *I believe my right work is attracted to me today.*
5. *I believe a wonderful new life opens up for me today.*
6. *I believe unlimited new opportunities will be offered me in miraculous and amazing ways.*

Keep up this practice and your subconscious mind will believe that which you believe to be the truth about you. It will go right to work to attract new opportunities to you. And the miracle-working power of your FAITH will have become your magical opportunity pass key to new employment. Remember, "And according to your faith, so shall it be done to you."

How an Actress Found Instant Work

At a social affair I met a young actress who had returned to New York after entertaining soldiers overseas and was desperately in need of employment. I explained the Laws of Mental Magnetism to her, and told her that, when she went looking for work the next day, she was *to believe she would receive work by 5 PM that day*. She visited several theatrical offices the following day and, in mid-afternoon, she was offered an opportunity to go to Paris, France, for a lucrative engagement. She immediately signed a contract and made arrangements to leave for that city. I was told later that this young lady phoned all of her friends and said, "I met a man last night who told me all I had to do to get a new job was to believe that I would get one before 5 PM today. I believed what he said and followed his instructions and what he told me to do really worked! I've got a wonderful new job and am flying to Paris tomorrow!"

How to Make the Right Decision

As a result of your using your power of faith, let us suppose two opportunities are presented to you at the same time and you do not know which one to accept. Here is an excellent method for arriving at a right decision. Weigh the good and bad points in both propositions and accept the one that contains the most benefits.

Get a sheet of paper and a pencil and write at the left top side of the sheet "Opportunity 1" and write "Opportunity 2" at the right top. Under each write "Benefits" and "Unfavorable Aspects." Ask yourself the following questions about each and put a check mark after those that benefit you and those that do not.

1. Which one gives me greater opportunity for progress?
2. Which one gives me greater financial income?
3. Which one would allow me freedom to express my talents best?
4. Which one would I feel more at ease with in regard to the people involved?
5. Which one has the better working conditions?

The Law of Unlimited Opportunity

For your convenience and to save time you can use the following check form:

OPPORTUNITY 1		OPPORTUNITY 2	
Benefits	*Unfavorable*	*Benefits*	*Unfavorable*
Q. 1	Q. 1	Q. 1	Q. 1
Q. 2	Q. 2	Q. 2	Q. 2
Q. 3	Q. 3	Q. 3	Q. 3
Q. 4	Q. 4	Q. 4	Q. 4
Q. 5	Q. 5	Q. 5	Q. 5

Now count the check marks which represent benefits and those that are check marked "Unfavorable" on this chart. Whichever opportunity contains the most benefits for you is the one you should accept. You can use this method in coming to a right decision regarding any matter by choosing that which is best for you.

Make Each Day a Golden Opportunity Day

My reader friend, I would have you know that no one can cause you to receive a new opportunity but you yourself. You have been given everything necessary to create your own opportunity. I ask you to stand on your feet and become a self-reliant person, responsible to no one for your success and growth but yourself. Do this and you will be the true self-sufficient person you were created to be, with all power to form and shape your own destiny into a richer and more expansive life.

So, go to it, friend. Use your *imagination* to visualize the right kind of opportunity for yourself. Then *desire* it with all your heart. Then spark it with the fire and ardor of your dynamic *faith* and cause it to become a reality.

Make each day a Golden Opportunity Day, a day in which you receive amazing new opportunities. Make each day a greater self-expression day. Make each day a day for personal advancement. Make each day a day in which you attract more of life's abundant riches. Do it today, good friend, for your power of faith is the great miracle working power of your life. It will attract every good thing to you when you firmly believe it will.

NEW OPPORTUNITY REMINDERS

1. Opportunity begins in your imagination. This is why people with great imagination have opportunities in abundance.
2. When a change takes place in your life, do not panic. See yourself in the new activity.
3. Remember how a woman with invincible faith found a rent-free apartment.
4. Remember the three rules for creating a new opportunity: (a) desire to become the greatest person ever in your field, (b) believe you will become the greatest in your vocation, (c) hold fast to the faith and you will demonstrate that which you believe.
5. How an amazing opportunity came to me "out of the blue."
6. You can create opportunity right where you are by putting your heart in your work. By giving better service. By making yourself extremely valuable to your firm. Do this and believe you will be promoted. Keep the faith and you *will* be promoted with an increase in pay.
7. Remember the part faith played in the Gilded Chestnut story.
8. Should you be the executive type, follow the example of the advertising woman who created her own new opportunity.
9. Memorize the Magical Key Method for gaining new opportunity.
10. How an unemployed actress found new opportunity by believing she would receive a contract by 5 PM the day she went looking for work.
11. The best method for making the *right decision* in choosing the opportunity which will benefit you the most.
12. Make every day a Golden Opportunity Day. Use the Miracle working power of your mind to attract more of life's riches each and every day.

10

The Unfailing Law of Prosperity

It is your right to have an abundance of money. Why? Because, money makes it possible for you to enjoy a higher standard of living. Is this the only reason? No. The principal reason is that you have a mind which has the power to produce wealth, and when you desire to receive wealth in the form of money and *believe* you will receive it, your power of mind will cause you to receive it. You will find many methods towards that end in this chapter. Put them to earnest and sincere practice, and you will open wide the door leading to greater financial security.

The Reason Why Some People Are Poor

The principal reason for a person being poor and without sufficient money is that such a person really believes in L-A-C-K, and not in ABUNDANCE. Such a one does not know that the source of all wealth is within him, nor does he know how to use the Law of Prosperity to produce his own wealth. As a well-to-do man expressed it to me, "Everyone was born to be successful, and if people are not, it is because of their own faulty thinking and believing." A belief in lack in our world of great abundance is not intelligent. However a large segment of the people do not realize this, and, it is their personal belief of lack which leads to poverty and want of every conceivable nature. Such people live in misery and want all of their lives.

The Basic Principle of Prosperity

The manner in which you use the power of your mind, i.e., Imagination, Desire and Faith, will determine whether you become poor or rich! Think and believe you will always be without money, and you will always be among the poor of this world. Think and believe that you will always be supplied with an abundance of money and you always will be. Why is this so? Because whatever you concentrate the power of your mind upon, strengthen your desire for, and believe you will receive, you attract. This Law of Mental Attraction is no respecter of persons. When used correctly anyone can prosper and become rich. *Any present failure can become a success with it*. Its prime purpose is to produce an abundance of all things that go to make for a prosperous life.

He Rose from Poverty and Prospered

One day a woman sent me a letter containing a check for ten dollars made out for cash. She asked me to give this check to a young concert singer who was in dire financial need. He, his wife, and their two small children had not even had sufficient food for several days. I got in touch with this man, and asked him to come to see me immediately. He did, and poured out his tale of woe to me in a pathetic manner.

I soon discovered he had completely lost sight of his real goal in life, that of becoming an outstanding concert singer. He had allowed money problems to so upset him that he could not think clearly, much less concentrate on his chosen profession. For six full hours I explained the basic principle of Prosperity to him over and over again. Then I told him to do the following:

I asked him to close his eyes and imagine himself as one of the greatest concert singers ever to have lived. I told him to *mentally visualize* himself appearing before huge audiences and to hear those audiences applauding him. I asked him to *believe* and *expect* he would receive word from his manager that a contract had been signed for a long concert tour. I told him to *believe* what he was imagining, and that I would add my own power of faith to cause what he was imagining to come true.

Five days later, I received a phone call from this man. In an excited voice he said, "A miracle has happened! My manager has just signed me for a long concert tour. I open next week at Boston. This is the most miraculous thing that has ever happened in my life!" You may never find yourself in exactly the same circumstance as this young man, but if you too have a need, you too can apply this principle! Use your imagination and faith to visualize yourself as being successful and receiving ample money in return for your talents.

How to Make a Money Goal

First I ask you to *banish the thought that the possession of money is evil*. This is not so, for money is the financial life blood of industry. It keeps the wheels of progress turning constantly for the betterment of all mankind. The more people who are gainfully employed, the better living conditions are for everyone. For this reason I ask you to make a money goal for yourself; a goal that will keep money in circulation; a goal that will give you and others more comforts of life. And here is a simple way to do it.

Think about how much money you would like to receive in a year. You can set your goal at $10,000, $25,000, $75,000, $100,000, or at a still higher figure. Look over these figures carefully. Be specific. Choose the one you honestly believe you can reach. Then put that figure down in the chart below as your financial objective to be achieved. Make that figure as large as a "bull's eye" to aim at.

THIS IS MY MONEY GOAL

1. I have decided to make the following sum of money the amount I am determined to receive within one year. That sum of money is:

   ....
   (Write your sum here)

2. I shall use all of my talents and abilities to the fullest towards causing my goal to become an accomplished fact.

   ....

3. I declare this to be true, and I know it to be true.

MY MONEY GOAL WILL BECOME A REALITY

....
Sign your name and date here.

Give Meaningful Purpose and Action to Your Goal

Dedicate yourself wholeheartedly towards causing your goal to become a success. Keep your goal ever before you in your mind as the one thing above all else you intend to achieve. Think of the many good things your goal will cause you to receive. Think of the financial security and peace of mind your goal will give you. Concentrate on doing the kind of work you are engaged in with greater efficiency. Bend every effort towards putting more heart and spirit into each thing you are given to do. Know that the greater service you give to others, the larger amount of money you will receive in return.

Back up Your Goal with Magnetic Faith

Faith is a powerful mental magnet, which draws to you that which you desire to receive. Why is this so? Because when you make up your mind to desire something of value, and *believe* you will receive it, it is FAITH, YOUR FAITH, that will cause you to receive it. This likewise includes an abundance of money. I am now going to ask you to back up your money goal with statements of dynamic, powerful, magnetic faith. Keep repeating the following affirmations to yourself each and every day, until they become firmly impressed upon your subconscious mind:

I firmly believe I will receive an increasing abundance of money this day and every day of this year. I firmly believe my money goal is now becoming a reality. I know this is true, I believe it is true, and nothing can change my strong, powerful, faithful conviction.

Do this and your money goal will become a 100 per cent success.

The Case of a Man Who Is an Amazing Believer

Recently I called on a man in New York City, and while waiting to be announced, I read an office brochure containing an outline of his successful achievements. I was particularly impressed with his latest gigantic goal. This man had imagined he would build an entire "new city," from the ground up, in the state of California. This is not a building-castles-in-the-air fable. No, because what he imagined is today becoming a reality.

First he selected the proper location for his "new city," and made arrangements to acquire suitable land. Then he had architects draw up plans for civic buildings, apartment houses, private houses, school buildings, churches, a theatre, a library, office buildings, stores, and other buildings to be found in a modern city. Then he arranged proper financing for this project. Next, he began his building operation and started erecting buildings, many of which are now completed. Today he shuttles back and forth by air between New York and California, supervising the balance of the buildings now being erected.

Talk about making a goal and staying with a goal until it becomes a reality! This man is a super-goal achiever. *Yet he is basically no different from you or me!* We have the same power of mind as he does, but *he used his imagination and faith* to an amazing degree. Consequently, he is prospering greatly for having so used the creative power of his mind. You, too, can imagine something really big and believe you can do it. When you do you will become exceedingly rich.

His Twenty-Five Dollars Became a Fortune

I know another man who, when I first met him, was out of work due to the fact that the firm he was with went out of business. He told me he had but $25. The next time I met him he had secured a line of merchandise to sell. At that time he said to me, "I am fed up with being without plenty of money. I have made up my mind to make $200,000 a year, and I am determined I will make it." Then I learned he had acquired several top-flight lines of merchandise to sell.

Two years later I visited him at the hotel where he was staying. He said to me, "Remember when I only had twenty-five dollars?" I replied, "Yes." "Well," he said, "today I have $40,000 in the bank, and I am now organizing my own national sales organization." Today, his volume of sales runs into several million dollars annually, and he has far exceeded his original money goal. His story proves that even in the direst circumstances, when you do not lose faith in yourself and your ability, and you make every effort to become rich, *you will inevitably become wealthy.*

Money Can Come to You in Many Ways

The unfailing Law of Prosperity never fails to produce wealth for anyone who desires to receive wealth. Failure to apply this Law is the only thing that can stop money from flowing into your pocket or purse. When you concentrate on attracting money, you set up a Mental Power of Attraction in your mind to attract money to you. Here are some ways money can come to you:

1. Thinking up new methods for doing things more efficiently.
2. Alertness in grasping new opportunities.
3. Creating something new that people desire.
4. Success in any business, profession, or enterprise.
5. Being left property as a legal heir.
6. Being declared a winner in a contest.
7. Through the mail or by telegraph.

A well-known songwriter has another way of receiving money. He is not in need of money. As a hobby, he believes he will find money on the streets. To date he has found several thousands of dollars in nickels, dimes, quarters, half-dollars, and dollar bills on the streets of New York City. This proves that what you concentrate on and believe you will receive, you receive.

However, the more you give of yourself and your talents for the benefit of other people, the greater measure of prosperity you will receive in return.

A Money-Attracting Technique

As you retire each evening, close your eyes and think of the amount of money you are determined to receive in one week, one month, or a year. Visualize that amount of money in your mind, paint a mental picture of it in your mind, and concentrate your attention upon that money picture for five minutes. Then speak to your subconscious mind. Say, "Subconscious Mind, I have given you a mental picture of the amount of money I desire to receive (name the amount and specified time). I now give you a direct order to go to work and deliver that sum of money to me." Then, go to sleep *knowing* that your desire will become a reality. I urge you to practice this method every night before you go to sleep. Keep it up for a period of six months and you will attract money in abundance.

Use This Self-Convincer Method Daily

You have no one to convince but yourself that your money goal will become a reality. You can do this wherever you are by making the following affirmations of faith to yourself. Say to yourself, "*I positively know my money goal will be reached. I firmly believe I will be rich and prosperous.*" Then take a giant step forward in faith and declare to yourself with intense feeling, "*I am rich and prosperous now.*" Keep up this practice every day and you will become exactly what you believe. Money in abundance will be attracted to you. And you will have become a person abundantly rich and wealthy.

Giving Thanks Will Cause You to Prosper

Each day count your blessings. Rise into the spirit of enthusiastic gratitude for the money you have claimed as yours, knowing that it is now being attracted to you. Take what money you now have, hold it in your hands, bless it, and give thanks to God for having received it. Then say, "*I now bless and multiply each piece of this money 100 times.*" If you truly believe what you have said, the money you now have will be multiplied 100 times, and find its way back into your hands. This is what is known as the Law of Increase. *Believe* that which you already have will increase and grow larger. *Believe* the money you already have will attract greater wealth.

Good Health and Prosperity to You

Allow me to extend to you my sincere desire that you enjoy a healthy and prosperous life. This is your divine birthright, and there is no reason for you not to have it. So, get busy. Practice the Law of Prosperity, and you will enjoy all the benefits that go to make for a happy and prosperous life. "*Peace be within thy walls, and prosperity within thy palaces.*" (Psalms 122:7) This is the Bible's way of saying to you, "Live and enjoy a peaceful and prosperous life."

LAW OF PROSPERITY REMINDERS

1. You have every right to live a prosperous life.
2. The reason some people are poor is their basic belief in *lack* rather than in *abundance*.
3. Your imagination, desire and faith will cause you to become either poor or rich.
4. The concert singer who rose from poverty to prosperity when he applied the Law of Prosperity to gain a lucrative concert contract.
5. How to make a Money Goal for the amount of money you desire to receive.
6. How to put meaningful purpose and action into your goal.
7. How to back up your goal with magnetic faith.
8. How a man with amazing imagination and faith caused his stupendous goal to become a reality.
9. How one man turned $25 into a fortune.
10. How money can come to you in many ways.

11. How to use the money-attracting technique.
12. How to use the self-convincer method to become rich.
13. How giving thanks for what you have will cause you to prosper.
14. Good health and prosperity to you. Receive it and enjoy it NOW.

11

The Ever-Present Law of Protection

When you came into this world as an infant you brought with you everything necessary for your development and growth towards a full and successful life. You also brought with you a built-in safety device—the power of your mind. Give close attention to this chapter and you will know how your mind can protect you from danger and harm.

Nothing Can Harm You but YOU

Personal safety is extremely important to you. It is life itself. A very wise man, Saint Bernard, knew this great truth and expressed it thus,

> **Nothing can work me damage except myself; the harm I sustain I carry with me; and never am I a real sufferer but by my own fault.**

The Ever-Present Law of Protection

In other words, each individual creates his own harm by faulty thinking and believing. Remember, what you *think* and *believe* *becomes* a *part* of *your actual living experience*. The Bible rule for safe living states: "*Discretion shall preserve thee: and understanding shall keep you.*" (Prov. 2:11.) This means that when you refuse to anticipate danger of any kind happening to you and, instead, believe that you will always be protected from harm, this perfect understanding of the protective life force within you will assuredly preserve and keep you each day in perfect safety.

Being Robbed Never Happened to Him Again

One day I called at the office of the owner of a wholesale business in Chicago, Illinois. The owner himself was not there, and I found that his wife was taking care of his business. I asked her where her husband was and she replied, "In the hospital—he was beaten up and robbed in this office two days ago." I told her to give him my best wishes, and that I would pray for his speedy recovery.

This I did by *mentally visualizing* him as restored to perfect health and by *believing* that he would be. About six weeks later, I called on this same wholesale firm again. The owner was in his office looking as happy and healthy as I had previously visualized him. I took him aside and asked him this question, "Did you ever believe you would be held up and robbed?" He replied, "Why, of course I did! Every merchant on this street has been robbed and I knew it was sure to happen to me."

I then gave him a brief talk on the Laws of Mental Magnetism. I explained to him how he had attracted what he feared. I then wrote down on a sheet of paper a few short sentences and told him to memorize them and *believe* in them. Here are those brief sentences:

> **I am divinely protected from all harm.**
> **My business is protected from all harm.**
> **Never again will anyone have a desire to harm me.**
> **I believe this is true, I know this is true, and I thank God that this is true.**

And, my friend, these simple affirmations of truth *became a fact* in this man's life, for from that time on, no one has tried to rob him or injure him.

Note carefully how, when this man changed his belief from anticipated danger to that of Divine Safety, complete safety became a manifest *fact* in his daily living. *You*, too, can use this same method for your own protection at all times. Make a copy of these affirmations for personal safety. Carry them in your wallet or purse. Memorize them. Look at them often. *Believe* in them, and you will be shielded from harm.

Wake Up to Your Safety Factor

The belief in harm is a *human invention* founded on superstition and ignorance. It has caused more misery and suffering to the human race than any other false belief that man has imposed upon himself through the ages. Have nothing to do with this utterly destructive belief! Why do I tell you this? Because having been endowed with free will you have the power to *choose* the kind of thinking which will benefit you, and self-preservation is a basic instinct, a law of all life. Therefore I say to you, make safety the law of your mind. *Believe* in safety with all your heart, and the ever-present Law of Protection will work for and through you to the very end of the pathway of YOUR life.

Safety Is a State of Mind

From the standpoint of the laws that govern correct thinking, you know, *or should know*, that you have the ability to distinguish between right and wrong, thereby using good judgment in choosing the kind of thoughts you allow yourself to think. Now, I am going to ask you a very important question.

"Do you think it is more intelligent to think and believe in safety, than to think and believe in harm?" Having just learned from these pages that *what you think and believe you attract*, you certainly know the right answer and that it is vital for you to believe in safety.

Yet, it is exactly at this point of decision that many people go wrong in the use of their mental faculties. They let their imaginations "run wild," thinking of all kinds of harmful things that might happen to them until they are walking about in complete fear. Then when some tragedy does strike their lives, they exclaim, "How could that have happened to me?"

The Ever-Present Law of Protection 117

To help YOU to discipline your imagination and "promote" your own safety factor, I have prepared the following safety methods for you to practice. Practice these methods *daily*, and you will soon come to realize that *safety* is a *state of mind*. Be constant in your practice, and you will become your own safety director, living in a safe and sound environment of your own making.

Home Protection Safety Method

Your home is more than a three-dimensional building. It is a dwelling place for you and your loved ones. As such it should be a place of safe-keeping in every respect. You can make it that kind of a place, first, by application of the practical elements, such as seeing to it that all electrical wiring is in good condition, by checking all electrical appliances and making sure they are in good working order. Should you have children, make certain that such things as matches and poisonous drugs are out of their reach. See to it that all rugs have "rug anchors" under them to avoid trips and falls. Place a rubber mat in your bath tub; keep a good bath mat on the floor to step on after a bath or shower. Check your heating equipment to see that it is in good order. Check the locks on your windows and doors to make certain they function properly. Remember, more accidents happen in homes than in any other place. These are simple precautions which will insure comfort and safety at home.

Now, secondly, memorize the following thoughts for home safety. Make them the code of your firm personal belief.

> **This house is a haven of safety. This home is the dwelling place of God. Nothing of a harmful nature can enter this house. The spirit of safety and protection stands guard over me and my loved ones, causing us all to dwell in perfect safety.**

Do this, and your home will never fail to be a haven of safety and peace.

Auto Protection Safety Method

Before you start out in your car, whether it be for a short run or a long trip, you should *condition your mind* with the right mental attitude regarding personal safety. You can do this very easily. It will only take a few minutes.

Sit down in a quiet place, completely relax, and close your eyes. Now imagine yourself as already being in the place you intend to visit. Visualize yourself as having already completed your trip back home in perfect safety. Believe what you imagine is the absolute truth. In other words, make a mental journey—in perfect safety—in your mind to the place you are going and back home before you have actually gotten into your car. Then, open your eyes, get up and go out into your car and drive confidently on your journey.

The reason I tell you to do this is that many, many people start on a trip with worry or fear in their minds that they will have an accident—and so they will "attract what they believe." Insurance companies have a term for these people—"accident-prone"—and you know now what this tendency to accidents is based upon.

Here is a good motto for safe auto driving which will serve you well if implicitly *believed* in. Say to yourself:

> **I always arrive at my destination safely. I am always protected while driving my car. This is the truth I believe in and the reason why I am always protected when I travel in my car.**

Air Safety Protection Travel Method

I have traveled more than 500,000 miles by land, sea, and air and have *always* arrived at my destination safely because I always *believed* I would. Before taking an airplane trip I have a special method for safety which I will share with you. I believe in this method and so it works like magic for me in carrying me to my destination safely. Here is my method—use it yourself the next time you plan making a trip by air.

Let's suppose you plan to fly from New York City to Los Angeles, California. The first thing to do, *before* you leave your home for the airport at New York, is to sit down in an easy chair, close your eyes and relax. Now imagine yourself boarding your plane at the New York airport. Mentally picture yourself taking a seat in that plane. Picture yourself fastening your seat belt. Imagine that your plane is taking off and soaring high in the air. Visualize yourself eating dinner on the plane. See yourself reading a magazine or two.

The Ever-Present Law of Protection

Now, imagine that the stewardess is saying, "Fasten your seat belts. We are about to land in Los Angeles." Picture yourself walking down the ramp onto terra firma at the Los Angeles airport, safe and sound and feeling wonderful. Then open your eyes, and get ready to go to the New York airport. Now, remember, what you have been doing by this method is to *actually create a safe air trip* for yourself, for what you create in your imagination becomes a fact when you firmly *believe in* the mental image of your own creation.

Now, when you reach the airport at New York City and board your plane for Los Angeles, sit down in your seat and affirm these thoughts to yourself.

> **This plane has a perfect take off. It will have a perfect flight and a perfect landing at Los Angeles, California. This is true because God is the real pilot of this plane.**

I have given this, my air safety method, to several airline pilots who believe it to be an excellent method. You, too, can use it the next time you travel by air to any destination. I ask you to use it and prove to yourself that this right mental attitude regarding air travel will dispel all sense of fear. I ask you to *believe* and to know you will always arrive safely at your destination any time you make a travel trip by air.

How to Protect Your Loved Ones

With the current world-wide unrest among nations, many young men are today being sent overseas for military service. Should you be a parent or sweetheart of such a young man, you are naturally concerned with his safety. I take it for granted that, in your own way, you will each day say a prayer for his safety. This is your duty, but there is something else you can do. You can use the ever-present Law of Protection in his behalf, in the following manner.

Once, twice, or three times a day, sit alone in a quiet place. Place a picture of the one whom you love on a small table in front of you. Gaze at that picture intently for two minutes. As you do this realize that he possesses the same spirit of life as do you. Realize that there is no separation between him and you in mind, and that the thoughts you are now holding regarding him will travel instantly to him; that he will be uplifted in spirit by them.

Now close your eyes and visualize your loved one possessing great courage and faith. Mentally picture him as being unafraid and very brave in heart. Picture him as being surrounded on all sides by the Divine Protection of God. Know for a certainty that no harm can ever come to your loved one. Now go a step further. Create in your imagination a vivid mental picture of your loved one *coming back home to you* TOTALLY UNHARMED. Feel this to be true, know it to be true. Now, enlarge your picture of him by seeing him actually coming back into your home, putting his arms around you, kissing you and telling you:

"*I knew it would happen! I knew I would come back home alive!*" Believe that what you have just been imaging for him will SURELY HAPPEN. Then, open your eyes and resume your daily duties. Keep up this practice for him every day while he is overseas. *Believe* in it wholeheartedly, and what you have imagined and believed will become a reality. This is how to use the God-given Power of your Mind for the one you love. This is the way to use the ever-present Law of Protection constructively for your loved one.

How to Protect Your Valuables

I know a man who owns a supermarket and is so afraid of being robbed that he has placed a large circular mirror in his store to detect any "character" in the act of pilfering. I told him he was attracting a very negative influence by this mental attitude of fear; that the Bible says, "What I feared came upon me." He replied, "Don't give me that 'hog-wash.'" Well, what do you suppose has happened to him as the result of his fear complex? Every month, almost regularly, some "character" does come into his place of business, threatens him with bodily harm if he yells and cleans out his cash register of the daily cash receipts.

The surest way to keep from losing anything of value is to REFUSE TO BELIEVE IN LOSS. This is really simple and, when you believe in it with all the conviction you can muster, *no one* will take from you what is rightly yours. This is another facet of the Law of Mental Magnetism, for whatever material thing of value you now own, you attracted that possession to you by the power of your mind. This is how it came into your private ownership. The only way you can lose it is to fear it will be taken away from you. To counteract and cancel out such fear, say to yourself repeatedly, "I CAN NEVER LOSE ANYTHING I RIGHTFULLY POSSESS." Believe this truth with all your heart, and you and your valuables will never know a parting. Practice this method NOW. Prove this method to yourself NOW.

Put Yourself "On Guard" Every Day

Just recently I spent an evening with some friends who are insurance executives. During our conversation the name of a certain man came up. One said, "Isn't it ironic that .... could go through the last War with General Patton, come home and work with us, and then, while walking across the street one day, meet with an accident and die instantly!" Although I said nothing to that gathering, in my mind I felt I knew the probable answer. This ex-soldier did not have his mind alerted to his present surroundings. Instead, he had allowed his mind to become absorbed with some unsolved problem, far removed from that street he was crossing.

The way to start your day right is to *know* and *believe* that you will be shielded from all manner of physical harm. But you must do your part on behalf of the Law of Protection by being on guard, and by crossing the street with the green light; by being sure to look in all directions to assure yourself that your pathway is clear.

Keep your mind in the present and alert in every type of circumstance. Be safety conscious. *Know* for a certainty that you will arrive back at your home safe and sound at the end of your day. Use this simple formula for personal safety and you will have it around the clock.

Safety Thoughts for Each Day

Now that you know all things begin in your mind as ideas and beliefs and then develop into your own experiences, it is important for you to give attention to your everyday safety. The following thoughts will greatly aid you in doing this, and I ask you to practice saying them to yourself often, until you can repeat them by heart wherever you are. Determine now to believe in the thoughts given below as quickly as possible, to insure safety for you and the ones whom you love and live with.

SUNDAY: *My home is a place of safety. All who dwell in it are protected from harm.*

MONDAY: *The ever-present law of protection is with me today. I use this law of safety all through this day.*

TUESDAY: *I use caution in walking and driving today. This practice gives me self-protection.*

WEDNESDAY: *I am completely safe today. I am safe on the street. I am safe while I work. I am safe while I play.*

THURSDAY: *The Law of Mental Magnetism protects me today, for I know and believe I am safe from harm.*

FRIDAY: *I live my life in complete safety today. I know this is true, and believe it is true.*

SATURDAY: *Today I give thanks for the safety of my loved ones. Today I give thanks for knowing I am forever protected and shielded from all manner of harm.*

Now, put the rules for safe and successful living that you have learned in this chapter into practice, and go forward into life with a sense of complete safety. Go forward with courage and the conviction that what you think and believe you already have—in this case, protection. Use this knowledge you have gained by applying the Laws of Mental Magnetism for your benefit. If you do this, nothing will obstruct your development for the enjoyment of a rich and happy life.

EVER-READY SAFETY REMINDERS

1. You have a built-in safety device. This instrument is your conscious mind.

2. Nothing can harm you, but your own wrong thoughts and beliefs.

3. When you refuse to anticipate danger, you will not attract injury or harm.

4. The man who changed his mind from anticipated fear to belief in safety, never was harmed again.

5. Wake up to your safety factor by making safety the law of your life.

6. Safety is a state of mind. Believe in safety and you will always be safe.

7. Use the safety method for home protection. Know that your home is a dwelling place of safety.

8. Use the method for safe auto driving and you will arrive at your destination safely.

9. Take a "mental" air trip before you board your plane, and so guarantee your landing at your destination safely.

10. Practice the Law of Protection for your loved ones overseas, and so "bring" them safely home to you.

11. Protect your valuables by believing that no one can take from you that which you rightly own through the power of your mind.

12. Do your part every day to invoke the ever-present Law of Protection which will shield you from all harm.

13. Practice the "Safety Thoughts for Each Day" method. Believe in them for a rich and happy life.

12

The Magnetic Law of Love

Your mind can think an unlimited number of thoughts and translate these thoughts into mental pictures with the power of your imagination; but nothing will happen as a result of your doing so until you put *all* your *feeling* into such thoughts and images. Why is this so? Because your intense feeling is *the one power of life* that gives meaning-action to what you think and imagine. More than this, *feeling* is the *magnetic power of the spirit of life* within you, and when you feel deeply about something, it matters not what that thing may be, the life power within you causes the object of your deep feeling to be drawn to you and become a part of your experience.

This chapter will deal with love as a human emotion. It will show you how this mighty feeling-power of life can be used in a variety of ways to aid you in living a happy, successful life.

What You Feel Love For—You Attract

When you become emotionally upset about something, this strong feeling causes high tension in every part and organ of your body. This tension blocks proper functioning of your body and so results in pain and disease; thus you become mentally depressed and physically ill. On the other hand, when you experience a tremendous feeling of love, this greatest and most beneficial of our emotional gamut of capabilities will cause you not only to feel uplifted in spirit, but every part of your physical body will react to the harmony of your feeling of love and will function perfectly. You will feel wonderful in every part of your being!

A Mental Magnet in Action

Recently I attended a picnic at the summer home of a member of my club. Over 60 people attended this affair, and after boating and picnicking, we all assembled on the back lawn of the estate. Suddenly a tall, handsome man came on to the scene with a guitar, and began strolling among us and singing love songs. His charm of manner and self-assurance instantly captured the attention of everyone. He continued to sing Neapolitan and American love songs for over two hours. Every woman at this affair gazed at him in complete abandon and fascination. The men, too, totally enjoyed him. Never have I seen any entertainer capture the attention of his audience and hold it for such a sustained period of time. In speaking with him later, he told me he was a professional builder of homes in the state of Florida, and loved to sing love songs to people for the pleasure it always seemed to give them. To me this man is a human *magnet in action*. Not only has he the power to express himself in song, but also the power to cause those who hear him sing to be uplifted by the feeling of love he puts into each song.

Love Built Their Dream House

A married couple living in Cincinnati, Ohio, who are friends of mine, often used to drive to the top of a mountain about 20 miles from that city on weekends. On one of their trips to this look-out spot, they discovered a deserted parcel of land that would be an ideal place to build the kind of a house they often dreamed about building. However, upon making inquiry they learned that this land was owned by an executive of a large Ohio corporation. They contacted this man and were told the price he was asking for it. It was much too high for their circumstances. This did not kill their dreams, however, and they continued to visit this location. They kept on imagining and feeling that some day they would build their dream house on this very spot.

Suddenly, as if out of the "blue," they received a phone call from the owner of the property. He said he was being transferred to another city and had to sell his land immediately; that he would take a big sacrifice in price in order to dispose of it. My friends immediately arranged to buy it and started at once to build their dream house. Today, they live in this dream house upon the mountain top. I have visited with them often and the view from it is simply magnificent. In the distance can be seen majestic mountains. Down below are the rolling lowlands and a silvery river. "Paradise on earth" is a fitting description of it. And it all came about because two people created a dream house in their imagination, loved the mental picture they imagined, and actually felt and believed their mind picture would become a reality. They put their Personal-Miracle Maker to work for them. Their Mental Magnetism, coupled with their love of their dream house, brought forth their dream as a realized fact.

You, too, can create a dream house in your mind, or anything else that you think will give you great pleasure. *You*, too, can love what you dream. *You*, too, can believe that your dream will come true. *You*, too, can feel that it will surely come true. And according to your strong *feeling* of faith, your dream will become a reality. DO IT NOW!

How Love Reunited Two Brothers

I know two brothers who have always had a deep feeling of love for each other. However, the younger of these two brothers disappeared and the elder one could not locate him for many years. A World War came along and this elder brother volunteered for the Army. He was soon shipped overseas, and his duties there included the inspection of taverns in Barle Duc, France, where soldiers on leave went for periods of relaxation in the evenings. One evening while on a tour of inspection he entered a certain tavern, and as he did so a "buck private" brushed past him. He turned around to interrogate this soldier and, much to his amazement, there stood his long lost brother, alive and in the flesh. He grabbed the soldier's arm and said, "Hello, Bill, my dear brother! I always had a feeling I would see you again but I didn't think it would happen in a war!"

The two of them sat down and had a great reunion that night, and many more after they came back to the States after the war. This is a graphic example of the cohesive quality of love. In spite of the apparent impossibility of finding someone in the upheaval of an active war, these brothers' love for each other was stronger than their circumstances. When you love someone with deep affection, you never can be separated in spirit from him.

How to Attract Your Life Partner

If you are currently a single person and are yearning to meet the "right" marriage partner, you can do something about this important matter without asking a man-made computer for advice. All you have to do is to use the Laws of Mental Magnetism you have already learned about in these pages to attract your right mate.

1. Start concentrating on the man (or woman) you desire to have in marriage by making it your number one desire from now on.

2. Think of the qualities you admire and respect in a person of the opposite sex, such as a sound character, an attractive appearance, a sense of responsibility and one who has interest in the same things as do you. Remember, marriage is a union of mind, spirit and body between two people. Therefore mental harmony is extremely important if two people are to get along with each other happily.

3. Seek out a quiet place where you can be alone. Sit in an easy chair and completely relax. Now close your eyes and imagine the kind of a person you would like to marry. Visualize that person being attracted to you. Visualize that person becoming engaged to you. Mentally visualize yourself attending an engagement party with this person. See yourself being showered with gifts. Now stretch your imagination, and imagine yourself at the marriage ceremony, then attending the wed-

ding reception and finally leaving on a honeymoon trip. Picture yourself being *happily married to that person for the rest of your life*. Believe this to be true. *Feel it to be true with all your heart.* Then open your eyes and go about your business certain in your heart and mind that you will definitely meet your Life Partner.

4. Go out in the world and meet people. Accept invitations that come your way with a sense of expecting to meet the "right" person. Live in a state of constantly expecting that you positively will meet the person who is best suited for you.

This is the way to use your powers of Mental Magnetism, and the only *sure* way to become happily married. So live your life to the fullest. Do it today. Practice this method each and every day. There is no time like the present. Go forth and attract your life partner and become happily married in truth.

The Healing Power of Love

The Bible tells us we should love ourselves and our neighbors. There is a good reason for this sound advice, for when we have love in our hearts it is impossible for us to condemn ourselves or others for past or present mistakes.

Self-condemnation is a vicious mental habit which serves no useful purpose. It causes us to live in fear and torment. It is a mental block that keeps us from making progress. Therefore, in order to live a successful life you will do well to forgive yourself for all past mistakes. Know that no one can *really* condemn you but you yourself. Learn to love yourself for the truly wonderful person you really are. A good way to do this is to say to yourself over and over again:

> **I forgive myself for every mistake I have ever made in my life. From this day on I am going to love myself with all of the power of my mind and spirit. From this day on I am going to have love in my heart for all people. From this day on I am going to express love in thought, deed, and action.**

Believe the words you say to yourself. Put a feeling of deep conviction into your words. Begin this today, and very soon you will become uplifted in mind and spirit. Every part of your body will function properly. You will have a new incentive to make something really great of yourself. And new doors of opportunity and success will open wide for you. Do it now! You will be amazed at what the miracle-working Power of your love will do for you.

A Miracle of True Love

A young woman phoned me one night at my hotel in Chicago, Illinois, and the tone of her voice was frantic. She said she had to see me at once on a very important matter which could not be discussed over the phone. My day had been a very active one and I told her I could not see her. She began pleading with me and I finally agreed to meet with her in a quiet restaurant. When we met she said, "My brother-in-law urged me to see you because he believes you are a very practical minded person. My trouble is that my own brother, whom I deeply love, is going to be placed in a mental institution. What can I do to help him?"

This young woman had a slight knowledge of the Laws of Mental Magnetism, but apparently not enough to meet this situation. I told her that constant negative thinking sometimes causes a person to lose control of his mental faculties, and that when this happens the subconscious mind of that person takes over, causing him to act without self-control.

I told her to go home, get a picture of her brother, sit down, and concentrate upon it. I told her to realize that her brother had been created in the image and likeness of God, i.e., perfect and whole. I told her to close her eyes and imagine that her brother would be completely restored to soundness of mind; to believe that this would surely happen. I told her to practice this method three times a day and that I, too, would be doing it along with her. She left me with her feeling of faith restored and a strengthening conviction that her brother *would* be restored to complete soundness of mind.

A few months later I was invited to luncheon by this woman's brother-in-law, who had sent her to me. With him was his wife, a young daughter, and a gentleman whose name I failed to catch when being introduced. This young man impressed me very favorably because of his good sense of humor and well-balanced manner of deportment. I asked my host's wife the name of this young man.

She said, "Why he is ...., my brother, the one my sister went to see you about a few months ago at your hotel. He has just been released from the mental institution and is completely normal." Upon hearing this good news an intense feeling of joy welled up in my heart, such as I had never before felt in my life. Here, right before me, was a living miracle, brought about by a young woman's devotion and love for her brother.

What you mentally visualize for yourself, or for another, will become a reality when you *feel* it will, and *know* that it positively will. This is how miracles happen, and the *only* way by which they do *happen*.

Love Is the Motivating Power of Success

Da Vinci, the artist, Einstein, the physicist, Edison and Tesla, the inventors, and Caruso, the operatic genius, all became successful and famous because they *loved* what they were doing. Why? Because love is the motivating power of life. When you put your heart into the thing you love to do it is impossible not to do it well.

Let us take some specific instances. If you are in business, put your heart, all the affection you can muster, into your business and love it with all the power within you. Do this, and a stream of new creative ideas for improving your business will flow into your mind. Some of these ideas will be just the right ones which will cause your business to expand and flourish. Why is this so? Because when you love what you are doing, you will attract the right thoughts that will cause what you are doing to become a success.

If you are in the entertainment or artistic field, love what you are doing with all your heart. Put your feeling of love into the songs you sing. Put your feeling of love into the part you are playing, or that instrument you play. Put a feeling of love into the picture you paint, the design you make, that form you are sculpturing, that scenario or book that you write. Whatever you are doing, learn to love doing it, and you will do it so well that you will attract the attention of people. When people see what you are doing, they will desire to pay you well for it, and your love for your work will motivate you on to greater success.

If, by chance, you are just starting out in life, choose something that appeals to you, that makes you happy. Learn everything you can about that field of work and everything connected with it. Make up your mind you are going to become an outstanding person in that field. Today the range is wide open for you in sports, mathematics, business, history, entertainment, politics, and writing, to name a few of the major fields. Whatever it is you choose as a career, put your heart and soul into your selected vocation. Make up your mind you will become a top-flight leader in that field. *Desire* to become it. *Believe* that you will become it. Develop that *feeling* of knowing that you positively will become a great success in your chosen field of endeavor. Do this, and you will not only become successful, but you will attract the respect and attention of many other people who, through similar beliefs, are the world-renowned personalities.

Let Love Make You Attractive

You no doubt have met some person at one time or another who, according to outer appearances, was not what you would term handsome or beautiful, yet who had an inner beauty of spirit which fascinated you and made you love to be in his company. You may have wondered what it was that gave that person such inner dynamic charm. I'll tell you what caused it. That person had allowed the highest emotion of life to come alive in his heart; namely, the emotion of love.

You, too, can let love come alive in your heart. How? By loving all that is good, with all your heart; and by expressing love and kindness to all people.

Do this and you will be amazed at the transformation that will take place within you for your own benefit. Do this and you will become a kind-hearted person. Do this and all the people you meet will greatly admire you. Do this and you will attract new friends and companions. Do this and it will be impossible for you not to become an outstanding success. Why is this so? Because LOVE is the mightiest Power in the Universe, a Power so great that it is like a great magnet, constantly attracting only the good in all things and circumstances. This is why you should learn how to use the Power of Love correctly as explained in this chapter. This is why you should use the magnetic Power of Love each day to draw to you everything necessary for you to enjoy all of the true riches of life.

The Rich Rewards of Love

When you have love in your heart, you will have peace in your mind. When you have love in your heart you will have an abundance of friends. When you have love in your heart, good health will be your constant companion. When you have love for the thing you are doing, your work will be crowned with success. When you truly have love in your heart you will have discovered your true self. And from that moment onward you will fully realize that you are a manifestation of the Supreme Power of Life, with free will to govern yourself and so shape your own rich destiny.

This is the true formula for becoming rich in mind and spirit. This is the true basis for all success in life. To prove to yourself that this really is the true way, let the amazing Power of Love dominate your every motive and action and you will find that you are well on your way to becoming a dynamic masterpiece of life, your true heritage.

LAW OF LOVE REMINDERS

1. Feeling is the magnet power of life. What you feel love for you attract.
2. Negative emotions cause high tension which blocks the normal functions of the human body, causing pain and disease. Feelings of love, on the other hand, uplift the spirit and establish perfect harmony in both mind and body.
3. How the singing of love songs caused a man to become a mental magnet in action.
4. How a married couple built their dream house with imagination, love, and faith.
5. How the magnetic power of brotherly love reunited two brothers in the midst of a World War.
6. The method for attracting your right life partner, and becoming happily married "forever after."
7. Why you should never condemn yourself for past mistakes. How the emotion of love can change your life and give you the incentive to make something really great of yourself.

8. How a sister's love for her brother, plus the use of her mental powers, restored him to soundness of mind.

9. Why you must love what you are doing to become a success. How the emotion of love will motivate you on to success.

10. You can become an attractive person by allowing love to come alive in your heart. An amazing transformation will take place within you and all your affairs.

11. The rich rewards are: peace of mind, abundance of friends, good health, assured success in your work, discovery of your true self. Through love you can become a dynamic masterpiece of life.

13

The Miracle-Working Law of Faith

What everyone calls faith is a personal inner conviction that something is true, and always has been, or can be proved to be true. This is as it should be, for if you believe something is not true, why waste time and energy on it? Yet many people have faith in all sorts of things that cannot benefit them. They discover eventually that their very faith has worked to their detriment. This is because "blind" faith is not founded on fact.

Do you know you cannot become a failure unless you believe in failure, and you cannot become a success unless you believe in success? This is fact, for what you believe about yourself causes you to become exactly like what you have put your faith in. Why is this so? Because the *magnetic power of your mind* takes hold of what you believe and draws to you either an inner experience or an outer concrete manifestation of your belief.

The Power of True Faith Never Fails

Take the idea of success, for instance. What does this idea mean? It means the prosperous termination of any enterprise; that which achieves favor and gain. Now, let us see what failure means. It means lack of effort, neglect, or just plain non-performance, or businesswise, the act of becoming bankrupt. Naturally, every human being wants to achieve success in life for the benefits it will give him; and it so follows that you must put forth effort to dissolve from your mind all doubts which will keep you from achieving your own personal success now in the present. Even the Bible confirms this truth when it says,

> **I say unto you that whomsoever shall say to this mountain (human doubt and unbelief) be thou removed, and be thou cast into the sea (of unreality), and shall not doubt in his heart, but shall believe that those things which he says shall come to pass, he shall have whatsoever he saith. (Mark 11:23.)**

Believe this dynamic statement of Faith with all of your heart and spirit. When any doubt comes into your mind, say to it, "You are nothing, get out of my mind and stay out of it!" Believe that any good thing you desire to have come into your life *will* come into your life. Believe that you will be successful in all you plan doing. Believe that you are successful NOW with all your heart; and what you genuinely believe will become a reality. This is dynamic Faith in yourself, the ONLY thing that can *guarantee your success*.

A Dramatic Example of Dynamic Faith

I was once the general manager of a large dramatic production whose star performer was a very beautiful and talented actress. One day, prior to the opening night of this show, the star's jealous ex-husband came into town and announced he was going to shoot this woman from an orchestra seat in full view of the audience.

This startling announcement created great excitement among the cast of players as well as among the stage hands and musicians.

I had a conference with Juliette, the star, and this is the gist of what she had to say. "I refuse to be scared by this threat against my life. I refuse to believe in fear, and I refuse to be intimidated. I believe in God, and I believe I will be protected from all harm. I love the part I have been given to play and I intend to go on and play it. So on with the show, and "let the chips fall where they may."

The next night, which was the opening night of this show, over 2,000 people filed into the theatre to see it. The orchestra stopped playing, the house lights were dimmed and the curtain went up. Juliette made her appearance with great self-confidence and courage. She put her heart into her part and played it with tremendous sincerity and dramatic ability. At the end of the first act she was given a rousing round of applause by the audience. She stepped down to the footlights and accepted 35 bouquets of flowers sent to her by her admirers and well-wishers.

At the end of the third act the audience gave the star curtain call after curtain call for her magnificent performance. She then changed to evening clothes and went out to attend a "victory" dinner given in her honor by her close friends and associates. How about her jealous ex-husband? I scanned everyone very carefully who entered the theatre that night and I did not spot him in the audience. But this I do know: he never tried to threaten this woman again nor did he ever again appear in her life.

This is dramatic proof that when you believe you will be shielded from harm, you will be, and when you love what you are doing, nothing can stop you from being successful if you have made up your mind to be successful.

How Faith Conquered a Suicide Impulse

What would you do if you had a man on your hands who was intent on committing suicide? Well, here is what I did. This man had been in an accident and had one of his legs amputated. He was in a very depressed state of mind and told me he intended to "end it all." I tried to talk him out of this destructive idea but got nowhere with him.

Suddenly, I remembered hearing of a young girl who had lost both of her legs in an accident, but refused to allow this incident to get her "down." I put through a phone call to this young lady,

The Miracle-Working Law of Faith

told her about my friend, and she agreed to meet with both of us at her home the next evening.

Here is the gist of the conversation that transpired between my friend and this young girl:

> **HE:** You and I are in the same boat, but I've got a great business proposition I just thought of to offer you.
> **SHE:** What is your proposition?
> **HE:** I have an idea to start a home for disabled people.
> **SHE:** What do you want me to do?
> **HE:** Take charge of the women.
> **SHE:** I should say not! I have my own business to look after, and besides, *I am engaged to be married!*

Then, arising and standing on her two artificial legs, this very attractive young girl put on her coat, bid her father, mother, and the two of us good night, walked swiftly out of the front door of her house, got into her automobile and drove away to meet the man she loved.

That did it! This girl's remarkable display of courage in the face of her physical handicap amazed and stunned my friend. We left almost immediately, and on the way home, he finally burst forth with this statement. "If that mere slip of a girl has the spunk to rise above her problem—so will I!" Then, he thanked me for all I had tried to do for him and we both went our ways. This man did keep his promise to rise above his problem, and today he is a successful businessman.

Sometimes it takes a complete shock to cause some people to "wake up" by seeing those who are worse off than themselves refuse to let anything defeat them. In the case of this man, it was the young girl's faith in herself and her desire to be happily married that caused him to change his mind. It gave him faith to carry on, too. It is faith in oneself that always gives one the courage to win out regardless of what obstacle stands in one's way.

The Miracle Pass Words

"*I Believe!*" These two little words are *Miracle Pass Words*. They will allow you to enter into a magnificent new life. You have no doubt used these two words often without realizing their dynamic potential. Now, nothing is good or bad "but thinking makes it so." Why is this so? Because no person or circumstance has any power to affect you until you *believe* in that person's power to do so, or to bring about certain circumstances. Then, BOOM! What you believe in becomes a part of your life and experience. Why? Because FAITH is the dynamo of Mental Magnetism that attracts to you what you think, desire and believe. Therefore, I urge you to *believe* in those things that can benefit you and advance you, and to *keep believing* until they do become a part of your life. Do this, and you will have proved to yourself that "I Believe" are indeed the Miracle Pass Words of Life that open wide the doors to all success.

The Faith of a Young Soldier

One cold, snowy day just before sunset, while I was walking from the Union Station in Detroit, Michigan, to the downtown district, I heard a voice behind me saying, "Mister, do you know where the Post Office is? I have to get a money order cashed." I turned around and there stood a good-looking young marine without an overcoat. After I had told him the Post Office was closed due to the lateness of the hour, he suddenly started jumping up and down in the snow, saying, "*It really happened! It really happened! It really happened!*" I asked him the cause of his great jubilation and he said, "Mister, I have just come back from the war in the Pacific. Every day I was in that war I said to myself, *I WILL GET BACK ALIVE!* And here I am back home alive again among the living! After the hell I have been through do you blame me for being so happy?" I said, "I certainly do not. I admire you tremendously for having so much courage and faith."

This is a perfect example of how heartfelt, positive faith becomes a reality in human experience. Whenever you have to take a long journey, know that you will return back home alive. Believe in this very simple creative idea, and like this young soldier, it will really happen to you.

His Faith Put Him in High Office

No one has a monopoly on faith. It is life's free gift to every man, woman and child. It will even bring success to a politician. One such incident comes to mind to prove what I am saying. Some time ago, as I was checking out of a hotel in a small mid-western town, the manager of the hotel rushed up to me and asked me if I would be good enough to share the taxicab, which I had waiting to take me to the railway station, with a state senator. I readily agreed. The senator told me he had to catch the same train as I in order to keep an appointment in a distant city with a candidate for the presidency of the United States.

We both sat together on the train and during a long conversation I explained the Laws of Mental Magnetism to him. I emphasized the Law of Faith. He, in turn, said he was giving up his state senatorship to run for a seat in the United States Congress. I asked him if he had an open mind and he replied, "Yes." He said, however, he was just beginning to campaign and was up against a tough opponent. I said, "Would you be willing to make a pact of faith with me right here on this train before you have even started your campaign?" He looked at me, and I said to him, "*You are already elected* to the United States Congress from your state." He replied, "Yes, I'll buy that idea." "Alright," I said, "shake my hand. You are already elected to Congress, and I am the very first person to congratulate you on your victory."

Election day came and this man was swept into office by an overwhelming majority of votes. After he was installed in Congress I visited him in his office on Capitol Hill. We went to his private inner office and he said to me, "If I hadn't met you that day you allowed me to share your taxicab, I would not be here in this office today. You gave me just the boost in spirit I needed that day. Believe me, I am grateful to you for the wonderful lesson in positive faith you gave me."

This is not the end of the story, for this Congressman went on to become the National Executive Director of one of our two great major political parties.

The Power of Personal Application

Whatever it is you have decided to do, *believe* that you are already doing it. Assume that you already *are* what you desire to be. Remember that when sincere desire is motivated by the power of complete faith, it becomes objectified, as a concrete reality. This is how your power of faith turns your greatest aspirations into demonstrated truth.

He Quickly Received a Big Promotion

While attending a convention of Mental Scientists at a hotel in Michigan a short while ago, I met the assistant manager of the hotel. "This is a fine group of people you are associated with," he stated. "What is the purpose of this convention?" I replied, "To show people how to use the power of their minds intelligently; to explain how the proper use of faith, will cause desires to be turned into realized facts." "That's very interesting," he said. "I would certainly like to get a promotion from the job I'm in. Frankly, I need a larger income. Would your ideas help me?" I said, "You are an intelligent man. How about you and I entering into a pact of faith right here in this very busy hotel lobby? Let's shake hands on the idea that you are being promoted immediately to a higher position with a big boost in pay. Let's *believe* this will surely happen to you." He said, "Give me your hand. Let's shake on that, and I promise to believe in your idea with all my heart."

In exactly two weeks' time this man was made the sales manager of a large hotel chain and moved to its headquarters in New York City. The next time I was in New York I visited with him at his office. As I entered and approached him, a big smile came over his face. "Welcome," he said, "my heartfelt thanks to you, I really made it." Then he said he was leaving for Philadelphia that very same day to try to sign up a large convention for his new hotel. I said, "All right, you and I know the Law of Faith. Let's you and I *know* and believe you *have* already the signed contract for that convention in your pocket." He agreed to this idea with complete faith. The next day he returned from Philadelphia, and actually did produce the signed contract from his inside coat pocket. Since that time, this man has become the president of his own hotel corporation, and so is a wealthy man in his own right.

If you desire a promotion in the work you are now doing, make a pact of faith with yourself in the following manner. Say to yourself repeatedly, with strong feeling:

I am going to be promoted to a better position with much higher pay immediately.

This is not difficult to do. There are only 15 words to this statement. Surely you can find time to memorize and repeat them at every free moment. Surely you can make the ideas they contain the goal of your life. Surely you can *believe* this simple self-promotion idea, and the more you persist in this thought, the more surely your subconscious mind will accept your beliefs, and go into action for you. The proper things and conditions will begin to develop and you will be promoted into that higher paying position. Surely you can perform this sample act of faith for your own benefit. Surely you can in this way convince yourself that according to your faith, so shall it be done unto you. Then you will *know*, as you step into that new position, that it was *your own faith* that brought about your heart's desire. Obviously, it is faith in yourself and your desires —unwavering faith—that will assure your progress in life.

His Faith Survived Three Wars

An ex-Marine friend of mine recently told me this story. He knows a Marine Sergeant who contracted malaria in the Philippines during an insurrection there many years ago. He was put in a tent as a "hopeless case," and overheard another soldier say he was certain to die of the fever. That night this man crawled out of his tent onto a barren field, and as he lay there he said to himself, *I believe I will live, I believe I will live, I know I will live!* The next day he was discovered by some soldiers in this field, and was taken to a field hospital for special treatment. Gradually the malaria fever left him and he was restored to good health.

His next assignment was in the Spanish-American War. He came out of this war in excellent physical condition.

When World War I came along, he was among the first Marines to enter that war. He fought at the Battle of Belleau Wood (Chateau-Thierry), where so many American Marines were killed in action. He was slightly wounded in that battle. Today this man is hale and hearty at the age of 88. He enjoys a happy, peaceful life in his home state of Virginia. This proves that where there is a desire to live, and a strong faith to live, faith will keep the spark of life glowing brightly.

How Faith Attracts What You Look for

A friend of mine, who is a successful attorney in Washington, D.C., asked me to come to see him. He said he had handled an insurance claim that had been successfully settled, but now could not find his client to give the money to. He asked me if I thought I could find this man in New York City for him. He had no clue for me to work on, not even a picture of the man. All he had was a general description of him and the name of the last firm he worked for. I told my friend I positively would find his client through the power of faith.

The firm in New York City knew nothing about the whereabouts of the man I was looking for. I made countless inquiries at hotel after hotel and neighborhood after neighborhood to no avail. The annual Hotel Show was in progress in New York City at this time, and I next decided to question every exhibitor to see if this would turn up any clues. I spoke to every exhibitor at this Hotel Show, and finally "struck gold." One man said, "I think the man you are looking for lives on Route 16, near Alexandria, Louisiana."

I immediately went to a Western Union office, and while I stood there wondering whether to wire the Mayor of Alexandria or the Chief of Police of that town, the Western Union girl suggested, "Why don't you wire Alexandria's Western Union office?" I did, and back came a telegram stating that the man I was looking for lived in Houston, Texas, and giving me his business address. I wired him in Houston and asked that he telegraph my lawyer friend. The case was settled satisfactorily. My friend's client received the money due on his claim.

How to Use the Mental Attractor Chart

When you make up your mind to find whatever you are looking for, you can and will find it, if you will but exercise your faith to the fullest. It can be a person, a new position, a valuable possession or a lost friend, even the right life-mate. The Bible says, "Seek and ye shall find." This really means that if you strongly desire strength, health, happiness, peace of mind, or success, you must seek within yourself for these true values of life. Be persistent in your search. Believe that you will find them. Believe you will receive the benefits that they have to give you and, according to your faith, you will have found that which can make you rich in mind and spirit.

To aid you in this direction, fill out the chart below, with all of the things you have been seeking but still have not found. Make it your own Seek-and-Finder Chart.

MY MENTAL ATTRACTOR CHART

Write down your secret desires on the following lines in their order of importance to you. To simplify this procedure, put just one desire on each line. Then look them over, think about each one, and decide that you will spend one full week on each, one at a time, to cause each to be a demonstrated reality in your life.

1. ....
2. ....
3. ....
4. ....
5. ....
6. ....

The following method of Magnetic Attraction should be adhered to in each case.

1. Each morning, after you have completed dressing, sit down in a chair for ten minutes, close your eyes and relax. Visualize the first desire you have decided to concentrate upon. Think about that thing as having real existence. Believe that it is the right thing for you. Now create a vivid picture in your mind of that thing. Then, mentally affirm to yourself, "*My desire is now being attracted to me. I feel my desire being attracted to me.*" KEEP ON FEELING IT BEING MAGNETICALLY ATTRACTED TO YOU. Feel the Power of the life force within you drawing to you that which you desire. BELIEVE THAT THIS IS TRUE, AND THAT YOU NOW HAVE IT IN YOUR POSSESSION. Open your eyes, and say to yourself with strong feeling, "I thank God my desire is already a demonstrated fact in my life."

2. At lunch time, get away alone for a few minutes, close your eyes, and imagine that your desire is now making an appearance in your life as an objectified fact. FEEL THIS TO BE TRUE WITH INTENSITY OF FEELING. KNOW THIS TO BE TRUE WITH A STRONG FEELING OF FAITH. Then open your eyes and be on your way.

3. As you retire in the evening, close your eyes and speak to your subconscious mind thus:
   I ASK YOU TO ATTRACT AND FULFILL MY DESIRE (name it) WHILE I SLEEP THIS NIGHT. I FIRMLY BELIEVE YOU WILL DO THIS FOR ME THIS VERY NIGHT.

Use this simple method three times a day for a full seven days for your first desire. Then you are ready to choose another desire. Use this same method three times a day for another full seven days. Then go on down your list until you have completed work in this way on every desire you have listed on your Mental Attractor Chart.

I tell you sincerely, my friend, that if you will but practice this method without fail, true miracles will happen in your life. So, why not get busy this very day and prove to yourself that your own faith *is* your Personal Miracle Maker. DO IT NOW!

It is *Faith* that produces all good things in life, and it is *Faith* that will cause you to develop a fruitful life for yourself, BUT DO IT NOW! Prove for yourself that dynamic, positive *faith* is truly the "supernatural" power of life, a power so great that it can and will give you every true treasure of life when you believe in its amazing Magnetic Power.

MIRACLE-WORKING FAITH REMINDERS

1. Faith is much more than trust and confidence. It is Mental Magnetism in action.
2. When you believe in your heart you will receive what you desire, whatever you desire will be attracted to you.
3. How the faith of an actress protected her from great harm.
4. The man who was healed of a suicide impulse by a girl who refused to be defeated.
5. "I Believe" are the Miracle Pass Words of life.
6. The young Marine who came out of a war alive and so proved that faith does work miracles.
7. The politician whose faith put him in high office.
8. The hotel man whose power of faith brought him unlimited opportunity and abundance.
9. The man whose faith caused him to survive three wars.

The Miracle-Working Law of Faith

10. How faith attracts what you look for.

11. How to use the Mental Attractor Chart to select your secret desires. How to use the three-time-a-day method for causing your desires to come true.

12. Prove to yourself that faith is the "supernatural" power of your own mind. Prove to yourself that dynamic faith is the Miracle-Working Power of your life.

14

The Creative Law of Cosmic Mind

YOU are one of the most intelligent and unique manifestations of life on earth. Yes, you are, and for a very good reason. Actually you are a conscious *inlet* and *outlet* whereby the creative ideas of the Cosmic Mind of the Universe can be expressed, in you and through you, for the benefit of yourself and your fellow man. However—and here is the rub—when you clutter up your mind with WORRY, you disconnect yourself from the source of life's goodness, just as water will cease flowing through a pipeline when you turn off the water faucet. This chapter will show you how to tune in to the source of all power, and how to use this power for your own benefit.

You Are Greater than You Think

Here is some startling news! You have within you a tremendous reservoir of untapped creative power which you have never as yet used. This is not only true of you; it is true regarding every human being. This power is an impersonal power; you make it personal to you by the manner in which you use it. Use it wrongly and you experience the consequences. Use it intelligently and wisely and it will be your great benefactor. Think big, imagine big, desire big—and you will become a creative giant. Think this over, my friend, and I believe that you will realize what I am saying is true.

The World's Most Amazing Inventor

It was my food fortune to have lived in the same hotel in New York City as did Nikola Tesla, considered by many to have been the world's greatest electrical inventor. It was also my good fortune to have met and talked with Mr. Tesla.

During his lifetime, Nikola Tesla's inventive mind conceived and produced artificial lightning. His mastermind conceived and invented over 90 original inventions, among which was the method for producing alternating current. He invented rotary motors, which operate by water or by gas, a wireless communication system, and many other unusual devices. He conceived of the induction-motor, perhaps his greatest invention.

Mr. Tesla was well aware of the Laws of Mental Magnetism and practiced these Laws, as you will soon see as he tells his own story in his own words:

> I began to travel, in my mind, of course, every night (and sometimes during the day). When alone, I would start on my journeys—see new places, cities and countries—live there, meet people and make friendships and acquaintances and, however unbelievable, it is a fact that they were just as dear to me as those in actual life, and not a bit less in their manifestation. This I did constantly until I was about 17, when my thoughts turned seriously to inventions. Then I observed, to my delight, that I could *visualize* with the greatest facility. I needed no models, drawings, or experiments; I could *picture them as real in my mind*. Thus, I have been led unconsciously to what I consider to be a new method of materializing inventive concepts and ideas, which is radically opposite the purely experimental and is, in my opinion, ever so much more expeditious and efficient. My method is different. I do not rush into actual work.

> **When I get a new idea, I start at once *building it up in my imagination*, and *make improvements and operate the device in my mind*. It is absolutely immaterial to me whether I run my turbine in thought or test it in my shop. I even note if it is out of balance. The results are the same. In this way I am able to rapidly perfect a conception without touching anything. When I have gone so far as to embody everything in my invention, every possible improvement I can think of, and when I can see no fault anywhere, I put into concrete form the final product of my brain. Invariably the device works as I conceived that it should and the experiment comes out as I planned. In 20 years there has not been a single exception.**

Let us analyze Mr. Tesla's unusual method for producing an inventive conception in concrete form without using pencil, paper, or drawing board. First, we note he could visualize mental pictures and make these pictures real in his mind. Next, we see that when he received a new idea he did not rush into actual work. Instead, he enlarged that idea by dwelling upon it in his mind. This action started the Law of Mental Magnetism in action to attract to him every other idea needed to cause the invention to function and operate perfectly.

In his "magnetic" frame of thought he was enabled to attract the right mathematical measurements for each and every part needed in his inventive device. He knew so much about such forces as magnetism that he could look "beyond" for inspiration. He had such faith in what he visualized that, once convinced that his inventive device worked perfectly in his mind, he put the final product of his brain into concrete form and it worked just as perfectly in substance.

Amazing? Yes. But you, too, have the power to use your imagination when you receive a new idea that will benefit you. You, too, have the power to visualize that idea and perfect it. You, too, have the power to desire the benefit that idea will give you. And you, too, have the power to believe that you *will* receive that particular benefit. So why not put your "magnetic frame of thought" to work for you and attract all of the good things of life that you are entitled to have by divine right?

The Real World You Live in

You may have been led to believe that the outer world around you is the only world. This is not so. The real world you live in and have always lived in is an internal world, the world within your mind. It is in this mental world within you that everything concerning you originates and takes place. This is a Universal Truth applicable to all people. If you do not like the kind of personal world you are living in, you have power to create a world more to your liking. How? By changing your conception of yourself, *and* by changing your conception of the environment in which you live. By imagining the kind of person you desire to be and by imagining the kind of environment you desire to live in. Then put your faith to work for you by believing that these wonderful changes will take place in your life.

All change *must* first take place in your mind. This is where all self-transformation begins. This is where all future experience begins. So if you desire to have a very unique and interesting life, create that new life for yourself in your imagination, desire to live in it, believe that you will live in it and express it, then use your power of faith to cause it to come alive within you.

Her Sudden Vision Became a Fabulous Reality

I know a widow who, while preparing breakfast in the kitchen of her home one morning, had a vivid mental picture flash into her mind. She saw herself in this picture seated in a large office in charge of 200 employees. For several days she continued to dwell upon this unusual picture that had appeared in her mind.

Prior to this unusual occurrence she had definitely desired to be gainfully employed in the business world. Finally, something within her impelled her to take a secretarial course. She completed the course and became the private secretary of a successful business executive. Sometime later, at a social affair, she was introduced to the president of one of the largest business concerns in the world. This man was tremendously impressed with her apparent efficiency, and offered her a position as his private secretary. She accepted the offer. In the course of events, this man had the problem of replacing a branch office general manager. He was unable to find what he considered the right person and finally decided to give this position to his very capable private secretary.

Arriving at her new assignment, this woman was amazed to find herself in a luxurious office and in complete charge of 200 employees. The scene she beheld was like the vision she had previously seen while preparing breakfast in the kitchen of her home. She later told me that in this management position she had the power to sign a company check as high as a half-million dollars. Since then she has traveled the world, meeting rulers of countries and important businessmen in the interest of her firm's products.

An intense desire to do something worthwhile often takes the form of a dream while you sleep, or appears as an imaginary mental picture in your conscious mind while you are awake. Should you have such an experience—*dwell* on the meaning of that experience; *desire* enlightenment regarding that experience; *believe* that you will receive the meaning of that experience. And if it is something that will benefit you, take the necessary steps to cause that mental picture to come true.

How Action Will Make a Dream Come True

One Sunday morning, as we were strolling together along Park Avenue in New York City, a good friend of mine said to me, "I had a dream last night and in this dream you appeared, big as life, giving a welcome home dinner for Allen, who has just arrived back from the army." I replied, "All right, I will show you how to make your dream come true." We both proceeded to a certain hotel, where I reserved the "Sky Garden Room" and arranged to have 75 dinners served in the near future for our friend who had just returned from the army. Then I went to work and sold tickets for that dinner, which included some choice entertainment. The "dream dinner" became a reality and was just the thing needed to give the honored guest a boost in spirit, and cause him to return to a successful civilian career. This is a concrete example of the fact that a dream is just a dream—until practical action is taken to make it a reality.

Whenever you have a dream about something that will benefit you, don't sit down and continue to dream about it. *Do* something practical about it. Make out a plan of action that will change your dream into a reality. Do this and you will know that it takes planning and action to make a dream come true.

Great Men Who Tuned in to Cosmic Mind

When Christopher Columbus received an idea regarding the existence of a new land, he built up this idea in his imagination until he was convinced that such a new land did exist. Then he had a consuming desire to discover the land which he had conceived in his imagination. This desire of his so impressed Queen Isabella of Spain that it is said she pawned several jewels to finance this unusual voyage in search of a yet undiscovered country. The rest is history. That which was but an idea in a man's imagination became a reality. The country of America came into being for all.

When Robert Fulton received an idea that a boat could be operated and run by steam, he conceived a steam engine in his imagination, concentrated upon making such an engine and, as a result, the steamboat came into being. Eli Whitney received an idea for creating a machine for clearing cotton fibers from cotton seeds. He went to work to change this idea into a reality. Thus the cotton gin came into being. Alexander Graham Bell received an idea that would make it possible for people to speak to each other over a wire. He built up this idea in his imagination and did what was necessary to cause what he had imagined to come true. Thus you can speak to anyone whom you care to over your telephone.

All through the ages, great men and women have opened their minds to new ideas, *put these ideas to work for them* and, as a consequence, we have great masterpieces of art, literature, music, and amazing scientific discoveries which enrich the lives of people around the world.

What You Concentrate upon You Attract

It is a Universal Law of Mind that what you concentrate your attention upon—you attract. *This is especially true when you concentrate upon worry*—you attract more things to you to worry about. However, when you concentrate your attention upon a basic idea that will be for your benefit, this basic idea will act as a magnet to attract to you other ideas that will benefit you. For example, the desire to explain the Laws of Mental Magnetism to you has caused me to concentrate my undivided attention upon writing this book. As a consequence, this book has come into being for the benefit of all who read it and practice the methods it contains.

He Concentrated on Success and Attracted Success

A good friend of mine decided to give up what he had been doing for years. A friend whom he knew secured a position for him with a large insurance company. This field was entirely foreign to him but he made up his mind to become a huge success in it. He concentrated his attention on the insurance business exclusively. He studied every bit of information he could find about this business. He literally breathed, slept, and lived insurance. Immediately he gained the attention of the top brass in this firm. He was promoted from one position to another, and another, and another, until he was given charge of 300 people in this firm. Today he lives on his own private estate, has two cars in his garage, and has adequate money at his command. This is a specific example of giving undivided attention and concentration to what one is engaged in—in this man's case, a determination to become a success. You, too, can accomplish amazing things by applying your power of concentration to that which you desire to accomplish. Do it today and you will be forever grateful to yourself that you did.

Practical Steps to a Richer Life

1. Get a sheet of paper and a pencil and write down the following paragraph:

As of this day, I am determined that every worry, fear and mistake that I have ever made is completely dispelled from my mind. I promise myself I shall never think of these worthless things again.

Memorize these thoughts. Believe completely in what you have written down.

2. Make up your mind that you will discipline your thinking in the following manner. When you arise in the morning, say to yourself:

> **I promise I will not give my attention today to any unhappy experience I have had in the past. The moment any such memory tries to come into my mind, I will rub it out by saying to it, "You have no power over me; you are nothing but a dead mental illusion."**

Repeat and practice this affirmation as much as possible for one full day. Then practice it the next day and each day thereafter until you have practiced this technique for seven days. This is the way to eliminate worry and anxiety from your mind. This is the way to open your mind to new creative ideas that will benefit you and enrich you. This is a very important procedure, so begin it at once.

3. Write down on another sheet of paper:

I DESIRE FRESH NEW IDEAS

Think about what you are most interested in. Make that thing the basic idea or mental magnet that will attract new ideas to you. Here are some suggestions: Health, Prosperity, Happiness, Peace of Mind, Courage, Strength, Right Activity, Companionship, Success. Whatever it is you desire to receive new ideas about, write that basic idea under the caption you have put down on your sheet of paper.

Now put your thinking processes to work and THINK about your basic idea and as soon as a *new thought* comes into your mind concerning it, write it down. Then THINK, and THINK again and again, and soon new ideas will flow into your mind. Then fill up your sheet of paper with all of the new ideas you have received concerning the one thing you are most interested in.

Carry a notebook with you at all times. When a new idea comes into your mind regarding your principal project, write that idea down quickly in your book. Do this for one week and you will be amazed how many new and unusual ideas will keep flowing into your mind.

4. Whenever you receive a new idea that will benefit you, build up that idea in your imagination. Visualize it. Picture that thing as being real. Concentrate on it continually. Plan to cause that thing to become a concrete reality in your life.

5. Once a day have a period of quiet meditation alone with yourself. Close the door of your office, or go to some quiet place where you can be alone without outside interference. Sit down and

completely relax. Still your conscious mind by remaining silent for a few minutes. Now imagine that the thing you have made real in your mind is created especially for you. Know that it is given freely to you by Divine Right. Accept it as a free gift of life to you. Take hold of it in your mind. Hold it closely to you in your heart. Love it for the enjoyment it will give you. Know that you already have it in your possession. Believe that this is true, then open your eyes and go about your business. Practice this method each and every day, and that which you have conceived in your imagination will be attracted to you by your own power of dynamic positive faith.

6. Whenever you receive a sudden impulse within you to do something or see someone that can be to your benefit, obey that impulse immediately. Do that something or see that someone at once! Why? Because this impulse is the intuitive prodding of the Spirit of Intelligence within you urging you to take the practical, necessary steps to cause what you desire to come true. Remember that many an opportunity and fortune have been lost by those who have failed to obey the "still small voice" of the Spirit within them. So when you get that "hunch" to do something that will benefit you, play that "hunch" for all it is worth. DO IT AT ONCE, for it is the Voice of the Universe speaking to you, telling you to take the steps that lead into a newer and richer life.

Practice and Action Attract to Yourself Life's Riches

As an individual you have been given everything necessary to create for yourself all of the things that go to make for a truly rich life. You have a mind which makes it possible for you to tune in to creative ideas that will benefit you. You have imagination with which to make what you desire real in your mind. You have unlimited faith to cause what you desire to be attracted to you. Now it is up to you to put into practice these great powers that have been given to you. Now it is up to you to make practical use of the stupendous power that has been given to you. Go into action immediately and use your God-given powers wisely and life's greatest riches will be made manifest in your life.

LAW OF COSMIC MIND REMINDERS

1. You are greater than you think. You have a tremendous reservoir of untapped creative power within you.
2. The world's most amazing inventor. His revolutionary creative method.
3. The real world you live in is a mental world. Change your mind and you change yourself and your environment.
4. How a widow's sudden vision became a fabulous reality.
5. How action made a dream come true.
6. Examples of great men who tuned in to Cosmic Mind.
7. What you concentrate your attention on, you attract. Concentrate on a basic idea and you will attract ideas for its fulfillment.
8. Practicing success brings more success.
9. How to take practical steps to richer living.
10. Practice *and* action attract life's riches to you.

15

The Tranquilizing Law of Peace

Someone once said, "A confused mind is the devil's playground." This is a truthful and penetrating saying. Confusion in mind is caused by disorderly thinking and lack of self-control. Mental confusion attracts tumult and strife. This is why you must have inner serenity in order to attract the good things of life. Furthermore, serenity of mind is a magic door-opener for great forces of magnetism to flow through you. When you have calmness of mind, this indicates that you have refused to be governed by shallow, mortal thinking. It indicates that you are master of your thoughts and emotions. And when your mind is calm and peaceful you are then able to use the Laws of Mental Magnetism skillfully and effectively to draw to you any good thing you desire.

How Serenity Increases Your Power of Attraction

When you are calm and serene, clouds of fear and doubt disappear. Your vision is clear. You can envision higher goals to achieve. Your imagination comes alive. You can then visualize clearly what you intend to accomplish. You can make a vivid mental picture of the thing you desire to attract to you. Then you can set into action the magnetic department of your mind to draw to you what you desire. And you can believe more firmly in the magnetic power of your subconscious mind to deliver to you that which you wish to receive.

If you really desire to enjoy a richer and happier life, it is extremely important that you have inner serenity and peace of mind. Many people try to gain this great gift of life by reaching for a tranquilizer pill. This habit gives them only temporary relief from nervous tension and fear, and at best creates a pill-taking habit. This chapter will show you how to so discipline your mind that you can remain calm and serene under all circumstances which may take place in your day-to-day living.

People Are Creatures of Habit

What do you suppose it is that causes nervous tension and discord within so many people today? Basically it is lack of self-control—control of thought and emotion. This is a fact. For instance, Jane B sees something or hears something unpleasant about herself or someone whom she knows. What does she do? She dwells on this incident, and continues to dwell on it. Then what happens? Jane B's subconscious mind immediately goes to work to cause her to feel terrible and, as a result, she loses complete control over her thoughts and emotions and flies into an emotional rage. On the other hand, Richard J has learned how to control his thoughts and emotions. When he sees something or hears something that is not good about himself or someone whom he knows, what does he do? He refuses to allow that incident to disturb or upset him. Then what happens? Richard J remains as calm and serene as he was before he experienced this incident. Yes, people are creatures of habit: those who lack self-control, lack peace of mind; those who do not allow what they see or hear to impress them in a negative manner enjoy peace of mind.

He Was a Human Volcano in Action

I once knew a man who went to his office every day in a very bad state of mind. Immediately he would pick an argument with one female employee after another, until he had all of the women in his office shaking and trembling with fear. One day I asked him, "What is bugging you that makes you so irritable and disagreeable?" He replied, "It is my mother-in-law. She came to visit my wife and me for a week, and stayed three years. All those years I have had to support her." "But why take your anger out on the women in the office?" I asked him. He replied, "Because my wife or my mother-in-law won't take any guff from me, so I have to give it to someone to get rid of it." I tipped these women off to this man's lack of self-control and told them to be courteous to him, but to treat him with silence. They did, and a measure of inner serenity came into their lives.

This man's constant dislike for his mother-in-law not only caused him to lose control over his thoughts and emotions, it caused him to become a very sick man and, later, to pass on. When a chronic complainer tries to argue with you, treat that person with courtesy. Never allow yourself to descend to his or her level of consciousness by becoming involved in an argument. Treat that person with *silence*. Do this and the person concerned will either leave you alone or make an effort to be friendly with you.

This Man Has Great Peace of Mind

Recently I spent a very enjoyable evening with one of the most peaceful men I have ever known. This gentleman is Mr. George A. Haines, who for many years had charge of the employee commissary for a large life insurance company. During his tenure with this organization he served 3,000 meals daily to the employees of his firm in a luncheon period of two-and-a-half hours. I asked Mr. Haines what it was that caused him to be so peaceful. He thought for a moment and replied, "I guess it is because I have never had any bitterness in my heart for any person. I like people and love to be with people."

Bitterness in heart towards another is personal dislike for another. Surely this mental attitude will not give you peace of mind. What it will do is give you mental disharmony and emotional discord. In order to like people you must first like yourself. Why? Because if you do not like yourself, how in the name of heaven can you like someone who is not as close to you as you are to your own self? You gain peace of mind when you have no dislike in your heart for anyone; when you like people and love people for the wonderful beings they really are.

Nothing Can Bring You Peace but YOU

You can travel the world over in search of peace of mind and you will never find it. Why? Because, "Nothing can bring you peace of mind but you yourself. Nothing can bring you peace of mind but the triumph of principles." (Ralph Waldo Emerson.) This is true. Peace of mind comes as a result of right thinking and believing. Peace of mind comes as a result of knowing how to control your thoughts and emotions. And peace of mind comes as the result of your treating other people as you would have them treat you.

A Home as a Haven of Peace

Two of my very good friends, a man and his wife, are two of the most harmonious, peace-loving people it has ever been my good fortune to know. They are both self-disciplined people who have gained mastery over their thoughts and emotions. In all of the time I have known them, never have I heard either of them say anything or do anything that is discordant or inharmonious. They both believe that to be a friend is to have a friend, consequently they have a great abundance of friends, some who travel thousands of miles each year to visit with them. Their home is like a heaven on earth. Great peace and harmony can be felt in every room of their house. These two wonderful people have true peace of mind, and they gained it by making a deliberate effort to become peaceful in mind and spirit.

They know, as do I, that when a negative thought or mental

image is impressed on the subconscious mind, the subconscious mind immediately produces a feeling in the individual which corresponds to the nature of the negative thought or image so impressed. Thus, when a person constantly dwells upon inharmonious thoughts, that person must experience discord and inharmony in his or her life. Conversely, they know as I do that constant dwelling upon peaceful and harmonious thoughts produces great feelings of peace within one's own mind and spirit. This is how to gain peace of mind. Concentrate your attention on harmonious and peaceful thinking and you will become the possessor of great peace of mind. "Great peace have they which love thy law." [Psalms, 119:165.]

Calm Down, There Is Nothing to Fear

Calm down, take it easy—there is absolutely nothing to fear. This statement is true. What seems to be going on in the world is but the result of people's imagined fear. Why let the outer world hypnotize you and try to make a coward of you? Pull yourself together, put on the armor of courage and let nothing hoodwink you into believing that it has any power over you. Do you know why you should do this? Because you are too important to yourself and your own well-being to allow anything, and I do mean anything, to keep you from your goal of living a richer and greater life. So stand up on your own two feet, without a quiver or a quake, and go forward in life and never allow anything to keep you from living and expressing a peaceful and serene happy life.

How to Relax in Mind and Body

Take time out each day so that you can be alone with yourself, away from all outer noise and disturbance. Should you be in your office, close the door; if at home, select a room where you can be alone.

Sit down in an easy chair, let go, and completely relax. Close your eyes. Think of peace as the absence of all discord. Think of quietness as harmony within mind and spirit. Now say to yourself silently but purposefully:

> **The peace of God is now flowing into every part of my being. His peace is now giving me peace in my mind, body, and spirit. I feel the peace of God flowing into my mind and through every organ, gland, atom, cell and tissue in my body. I feel peaceful, I am peaceful. I thank God I really and truly am peaceful.**

Then open your eyes. Repeat this affirmation once a day for a full 30 days, and if you are faithful in your practice, you will become a very peaceful person.

How to Control Your Emotions

Have you ever tried to ride a wild horse that has never been ridden? I have, and discovered that unless I controlled that horse it would unseat me and hurl me to the ground. This same thing will happen to you unless you learn how to control your emotions—they will control you and toss you for a loss you will never forget.

What is an emotion, you may ask? That is a good question. An emotion is a feeling. How many emotions are there? Innumerable, beginning with the most sublime and peaceful to the most violent and harmful. How is an emotion created? All emotions begin as ideas you entertain in your mind. Then when you concentrate on them they become impressed on the subconscious part of your mind, which is the powerful life force within you. This subconscious power within you causes you to feel the effects of what you have impressed upon it. If your thinking has been calm and serene, you will feel peaceful. If your thinking has been of a violent nature, it will cause you to feel and act violently.

1. Whenever a thought regarding yourself or something that is not good tries to enter your mind, stop it dead in its track. Refuse to allow it to enter your mind. How? By instantly replacing it with another thought. Say to yourself quickly, "*God is the only presence and power in my life.*" Keep repeating these words over and over to yourself. What will you have done by taking this instant action? You will have made it impossible for that bad thought or whatever it was to enter your mind, and you will have gained control over what would have otherwise developed into a bad emotional experience.

2. Should anything happen in your presence which might have a tendency to upset you, REMAIN CALM. Refuse to give that thing any power over you. Keep repeating to yourself over and over, *I am calm, poised and serene.* Keep your mouth shut if someone tries to involve you in an argument. Close your ears tight to bickering. Say to yourself, *I am the master of this situation.* Do this, and you will have gained mastery over your own emotions.

3. Make it your duty to associate with harmonious people. Remember, birds of a feather flock together. Trouble-makers attract trouble-makers. Scandal-mongers attract scandal-mongers. Select some well-balanced, peaceful person as a companion and you will discover you are in the right company.

Begin Each Day With A Peaceful Attitude

As soon as you have finished dressing each morning, go to your mirror and look at yourself. Keep looking in your mirror and as you do, say to yourself, with plenty of feeling, "*This is going to be the most peaceful day I have ever had in my life.*" Then go about your business. Should anything happen during the day that is disturbing, quickly say to yourself, "*This is the most peaceful day in my life. Nothing in the world can disturb me today.*" Practice this method for 30 days and you will be amazed how peaceful your days will become.

A Peaceful Walk Each Day Is Good Therapy

Walking is good exercise, as you well know. I know a man who came out of a war in a very fearful state of mind. His doctor suggested he walk four miles a day; he did, and he told me, "After two months of this practice all of my fears left me." You should take a short walk every day; it will do you much good. When you walk, say to yourself, "*I am peaceful.*" Now break this statement up into four parts to match every four steps you take. For example, as you walk, say to yourself: *I am peace-ful, I am peace-ful, I am peace-ful, I am peace-ful, I am peace-ful, I am peace-ful, I am peace-ful.*

Notice how what you say to yourself will put you in rhythm with your walking. It will do much more than that for you, for when you make these statements to yourself, you are affirming to yourself that YOU ARE PEACEFUL. These thoughts will then be impressed on your subconscious mind, which will accept your thoughts as valid and go to work to cause you to feel peaceful. Practice this method while walking one block, two, three, five, ten or more every day and you will create for yourself better health and greater peace of mind.

Some Peaceful Thoughts to Keep Worry Away

Memorize the following thoughts. Say them to yourself in your home, office, or wherever you are. They will aid you in gaining peace of mind.

SUNDAY: *I will remain calm, serene and peaceful today. This is my day to take a peaceful day's rest.*

MONDAY: *I will act kindly and friendly to people today.*

TUESDAY: *I shall calm down and be peaceful at every opportunity today.*

WEDNESDAY: *I am at peace with myself and the world today.*

THURSDAY: *I feel peace in my mind and heart today. I shall express this peace to all whom I meet.*

FRIDAY: *I am determined that I will be harmonious and peaceful every single moment of this day.*

SATURDAY: *I am peaceful in mind, I am peaceful in spirit, I am relaxed in body, too. This is the natural and normal state of my being, and I intend to keep that way.*

A Bedtime Treatment to Gain Peace

Upon retiring each night, lie down, stretch out, and completely relax. Now silently thank God for all of the blessings you have received. Now imagine that you are surrounded with an all-pervading presence of peace that permeates every part of your being. Feel this PRESENCE OF PEACE in you and around you. Claim this peace as your rightful heritage. Then close your eyes and have a peaceful night's sleep.

The Rich Rewards of Peace of Mind

A reward is something given for having done something good. I must remind you that nothing can give you peace of mind but you, yourself. What have you been doing by practicing the methods in this chapter? You have been doing something good for yourself and therefore you are entitled to receive the rich rewards of peace of mind. What are these rewards? Peace and harmony within your own self. A clear mind. Good health. Renewed strength and vitality. Good fellowship with other people. The ability to make your own success. The ability to earn a good living, and to really enjoy life. Therefore, my friend, I urge you, with all my heart, to practice what has been said in this chapter. Turn to its pages any time you need a quick pick-up, and you will enjoy all of the rich rewards that are rightfully yours for having gained a serene and peaceful state of mind.

LAW OF TRANQUILIZING PEACE REMINDERS

1. People are creatures of habit. Those who lack self-control lose control of their emotions. Those who have self-control remain calm and serene in all circumstances and conditions.
2. Never allow one who is emotionally upset to disturb you. Treat that one with courtesy and silence.
3. Have no bitterness in your heart for another. Like yourself, and you will then be able to have a liking for other people.
4. Nothing can bring you peace of mind but yourself. Nothing can give you peace of mind but the practice of peace-making principles.
5. How one home is made a haven of peace.
6. Calm down, take it easy, there is really nothing to fear.
7. How to relax in mind and body.
8. How to control your emotions and gain peace of mind.
9. Begin each day with a right, peaceful attitude.

10. Take a peaceful walk each day. Practice the rhythmic peace-producing method.
11. Some peaceful thoughts to practice to keep worry away.
12. A bedtime treatment to gain peace.
13. The rich rewards of peace of mind are always available.

16

The Exhilarating Law of Happiness

Everyone wants happiness, but not many make a sincere effort to obtain it. This is ironic, for happiness is one of the greatest and richest treasures of life. Do you know that if you possessed all of the money in the world, you could not buy happiness? Know why? Because happiness is a thing of the spirit and it can only be obtained by using the creative powers of your mind intelligently and wisely—then happiness will become a natural part of your life.

Why Some People Are Unhappy

These are the people who refuse to face up to life. They blame everything that happens to them on someone else, not knowing that they are the prime cause of their own unhappiness. They react to everything that their five senses convey to their brain as if that thing were a mortal enemy, out to get them and do them wrong. They see nothing good in themselves or in anyone else. They are the chronic complainers and whiners of life, who not only make themselves feel miserable but also everyone else whom they can get to listen to them.

Why Some People Are Happy

These are the people who take a real interest in life. These are the ones who have set their aim high to do something constructive with the creative power that has been given them. They gain satisfaction and happiness in the work they are doing by doing what they do well. They like themselves and they like people. They are too busy to spend time on idle chatter. They have a sense of humor and enjoy a good laugh. They look at the bright side of life. They are cheerful and well-mannered, and to associate with them frequently is to have some of their happiness rub off on you.

Sudden Good Fortune Gave Her Great Joy

I know a cashier in a New York City shop who had a burning desire to visit her children in California, but who did not have enough money to make such a trip. I told her to fix her mind and believe that something unusual would happen that would make such a trip possible. She accepted my suggestion. Three weeks later I saw this same woman again. This time she was in a happy state of mind. She said, "The unusual has just happened to me. Recently I ran into a friend of long standing whose wife was a school chum of mine. This man was in very high spirits. He told me he had just inherited a large sum of money. I congratulated him on his good fortune and mentioned I wished something good like that would happen to me so I could visit my children in California. He asked me to meet him the next day, and I did. He then produced a large roll of money and said, "Here, take this. This money will make your dream come true. Now, go visit your children in California. Don't skimp with this money I have given you; if you need more, all you have to do is to telephone me."

Note carefully how this woman's burning desire remained just a burning desire until I told her to believe that something unusual would happen that would make her trip to California possible. She accepted this idea on its face value and believed in it. This action on her part set up a magnetic power of attraction to attract just the right person to give her the money to make this trip. To merely have an intense desire to do something or have something is not enough to make a desire come true. You must use your faith by believing that everything necessary for the fulfillment of your desire will be attracted to you so that your desire will come true.

She Exchanged Her Sorrow for Happiness

What do you do when you buy something in a department store that is unsuitable for you? You simply take that thing back and exchange it for something more suitable. How about sadness? Can you exchange that for joy? Yes, you can, and the following story will prove that you can.

One evening, while having dinner at the home of a good friend, a woman of considerable wealth sat opposite me at the table. I noticed that this woman was in a very depressed state of mind. After dinner I asked my host the reason for this woman's apparent unhappiness. He replied, "She has been in deep sorrow for months since her husband passed on and I am doing my best to snap her out of her sorrowful mood."

When the right opportunity presented itself, I asked this woman to take a walk with me in the fresh air. She accepted my invitation.

As we walked together along tree-lined streets that evening, I had a heart-to-heart talk with her. I said, "It is only natural that when someone whom we love passes on, we experience a deep emotional shock. I had that experience when my brother, whom I dearly loved, passed on. At such a time it is the part of wisdom to have a good cry in order to release emotional tension, but to go on feeling sorry for one's self day in and day out is a very harmful practice. Keep it up and you will wind up being a chronic invalid. Why don't you release your husband to God as I did my brother, and start living?"

As we arrived at a street light, I stopped and wrote some thoughts down on a sheet of paper. I gave her the paper and told her to memorize the thoughts I had written down, and to repeat them to herself 100 times a day for the next 30 days. Here are those thoughts:

I release my husband to God, his Maker. I promise myself I will pull myself together. I promise myself I will look on the bright side of life. I promise myself to live a new, happy

The Exhilarating Law of Happiness 169

life. I shall dedicate myself to the giving of happiness to others, knowing that as I do I will be bringing happiness and joy to myself.

Ninety days later I met this woman again and the change that had taken place within her was simply miraculous. She was an entirely new woman. This time she had a big smile on her face. Her eyes shone with new sparkle and light. She was lighthearted, happy and gay. She said, "I must tell you the good news. I have just been elected president of my club. I have so much to do these days I haven't time to give a thought to sadness or worry." I have learned since that she has remarried, and is indeed a happy woman.

It may surprise you to know that both joy and sorrow are emotions. Yes, they are, and this is the reason why: When you like something or someone very much, it makes a strong impression upon your subconscious mind which causes you to experience a feeling of joy towards that person or thing. Thus you become emotionally attached to whatever it is you admire and adore. However, when the object of your fond affection is taken away from you, the emotional tie which held you and the object of your affection together is severed. What happens then? You immediately begin to develop a sense of loss. It is this sense of loss you now impress upon the feeling power of your subconscious mind, and as a result you experience a strong feeling of sorrow. Thus, it is *how you use* the creative power of your mind, and the *way you react* to things and events that causes you to feel joyful or sad. However, it is a fact that in the midst of any circumstance, regardless of its nature, you can always take a new liking to something or someone else and create for yourself renewed joy and happiness. This is why you should make a determined effort to rise above sorrow and so create for yourself that joyous feeling that makes life a grand and glorious experience.

Music Will Put You in a Happy Mood

Music is a universal language of harmonious sounds that speaks to the hearts of people. When you feel blue, listening to good music will drive your troubles away and cause you to feel lighthearted and gay. For this reason, you will indeed be wise to listen to as much good music as you possibly can. Your appreciation of it can attract wonderful things to you.

I once knew a famous orchestra leader whose music gave great happiness to millions of people. This man believed that giving happiness to people through the art of music was the greatest science man could be engaged in. Incidentally, he was keenly aware of the Laws of Mental Magnetism and used them often in the following manner. He would sit at his desk and imagine a new musical show he intended to produce for radio or TV. Then he would visualize the artists he intended to have in that show. Next he would expect these artists to come to him and sign contracts with him. And they did. When he subsequently produced the shows he had conceived in his mind, the fine music and artistry gave great happiness to many people.

I urge you to tune in to good music on your TV or radio. Hear a good concert. Go to the opera or to a good musical comedy show. Listen to music frequently, for it will put you in a gay, happy mood.

How One Woman Found Happiness

Following a lecture I had given one evening, a woman came to me and said, "I am very unhappy because my husband always finds fault with me. Do you think I should break up our marriage and leave him?" I asked her if she had relatives or friends to live with, or if she had enough money to support herself. She answered "No" to both of my questions. I said, "Well, why not try finding a job for yourself? That will take your mind off of your problem." She replied, "I have thought of that, but now that you have reminded me, I think I will do just that."

Six months later I met this woman again, but this time she was bubbling over with happiness. With great enthusiasm she said, "Something really wonderful has happened to me. Right after seeing you the last time, I went out looking for work. I finally landed a position as a school teacher, teaching a class of little children. This work is very interesting. I love these children and I feel certain that they love me. But here is the big news! My husband no longer finds fault with me. He is kind and considerate. He has just bought a magnificent new house for us and he has given me a present of a new car."

The Exhilarating Law of Happiness

Let us analyze this woman's story. Here was a woman who had previously sat at home every day, letting her imagination run wild. She worried about this thing and that thing until she became mentally depressed. Now, if you were a man, how would you like coming home to that kind of a woman after a day's work? If you are human you would get fed up with that kind of married life. Ah, but here is the magic in this story: the moment this man's wife found something interesting and constructive to do with her life, his attitude towards her changed to kindness and consideration, and harmony and happiness were restored in both of their lives. Should you be married, occupy your mind by doing something constructive, and you will be too busily engaged in what you are doing to waste time and energy in finding fault with your mate or yourself.

You Have a Decision to Make

If at present you are unhappy about something, this means you have an important decision to make: either to remain unhappy or to make up your mind that you can and will be happy. No one can make this decision for you; you must make it for yourself. So why not make up your mind to be happy now, and to make happiness the supreme goal of your life? DO IT NOW, and you will forever be glad that you did.

Some Things That Will Give You Happiness

Having a love for music will give you happiness.
Reading a good book will lift you up in spirit.
Being in good company will give you a feeling of happiness.
Listening to good conversation will brighten your day.
Seeing a good comedy show will cause you to be gay.
Doing something good for another will give you great joy.
And making up your mind that you will be happy, will cause you to feel happy every moment of the day.

Three Magic Steps to Happiness

As only practical work done by you in your own mind will make it possible for you to enjoy true and lasting happiness, I have prepared a plan of action for you which is as follows:

1. Get yourself a sheet of paper and a pencil and write down at the top, "THINGS THAT MAKE ME UNHAPPY." Now, be frank with yourself. Think of all the things that cause you to feel unhappy and write them down under this heading. After you have done so, look over those things and say the following to yourself:

> **These things have no power to make me unhappy. I cast them out of my mind forever. I create my own happiness by what I think, imagine and believe. This day I am determined that I will create my own happiness. This day I am determined that true happiness will be my principal objective in life.**

Now tear up your unhappy list and put it in your waste basket as something that not even a garbage collector would be interested in.

2. Now get another sheet of paper and make a copy of the following new basic goal as shown below. It took me some time to think this one out. Surely you can take a little time and copy it as a reminder to carry with you in your pocket or purse. Here is your new goal.

My New Life Goal

```
        H
        A
        P
        P
HAPP I NESS
        N
        E
        S
        S
```

Note the *I* in the center of this diagram. It means you! You are the one who is going to create your own happiness. Remember this, *you are the only one in the world who can create* YOUR HAPPINESS.

The Exhilarating Law of Happiness

3. Now fill in the following chart with everything you can imagine that you think will cause you to be happy.

1. ....
2. ....
3. ....
4. ....
5. ....
6. ....

Look at this chart once, twice, or three times a day for three days. This practice will keep your attention on those things you think will be instrumental in bringing happiness to you.

Now choose one particular thing you have written down on the chart and desire to have demonstrated in your life. After you have done this, go to a quiet place alone, sit down in an easy chair, relax and close your eyes.

You are now ready to give reality to the thing you have chosen and cause it to be made manifest in your life as a demonstrated fact. Now do the following:

Make a vivid mental image of whatever it is you desire to happen to you. Do this in your imagination. For example, if your desire is to meet someone whom you love, imagine yourself being in the company of that person in real life, with both of you having a most remarkably good time. If it is to have a new home, visualize yourself actually living in a beautiful new home. An invitation to a dinner party? Imagine yourself actually seated at a table at that party in the company of very happy people, enjoying yourself and having the jolliest time of your life. If it is more money that you think will cause you to feel happy, imagine yourself receiving the exact amount of money you desire. Feel the thrill this experience will give you. Greater success? Visualize yourself doing those things that will cause you to become a great success. More health and vitality? Make a vivid mental picture of yourself as being whole, well, strong and perfect. Whatever it is that you think will give you happiness, make a real, life-sized picture of that thing in your imagination.

Now take hold of the thing you desire and have imagined.

Breathe the breath of life into it by believing it is something very real, something that will surely happen to you, something that will give you great happiness. Feel the joy and pleasure that this thing will give you. Let this feeling of joy and pleasure be felt in the depths of your heart and soul. Bathe in this feeling of absolute conviction and certainty for a few moments. This action on your part will cause your subconscious mind to go into action on your behalf and attract to you what you desire, have imagined, and believe will give you happiness. Now open your eyes, fully convinced that you *will* receive a great abundance of happiness and joy as the result of your own use of the Laws of Mental Magnetism.

How to Attract Every Day as a Happy Day

Each morning, right after dressing, go to your mirror, take a good look, and say to yourself, with feeling: *I look wonderful today. I feel marvelous today, this is going to be the happiest day of my life.* Now look at yourself in your mirror again and say to yourself: *I am determined to be lighthearted and gay today. I am determined to keep a happy smile on my face today. I am determined to be happy today.* Now go out into the world and act out the part of what you have promised to yourself. Under no circumstance allow any person, thing, or condition to disturb you or cause you to get off of your HAPPINESS BEAM. Know that nothing in the outer world has any power to make you unhappy. *Let your sunny disposition and spirit of good will bring happiness to others. Be cheerful, happy and gay every minute and hour of the day.* Do this for one day, then two, then three, four, five and ten days, until happiness becomes a way of life with you and your every day will be filled with great joy and true happiness.

The Rich Rewards of Happiness

Happiness will lift you up in mind and spirit. It will give you a feeling of complete well-being. When you are happy in heart, everything good will be attracted to you. Your relations with people, your employment, your environment, and your health will improve, because your harmonious nature sets into action the Universal Law of mutual attraction. This, my friend, is the reason you should make up your mind to be happy and stay happy. Do this and you will become one of the most happy and joyous persons alive. DO IT NOW.

LAW OF HAPPINESS REMINDERS

1. Unhappy people are those who believe other people are the cause of their unhappiness. These are the people who do not know they create their own unhappiness.
2. Happy people are those who look at the bright side of life. They have no bitterness in their hearts towards anyone. They are cheerful and happy in every circumstance and condition. They like people and love to be with people.
3. How sudden good fortune brought happiness to one woman.
4. How a woman exchanged her deep sorrow for happiness and joy.
5. How one person's music brought happiness to millions of people.
6. How a new interest brought happiness to a woman.
7. You have an important decision to make—NOW.
8. Three magic steps to happiness show you how to gain true happiness.
9. How you can attract every day as a happy day.
10. Claim your rich rewards of happiness NOW.

17

How to Attract Happy Happenings

By using the Magnetic Power of your mind, you can attract many happenings you never believed you could receive. This chapter will show you how to use the Law of Mental Magnetism in a variety of ways to attract and experience many happy happenings.

All Good Things Exist for Your Benefit

I am going to ask you a question. Why do you have the power to desire something that will benefit you? Because everything that will prove to be for your welfare already exists in a completed state. Then why do you not have all that you desire? Because you have not used the magnetic power of your mind to reach out and attract what you desire. You have not as yet used your own power of Mental Magnetism in a skillful and effective manner.

How to Use Your Magnetic Subconscious Mind

Your subconscious mind is extremely magnetic. It knows how to attract everything necessary to keep your physical body in good condition. You use its magnetic power of attraction every time you draw in a breath of fresh air. This action on your part keeps you alive. You also use the same magnetic power of your subconscious mind to desire and believe with. Then why do you not always receive what you desire? Because you have not developed enough faith to believe in the magnetic power of your subconscious mind. You do not believe you will receive what you desire to receive. The following methods will show you how to use the Laws of Mental Magnetism intelligently and effectively.

1. In order to attract anything good, you must first use your imagination. You must make a clear mental picture of the thing you intend to attract. You do this by visualizing that thing. You do this by making a vivid picture of that thing in your imagination.

2. Next, you must desire to have the thing you have pictured in your imagination. You do this by taking possession of it mentally, that is, by taking ownership of it in your mind. After having done this you must make up your mind to attract that thing to you.

3. Finally you must make a deep impression of the thing you have visualized and desire to receive upon your subconscious mind. You are to firmly believe that the magnetic power of your subconscious mind will reach out and draw what you desire to you. You are to believe that you positively will receive the thing you desire. You are to keep believing that you *will* receive what you desire until you actually *do* receive it.

Do this and the magnetic power of your subconscious mind will go to work for you and cause you to receive whatever you desire as a demonstrated fact. This is the secret of using Mental Magnetism skillfully and effectively. This is the secret of receiving any good thing you desire to receive.

How to Attract Your New World

Now, let's talk about you. You are the result of your upbringing by your parents, plus what you have learned in school. During this time you have taken on many thoughts and beliefs. Basically, however, YOU ARE AN UNLIMITED PERSON, and the time has now come for you to take control of your life and start it in a new direction by practicing the Laws of Mental Magnetism.

HERE IS BIG NEWS! If you do not like the kind of a world you are living in, *you can change it.* You can attract and live in a world more to your liking. How? By picturing yourself as a terrific success in the work you are engaged in. By visualizing yourself in a magnificent environment home-wise. By imagining yourself being associated with very successful and harmonious new friends and companions. You can do this by doing the following:

Each day arrange to have a period of silent meditation by going to some quiet place, sitting in an easy chair, relaxing, and closing your eyes.

In this stillness, *imagine yourself being outstandingly successful in the work you are engaged in. Picture yourself living in a magnificent new home or apartment. Visualize yourself being associated with successful, good-natured new friends and companions. Picture yourself living in a completely new, interesting world.*

Develop an intense desire to attract and live in the new world you have pictured in your imagination. Make up your mind that you will live in it.

Now put the magnetic power of your subconscious mind to work for you. Believe that everything needed to cause you to become an amazing success will be attracted to you. Believe you will become an outstanding success in an astonishing manner. Hold this firm positive conviction for a few minutes, then open your eyes and be on your way. Be sure to practice this method every day without fail. Do so, and what you have visualized and believed will become a reality.

The only way you can unglue and free yourself from any adverse situation is by imagining yourself in a more favorable circumstance. Then put the Law of Mental Magnetism to work by believing what you have imagined will become a reality. The above method is "sure fire" in this respect, for when you *persistently practice* it, what you imagine, desire and believe will happen, most assuredly will happen.

How to Attract New Friends and Companions

It is a known fact that like attracts like on all levels of life. This is especially true regarding human beings. Friendly people attract friendly people. Unfriendly people attract people of like mental disposition. This Law of mental attraction operates in the lives of every member of the human race. Thus, the first thing you must do in order to attract new friends to you is to be a friendly person yourself.

You can do this by expressing good will and friendliness to others. By being cheerful and good-natured. By treating people as you would like to have them treat you. The methods contained in Chapter 8 of this book, "How to Gain a Magnetic Personality," will aid you in becoming a more friendly and likeable person. I suggest you practice the methods contained in that chapter. Do so, and you will become a more friendly and magnetic person.

Each day you should have a quiet period of meditation with yourself. Sit in an easy chair, completely relax and close your eyes.

> **Visualize yourself as being a very friendly person. Picture yourself as being the kind of person people take an instant liking to. Reach out and desire to attract many new friends to you.**
>
> **Now, firmly believe that the magnetic power of your subconscious mind is attracting many new friends to you. Hold this firm conviction for five minutes and expect what you have imagined and believe will come true.**

Now open your eyes and be on your way. Practice this Law of Mental Attraction every day and you will attract to you many interesting and wonderful new friends. Should you be lonesome, let me tell you that loneliness is a result of a refusal to face up to life. It is a refusal to enjoy many of the joys and blessings of life. Allow me to tell you that the right companion for you exists, but in order to attract this person to you, you must make up your mind to attract him/her. The following will show you how you can do this.

Refuse to live a solitary and uninteresting life. Decide to be friendly to people. Decide to get out and mix with people. Sit down in an easy chair, relax and close your eyes. Now practice the Law of Mental Magnetism thus:

Desire to attract your right companion to you. Imagine that a most likeable and friendly person is being attracted to you. Imagine the joy and happiness that person's companionship will give you. Dwell on these thoughts for three or more minutes.

Next, BELIEVE that your right companion is being attracted to you. BELIEVE that a most friendly and likeable person is being attracted to you. EXPECT to meet your right companion in person. BELIEVE you positively will meet your right companion. Now open your eyes. Practice this method every day without fail. Do so, and the Law of Mental Magnetism will go to work for you to attract a most interesting and enjoyable constant companion to you.

How to Attract Things for Your Pleasure and Comfort

You do not have to wait until the Christmas season rolls around to receive specific items that will give you pleasure and joy. The Law of Mental Magnetism can be used just as effectively to cause you to receive material things as it can be used to attract health, happiness, or any of the intangible experiences for greater joy in living.

First, I must tell you there is nothing wrong in desiring to receive any kind of a material thing. To believe otherwise is to believe in lack. Keep believing in lack and you will never receive any good thing. Furthermore, every material thing was once an idea which someone believed in and then produced by using imagination and faith. You can have an idea for something you would like to have. You can start your power of Mental Magnetism in action to draw whatever you desire to you. You can believe that you will receive what you desire, and according to your faith you will receive it.

Here are a few things you may have a desire to receive: a color TV set; a fast-action camera; a new wardrobe of clothes; a fur coat; a traveling bag; new home furnishings; a diamond ring; a pearl necklace; wrist watch; motor boat; camping equipment; or a shiny new car. These things do exist as you well know, and the only way by which you can draw any of them to you and receive them is by believing that you *will* receive them. The following method will aid you in doing this.

Sit down in a chair and close your eyes. Think of the thing you would like to receive. Think of the pleasure that thing would give you were you to have it. Then do the following:

> **Visualize the thing you would like to receive. Make a vivid mental picture of that thing in your imagination. Reach out and take hold of that thing and claim it as your own. Hold it tight to you with strong feeling. Now imagine that the thing you have so vividly pictured and claimed as your own is being attracted to you. Now hold this firm conviction in your consciousness for five minutes.**

Now, BELIEVE you will receive the object of your intense desire and affection. BELIEVE it is already on its way to you. EXPECT to have that thing delivered to you, and KNOW that it positively will be delivered to you. *Keep believing that you will receive it for ten minutes.* Now open your eyes and go about your business.

The object of your desire can come to you in many ways. It can come as the result of your being given a sudden raise in pay which will enable you to buy it. It can come to you as a gift from a friend or admirer, or by your winning it on a TV program or in a prize contest. It can come by your having been named as an heir in a will, or as a gift to you from a business or social club. Or it can come to you from someone you have never met in your life. The main thing to remember is:

> **The power of your mind is magnetic. When you desire anything, the magnetic department of your mind reaches out and attaches its magnetic power of attraction to that thing. Then, when you believe you will receive the thing you desire, the magnetic power of your own faith makes it possible for you to receive it.**

How to Cause Good Fortune to Happen to Another

You can practice the Law of Mental Magnetism for someone other than yourself, especially if that someone is a relative or a friend. You can do this by visualizing something very good for that other person and by believing this good will happen. I have done this for many people with amazing results.

For example, a private secretary to the president of a business concern in a large city came to me one day and said, "The firm I am with is on the verge of bankruptcy due to a shortage of working capital. I have attended some of your lectures and now ask you, will the Laws of Mental Magnetism work in this situation?" I told her that *they would if she really believed they would.* She then asked how she could apply these Laws for her employer's benefit. I told her to do the following:

Close your eyes while you are in the chair you are now sitting on. Visualize a large sum of money now being given to your employer. Picture this sum of money coming to him in a most unusual way. Desire money in abundance to flow into the hands of your employer. Hold these pictures in your mind for ten minutes.

Then BELIEVE that a large sum of money actually is being given to your employer. BELIEVE that a miracle will happen that will keep the firm you are with in business. BELIEVE that your employer is now receiving an abundance of money. Hold these firm beliefs in your mind for ten minutes. Then open your eyes.

Immediately after this young lady had left me, I closed my own eyes and visualized her coming back to see me in a few days and telling me, "A miracle has happened!" I pictured her saying to me, "My boss has received plenty of money, which will enable him to stay in business." And I positively believed she would do as I had visualized her doing.

One week later this young lady did come to see me again. In great jubilation she exclaimed, "A miracle has happened! Two days after I last came to see you, as if 'out of the blue' a man called on my boss and asked to see an empty warehouse building he owned but had been unable to sell for many years. This man was shown the building and was so impressed with it he made a huge down payment to purchase it and gave my boss this 'earnest money.' He also agreed to pay the balance in cash the moment title to this building is delivered to him."

I have since learned this man did take full possession to the building, and that the lady and her boss are still in business and doing very well.

Fantastic? Absolutely not. When you visualize any particular good fortune happening for another and positively believe that good fortune *will* happen, it will happen. I have used this method of hearing people come to me and saying, "A miracle has happened," with astonishing success. I assure you, when you do experience such a happening, you will have such faith in the Law of Mental Magnetism that no circumstance or condition will ever shake your faith in this miraculous Law of Laws.

Here is a constructive suggestion: *Never allow yourself to be emotionally upset by any negative story anyone tells you regarding him- or herself. The best way to give aid and comfort to such a person is to reverse the negative pictures that one is visualizing and believing in, in the following manner.*

For instance, suppose someone tells you he or she cannot find employment. Don't buy or accept that idea. Instead, instantly picture that person receiving a very lucrative offer of employment and accepting that offer. *Believe* this will surely happen to that person. Picture that same person coming to you again and saying to you, "A miracle has happened! I have just landed the best-paying job I have ever had in my life." *Believe* what you have imagined for that person. *Believe* what you expect that person will tell you, and what you have visualized and *believe* will surely happen.

Suppose someone tells you he is in poor health. The best deed you can do for that person is to picture him being completely restored to perfect good health. Sit down in a chair, close your eyes and visualize that person coming to you and saying, "A miracle has happened! I am enjoying wonderfully good health." *Believe* what you have visualized for this other person will happen. *Believe what you believe will surely happen.* Do this and you will attract this other person to you expressing abundant good health.

This same basic principle of the Law of Mental Magnetism will work for you in any circumstance or condition for the benefit of another person. For example, one time a well-known actor friend of mine had a very severe case of laryngitis, so much so he could not speak. This man had a very important speaking engagement booked on the evening of a particular day. According to human logic and reasoning this engagement would have to be cancelled. I asked him if he intended to go ahead with his speaking engagement and he gave me a nod, meaning yes. That was all I needed to go ahead and do the following.

At two o'clock on the afternoon of that day, I sat down and closed my eyes. In the stillness I pictured my friend standing on a platform before a large audience giving a marvelous talk in a strong, powerful, resonant voice. I visualized everyone in his audience going to him after he had given his talk and complimenting him for having given such a powerfully inspiring and dynamic talk. I practiced this method of mental visualization for three solid hours.

Next, I convinced myself that that which I had pictured on behalf of my friend would surely happen. I did this by constantly knowing that what I had imagined and pictured positively would happen.

That evening my friend walked onto the platform. He smiled at his audience and began to speak. He spoke in a strong, powerful, dynamic voice, as I knew he would. He completely captivated and enthralled his audience with a most interesting talk. After he had finished speaking I noticed one person after another rushing up to him and congratulating him for having given such an inspiring and uplifting talk.

At two o'clock the following morning we sat together in the same hotel room where, 24 hours earlier, this man could not speak a word. This time my friend's voice was completely restored and we had many laughs together regarding this most amazing happening. This incident has given me even greater faith in the Laws of Mental Magnetism. You, too, can use this method of seeing and knowing good fortune will happen for another when you firmly believe it will.

Suppose you know someone close to you who is involved in the litigation of settling a will. Have that person tell you the exact contents and disposition of that will. Be sure to have him tell you that he is a rightful legal heir in that will. Then sit down, close your eyes and do the following.

Visualize true justice being done for your friend in the final settlement of the will. Know that that which is his by divine right cannot be taken from him. Visualize your friend's face. Picture him coming and saying to you, "That will case has been settled and I have been awarded my rightful share in it." Do this for your friend and he will come to you and tell you about his good fortune.

How to Attract Happy Happenings

It is a fact that nothing ever happens by chance. Everything happens according to a Law. This is true. In order to produce any effect there must always be a cause to produce an effect. Not too many people are aware of this important truth. This is why the Law of Mental Magnetism is so important to you. If you want something wonderful to happen to you, you must set the right cause in motion to enable that thing, whatever it is, to happen.

One spring, while giving a series of lectures, I suddenly developed a consuming desire to spend the summer away from the hustle and bustle of a large city. I had no specific place in mind, just an intense desire to spend the summer at a charming country home near a river or ocean.

The following week a lady, who had evidently attended several of my lectures previously, and whom I had never met, came to me and showed me a picture of her beautiful country estate. I remarked, "You certainly do have a beautiful home in the country." For several weeks thereafter she spoke to me after each of my lectures, and finally invited me to spend the oncoming summer at her country estate. I accepted her invitation to do so.

Arriving at this lady's beautiful place, I was given a charming cottage to live in. I was even offered the services of a private secretary to assist me with my writings. I enjoyed fishing, boating and swimming in the river which flowed in front of this lady's magnificent home. I had a most glorious and wonderful time with this lady and her husband all through that summer.

When we have an intense desire for something wonderful to happen and believe that something good will happen, it will most surely happen.

Another time I had a desire to be given a birthday party on a New Year's day. This was a deliberate intention on my part. I sat down and visualized this party being given for me. I even pictured certain singers and musicians whom I know performing at it. And I firmly believed a party would be given me.

I mentioned this idea to a friend of mine; she thought it was a great idea and mentioned it to a friend. This friend enthused about the idea and arranged to give me the party.

On the evening of my birthday I was ushered into a luxury apartment located on Fifth Avenue in New York City. As I entered I was greeted by a host of friends and new friends to be. The singers and musicians I had formerly visualized were present. On a table reposed a large birthday cake with one lighted candle upon it. Soon the music began to play, people sang and laughed and had a jolly time. This just goes to show what can be accomplished when you desire something wonderful to happen, picture it happening, and believe it will positively happen.

What Happy Event Do You Want to Happen?

What wonderful event do you want to happen for you? Here are a few suggestions: a big raise in pay; an important contract to be signed; a luxury vacation trip; a birthday party given in your honor; a new home to live in; an invitation to a big dinner and dance party; a proposal of marriage; a trip to Europe. These are a few ideas that will stimulate your imagination and cause you to desire something wonderful to happen to you. After you have selected the one most important event you desire to happen, do the following:

Go to a quiet place where you can be alone each day. Sit in a comfortable chair, relax and close your eyes.

How to Make a Happy Event Happen

> **Visualize the thing you most want to happen. Make a mental picture of that event clearly and vividly in your mind. Should it be a raise in pay, picture your employer handing you a raise in pay; an important contract to be signed, picture yourself and the parties concerned sitting at a table signing that contract; a trip to Europe, visualize yourself stepping off your plane at London, Paris, or another European country you intend visiting. Whatever it is you desire to happen, make a realistic picture of that event in your imagination, and decide to make that picture come true.**

After you have visualized and pictured in your mind the thing or event you desire to happen, you are to put the magnetic department to work for you. You do this by *believing* that which you have

How to Attract Happy Happenings

imagined and desire to happen will happen. Do this, and the Law of Mental Magnetism will attract everything needed to cause what you *believe* will happen. Now open your eyes and be on your way. Practice this method once, twice, three times a day or more often. And when you get that sudden, "I know it is going to happen" feeling, this is a "sure sign" your happy event will happen.

As you are about to retire each evening, lie on your bed, close your eyes, and speak to your subconscious mind, making certain to mention your happy happening desire. "*I give you a firm order to attract everything needed that will cause my happy event to happen.*" Now close your eyes and go to sleep.

If at any time when you are practicing these methods, any doubt enters your mind as to the fulfillment of your desire, this means you do not believe in what you have practiced. The Law of Mental Magnetism will definitely attract what you desire to receive, but you must fully *believe that it will*. So make it a firm rule to practice these methods of magnetic mental attraction, and you will experience and enjoy many new and eventful happy happenings.

LAW OF HAPPY HAPPENING REMINDERS

1. Everything for your greatest good already exists in a completed state. Then why do you not have all you desire? Because you have not as yet used your power of Mental Magnetism to reach out and attract what you desire to you.

2. The secret of attracting what you desire is to use your imagination, desire, and faith skillfully. Set the *magnetic power* of your mind in action to attract what you desire to you.

3. You can attract an entirely new world to live in by picturing yourself as an outstanding success in the work you are engaged in, by visualizing yourself living in a magnificent new environment, by seeing yourself associating with successful companions, and by believing what you imagine and desire will happen to you.

4. You can attract new friends and companions by giving your subconscious mind an order to attract new friends and companions to you.

5. You can attract many things that will give you pleasure and comfort by making a picture of what you desire to receive, and by firmly believing you will receive that which you desire to receive.

6. You can picture good fortune happening for another by visualizing that thing happening in your mind and by believing a miracle of good fortune will surely happen for the benefit of that other person.

7. How the author used imagination and faith to cause him to receive and experience two wonderful happy happenings.

8. How you can select any happy event you desire to happen and use the Laws of Mental Magnetism to cause that event to happen for you.

9. How the magnetic department of your mind can attract to you many happy and enjoyable experiences.

18

How to Attract Phenomenal Personal Success

My friend, you are living in the greatest scientific age in the history of mankind. You are living in an age of miracles. Today, what man can conceive, he can achieve. This all came about through the use of scientific knowledge. Just what is science? It is a systemized knowledge of any one department of mind or matter. This book is concerned with the magnetic department of mind, your mind, which will draw to you everything that will cause you to experience great joy in living. The Art of Successful Living is the greatest of sciences. Following the Laws of Mental Magnetism in daily practice for your own benefit can make you phenomenally successful in anything you put your mind to.

The Secret for Gaining Fame and Fortune

What do you suppose it is that causes one person to become a famous celebrity, and another, with apparently equal talent, to remain unknown? The answer is simple. The one who has gained notable recognition and renown had complete *FAITH* in his talent and ability and used it to its fullest capacity. The other person did not.

What are you attracting to yourself at this very moment? Are you attracting public acclaim for having used your talent in an astonishing manner? Or are you still unknown as the result of not having used your talent and ability successfully? If the latter is the case with you, you can reverse this situation by making use of your talent to its fullest potential. The following classic lines state a success formula for your immediate adoption:

> **Lose this day loitering—'twill be the same story**
> **Tomorrow—the next day more dilatory.**
> **Then indecision brings its own delays.**
> **And days are lost lamenting over days.**
> **Are you in earnest? Seize this very minute—**
> **What you can do, or dream you can, begin it.**
> **Courage has genius, power, and magic in it.**
> **Only engage, then the mind grows heated.**
> **Begin it and the work will be completed.**
> **—Goethe**

You Have the Unfailing Power to Attract Success

Regardless of what place in life you are now in, you have the power to rise higher. You have the power to begin an entirely new life any time you decide to do so. This decision is entirely up to you. You can remain just where you are year after year without making progress, or you can come to a quick decision and make up your mind you will become an outstanding success. The royal road to success is always wide open to you. Make up your mind that you will be a success and you can't miss becoming a success. Practice the Laws of Mental Magnetism daily and everything needed for your gaining success will be attracted to you.

The Magnetic Law of Mental Telesis

There is a magic Law for gaining success in any human endeavor. Simply stated, this Law reads as follows: *Progress clearly planned and directed is consciously directed effort.* Just what do these words mean? They mean that you must have a clearly defined plan to achieve what you intend to accomplish in order to achieve what you plan. This is simple enough language, but there is a certain magical element contained in this Law which is as follows.

When you plan to do something that will benefit you, your very act of making a plan works like a magnet to attract to you every idea which will cause your plan to be a success. In other words, your original idea for success will attract other ideas for the success of your plan. This again is my previous statement that like attracts like. Think success and plan success and every idea for the success of your plan will be attracted to you. The following diagram will show you what it takes mentally to climb the ladder of personal success.

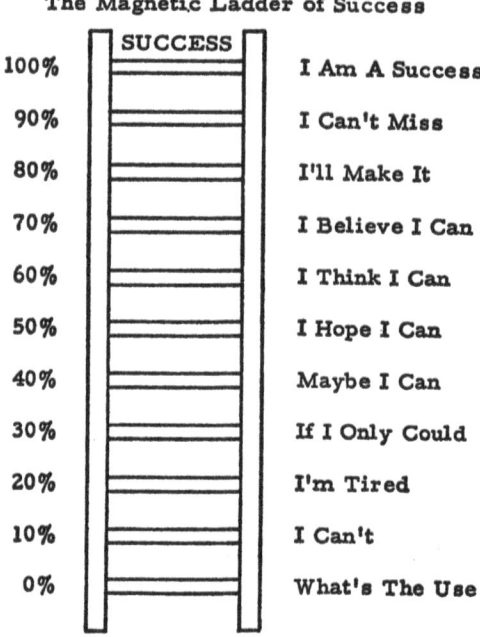

Make a Talent Goal for Outstanding Success

Get a sheet of paper and a pencil. Write down on that paper what you consider to be your best natural talent, the thing you can do naturally and easily. For instance, if you have a natural talent for selling, write that down. A natural talent for singing, write that down. A natural talent for business management, write that down. A natural talent for musical composition, write that down. Whatever comes naturally to you and you know you can do best, write that thing down on your sheet of paper. Now fill in the following form.

MY TALENT GOAL FOR PHENOMENAL SUCCESS

1. (Write your best talent here) ....
   ....

2. Write the following statement on the lines below it.
   I promise myself I will make my best talent the supreme goal of my life to attract phenomenal success.

   ....
   ....
   .... (Name your talent)

3. Write the following statements on the lines below them.
   I promise myself I will dedicate myself to my talent.
   I promise to use my talent for the benefit of all people.

   ....
   ....

4. Write the following statements on the lines below them.
   I promise to put my heart and soul into my talent each and every day. I promise to practice the laws of mental magnetism to attract everything needed to cause my talent goal to become a phenomenal success.

   ....
   ....
   ....
   ....

   Date here. .... Sign your name here ....

Attract Phenomenal Personal Success

By signing your name to this Talent Goal form you have made some vital promises to yourself. This act on your part is a *magnetic* action which will draw all manner of good fortune to you, provided you keep these promises you have made to yourself. When you make a goal to be realized and achieved, this action starts the magnetic department of your mind in action to attract the right circumstances needed to give you success in what you are determined to accomplish.

Determine to Play a Star Part in Life

Shakespeare was right when he wrote, "All the world's a stage and men and women merely players...." (*As You Like It*, Act 2, Scene 7.) Some people play "bit" parts all of their lives, not knowing that they only have to call upon their Powers of Mental Magnetism to become "stars" in the great amphitheater of life. This need not happen to you, for simply by putting your heart into your talent and using it to its fullest capacity, you can rise to stardom in life.

Picture Yourself as Having Great Talent

In order to convince yourself you can really gain phenomenal success by using your talent, you must *believe* you have tremendous ability for expressing your talent in an amazing manner. You can do this by sitting in a chair, alone, relaxing, and closing your eyes. Then do the following:

> **Imagine that you have tremendous ability. Picture yourself as being extraordinarily gifted. Visualize yourself as being exceptionally skillful in expressing your talent. Picture yourself as being a phenomenal success as the result of having used your talent to its fullest capacity. See yourself as becoming world-famous and attracting great good fortune as the result of having used your great ability successfully.**

This will make a deep impression of what you are imagining, visualizing and picturing upon your subconscious mind.

At this same time of silent visualization, do the following:

BELIEVE you have tremendous talent and ability. *BELIEVE* you are extraordinarily gifted. *BELIEVE* you are skillful in expressing your talent. BELIEVE you ARE a phenomenal success. BELIEVE you ARE world famous. BELIEVE that good fortune in the form of wealth IS BEING attracted to you. BELIEVE that the magnetic power of your subconscious mind is attracting everything necessary to cause you to BE a phenomenal success. Then open your eyes and be on your way. Practice this method every day without fail.

Practice Will Gain "High Voltage" Confidence

As you put your powers of Mental Magnetism to work by thinking and believing in your heart, you are also building confidence in yourself and your ability. This can only be acquired by constant practice—by convincing yourself that you are really great and will reach the pinnacle of success by using your talent for the benefit of others. In other words, you must sell yourself to yourself.

You can do this by going to your mirror at any time and taking a look at yourself. As you do, say to yourself, and mean what you say,

> "I have supreme confidence in myself and my ability. I am determined to become a phenomenal success in life. I shall think I am a success. I shall believe I am a success. I shall keep knowing I am a success and as I do I shall attract every circumstance to me that will cause me to be an outstanding success."

Practice this technique every day without fail. As you do, you will become such a positive, self-confident person that nothing will stop you from becoming that phenomenal success.

Give Your Subconscious a "Success Order" Each Evening

As you are about to retire each evening, sit in a comfortable chair and close your eyes. Tell your subconscious mind to attract to you new ideas for greater usages of your talent. Tell it to open the door of greater opportunity for you. Tell it to attract to you the people who will enable you to express your talent more fully. Tell your subconscious mind:

> "Attract everything to me that will cause me to be a phenomenal success in life. Draw to me people, things, and circumstances that will cause me to be famous for having used my talent successfully."

Then go to bed believing that while you sleep your subconscious mind will be attracting everything to you that will cause you to accomplish your desire.

How Your Talent Will Act as a Magnet for You

When you express your talent to its fullest capacity, people will stand up and take notice of you. Many will become interested in you. New doors of opportunity will open wide for you.

Today there is an enormous demand for new talent in every conceivable field. When the word gets out that you have exceptional talent, today's so-called "talent scouts" will discover you. Therefore, through your own powers of Mental Magnetism, keep developing your talent, and circumstances necessary for your recognition by others who can use your great ability will be assured.

A Famous Star's Secret for Success

I once met Ted Lewis, the famous stage, moving-picture and TV star, on a Thanksgiving Day in Milwaukee, Wisconsin. As I wanted to pass on some success ideas to my audience later that day, I asked Mr. Lewis what his secret for gaining success was. He replied, "Always do the right thing and you can't keep from being a success; it comes naturally." This is very important, for when your motive is right, you will always do what is right. Be sure to see to it that your motive in using your talent is right, that what you do will benefit people. With this motive you cannot keep from becoming an outstanding success.

The Value of Stick-To-It-Tiveness

We have been told, "Having once put your hand to the plow, never look back." This means that having made up your mind to use your talent for personal success, you must stick to your intention. You must keep your attention focussed on developing your talent to greater proportions. You must learn by doing everything practical you can find to do with your talent. You must constantly bear in mind that the more you use your talent, the greater it increases in value. You must stay with your talent goal for success regardless of what happens on your pathway to success, and always firmly believe you will reach your goal.

The Value of Associating with Successful People

The president of a firm I was once with insisted I stop at the best hotel in every city I visited when selling his products. He said, "If I ever learn that you are stopping at a second- or third-rate hotel, I shall immediately ask for your resignation." He had a very good reason for making this statement. It is a well known fact that when a representative of a firm stops at a first-rate hotel in any city, buyers of his kind of merchandise will have a high regard for him and his firm. They will know they are doing business with a successful business firm and its representative. It is also a fact that first-class hotels attract success-conscious people and by living among them, one keeps on the success-minded beam.

You can gain nothing by associating with failure-conscious people. The only thing such people will do for you is to attract you down to their level of hopelessness or frustration. So make up your mind that you can and you will associate with successful people. The following is how you can attract such people to you. Sit down and close your eyes.

> **Visualize yourself being attracted to successful people. Picture very successful people being attracted to you. Imagine yourself meeting successful people every day. See these people taking a liking to you. Picture yourself having lunch with these kind of people. See them introducing you to their circle of friends. Believe what you have imagined, pictured, and visualized will surely happen.**

Then open your eyes and be on your way. Practice this method every day without fail and you will find yourself associating with many successful people.

Use Every Opportunity to Express Your Talent

Whenever an opportunity comes your way that will allow you to express your talent, accept that opportunity immediately. Remember you have been practicing the Laws of Mental Magnetism to attract opportunities to you.

When I first discovered I had a natural singing voice and decided to make singing a profession, this decision on my part drew many opportunities to me. Once I was given an opportunity to give an audition for a certain man. The place of this audition was 18 miles away and I had no means of transportation to get to this place. What did I do in this situation? I walked 18 miles through a blizzard to give this audition. As a consequence I landed a well-paying singing job, which led to many other excellent singing engagements.

One time I had a consuming desire to speak on radio, and believed that I would. Several weeks later I met a friend who had a radio program and who, on one hour's notice, asked me to speak for 45 minutes on that program. I accepted this offer immediately. Another time I had an intense desire to appear on television. Shortly thereafter I met a public relations man. I gave him a briefing on some interesting experiences I had had. The next day he phoned me to tell me I was to appear on a national color TV program the following day. I did, and it was the easiest thing I have ever done in my life.

So take advantage of every opportunity that comes your way, no matter how difficult you may think that opportunity is. The person who could be your greatest benefactor may see you at work or hear about your unusual ability. Do so, and at any moment you may become known as a person who is in great demand talent-wise and money-wise.

Think Success! Believe Success! Be Success!

Having made up your mind to play the part of a "star" actor or actress in life, you must think and act like a "star." You must *think* you are great and *believe you are great*. You must assume the attitude of being really great. Do this and every act that you do will tell people you are a man or woman of exceptional talent and ability.

Do everything you do with tremendous self-assurance. Do what you are doing so well that people will think you are a genius. Keep everlastingly at what you are doing and what you are doing will result in phenomenal success.

The Rich Rewards for Using Mental Magnetism Successfully

Once you have applied the Law of Mental Magnetism successfully, you will become more and more conscious that this great Law is your own Personal Miracle Maker to attract success to you.

With this realization you will know that by doing something practical about your needs and desires you will, at the same time, be eliminating the bad habit of worry from your mind. Thus, having freed your mind for *constructive action,* you will know how to think and plan more clearly. Your new-found *self-confidence and courage* will give you the "How-to-do-it," and "I-can-do-it" spirit so necessary for attracting and gaining success.

Your new freedom of action will involve you in meeting with more people, many of whom will be helpful to you. You will find your relations with people will become increasingly more harmonious and beneficial.

Through the *inner harmony* you will have received you will experience true *peace of mind.* As this occurs, and it will, you will be able to concentrate your attention on attracting more and more of the good things of life to you.

By having made a talent goal for phenomenal success and by practicing the Law of Mental Magnetism conscientiously and persistently, you will attract everything to you that will cause you to become a tremendous success in what you are doing. Thus the Law of Mental Magnetism will have made of you a maker of miracles, a miracle-worker who can attract and receive all of the good things that will bring a healthier, more peaceful, more enjoyable and a more prosperous life.

Put Your Get-Up-And-Go Power into Action

As no good thing will be attracted to you until you put what you know and believe into action, you should practice every method

Attract Phenomenal Personal Success

I have given you in every chapter of this book. Then go forth into life as the very talented and capable person that you are. As you do, think like a genius, talk like a genius, work like a genius, and act as the true genius should.

Assume the air and manner of being a phenomenal success in life. Believe that you are a phenomenal success in life. Know that you are a phenomenal success in life. Breathe success, live success, attract success with every heartbeat. Do this every moment of your waking hours, and the magnetic department of your mind, your subconscious, will crown you with health, wealth, happiness and great peace of mind. The "crown" that rightly is yours will be yours for having practiced the Laws of Mental Magnetism to the point of having gained personal success and renown. Go forward, my friend. Put your "get-up-and-go" power into action and live the life of a dynamic, prosperous, joyous human being.

I now ask you to go back to the beginning of this book and read every page very carefully. Then go back to the beginning once again and read over the "Reminders" at the end of each chapter. Mark carefully those things you feel most in need of in your life and promise yourself you will practice the methods for attracting what is required to satisfy those needs. Your conscientious development, in this manner, of your own powers of Mental Magnetism will guarantee a new, dynamic, powerful life for you.

Many books have been written about the mind, but this book is unique in that it shows you how to USE the magnetic powers of your own mind to *actually receive* what you desire in life. Therefore, I urge you to practice the miracle-working Laws of Mental Magnetism explained in this book *every single day without fail*. Do so, and miracles of prosperous, happy, joyful living will be yours.

Begin living a rich, happy life today. Go forth into life with self-confidence and courage. Let your dynamic personality light up the place wherever you may be. Let the joy in your heart give inspiration and good cheer to others. Go to it, my friend, and shine as the "star of success" that you are, and good health, wealth, and prosperity to you.

Now turn the page . . .

19

Quick Magic Magnetic Reminders for Daily Use

The Ready Reference Guide below has been especially prepared for you to give you a quick lift in spirit any time during the day or night, as well as for programed daily use for one month. Make the powerful thoughts it contains the nucleus of what you desire to *attract* and also *receive*. Remember, WHAT YOU THINK, IMAGINE AND BELIEVE, YOU ATTRACT. So make this guide your constant companion. Turn to it often. Practice the Laws of Mental Magnetism every day as set out in this book. Do so, and you will experience the joy of living the abundant life, and attract all good to you at all times.

1. HEALTH — I am healthy in mind, I am healthy in body, I am healthy in spirit today. I shall repeat these thoughts often to myself today. This action on my part will attract to me a good health condition.

2. CONFIDENCE — I have tremendous confidence in myself and my ability. I am a very important person. This day I think with confidence and act with confidence. This day I am a very self-assured person.

3. COURAGE — I am strong, powerful, and courageous. Nothing has power to harm me. I am brave in heart today. This day I am the master of all I survey.

4. ATTITUDE — I take the right attitude towards everything today. I take a new outlook on life today. Old things have passed away. All things become new for me today.

5. FRIENDSHIP — This day I will be a friend to myself. This day I will act friendly to all people I meet. This day I will express good will and cheer. This day my friendly attitude will attract friendly people to me.

6. PERSONALITY — This day I will keep a smile on my face. This day I will laugh. This day I will project my magnetic personality towards everyone I meet. This day I will express myself in a positive, self-confident manner.

7. LOVE — Today I shall love the work I am engaged in. This day I shall love my neighbor as I love myself. This day I shall let love motivate my every action. This day I shall love putting my very best into my work.

8. CHANGE — I welcome change as an opportunity to advance and make progress. I know that when one door closes a better door opens for me. I firmly believe that new opportunities are now being given me. This day I shall take advantage of every new opportunity that comes my way.

9. BEGINNING — I am ready and eager to begin a new life. Gone are the fears and worries of yesteryear. Today I begin the best year of my life. Today I attract the best things in life to me.

10. YOUTH — I believe in youth. I do not believe in old age. I am young in mind today. I am young in spirit today. I am young in body today. Each and every day I am getting younger, and according to my belief so shall it be done unto me.

11. FAITH — I know that if I do not believe in myself no one will believe in me. This day I believe that I can achieve anything. I make up my mind to achieve great things. This day I believe a great miracle of good fortune will happen to me. This day I know that a miracle of good fortune will happen to me.

12. HARMONY — Everything in my life is harmonious today. Everything is harmonious where I work. Everything is harmonious where I live. Complete harmony is established in all my affairs.

13. BUSINESS — My business is in excellent condition. My business prospers and grows by leaps and bounds. My business is very good and as it increases, I enjoy greater and greater prosperity.

14. FEELING — I have a feeling that something wonderful is going to happen to me today. This feeling makes me feel wonderful. This feeling makes me feel marvelous.

15. STRENGTH — I am strong and powerful today. New strength and power flows into every part of my being. I am strong in mind, body,

Quick Magic Magnetic Reminders 203

and spirit today. And I intend to keep myself feeling that way.

16. **SAFETY** — I am always divinely protected wherever I may be. I am protected on the street. I am protected at home. I am protected at work. I am protected while traveling by train, automobile, or while flying in the air.

17. **IDEAS** — I always have an abundance of right ideas. Anytime I need ideas that will solve a problem, I tell my subconscious mind to attract them to me, and it does.

18. **EFFORT** — I make every effort to be a more likeable person. I make every effort to achieve what I desire to accomplish. I make every effort to be happy and gay. I make every effort to practice the laws of mental magnetism each day. And my effort rewards me handsomely in greater joy in living.

19. **THANKS** — I give thanks every day for all the blessings I have received. I give thanks each day for the blessings I am about to receive. This action on my part opens the flood gates of good fortune for me, and causes me to receive greater prosperity.

20. **GOAL** — My goal is to live and enjoy a happy, successful life. I keep my mind on my goal constantly. I remind myself I am happy and successful now. This mental action on my part draws to me every circumstance and condition that will cause me to experience happiness and success in my life.

21. **MIRACLES** — I believe that miracles can and do happen. I believe that miracles will happen to me. All I have to do to have an unusual event take place in my life is to visualize that

event and believe it will happen, and according to my faith in the laws of mental magnetism, so shall a miraculous event take place in my life.

22. MONEY — I believe that I will have all the money I can use to satisfy my every need. I know I am always receiving all of the money I can use wisely. Money flows to me in a steady stream this day and every day. I am always supplied with an abundance of money.

23. PEACE — I am at peace with myself. I am at peace with the world. I am serene in mind and spirit. My calmness of mind enables me to think clearly and plan clearly. Peace gives the magnetic forces within me greater opportunity to attract what I desire to me. Thus the more inner serenity I have, the more good things I attract and receive.

24. PROSPERITY — I believe in prosperity. I believe in having an abundance of all good things. The magnetic department of my mind is constantly attracting good things to me. This day I am prosperous in mind and in all my affairs.

25. HAPPINESS — I am happy today. I shall stay happy all day. This day I firmly believe will be the happiest and most enjoyable day of my life.

26. JOY — I begin this day with great joy in my heart. All through this day I will have joy in my heart. I shall bring joy to someone I know today. This day the joy I give away will come back to me.

27. ENTHUSIASM — This day I will put enthusiasm into my work. This day I will express enthusiasm

when greeting people. This day I will express enthusiasm in my living. This day I will take an enthusiastic new interest in life. This day I will express great joy in my daily living.

28. **ZEST** — I will have great zest for accomplishment today. I will put great zest in my living today. I will come alive with dynamic power today. I will work with gusto and pleasure today.

29. **TALENT** — I will use my talent to its full capacity today. I will express my talent at every opportunity today. Today I will use my talent for the benefit of people. Today I shall believe I will gain fame and fortune by using my talent successfully.

30. **SUCCESS** — I believe in success. I believe I am a success. My subconscious mind knows that I am a success. It now attracts to me everything needed to cause me to be an outstanding, phenomenal success in life.

31. **VICTORY** — I have gained victory over my former thoughts and beliefs. Today I am a well-balanced, successful individual. Today I know how to attract all good things to me. Today I am a new, dynamic, magnetic person.

Défaite : Copyright © 2018 par Jessa James
ISBN: **978-1-7959-0280-9**

Tous droits réservés. Aucune partie de ce livre ne peut être reproduite ou transmise sous quelque forme que ce soit ou de quelque manière, électrique, digitale ou mécanique. Cela comprend mais n'est pas limité à la photocopie, l'enregistrement, le scannage ou tout type de stockage de données et de système de recherche sans l'accord écrit et exprès de l'auteur.

Publié par Jessa James
James, Jessa
Défaite
Design de la couverture copyright 2018 par Jessa James, Auteure
Crédit pour les Images/Photo: Fotolia: stryjek

Note de l'éditeur :
Ce livre a été écrit pour un public adulte. Ce livre peut contenir des scènes de sexe explicite. Les activités sexuelles inclues dans ce livre sont strictement des fantaisies destinées à des adultes et toute activité ou risque pris par les personnages fictifs dans cette histoire ne sont ni approuvés ni encouragés par l'auteur ou l'éditeur.

DÉFAITE
LE CLUB V - TOME 2

JESSA JAMES

À PROPOS DE DÉFAITE :

Taylor Dawson passe ses journées à se salir les mains en tant que mécanicienne dans le garage de son père, plutôt qu'avec un mec sexy.

À dix-neuf ans, elle est impatiente de perdre sa virginité, mais elle n'a pas encore trouvé l'homme qu'il lui faut. En allant chercher sa colocataire au travail au Club V, Taylor tombe sur le propriétaire du club, Jake Mesa, en train de donner une leçon de soumission. Tay ne pense pas être capable d'obéir comme la femme au collier qui se trouve à la merci de Jake, et elle quitte la pièce sans se faire remarquer.

Cependant, les caméras de sécurité de Jake ont repéré la jolie voyeuse, et à présent, elle a toute son attention. Lorsque le père de Taylor lui avoue qu'il a commis une erreur catastrophique qui pourrait lui coûter non seulement son garage, mais aussi la vie, elle ne sait pas vers qui se tourner. Puis Jake lui fait une proposition... Arrivera-t-elle à y résister, ou sera-t-elle défaite ?

Si les héros sublimes, les coups de foudre et les moments sensuels sont votre truc, poursuivez votre lecture...

NOUVELLES DE JESSA JAMES

Abonnez-vous à ma liste de lecteurs VIP français ici : http://ksapublishers.com/s/jessafrancais

CHAPITRE 1

J'attrapai un torchon sur la patère et essuyai mes mains pleines de graisse avec le tissu rêche. Du dos de l'avant-bras, j'essuyai la sueur qui me coulait sur le front pour l'empêcher de me piquer les yeux. Les portes du garage étaient ouvertes et laissaient entrer une petite brise, mais dans la chaleur de l'été, ça ne suffisait pas pour refroidir la pièce.

Je jetai un coup d'œil à la pendule fixée au mur ; juste au-dessus du calendrier élimé qui montrait Miss Mars, que l'un des employés de mon père avait fixé au mur et n'avait jamais décroché.

Apparemment, tout le monde était tellement satisfait de l'apparence de Miss Mars qu'ils l'avaient laissée résider sur le mur du Garage Dawson ces dix dernières années. Il était seize heures cinquante, et pourtant, trois voitures attendaient et je savais que je ne sortirais pas du travail avant des heures. Mon père avait besoin de moi, et je détestais partir en avance, surtout les jours où peu d'employés étaient présents. Les affaires marchaient bien, mais comme beaucoup d'autres entreprises, elles avaient pris un coup avec la crise. Les gens continuaient à faire réviser leurs voitures, mais ils attendaient un peu plus longtemps entre deux visites, et ne venaient pas tout de suite lorsque leur véhicule commençait à faire des siennes. On finissait par avoir plus de boulot, et pas du genre qui nous plaisait. Mon père estimait qu'il fallait chouchouter sa voiture, et je suivais ses enseignements.

— Si tu veux qu'elle ronronne comme un chaton, il faut la gratter derrière les oreilles de temps à autre, me disait-il souvent.

Je l'avais entendu répéter ça un nombre incalculable de fois à ses clients au fil des ans. Comme ma mère était décédée en me mettant au monde, j'avais passé tout mon temps avec mon père. Nous avions un lien assez différent de celui que mes amies entretenaient avec leurs parents, en partie parce que nous passions tant de temps ensemble, mais aussi parce qu'il me traitait comme une associée au garage.

Depuis que j'étais petite, il avait fait en sorte de m'apprendre un maximum de choses sur ce qui se passait sous le capot d'une voiture. À dix ans, je savais repérer un problème mécanique à l'oreille à des kilomètres. En vieillissant, je m'étais mise à passer de plus en plus de temps au garage, à passer mes fins d'après-midi au milieu des pots d'échappement et des bidons d'huile. Ça me faisait de l'argent de poche que je dépensais lorsque je voyais mes amis, et j'avais pu en mettre un peu de côté. Après le bac, quand j'avais pu travailler à plein temps, j'étais devenue la meilleure employée de mon père, et de loin.

Je jetai un coup d'œil à Rodrigo, qui était allongé sur le dos sous une Mustang qui avait bien besoin d'un coup de peinture. En voyant ses cuisses épaisses et musclées sortir de sous le véhicule, je repensai aux nombreuses fois où nous nous étions amusés dans l'arrière-boutique, où à la fois où je l'avais attiré à l'étage pour mon dix-huitième anniversaire. Rodrigo était un type génial, mais il travaillait ici, et il était clair qu'il n'y avait rien entre nous, à part une alchimie sexuelle. Et si mon père apprenait ce qui s'était passé entre Rodrigo et moi... Eh bien, je ne préférais pas penser aux conséquences pour Rodrigo.

Être fille unique était une chose. Être la fille unique d'un père qui m'avait élevé seul depuis le premier jour en était une autre. Rien n'était jamais simple. Il avait beau me faire confiance de manière générale, il ne faisait pas confiance au monde extérieur au garage, et encore moins aux garçons susceptibles de me briser le cœur. J'étais sortie avec quelques garçons ça et là, mais la plupart de ceux avec qui j'étais allée à l'école avaient tellement peur de mon père qu'il ne valait pas le coup d'essayer de sortir avec eux. J'avais quand même réussi à aller au bal de promo accompagnée sans trop de mal, mais depuis la fin du lycée, un an plus tôt, c'était la panne sèche. Ça me dérangeait un peu, même si je savais que je pouvais faire l'amour quand je voulais avec qui je voulais, que je n'avais qu'un mot à dire.

Il y avait les mecs qui passaient avec leurs voitures de sport, ceux qui faisaient des courses le week-end, et ceux qui avaient hérité de l'argent d'un lointain parent. Cette dernière catégorie s'y connaissait rarement en voiture, et c'était ces hommes qui étaient les plus impressionnés par mon talent en mécanique. J'aurais pu en attirer plusieurs dans l'un des placards à fournitures pour arriver à mes fins, mais j'étais vierge depuis si longtemps que je n'avais pas l'intention de perdre mon pucelage avec l'un de ces gosses de riches incapables de se contrôler quand ils me voyaient dans mon bleu de travail et mon débardeur.

Je les voyais mater mon bonnet C, à peine contenu par mon soutien-gorge et mon haut. Mes débardeurs préférés étaient ceux avec un décolleté profond, car je pouvais faire en sorte qu'un peu de dentelle de mon soutien-gorge dépasse. J'attirais plus l'attention de cette façon - non que je cherche à tout prix à me faire remarquer. Il était évident que ces mecs n'attendaient que ça et qu'ils seraient prêts à tout pour m'avoir, ou au moins, pour voir ce qui se cachait sous le capot. J'en avais vu plus d'un être obligé de se remettre le paquet en place quand ils croyaient que je ne les voyais pas. Certains avaient même l'audace de se lécher les lèvres, de s'approcher de moi, et de me souffler doucement dans le cou, me faisant savoir sans le moindre doute ce qu'ils voulaient me faire dans le Coupé Chrysler 200 G dont ils avaient hérité. Cette dernière proposition m'avait tentée, parce que j'étais particulièrement excitée cette après-midi-là, et j'étais plutôt sale, alors j'avais laissé passer ma chance. Ça ne m'avait pas empêchée de me jeter sur mon vibromasseur à peine arrivée chez moi et de me caresser le clitoris jusqu'à atteindre un orgasme qui m'avait fait gémir et me tortiller sur mon lit.

— Oh la vache, dis-je tout bas alors que mon vagin se contractait à ce souvenir.

Je jetai un nouveau coup d'œil à la pendule. Il allait falloir que j'y aille bientôt, de toute façon, si je voulais avoir le temps de passer chez moi, de me doucher, me changer, et d'aller chercher Samantha au travail. Le Club V n'était pas très près de notre appartement, mais je lui avais promis d'aller la récupérer pour lui éviter de prendre les transports en commun en pleine nuit. Si je partais avec quelques minutes d'avance, j'aurais peut-être même le temps de soulager un peu ma frustration.

Mes yeux tombèrent sur Miss Mars et ses mains qui soutenaient ses seins pour les soulever, faisant pointer ses tétons vers l'appareil. Elle était sexy en diable, et si je ne quittais pas le garage bientôt, j'allais devoir me doigter derrière un tas de pneus en m'imaginant Miss Mars presser ses seins contre mon visage. Je ne suis pas lesbienne ni rien, mais bon, je ne suis qu'humaine.

— Hé, papa ? dis-je en passant la tête dans son bureau, pressée de quitter le garage et de regagner mon appartement le plus vite possible.

— Mmm ?

Les réponses monosyllabiques étaient la norme pour lui.

— J'y vais. Je dois passer prendre Sam tout à l'heure.

Il hocha la tête sans quitter son tas de factures des yeux.

— D'accord, Tay. À demain.

Je me précipitai vers ma voiture et bondis à l'intérieur après m'être assurée que mon derrière n'était pas couvert de graisse de moteur. J'avais une douche et un sex toy waterproof à rejoindre.

Le mitigeur grinça lorsque je le fis tourner et les tuyaux rugirent derrière les murs du vieil immeuble. Il faudrait au moins cinq minutes à l'eau pour chauffer suffisamment, et je me déshabillai, secouai mes cheveux et me les brossai en attendant.

Mes longues mèches brunes tombaient en une cascade d'ondulations qui atteignaient à peine le bout de mes seins fermes. Mes tétons durcirent alors que l'air frais les accueillait.

Le miroir en pied me donnait une bonne vue de mon corps musclé. Avec mon mètre soixante-huit, j'étais de taille moyenne. Je souris à mon reflet. J'avais dû hériter certaines de mes caractéristiques de ma mère, songeai-je en me retournant pour admirer les fesses rondes. C'était sans aucun doute l'un de mes plus grands atouts. Fermes, mais moelleuses et pulpeuses, mes hanches s'élargissaient à partir d'une taille fine, et je savais que mon corps était de ceux qui faisaient fantasmer les hommes. Les femmes aussi, d'ailleurs. J'en avais vu pleins au garage au fil des années, hommes comme femmes, et dès que j'étais devenue majeure, les gens n'hésitaient pas à me faire connaître l'intérêt qu'ils me portaient, quand ils se retrouvaient seuls avec moi.

Je poussai un soupir. Je pouvais avoir n'importe qui. Et pourtant, rien ne se présentait à l'horizon. J'avais beau être séduisante, personne ne me tentait. D'accord, certains mecs m'excitaient et me faisaient fantasmer sur ce qu'ils pourraient me faire sur le capot de leurs voitures. Mais au fond, je savais que je voulais plus. Je voulais que ma première fois soit spéciale. Mais pas de manière cul-cul. Non, je voulais me faire prendre bien comme il faut. Je voulais mettre la barre très haut.

Je me tournai et regardai mes seins. Ils étaient hauts et ronds sur ma poitrine, mes tétons bien centrés, de la taille d'une pièce de vingt-cinq cents, rose foncé et aussi durs que les galets que je ramassais l'été sur la plage. Je pris mes tétons entre mes doigts et poussai un soupir en serrant les jambes. Je me caressai les seins en me regardant dans le miroir. C'était sexy, et cette image m'excitait davantage. J'étais vraiment prête pour le sexe, mais en attendant, mon vibromasseur allait devoir suffire.

Avec la vapeur qui envahissait la salle de bains, je savais que l'eau était assez chaude, et j'entrai dans la baignoire en fermant le rideau derrière moi. Je posai mon vibromasseur sur le rebord, en me disant qu'il fallait que je me lave avant de me laisser aller. Cela m'encouragea à me laver les cheveux et à me savonner le corps rapidement. Alors que mes mains passaient sur mon pubis, puis sur mes tétons toujours durs, je poussai une exclamation et me saisis de mon vibromasseur préféré.

Il était rose et or, avec une forme parfaitement adaptée à mon anatomie et deux petits doigts en silicone qui m'entouraient le clitoris. Il m'allait comme un gant, et je devais me montrer raisonnable lorsque je m'en servais. Je savais exactement où le placer pour atteindre l'orgasme en moins d'une minute, mais j'avais un peu de temps devant moi et je voulais profiter de l'un de mes rares moments de solitude dans l'appartement.

J'enclenchai la première vitesse, et le léger bourdonnement résonna contre les murs de la salle de bains. Je m'allongeai contre les carreaux et fermai les yeux, tout en me pinçant le téton gauche et en guidant le vibromasseur contre mon clitoris à l'aide de mon autre main. Je fouillai dans ma mémoire et pensai à la scène de film pornographique la plus sensuelle que j'avais vue récemment, une scène si alléchante qu'elle avait presque été douloureuse à regarder. Un mec sublime avec un sexe dur comme du bois était sur le dos, en train de se faire masser par une fille. Elle taquinait les alentours de son pénis durant une dizaine de minutes, avant d'enfin le toucher du bout de la langue. Lorsqu'elle avait fait ça, le type avait presque bondi de son lit, mais il s'était contenu, et au final, ça avait payé. Alors qu'il attendait impatiemment qu'elle le prenne dans sa bouche, il la léchait.

Je n'aurais pas pu me retenir. Son membre était long et épais, et il ressemblait à une sculpture magnifique. Je m'imaginai le sucer profondément, ou faire glisser mon sexe humide sur sa langue.

Je me cambrai et pressai le vibromasseur contre mon intimité avec plus de force, avant d'en augmenter la puissance. Pas trop fort... non. Ça irait trop vite.

J'imaginai la langue du type me pénétrer, goûter à mon humidité et boire chaque goutte de moi. Me caresser avec ses doigts avant d'en glisser deux en moi tout en me suçant le clitoris, me faisait gémir. Je passai à mon téton droit et tirai dessus, l'étirant légèrement avant de le relâcher. Avec mes doigts pleins de savons, je le pétris, sentant mon téton dur contre le poids de ma paume.

— Oh putain, gémis-je tout fort.

J'avais des voisins et les murs étaient fins, mais je me

foutais complètement qu'ils m'entendent.

J'augmentai de nouveau le réglage du vibromasseur, avant de le faire bouger en rythme contre mon clitoris. Oui, comme ça. Je me laissais porter par la vague qui allait m'emmener aux sommets désirés. Je sentais la chaleur s'étendre entre mes jambes, s'accumuler dans mes cuisses, le long de mon échine. Ça allait être tellement bon...

Une fois sèche et satisfaite, je sortis de la douche avec un sourire au visage et je m'enveloppai dans une serviette propre. Le miroir était trop couvert de buée pour que je voie quoi que ce soit, mais je savais que je devais avoir l'air contente de moi.

— Pas besoin d'un homme, dis-je à voix haute face à mon reflet flou en attrapant un tube de crème hydratante et en l'appliquant sur ma peau légèrement bronzée.

Mais en vérité, j'en avais peut-être besoin. Enfin, pas vraiment besoin, mais la présence d'un homme me paraissait attrayante. Je n'avais jamais eu de petit ami sérieux, grâce à l'omniprésence de mon père dans ma vie. Bien sûr, il m'avait sans doute épargné beaucoup de souffrances en faisant fuir les losers avec qui j'allais au lycée. Mais je ne pouvais pas m'empêcher de me demander si cela ne m'avait pas empêché de vivre des choses importantes pour le développement et pour former des relations romantiques formatrices.

Je me séchai les cheveux avec ma serviette et me les brossai avant de sortir le sèche-cheveux pour terminer le travail. J'avais la chance d'avoir des cheveux disciplinés et faciles à entretenir. Je n'avais pas besoin de passer des heures dessus, ce qui était une bonne chose, car mon père s'attendait à ce que j'arrive au garage à l'aube tous les jours. En fin de compte, il ne servait à rien que je me pomponne pour passer la journée au travail. À midi, j'avais déjà le visage baigné de sueur, de toute façon.

Mais ce soir, j'allais chercher Samantha, et je voulais être à mon avantage. Pas pour mon amie... pas du tout. Elle m'avait vu dans mes pires moments, et je savais que je n'avais pas besoin de faire d'efforts en sa présence. Nous étions meilleures amies depuis que nous étions petites, à l'école primaire. Après le lycée, nous avions décidé de prendre un appartement ensemble pendant qu'elle travaillait et allait à la fac, payant ses frais de scolarité grâce à son nouveau boulot au très sélect Club V.

Je me glissai dans un jean slim et un tee-shirt blanc moulant, avec un blazer noir à manches courtes par-dessus. J'ajoutai un collier en onyx et admirai mon reflet une dernière fois tandis que je me mettais du mascara et du rouge à lèvre rouge. Ce n'était pas mon look habituel, mais un peu d'originalité ne faisait pas de mal, de temps en temps. Et le Club V était le genre d'endroits où j'avais envie d'être sur mon trente-et-un. J'y boirais sans doute un verre avant que Samantha quitte le travail, de toute façon, et je n'avais pas envie d'attendre au bar avec l'air dépenaillé.

Prête à partir, je descendis les escaliers du bâtiment quatre à quatre jusqu'à ma voiture, que j'avais garée dans la rue. Le trajet ne me prit pas très longtemps, et en un clin d'œil, je me garai à l'extérieur du Club V. Curt, l'un des voituriers, me reconnut grâce à mes nombreuses visites pour chercher Sam, et il hocha la tête, m'indiquant que je pouvais me garer sur le parking situé derrière le grand bâtiment industriel réservé aux employés.

Le parking était presque plein, mais je réussis à trouver une place et après avoir vérifié mon rouge à lèvres une dernière fois dans le rétroviseur, je sortis et me dirigeai vers l'entrée de derrière. Dès que j'eus ouvert la lourde porte, je fus accueillie par la musique aux basses assourdissantes qui émanaient de la pièce principale, et je me faufilai jusqu'au bar du Club V.

CHAPITRE 2

Je savais de quel genre de club il s'agissait, alors rien ne pouvait me surprendre en ces lieux, même si je n'avais pas beaucoup d'expérience en matière de sexe. Le bar se trouvait à l'écart des attractions principales de la salle, contre l'un des murs de la grande pièce principale. De l'autre côté se trouvait une piscine, et je m'aperçus qu'il s'agissait d'une soirée très animée.

Des couples s'embrassaient dans toutes les directions, certains s'adonnant à des actes plus poussés que les autres. Je vis plusieurs filles en train de travailler en salle, pour chercher un homme seul à divertir. Samantha m'avait parlé des filles aux colliers, m'avait dit ce que signifiaient les colliers en question, et ce que faisaient ces filles. Je savais que ça ressemblait à de la prostitution, mais je devais bien admettre que ce travail ne semblait pas si mal. Comme j'avais toujours eu une place dans le garage de mon père, je n'avais jamais eu à m'inquiéter pour l'argent. Je ne roulais pas sur l'or, mais je vivais la vie que je voulais, et je ne savais pas ce que j'aurais pu demander de plus.

— Salut, Taylor, me lança Céleste, la barmaid en chef, quand elle me vit sur le seuil de l'entrée privée.

Je lui lançai un sourire et allai m'asseoir sur l'un des tabourets inoccupés.

— Soirée animée ? demandai-je.

Céleste leva les yeux au ciel.

— Oh putain, dit-elle en murmurant à moitié. Encore une fichue pub dans un magazine d'avion. On reçoit tellement de clients ces soirs-là. Samantha travaille dans plusieurs des salles privées, parc que des tonnes de nouveaux venus préféraient aller là-bas et dans les alcôves plutôt que de venir commander au bar. Alors je n'arrête pas de préparer des boissons, mais personne ne me tient compagnie ce soir.

— C'est bien que ça ait du succès, j'imagine, dis-je.

Elle hocha la tête.

— Mais étonnamment, aucun de ces petits nouveaux ne semble timide. Ils se sont tous jetés sur les filles à peine arrivés.

Elle fit un signe de tête en direction d'un homme, qui avait le visage entre les cuisses de l'une des filles à collier.

— Bon, sang, dis-je en observant ce qui se passait.

L'homme avait beau ne pas être très séduisant, il semblait savoir exactement quoi faire de sa langue, et la fille au collier avait l'air de s'éclater. Soit ça, soit il fallait lui donner un Oscar. Elle avait rejeté la tête en arrière, ses mains enfoncées dans les cheveux de l'homme, le pressant contre elle alors qu'il la léchait. Toutes les quelques secondes, elle poussait un petit cri gémissant. Même si je venais de me donner un orgasme très intense moins d'une heure plus tôt, voir une scène pareille me laissa un peu haletante, me faisant regretter de ne pas pouvoir m'amuser, moi aussi.

Céleste claqua des doigts devant mon visage. Lorsque je me tournai vers elle, elle souriait.

— Qu'est-ce que tu veux que je te serve ? demanda-t-elle. Le cunnilingus n'est pas au menu.

— Et c'est bien dommage, dis-je en me tortillant dans mon siège et en me tournant de nouveau vers le bar.

— Mais on a un nouveau cocktail appelé « Broute Minou », si tu veux essayer.

Elle rit, et je ne pus m'empêcher de sourire.

— Un « Broute Minou » pour moi, s'il te plaît.

Céleste alla chercher les ingrédients pour ce qui se révéla être une boisson très compliquée pendant que je restais là à faire comme s'il ne se passait rien derrière moi, mais les gémissements persistants me compliquaient la tâche. Comment les gens étaient-ils capables de travailler ici sans se déshabiller et se frotter à la personne la plus proche ?

Taylor, faut que tu te reprennes, ou que tu te fasses baiser, songeai-je.

Comme s'il avait lu dans mes pensées, un homme vint s'asseoir à côté de moi.

— Si c'est un broute minou que vous cherchez... eh bien...

Il se montra du doigt avec un sourire.

Je tentai de ne pas lever les yeux au ciel. Le Club V était fait pour ça, je le savais, mais je n'étais pas venue dans ce but. Je n'avais même pas le droit de participer si j'en avais envie. Il fallait être un membre payant du club pour prendre part à ces activités, et malheureusement, mon travail au garage ne suffisait pas à financer ce genre d'activités.

Je secouai la tête en direction de l'homme alors que Céleste revenait avec mon cocktail.

— Non merci, je pense que la boisson me suffira, dis-je.

J'étais capable d'envoyer chier les mecs, mais j'étais là pour chercher Samantha, pas pour offenser l'un des membres payants.

Céleste prit la situation en mains.

— Dave, t'es en train d'embêter ma copine ?

Elle aussi savait qu'elle devait se montrer prudente. Elle était à la tête du bar, et elle savait gérer ce genre de situations tendues, mais elle devait également garder à l'esprit que ce type était un membre du club. Mais c'était à elle de veiller au respect du règlement au bar, et elle était inflexible.

— Je l'embête pas, dit le type avec un demi-sourire en levant les mains en l'air. Je lui faisais juste une... proposition.

— Eh bien, je suis désolée de te l'annoncer, mais elle n'est pas dispo, dit-elle avec un sourire séducteur en se penchant sur le bar pour lui murmurer à l'oreille. Mais je vais te dire qui l'est. Regarde par là-bas, dans le coin. C'est Dana. Elle est nouvelle, mais elle est très douée, et je pense que vous pourriez bien vous amuser, tous les deux. Et si tu allais lui dire bonjour ?

Cela suffit à détourner l'attention de Dave, et peu de temps après, il était en train de flirter avec la fille à collier, qui le guida vers l'une des alcôves avec un petit rire.

— Merci, dis-je en sirotant mon cocktail.

Il contenait tant de saveurs : canneberge, vanille, pêche, et... quelque chose que je ne reconnaissais pas.

— C'est du jasmin, le goût que tu sens, dit Céleste avec un sourire. De la vodka infusée au jasmin fait maison. Une petite invention à moi.

— C'est incroyable, dis-je.

Et c'était la vérité. Je pris une autre gorgée et sentis l'alcool me parcourir jusqu'aux genoux, me détendant légèrement.

— Au fait, reprit-elle, je sais que tu es capable de te débrouiller toute seule. Je t'ai vue le faire plein de fois. Mais je voulais t'éviter des embrouilles avec ce client. C'est la première fois qu'il vient ici, mais c'est un membre de longue date. Il passa la plupart de son temps au club de Seattle. C'est un grand investisseur dans le monde de la technologie, et tu ne veux surtout pas te retrouver sur son compte Twitter, dit-elle en grimaçant.

— Beurk. Merci, Céleste.

— pas de problème, répondit-elle avant de jeter un coup d'œil à sa montre. Je ne sais pas si Samantha va tarder. C'était un groupe de huit personnes, et elle était censée leur préparer des boissons dans l'une des pièces privées. En gros, elle est obligée de rester jusqu'à ce qu'ils aient fini, et... bon, ils sont huit là-dedans.

Je ris.

— je comprends. Ça va prendre un moment. C'est pas grave, je vais rester assise ici à boire mon cocktail.

— Et le travail ? s'enquit-elle en commençant à nettoyer une portion du bar. Tu bosses toujours pour ton père ?

Je hochai la tête.

— Ouais, on est que tous les deux la plupart du temps. Rodrigo et un autre type travaillent toujours pour nous, mais les gens viennent de moins en moins régulièrement. Beaucoup ont des problèmes d'argent.

Céleste poussa un petit grognement amusé.

— Ne m'en parle pas. Entretenir une famille semble presque impossible, parfois. Sus mon conseil, et reste célibataire et sans enfants le plus longtemps possible. Bien sûr, quand on est ici, on a du mal à imaginer que des gens puissent galérer.

Elle avait raison. En plus des lumières tamisées et de la musique qui résonnait, tout était recouvert de tissus somptueux et l'on se serait cru dans un film français représentant une époque antérieure à la décapitation des nobles. Au Club V, tout était décadent. Les membres pouvaient venir ici et tout oublier de la vie à l'extérieur. Ils laissaient leurs ennuis à la porte et s'adonnaient à leurs fantasmes les plus sombres.

— Je ne sais pas comment tu fais pour travailler ici tous les jours, dis-je. Ça ne t'atteint pas ?

— Tu me demandes si ça m'excite ?

Elle rit et hocha la tête, puis ajouta :

— Si, mais je crois que ça a une influence positive sur ma relation. Tu savais que j'avais rencontré ma femme ici ?

Je secouai la tête.

— Je ne savais pas que tu étais mariée.

Céleste hocha la tête et baissa les yeux sur son annulaire nu.

— Je ne porte pas mon alliance au travail. Elle a tendance à décevoir les membres du club, s'ils pensent n'avoir aucune chance de me séduire. Premièrement, je ne suis pas attirée par les hommes. Deuxièmement... eh bien, les visiteuses ne le savent pas, mais ma femme et moi, on est assez ouvertes. Je l'ai rencontrée ici, après tout.

Voilà qui me rendait curieuse. Je me demandais si Samantha était au courant que Céleste et sa femme s'étaient rencontrées ici. Elle avait peut-être simplement eu la délicatesse de ne pas me le répéter.

Je souris.

— D'accord, Céleste. Il faut que tu me racontes comment s'est passée votre rencontre. J'adore ce genre d'histoires.

— Ce n'est pas aussi romantique que tu te l'imagines ! Mais c'est plutôt sexy.

Elle se pencha sur le bar et poursuivit :

— Elle avait commencé à travailler au bar, et à l'époque, c'était mon employée. Le courant passait bien, mais elle était beaucoup plus jeune que moi - je sais que je n'en ai pas l'air, mais j'ai quarante-trois ans. Je pensais qu'il n'y avait aucune chance pour qu'il se passe quoi que ce soit. Et puis, comme je l'ai déjà dit, elle bossait pour moi. On a des règles, ici. Il n'y en a pas beaucoup au Club V, mais celle-là est très claire. Ne pas coucher avec les autres employés, surtout si celui-ci est notre subordonné.

Elle leva les yeux au ciel, puis reprit :

— Enfin bref. Elle a décidé qu'elle voulait grimper les échelons au club. Il y avait une place pour bosser en salle, et elle a sauté sur l'occasion. Et donc, quelques semaines plus tard, après sa formation, voilà qu'elle se présente en salle, du haut de son mètre quatre-vingt - c'est une déesse, soit dit en passant - vêtue de rien d'autre que ce putain de collier.

Je pris une inspiration. La couleur du collier indiquait ce que chaque fille était prête à faire.

— Je savais que j'allais assister à ce qu'elle ferait en salle. Tu sais que les trucs les plus hardcore se pratiquent dans les alcôves ou les salles privées, mais parfois, les gens se laissent emporter. Enfin... tu sais. C'est en train de se produire en ce moment même.

Céleste ne plaisantait pas. Du coin de l'œil, je voyais que le type qui avait plongé sa tête entre les jambes de la fille était à présent en train de la prendre fougueusement, et à en croire les bruits qu'elle faisait, elle en appréciait chaque seconde.

— Je savais que j'allais la voir faire des choses, reprit Céleste, mais souviens-toi qu'à ce moment-là, je croyais qu'il ne s'agissait que d'une apparence passagère et non réciproque. J'ignorais complètement qu'elle ressentait la même chose que moi. Mais la première fois où je l'ai vue nue, mon Dieu, j'ai cru que j'allais perdre la tête. Elle était à couper le souffle, et je savais qu'un mec allait l'avaler toute crue. Elle m'a fait un clin d'œil en passant devant le bar ce soir-là, alors qu'elle allait dans une pièce privée, et... je ne suis pas religieuse, mais j'ai prié pour elle. Les membres sont sélectionnés avec soin, ici, mais de temps à autre, on a des clients avec un goût pour la violence. J'ai essayé de me chasser cette pensée de l'esprit en travaillant ce soir-là.

Elle haussa les épaules et poussa un soupir.

— Je ne savais pas dans quelle pièce elle se trouvait, et on manquait d'employés, ce soir-là. Je suis allée servir des boissons dans l'une des pièces. Les clients avaient demandé à ce que quelqu'un vienne les servir, et ce n'est pas mon boulot, mais c'étaient des gros bonnets. Je savais qui ils étaient, parce que je les avais déjà servis avant. Un couple qui veut rester anonyme. Ils sont assez connus à New York, et je comprenais pourquoi ils entraient toujours par l'entrée privée et prenaient une pièce privée. Ce que je veux dire, c'est que ce sont des grands noms de la politique.

Céleste agita les mains nonchalamment, et poursuivit :

— Je savais que c'était important, et le fait qu'Amber ait été choisir par ce couple était un grand coup pour sa carrière. Ils avaient tendance à choisir toujours les mêmes filles. Et vu l'argent qu'ils avaient, ils payaient très cher pour avoir une fille pour eux tout seuls... Bref, je ne voulais pas m'immiscer. Les gens ne se rendent pas compte du fric que se font les filles en salle. Avec ce genre de couples... Ils payent souvent pour que la fille qu'ils ont choisie ne voie personne d'autre en leur absence, ou pour pouvoir choisir ce qu'elle a le droit de faire avec d'autres clients. C'est assez rare, mais la direction le leur permet, quand ils agitent une liasse de billets pareille.

Céleste prit une grande inspiration.

— Enfin, je ne savais pas qu'Amber se trouverait là quand je suis allée dans la salle privée pour leur faire le service. Je ne savais pas qu'elle serait à quatre pattes, en train de se faire pénétrer par le mec pendant que la femme de celui-ci serait en train de lui lécher le clitoris comme une folle.

— Nom de Dieu, lâchai-je en prenant une gorgée de ma boisson.

Céleste sourit.

— Ce n'est pas trop cru pour toi, si ? Normalement, je ne parle pas de ce genre de choses avec les non-membres, surtout pas quand c'est aussi personnel. Tu sais, pour moi, ce qui est important, c'est de donner l'illusion aux clients qu'ils ont une chance, alors que c'est très loin d'être la vérité.

Je secouai la tête.

— Non, ça va, mais tu as raison. C'est très sexy. Je ne sais pas comment tu fais pour bosser là sans... tu sais... ans te masturber furieusement toutes les demi-heures.

Céleste éclata de rire et me toucha la main.

— Oh, ma belle, je peux t'assurer que ça nous arrive.

— Alors, comment est-ce que vous vous êtes mises ensemble, après ça ?

Elle se pencha sur le bar et me prit le menton dans les mains.

— Eh bien, comme je le disais... je suis entrée dans la pièce, et je me suis retrouvée nez à nez avec cette scène. Il fallait que je me comporte normalement, que je garde mon calme, sans faire attention au fait que la femme que je désirais plus que tout était en train de se faire prendre par ce type - ce type qui pourrait très bien devenir président un jour -, et il fallait que je fasse mon boulot. Ils ont fait une pause pour passer commande, puis ils s'y sont remis. Cette fois, Amber était à genoux devant la femme, en train de la doigter et de jouer avec son clitoris. Le type avait déjà joui sur les seins de sa femme, et il était en train de les sucer en matant Amber. Je me suis placée derrière le bar et j'ai essayé de ne pas regarder, mais elle attirait l'attention. Elle avait les yeux sombres, et alors qu'elle sortait la langue pour lécher le sexe de la femme, elle m'a regardé. Le couple était trop distrait pour le remarquer, mais pendant les quinze minutes qui ont suivi, alors qu'elle donnait du plaisir à la femme, elle ne m'a pas quitté des yeux.

Je m'éventai.

— Tu plaisantes ? Ça m'aurait rendue dingue !

J'arrivais parfaitement à m'imaginer la scène, même si j'ignorais complètement à quoi ressemblait Amber. Céleste était sublime, et j'étais persuadée que la femme qu'elle avait rencontrée au Club V devait être à tomber par terre.

— J'ai failli avoir un orgasme rien qu'en la regardant. La façon dont ses yeux se posaient sur moi, la façon dont elle léchait cette femme en me regardant pendant l'acte. À ce moment précis, j'ai su que je n'avais pas imaginé le courant que j'avais senti passé entre nous. Elle ressentait la même chose. Quand ils ont eu fini et que j'ai pu retourner derrière le bar, j'avais presque terminé mon service. Je suis allée dans le vestiaire pour récupérer mes affaires et me préparer à partir, en sachant que la première chose que je ferais en rentrant chez moi, ce serait de sortir mon vibro préféré et de penser à Amber. Franchement, je n'étais même pas sûre de pouvoir attendre d'être à la maison. Heureusement, je garde un sex toy dans ma voiture.

Elle me fit un clin d'œil et un sourire.

— Mais les choses ne se sont pas déroulées comme ça, reprit-elle. Amber se trouvait dans le vestiaire. Elle venait d'enfiler un legging et un débardeur, et venait de prendre une douche après une longue journée de travail. Elle était assise là, en train de m'attendre. Elle s'est levée, m'a embrassée doucement sur les lèvres, et m'a dit qu'elle rentrerait avec moi ce soir-là.

C'était sexy, mais aussi très mignon. En général, je n'étais pas touchée par ce genre d'histoires, mais en sachant qu'elles étaient toujours heureuses ensemble suffisait presque à faire fondre mon cœur de glace.

— C'est le truc le plus adorable que j'aie jamais entendu, Céleste.

Elle hocha la tête avec un sourire.

— Depuis, on est inséparables. Alors pour répondre à ta première question, comment je fais pour supporter la frustration ici ? Je me défoule sur ma femme tous les soirs, dit-elle en éclatant de rire. Mais un peu moins souvent que ça en ce moment, parce qu'elle est un peu fatiguée. Elle accouche dans quelques mois.

— Tu rigoles ? Céleste, c'est fantastique !

Je me levai et me penchai sur le bar pour la prendre dans mes bras, un peu pompette. Elle me donna de petites tapes dans le dos, et je voyais bien qu'elle essayait de contenir son émotion.

— Ouais, ouais. Qui l'eut cru, hein ? Merci de m'avoir écoutée. C'est rare que je puisse me confier, ici. En général, c'est plutôt le contraire.

Je lui souris.

— Tu sais, je me demande souvent si je crois en l'amour, et la plupart du temps, je me dis « pas du tout », mais ton histoire risque de me faire changer d'avis. Je suis très contente pour toi.

C'est là que je sus que l'alcool commençait à me faire de l'effet. J'allais peut-être devoir demander à Samantha de nous reconduire chez nous.

— Excuse-moi une minute, il faut que j'aille aux toilettes, dis-je en sautant de mon tabouret.

— Oh, attends une seconde, me dit Céleste en se souvenant soudain de quelque chose. Celle des employés est hors service. La tuyauterie sera réparée demain. Mais tu peux te servir de celui qui se trouve près de mon bureau. Prends le couloir. C'est presque au bout, tu ne pourras pas le rater.

Je la remerciai et me dirigeai le long du couloir dans la direction qu'elle m'avait indiquée, en tâtonnant dans le noir dans la zone de bureau qui semblait inoccupée à cette heure tardive. Des petites lumières rouges illuminaient le sol, mais elles étaient plus décoratives qu'autre chose.

J'atteignis une porte que je croyais être celle que je cherchais et l'ouvris. Elle était étrangement silencieuse et ne produisit aucun bruit en s'ouvrant et en se refermant derrière moi, mais il faisait noir et mes yeux mirent un moment à s'ajuster à la lumière tamisée venue d'un coin de la pièce. Quelle drôle d'idée, d'éclairer des toilettes aussi faiblement !

Puis je la vis. La fille au collier, assise dans un siège qui semblait fait pour une reine. Elle était nue, à l'exception de son collier en diamant, et ses jambes étaient grandes écartées, attachées aux pieds de sa chaise-trône. Entre elles, agenouillé pour la vénérer, se trouvait un homme aux cheveux noirs retenus en une courte queue de cheval. L'orgasme soudain et sonore de la fille couvrit le bruit de mon exclamation.

CHAPITRE 3

Je plaquai une main sur ma bouche. Ce n'était pas les toilettes des femmes. Je ne savais pas où je me trouvais, mais je restai là, clouée à l'endroit où je m'étais arrêtée en entrant dans la pièce. Lorsque je regardai autour de moi, je remarquai que je me trouvais dans un bureau, mais un bureau qui appartenait clairement à un homme avec des goûts particuliers. Il contenait ce qui ressemblait à un divan dans un coin, le trône où était assise la fille au collier, et un énorme bureau en acajou au centre de la pièce. Il semblait y avoir des fenêtres, mais elles étaient obscurcies, et le peu de lumière qui aurait pu filtrer depuis l'extérieur était étouffé avant de pouvoir pénétrer dans la pièce.

Il était en train de la lécher, se délectant de chaque goutte. J'avais beau savoir qu'il fallait que je m'en aille et que je sorte de ce bureau avant qu'ils réalisent qu'ils avaient un public, bon sang, j'avais vraiment envie de regarder ce qui se passait entre eux.

Il leva les bras et attrapa les seins de la fille, pas très gros, mais avec de gros tétons durcis. Il tira dessus, la forçant à se cambrer et à lancer :

— Baise-moi, Jake !

Soudain, l'homme se retira. Je priai pour qu'il ne me voie pas, debout dans l'ombre près de la porte, mais il était clair qu'ils étaient tout à leur tâche.

— Qu'est-ce que je t'ai dit ? rétorqua-t-il d'une voix rauque et sexy, sans doute rendue plus grave par son excitation. Comment ne pas être sur le point d'exploser, en faisant ce qu'il faisait ?

Elle prit une grande inspiration haletante.

— Je suis désolée, dit-elle. Mais je... j'ai tellement envie que vous me preniez maintenant.

Il se leva, puis recula, toujours tourné vers elle.

— Qu'est-ce que je t'ai dit ? répéta-t-il.

Elle déglutit et se mit à bouger les mains, puis elle se souvint qu'elle était attachée à son siège.

— Vous m'avez dit de vous appeler Monsieur Mesa. Mais je suis tellement près du but... Oh, pitié...

elle gémissait, et ses yeux étaient clos.

Il hocha la tête.

— Et qu'est-ce que je t'ai dit qu'il arriverait, si tu ne faisais pas ce que je t'ai dit ?

— Vous m'aviez dit que vous ne me laisseriez pas jouir.

Il hocha de nouveau la tête.

— Et quoi d'autre ?

Elle déglutit.

— Vous aviez dit que je serais punie.

Il hocha encore la tête et marqua une courte pause, avant de lui détacher les chevilles et les poignets. Elle referma les jambes, et je vis qu'elle était en train de se frotter à la chaise, jusqu'à ce qu'il lui attrape les cuisses et les lui écarte à nouveau.

— Non, interdiction de faire ça, dit-il. Quand est-ce que tu pourras jouir ?

Elle poussa un profond soupir.

— Quand vous m'y autoriserez.

— C'est ça. Maintenant, lève-toi et tourne-toi. Tu vas recevoir ta punition.

Je fus choquée de la voir faire exactement ce qu'il lui ordonnait de faire. La fille se pencha en avant et se rendit contre le siège, exposant ses fesses à l'homme. Il se tourna et se dirigea vers le mur situé derrière son bureau, avant de sélectionner l'un des douze fouets et cravaches pendus au mur. Il rejoignit la fille et lui massa lentement les fesses avec les mains, avant de se pencher pour les embrasser tour à tour.

— Comment je m'appelle ? demanda-t-il.

— Monsieur Mesa.

Les lanières du fouet en cuir glissèrent entre ses fesses alors qu'il la stimulait avec. Puis soudain, il le brandit et l'abattit sur elle. Elle sursauta, mais ne dit pas un mot.

— Quand est-ce que tu pourras jouir ?

— Quand vous m'y aurez autorisée, gémit-elle.

Il abattit de nouveau son fouet, plus fort cette fois.

— À qui appartient ta chatte ?

— À vous, s'écria-t-elle en attendant un autre coup de fouet.

Je réalisai que nous l'attendions toutes les deux lorsque je grimaçai, prête à ce qu'il abatte de nouveau son instrument de torture sur les fesses rouges de la fille.

Au lieu de cela, nous surprenant toutes les deux, il se mit à genoux et lui écarta les fesses, la léchant du sexe jusqu'à l'anus, avant de plonger les doigts en elle et de lui sucer le clitoris.

Elle était tellement à bout qu'il la conduisit droit vers un autre orgasme qui la fit crier et se frotter contre son visage.

Je réalisai que j'avais serré les jambes et que j'étais moi aussi au bord de la jouissance. Il fallait que je sorte de là.

Je repris mes esprits et me glissai par la porte sans me faire remarquer. Une fois de retour dans le couloir, je regardai autour de moi, en espérant trouver les toilettes, cette fois-ci, et y entrer avant que l'un des deux occupants du bureau n'en sorte. Quoique ça ne risquait pas d'arriver tout de suite. Les toilettes étaient là, avec une petite pancarte sur la porte. Facile à rater dans l'obscurité du couloir, songeai-je en ouvrant la porte et en entrant, avant de fermer à clé derrière moi.

— Putain, m'exclamai-je.

Je me regardai dans le miroir, et sans y repenser à deux fois, j'ouvris la fermeture éclair de mon jean et je glissai mes doigts dans ma culotte. J'étais trempée, et mon clitoris était brûlant et durci, réveillé par la scène érotique à laquelle j'avais assisté dans le bureau. Je me caressai avec mon majeur, m'imaginant ce type, qui qu'il soit, agenouillé face à moi, en train de me sucer le clitoris comme si c'était la chose la plus délicieuse qu'il ait jamais goûtée. Puis la scène où il fouettait la fille me revint à l'esprit, et voilà... C'est cette scène qui me fit basculer. La pensée d'une douleur exquise contre mes fesses, en train de m'apaiser de la manière la plus agréable possible. Je m'adossai au mur en balançant les hanches contre ma main.

Quand ce fut fini et que je fus capable de rassembler l'énergie nécessaire pour faire pipi et me laver les mains, je me regardai dans la glace. On aurait dit que je venais de baiser. Je savais à quoi ça ressemblait. J'avais déjà vu Samantha sortir de sa chambre après une soirée avec l'un de ses amis. J'avais aussi vu la même chose en salle, ici au Club V. Le sexe, ça se lit dans les yeux des gens. Pupilles dilatées, visage rougi... je baissai le regard. Tee-shirt froissé... Oh, tant pis, au moins, j'étais allée aux toilettes, même si Céleste allait sans doute se demander si j'avais un problème, avec tout le temps que j'avais mis.

Je quittai les toilettes et repris le couloir dans l'autre sens pour regagner le bar. Il y avait moins de monde dans la salle principale, et j'étais soulagée. J'avais eu ma dose pour la soirée.

— Ça va ? me demanda Céleste en se dirigeant vers l'endroit où je m'étais rassise.

Elle venait d'apporter un verre à un client à l'autre bout du bar, et elle revint vers moi avec un air inquiet.

— Ouais, c'est juste... J'ai dû manger un truc pas frais. Ne t'en fais pas. Ça ira.

Elle plissa les yeux et me regarda de la tête aux pieds, puis elle sourit.

— C'est ma petite histoire sur ma rencontre avec Amber qui t'a fait de l'effet ? Tu es allée t'occuper de toi ? Je sais que je ne devrais vraiment pas te demander ça, vu que tu es une cliente et tout ça, mais tu n'es pas membre. Et tu es la colocataire de Sam. Je te considère comme une amie.

— Euh, ouais. Désolée, c'est tellement gênant.

Mais pas aussi gênant que d'admettre que j'étais entrée dans ce bureau et que j'avais vu un certain Jake faire... des choses à la fille au collier.

— Tu veux un autre verre ?

Je hochai la tête.

— Oui, je veux bien. Je crois que je vais demander à Sam de conduire jusqu'à chez nous.

Céleste sourit.

— Je te l'apporte tout de suite.

J'attendis mon verre et gardai les yeux sur le bar, observant les rangées de liquides colorés qui se trouvaient derrière, joliment arrangés et luisants à cause des lumières noires. J'avais du mal à ne pas repenser à ce que j'avais vu dans le bureau. Qui était Jake... M. Mesa ? Samantha m'avait parlé de ses collègues, mais les personnes qu'elle fréquentait la plupart du temps étaient les barmaids... Pas des types assez importants pour avoir un bureau au Club V. ce devait être l'un des managers, ou l'un des propriétaires. Le club était assez grand pour les dirigeants soient extrêmement riches. Jake Mesa devait être très haut placé dans l'entreprise.

J'aurais pu interroger Céleste à son sujet, mais je ne voulais surtout pas admettre ce que j'avais vu. J'étais sûre qu'elle garderait le secret, mais j'avais l'impression que c'était quelque chose que je ne devrais pas partager. Et si elle était obligée de le signaler à quelqu'un ? Et si ce type faisait des choses qu'il n'était pas autorisé à faire ? Enfin, j'avais réussi à tomber sur eux par hasard sans trop de difficultés. Quand on s'adonnait à ce genre d'activités, on fermait la porte à clé, en général. C'était peut-être son délire... que des gens le surprennent.

Au moins, j'avais la certitude qu'il ne m'avait pas vue. Dans le cas contraire... eh bien, ça aurait été une tout autre histoire. On m'aurait sans doute jetée dehors, et je n'aurais jamais été autorisée à revenir. Était-ce une entrée par effraction ? Est-ce que l'on m'aurait cru, si j'avais dit que je cherchais simplement les toilettes ? C'était crédible, étant donné que la porte des toilettes se trouvait juste à côté. Il fallait vraiment qu'ils installent un meilleur éclairage dans ce couloir.

Céleste posa le verre devant moi et y plaça une petite paille à cocktail noire.

— Tu as l'air troublée, Taylor. Qu'est-ce qui se passe ?

Je haussai les épaules. Céleste était douée dans son travail, et je n'étais pas d'humeur à lui dévoiler ce genre de choses.

— Oh, tu sais. Je pense à l'argent, c'est tout, dis-je en agitant la main comme si ce n'était pas bien grave.

Céleste hocha la tête.

— J'aurais pu deviner. C'est marrant, je voulais justement te poser une question.

Je lui jetai un regard en coin.

— Quoi ?

— Bon, recruter des filles pour la salle, ce n'est pas mon boulot - pas mon domaine -, mais si tu cherches un petit job supplémentaire, je pourrais te recommander. Je suis sûre qu'il y aurait de la place quelque part pour toi.

Elle se pencha davantage et ajouta :

— Je ne te drague pas, mais tu as un corps sublime, et tu es exactement le genre de filles qu'ils adorent embaucher, ici. Du moment que tu es dégourdie...

Je poussai un soupir.

— Écoute, voilà le truc. Ça a beau me paraître vachement sympa - vraiment, tu peux me croire, j'ai un appétit insatiable -, je ne sais pas si je suis faite pour ça, et il y a un petit truc dont il faudrait que je m'occupe avant de passer aux choses sérieuses.

Céleste me regarda à nouveau, examinant mon visage un instant avant d'écarquiller les yeux.

— Bon sang. Normalement, je les repère à des kilomètres. Je n'aurais jamais deviné que tu étais vierge.

C'était à mon tour de la regarder avec de grands yeux.

— Comment tu as deviné ? demandai-je en chuchotant d'un ton pressant.

Elle sourit.

— Tu as dit qu'il fallait que tu t'occupes d'une petite chose avant. Et vu le contexte...

Elle se tapota la tempe et poursuivit :

— Enfin, il ne faut pas que ça s'ébruite, mais ici, il y a aussi un endroit pour les vierges, si ça t'intéresse.

Je secouai la tête. J'avais entendu des rumeurs à ce propos. Si j'étais désespérée, je l'aurais peut-être envisagée, mais je n'avais aucunement l'intention de vendre ma virginité au plus offrant.

— Non merci, dis-je. Je crois que je ferai ça à l'ancienne. Je ramènerai peut-être l'un de ces mecs avec moi en rentrant, ou un truc comme ça.

Elle rit.

— Hors de ces murs, tu fais ce que tu veux avec les clients du club, mais je te préviens, en sortant, ils sont vidés et ils mettent un moment avant de redémarrer, en général.

— J'imagine.

Céleste me laissa finir mon verre, et je restai assise là, à penser à l'avenir. Travailler dans un endroit tel que le Club V n'était pas du tout pur moi. Je n'avais jamais été barmaid, alors je ne serais pas capable de faire ce travail-là. Et les autres postes disponibles ici... ne me semblaient pas très adaptés à mes compétences. Je pensais que je serais sûrement douée au lit, mais je voulais le découvrir avec quelqu'un que j'aurais choisi moi-même.

Quelqu'un qui savait ce qu'il faisait. Pas un type qui aurait payé pour. Je ne cherchais pas le grand amour, mais j'étais à la recherche d'un désir assez fort pour que mon partenaire soit complètement à ma merci.

Je réalisai que ce qui m'avait attiré à ce point dans ce que Jake faisait à la fille au collier en diamant était le pouvoir qu'il avait sur elle. La façon dont elle se soumettait à sa volonté, l'autorisant à l'attacher au siège et à la fouetter lorsqu'elle n'obéissait pas à ses ordres. Je m'imaginai ce que cela me ferait d'être à sa place - vouloir atteindre l'orgasme plus que tout, et qu'on me le refuse. Je ne m'étais jamais retrouvée dans cette situation. La plupart de mes orgasmes avaient été provoqués par ma propre main, et je n'étais certainement pas assez disciplinée pour me retenir. Par le passé, j'avais tenté de patienter, mais j'avais le sentiment que c'était plus facile quand quelqu'un d'autre maniait le vibromasseur.

Je recommençais à me tortiller dans mon siège, et je m'efforçai d'arrêter, peu désireuse d'attirer davantage l'attention sur moi, celle de Céleste ou de qui que ce soit d'autre. J'eus le souffle coupé lorsque je levai les yeux et que je l'aperçus debout dans l'encadrement de la porte, de l'autre côté du bar.

Quoiqu'il arrive, ne surtout pas le regarder dans les yeux. Ces mots me tournaient en boucle dans la tête. J'étais convaincue que la plupart de mes émotions se lisaient sur mon visage, et j'étais incapable de les masquer. J'étais sûre que s'il passait à côté de moi, il sentirait que je l'avais vu seulement quelques minutes plus tôt, le visage enfoui entre les jambes de la fille dans son bureau. Quelques secondes plus tard, la fille arriva derrière lui, un grand sourire aux lèvres. Elle portait un haut de maillot de bain en diamants avec un string assorti, et alors qu'elle le dépassait, il lui donna une claque sur les fesses, et elle se dépêcha de rejoindre la pièce principale en riant.

Je gardai les yeux baissés sur mon verre, en espérant qu'il ne me remarquerait pas, mais je manquais de chance. Je le sentis approcher alors qu'il s'asseyait à côté de moi au bar.

— Je ne crois pas vous avoir déjà rencontrée, dit-il en me regardant d'un air curieux. Nouvelle membre ?

Je secouai la tête en levant enfin les yeux pour rencontrer son regard. Pourquoi fallait-il qu'il ait de si beaux yeux, bon sang ? Ils se mariaient à merveille avec ses traits sculptés, sa peau très bronzée, ses cheveux noirs et sa barbe légèrement mal rasée pour le rendre si délicieux et sensuel que je dus lutter contre l'envie de lui sauter dessus. Cet homme n'était pas mon genre. Je voulais un mec qui ferait exactement ce que je lui dirais, qui chercherait à me faire plaisir d'abord, et qui ne s'imaginerait jamais qu'il pouvait m'utiliser comme bon lui semblait.

— Non, je viens seulement chercher une amie. Elle est barmaid ici.

Un air de compréhension lui traversa le visage, et il hocha la tête en me tendant la main droite.

— Je suis Jake Mesa. Et vous ?

Je lui serrai la main, réalisant ce faisant qu'elle s'était trouvée il y a peu entre les jambes de la fille.

— Taylor Dawson, dis-je en avec un sourire poli.

— Enchanté, Taylor.

Il me lâcha la main, mais ne fit pas un geste, prenant son temps pour m'examiner. Je ne m'étais jamais sentie être dévorée ainsi par les yeux de quelqu'un. C'était comme s'il m'assimilait toute entière, jaugeant mes traits, me pesant dans sa tête et décidant ce qu'il pensait de l'ensemble.

Il sourit.

— J'ai vraiment cru que vous étiez membre du club. Quel dommage ! On aurait bien besoin de sang neuf, par ici.

Je penchai la tête en direction de sa jeune amie, qui dégoulinait de diamants.

— On dirait que vous avez plein de sang frais, par ici.

Son sourire disparut, et il se pencha près de ma joue pour me murmurer à l'oreille :

— Frais, j'ai dit.

Je déglutis et pris une gorgée de ma boisson.

Il recula lentement.

— Si devenir membre du club vous intéresse un jour, prévenez-moi. J'ai des relations.

Il sortit une carte de visite de sa poche et me la glissa sous la main.

— Vraiment, n'hésitez pas à m'appeler.

Jake Mesa se leva et s'en alla. Alors que je tournais sur mon tabouret de bar, je réalisai que ma culotte était complètement trempée, rien qu'à cause de la présence de cet homme.

Céleste vint vers moi.

— Désolée, avec celui-là, je ne peux pas t'aider.

Je secouai la tête, en baissant les yeux sur la carte qu'il m'avait donnée, sur laquelle figurait le logo du Club V d'un côté. De l'autre, il était écrit : « Jake Mesa, Propriétaire ». L'inscription était suivie de son numéro de téléphone professionnel et de son e-mail, et tout en bas, écrit au stylo, il avait ajouté « Numéro de téléphone personnel », suivi par sept chiffres.

— Sois prudente, me dit Céleste avec un clin d'œil.

— Qu'est-ce qu'elle fabrique, Sam ? demandai-je sur un ton exaspéré.

J'étais restée au Club V beaucoup trop longtemps, ce soir-là, même si en réalité, peu de temps avait dû s'écouler. Cet endroit me jouait des tours.

Comme si je l'avais fait apparaître de nulle part, Sam arriva.

— Je suis juste là ! Tu es prête à partir ?

Je hochai la tête et me levai, avant d'engloutir le reste de mon verre.

— C'est toi qui conduis, lui dis-je en lui tendant les clés.

— Pas de problème, répondit-elle alors que je la suivais hors du bar, jusqu'au parking, contente de retrouver l'air frais et de quitter le Club V - loin de Jake Mesa.

CHAPITRE 4

À l'aise dans mon jogging et un vieux tee-shirt, je m'installai sur le vieux canapé pour regarder une télé-réalité affligeante et discuter un peu avec Samantha après sa longue journée de travail et ma drôle d'expérience au Club V.

— Sérieusement, je ne sais pas si je t'ai déjà dit à quel point ton lieu de travail est bizarre, mais je crois que j'ai eu ma dose, aujourd'hui.

Samantha eut un petit rire joyeux en sirotant une tasse de thé et en passant les chaînes en revue.

— Je ne vois pas du tout de quoi tu parles, dit-elle d'un ton sarcastique.

En vérité, elle savait très exactement à quel point le Club V était bizarre. Elle devait s'y rendre tous les jours pour travailler.

— Je ne sais pas comment tu fais, Sam. Tous ces gens allongés partout, en train de baiser, d'attendre de baiser, de chercher quelqu'un à baiser, de s'asseoir à côté de moi au bar en regrettant que je ne sois pas au menu.

Elle haussa les épaules et hocha la tête.

— Ouais, certains d'entre eux sont spéciaux. Tu sais, ils ne sont même pas censés faire des avances aux barmaids. C'est le règlement, et ils le savent tous très bien, mais je crois que c'est ça qui les excite encore plus. C'est interdit, alors c'est plus attrayant. Ils veulent voir s'ils peuvent être le seul et l'unique à dépasser ça pour nous convaincre qu'ils valent le coup qu'on perdre notre boulot pour eux. Les membres sont exclus et les barmaids se font virer. Tout le monde est perdant. Quelqu'un est venu t'embêter ?

Je pris l'air détaché.

— Un type, c'est tout. Ce n'était pas grand-chose, et Céleste était là. Non que j'aie eu besoin de son aide, mais sa présence était rassurante, au cas où. Il ne semblait pas du genre insistant. Mais on ne sait jamais.

— Tu as bien raison.

Samantha choisit une émission de rencontres, mais le volume était mis au minimum alors qu'elle reprenait :

— J'ai de la chance que Céleste soit ma patronne. Elle veille vraiment sur nous. Certains types, et même quelques femmes, peuvent vraiment être ingérables, mais elle les remet à leur place en deux secondes.

Je hochai la tête et regardai la télé, en me demandant s'il était approprié que je lui parle de la conversation que j'avais eue avec Céleste ce soir-là. Si Jake Mesa était le propriétaire, ça signifiait qu'il était le patron de Samantha. Je n'avais jamais entendu mon amie parler de lui, sans doute parce qu'elle ne croisait pas souvent les membres de la direction, mais elle pourrait peut-être m'en apprendre plus sur lui.

— Céleste m'a proposé de venir travailler au club.

Samantha me regarda d'un air un peu surpris.

— Ah bon ? Mais tu n'as jamais travaillé dans un bar. Elle ne prend que des gens avec beaucoup d'expérience au bar.

— Oui, enfin, elle ne parlait pas de tenir le bar.

Samantha comprit soudain de quoi je parlais.

— Oh. Ouah. D'accord. Eh bien, c'est quelque chose que tu envisages ?

Je voyais bien qu'elle était choquée. Elle me connaissait depuis une éternité, alors c'était forcément surprenant pour elle.

Je secouai la tête.

— Nan. Enfin, je suis sûre qu'il y a beaucoup d'argent à se faire, mais je lui ai dit qu'il fallait d'abord que je m'occupe de quelque chose.

— Et par « chose », tu veux dire ta virginité, hein ? demanda Samantha du tac au tac.

— Ouais.

— Eh bien, Tay, tu sais que je t'ai toujours dit que je pensais que tu y accordais trop d'importance. Je sais que tu as une carapace et que tu veux que tout se passe comme tu l'as décidé, mais tu devrais peut-être tenter quelque chose, te laisser aller. On ne sait jamais où ça pourrait mener. Et même si ça ne mène nulle part, ça t'aura fait une expérience. Il n'y a rien de mal à ça.

Je digérai ses mots en silence. De nombreuses occasions s'étaient présentées à moi, et continuaient de se présenter. Je pouvais décider quand je voulais de laisser quelqu'un devenir mon premier. Je devrais peut-être jeter mon dévolu sur le prochain mec qui entrerait dans le garage.

— Tu devrais peut-être draguer quelqu'un, ajouta soudain Sam. C'est justement ton genre de truc. Tu aimes les défis.

Je souris et levai les yeux au ciel.

— Non, mais franchement, poursuivit-elle. Mets la barre haut. Peut-être un des types du garage. Un avec une bagnole super chère. Fais des recherches dès que tu obtiens son nom, assure-toi qu'il ne soit pas marié, et ensuite, baise-le sur la banquette arrière de ta voiture pendant ta pause déjeuner. Ça ne doit pas être bien compliqué, avec un physique comme le tien.

— Euh, merci, dis-je, sans trop savoir comment le prendre.

— Hé, tu sais que je te dis ça comme un compliment. Tu es sublime, Tay. Tu pourrais avoir tous les mecs que tu veux. Je sais que tu veux t'assurer qu'il sache ce qu'il fait, mais franchement, depuis le temps, tu dois être tellement douée avec ton vibro, qu'aucun mec ne doit être à la hauteur de tes attentes.

Je lui jetai un élastique et lui adressai un regard noir.
Samantha rit.

— Tu sais très bien que c'est la vérité. Sérieusement, si tu veux prendre ça en mains, choisis un mec, et puis c'est tout. Fais-le une bonne fois pour toutes. Et ensuite...

Elle me sourit d'un air incroyablement malicieux, et reprit :

— Ensuite, tu pourras les enchaîner. Il y en a tellement, là dehors. Imagine tous les mecs que tu pourrais trouver dans les bars. Franchement, je suis jalouse.

— Ce n'est pas comme si tu n'avais pas le même échantillon de mecs à portée de main ! m'exclamai-je.

Elle secoua la tête.

— Ouais, mais j'ai l'impression que de grandes choses t'attendent. Tu ne l'as encore jamais fait, tu es plus vieille que la plupart des gens quand ils font l'amour pour la première fois, et tu sais ce que tu veux. Je pense que les choses s'annoncent bien pour toi.

Je sortis la carte de visite de ma poche et la plaçai sur la petite table, avant de la faire glisser vers Sam. Elle l'attrapa et vit le nom qui y était inscrit. Elle leva les yeux vers moi avec surprise, et prit la parole d'une voix inquiète :

— Où est-ce que tu as eu ça ?

— Il me l'a donné, répondis-je.

Ses yeux s'écarquillèrent légèrement.

— Ouah. C'est... quelque chose. Mais je serais toi, je ne sais pas si je l'appellerais. Enfin, si c'est toujours en rapport avec la conversation qu'on vient d'avoir.

— Il doit avoir de l'expérience, dis-je.

Samantha s'éclaircit la gorge.

— Si on veut.

Je penchai la tête de côté et la regardai, les yeux plissés.

— D'accord, mais qu'est-ce que tu as à dire à son sujet ?

Elle haussa vaguement les épaules.

— Je dirais qu'il a une certaine réputation au club. Ça doit rester entre nous, bien sûr, et je n'ai aucune certitude. Mais quand on travaille au Club V... On entend des choses. Je suis employée là-bas depuis assez longtemps pour avoir entendu des histoires dingues sur les propriétaires.

— Qu'est-ce que tu sais sur eux ? demandai-je avec une curiosité non feinte.

J'avais pu me faire une idée sur Jake Mesa ce soir-là, mais je me demandais ce que Sam savait d'autre. Elle était bien placée pour connaître tous les ragots sur son lieu de travail, et s'il faisait ce qu'il avait fait à Miss Collier et Diamants à d'autres filles qui travaillaient au club, j'étais persuadée que le bruit devait courir vite, parmi les groupes d'employées.

— D'accord, alors, le club a été fondé par trois amis, alors qu'ils étaient à la fac. C'est toujours les propriétaires du club, et ils sont toujours très impliqués, même si je n'ai jamais vraiment travaillé avec aucun d'entre eux. Je ne suis pas très haut placée au bar. Ils ne nous parlent pas souvent. Enfin bref. Ils étaient tous amis à la fac et ont décidé de créer le Club V. Ils ont commencé par un club, et ensuite, comme tu le sais peut-être, ils en ont monté d'autres dans tout le pays. Ils en ont un dans chaque grande ville, ou presque.

— Alors ces types roulent sur l'or ?

Elle m'adressa un hochement de tête théâtral.

— Ils se font des couilles en or. Les gens viennent des quatre coins du monde pour devenir membres, et les abonnements pour les étrangers coûtent un bras - plus que pour les gens du coin. Ils se font des montagnes de fric, et ça ne risque pas de s'arrêter.

Je me mordillai la lèvre. Tout ça, je le savais déjà, mais je n'osais pas trop insister pour qu'elle me donne plus d'informations sur Jake Mesa en particulier. Elle ne semblait pas beaucoup fréquenter les propriétaires du club.

— Et qui sont-ils ? demandai-je.

— Neil, Pete, et celui qui t'a donné sa carte, Jake. J'ai surtout vu Neil, mais Jake a une certaine réputation avec les filles du club. Quelques-unes ont couché avec lui, et elles ont démissionné peu de temps après.

Je fronçai les sourcils. Ça n'était pas bon signe du tout.

— Pourquoi ?

Elle haussa les épaules.

— J'ai entendu des choses. Ce n'est pas comme s'il avait fait des choses pas claires ou illégales, mais je crois qu'il s'intéresse à des pratiques que les filles n'aiment pas trop. Et il est un peu effrayant, extrême. C'est vraiment un mâle alpha, un mec ténébreux.

— Ça, j'avais remarqué, dis-je à voix basse en prenant la carte de visite, que je fis tourner dans mes mains.

— Il t'a donné son numéro de portable.

— En effet, dis-je en hochant la tête.

— Est-ce qu'il s'est pointé au bar pour te le donner ? Comme s'il flirtait avec toi, ou un truc dans le genre ?

— Je ne sais pas trop, mais il essayait peut-être de me convaincre de devenir membre, ou quelque chose comme ça. Il a parlé de « sang frais ».

— Nom de Dieu, Tay. S'il te plaît, ne l'appelle pas. Je ne

pense pas qu'il soit dangereux, mais ça m'étonnerait que ce soit le genre de gars que tu voudrais fréquenter. Ce n'est pas le genre de mecs que tu cherches. Il te fera peut-être passer un bon moment, mais je crois que par « bon moment », il ne veut pas dire la même chose que toi.

Je hochai la tête.

— Je sais.

Samantha s'interrompit dans sa gorgée de thé.

— Comment ça, tu sais ?

Je levai les yeux vers elle, réalisant ce que je venais de dire. J'avais hésité à lui révéler ce que j'avais vu, mais d'après ce qu'elle savait de lui, elle ne risquait pas d'être trop surprise par ses activités.

Je pris une grande inspiration.

— J'essayais de trouver les toilettes ce soir, parce que celles des employés étaient hors service, et je suis accidentellement tombée sur son bureau.

Samantha reposa sa tasse de thé.

— Oh non. On se croirait dans la Belle et la Bête : ne surtout pas entrer dans l'aile ouest. Dis-moi que tu as fait demi-tour et que tu t'es tirée de là bien vite.

Je tentai un sourire, mais il se transforma en grimace.

— Eh merde, dit-elle. Est-ce que quelqu'un sait que tu y es allée ? C'est pour ça qu'il t'a donné sa carte de visite ?

Je secouai la tête.

— Personne n'est au courant. Céleste a cru que j'étais restée longtemps aux toilettes pour me masturber... C'était le cas, mais ce n'est pas la question. Elle ne sait pas que je suis entrée dans le bureau. Et plus important encore, il ne sait pas que j'étais dans le bureau.

Samantha poussa un soupir de soulagement.

— Oh la vache, heureusement. Bon sang, on aurait pu avoir de sacrées emmerdes, toi et moi.

— Ouais, alors personne ne sait que j'y étais, mais... j'ai vu des choses.

Elle se prit la tête dans les mains.

— Tu ne devrais pas remettre les pieds au club avant un petit moment.

Visiblement curieuse d'en savoir plus, elle dit tout de même :

— Oserais-je demander ce que tu as vu là-dedans ?

— Beaucoup de choses, répondis-je avec un rire nerveux. Des fouets, une fille attachée à une chaise, lui en train de la lécher. Et ensuite, il l'a fouettée.

Sam déglutit.

— Ouais, ça lui ressemble bien, mais je ne pense pas qu'il s'arrête là. Tu vois ce que je veux dire ? C'est vraiment pas ton genre de mec. Il est super autoritaire, très exigeant avec ce qu'il demande aux femmes avec qui il sort. Tu n'as pas besoin d'être avec un type comme lui.

— Ouais, je sais. Tu as raison.

Je gardai le silence en réfléchissant à ce que mon amie me disait. D'accord, ce mec était du genre dominant. Moi aussi. Ou en tout cas, je l'étais dans mes fantasmes. Je m'imaginais toujours en train de donner des ordres à un homme, de lui dire de prendre soin de moi sans penser à son propre plaisir. Je savais que j'étais un peu égoïste, mais j'avais réalisé il y avait bien longtemps que j'avais un appétit sexuel très développé.

Tout de même, quelque chose chez cet homme m'attirait beaucoup. Je n'arrivais pas à mettre le doigt dessus, mais l'idée de me soumettre à Jake Mesa m'intriguait. Il semblait savoir très exactement ce qu'il faisait, et n'était-ce pas ce que je cherchais, après tout ? Un type qui savait comment faire plaisir à une femme, et sublime, pour ne rien gâcher ? Il n'était peut-être pas exactement ce que je désirais, mais il pourrait être ce qu'il me fallait. Cette idée me fit frémir. J'ignorais si ce frisson était dû à l'excitation... ou à la peur.

— Tu fais ce que tu veux, reprit Samantha. Je pense que tu sais ce qui est bon pour toi. Mais tu comptes pour moi, et je ne veux pas que tu souffres. Ce qui me fait te dire de ne pas t'approcher de ce type, c'est que je connais son passé avec les femmes. Je sais qu'il les prend et s'en sert pour son propre plaisir pendant un moment, et ensuite, il les jette. Je ne voudrais pas qu'il te fasse du mal.

Je lui adressai un sourire chaleureux. Son inquiétude me touchait beaucoup, mais je savais que j'étais capable de prendre soin de moi.

— C'est peut-être tout ce que je veux, dis-je. M'amuser un peu avec un mec avec qui je ne compte pas avoir la moindre relation sérieuse.

Je me levai et éteignis la lampe qui se trouvait à côté de moi.

— Je crois que je vais aller me coucher, annonçai-je.
— N'oublie pas ton vibro, me lança Sam. Il est sur le meuble de la salle de bains.

J'éclatai de rire.

— Merci, Sam.

J'allai dans la salle de bains pour me brosser les dents et me préparer à aller au lit, puis j'attrapai mon vibromasseur avant d'aller dans ma chambre. Notre appartement était petit et vieillot, mais il était parfait pour nous deux. Et il était évident que les bruits de vibration ne dérangeaient pas Sam.

J'enclenchai la vibration la plus faible alors que je m'allongeais contre mes oreillers, en repensant à Jake et la fille au collier de diamants. Elle s'était amusée. Rien ne m'empêchait d'appeler ce mec et d'obtenir le même traitement. J'augmentai le niveau de vibration d'un cran en le revoyant se mettre à genoux et plonger entre les jambes de la fille, sa langue léchant son clitoris.

Mon vibromasseur n'avait rien à voir avec une langue, ça, je le savais, mais c'était ce qui s'en rapprochait le plus, et je m'imaginai ce que ça ferait d'être à la place de la fille au collier en diamant, offerte devant un homme comme Jake Mesa. C'était le genre d'homme qui savait précisément ce qu'il voulait et qui l'obtenait. La fille avait été contente de l'expérience, je l'avais remarqué lorsqu'elle avait regagné la salle principale du Club V.

Je pressai de nouveau le bouton de mon vibromasseur, et ses vibrations me coupèrent presque le souffle. Pourquoi ne pas laisser Jake Mesa devenir mon premier amant ? me demandai-je en me caressant. Tout ce que je cherchais, c'était du sexe - une bonne baise, bien sauvage. Au moins, il semblait en mesure de m'apporter ça. Je pouvais lui laisser une chance, voir où ça mènerait, et le laisser tomber au bout de quelques jours ou quelques semaines. Tant que le sexe serait agréable et que je serais contente, ça me suffirait. Pourquoi ne pas laisser un propriétaire de club riche comme Crésus - le propriétaire du Club V - me prendre ma virginité ? Même si je n'avais pas beaucoup d'informations sûres sur cet homme, à part ce que j'avais vu de mes propres yeux, j'avais le sentiment qu'il aurait du mal à refuser une proposition de ce genre.

— Bon sang ! m'écriai-je alors que j'atteignais l'orgasme.

Je maintins le vibromasseur en place, me forçant à soutenir la sensation. Elle était presque douloureuse, presque insupportable, mais je voulais avoir l'impression d'avoir quelque chose qui refusait de s'arrêter entre les jambes, malgré mes cris.

Enfin, je me laissai aller et me détendis sur les oreillers, vidée et épuisée. Jake Mesa semblait être bon au lit, mais valait-il le coup ? Avais-je vraiment envie de me frotter à l'ego d'un mâle alpha qui croyait pouvoir obtenir tout ce qu'il voulait, rien qu'en claquant des doigts ? Quelque chose là-dedans ne me plaisait pas du tout. Au moins, les types du garage semblaient accorder de la valeur à l'attention que je leur consacrais. Avec Jake, j'avais l'impression que ce serait une chose qui allait de soi pour lui. Toutes les femmes qu'il croisait lui tombaient sans doute dans les bras sans qu'il ait à bouger le petit doigt.

Je souris en commençant à m'endormir, réalisant que Jake Mesa et moi avions au moins une chose en commun.

CHAPITRE 5

Le lendemain, j'arrivai au garage à l'aube. Mon père descendait les escaliers pour préparer du café dans la salle de pause située dans un coin du garage, comme il le faisait tous les matins. Rodrigo était déjà présent, et travaillait sur une voiture surélevée. C'était un travail difficile, mais il était prêt à s'en occuper seul, car il avait beaucoup d'expérience avec le problème mécanique de cette voiture.

Quant à moi, ça ne me dérangeait pas du tout d'avoir une bonne vue sur le marcel moulant de Rodrigo, coincé dans son bleu de travail, qu'il avait déboutonné jusqu'à la taille. Il était musclé et bronzé, et rien qu'en le voyant, je me léchai les lèvres. Cela faisait plus d'un an que je le suppliais de me suivre à l'étage, dans la chambre que j'avais occupée lorsque je vivais avec mon père au-dessus du garage.

Avant ce jour-là, nous n'avions fait que nous amuser un peu. Nous avions presque le même âge, et au lycée, nous étions dans la même classe. Il y avait toujours eu ce non-dit entre nous, mais lorsque Rodrigo était enfin venu travailler pour mon père, j'avais tenté de chasser ces sentiments de ma tête. Une branlette de temps en temps, des baisers échangés derrière le garage dès que j'étais sûre que mon père ne pourrait pas nous surprendre. C'était simplement pour s'amuser, et ça avait continué comme ça pendant un moment. Rodrigo savait que les choses ne pourraient jamais devenir sérieuses entre nous, et dans l'ensemble, il semblait l'accepter.

C'était un jour froid de novembre, et ma fête d'anniversaire n'aurait lieu que le week-end. Le jour J tombait en milieu de semaine, et j'avais voulu marquer le coup. J'avais poursuivi Rodrigo toute la journée, en lui disant qu'il fallait qu'il m'offre quelque chose ou qu'il trouve le moyen de rendre ma journée exceptionnelle. Il n'arrêtait pas de dire qu'il ne serait payé que la semaine suivante, qu'il n'avait pas d'argent, et qu'il m'aurait bien acheté des fleurs, mais qu'il avait oublié quel jour c'était.

Je lui avais dit que ce n'était pas grave, et que j'avais une autre idée. Puis, après le travail, lorsque mon père était allé s'occuper de la voiture d'un client à domicile après que le véhicule avait failli exploser dans une allée, j'avais dit à Rodrigo que je voulais lui montrer quelque chose à l'étage. Je l'avais traîné dans les escaliers. Il hésitait, car il savait que mon père avait toujours dit que l'appartement lui était interdit d'accès. Je crois que mon père savait ce que je ressentais pour Rodrigo, ou qu'en tout cas, il craignait que nous couchions ensemble, et la dernière chose qu'il voulait pour moi, c'était que je tombe enceinte. Mais ça ne risquait rien. Ce n'était pas ce que j'avais en tête pour mon anniversaire.

Après des rires et des encouragements, j'avais réussi à traîner Rodrigo à l'étage, et une fois seuls derrière la porte de ma chambre, je l'avais plaqué contre le mur et je l'avais embrassé passionnément, lui faisant savoir sans le moindre doute ce que j'attendais de lui. Il était gentil et un peu timide, et il ne voulait pas me pousser à faire des choses que je n'avais pas envie de faire, mais je lui avais assuré que c'était précisément ce que j'avais prévu pour mon anniversaire, et que s'il gâchait tout, je serais très triste.

Nous nous étions rendus dans ma chambre, et je voyais bien qu'il hésitait toujours à sauter sur cette occasion.

— Écoute, lui avais-je dit pour essayer de le rassurer. Je suis vierge, et je ne compte pas remédier à ça tout de suite. Mais je veux que tu me goûtes.

Je n'eus pas besoin de le lui dire deux fois. En un quart de seconde, j'étais sur mon lit, et il m'enlevait mon jean, ma culotte, et enfouissait la tête entre mes cuisses. Je ne savais pas vraiment à quoi je m'étais attendue, mais je n'avais pas pensé qu'il serait aussi enthousiaste. Il m'avait fallu une minute pour m'habituer à lui et trouver le bon rythme. En fin de compte, ça avait été super, et j'avais réussi à faire sortir Rodrigo du garage avant que mon père rentre ce soir-là.

À présent, alors que je le regardais travailler sur la voiture à l'autre bout du garage, ce souvenir m'émoustillait un peu. Je n'avais jamais été plus loin avec un mec. Mais j'avais le sentiment que ça n'allait pas tarder à changer. Je savais qu'il ne se passerait plus jamais rien entre Rodrigo et moi, mais c'était un bon souvenir.

J'allai dans la salle de pause, où mon père avait fini de faire du café et nous versait une tasse chacun. Je lui souris.

— Bonjour.

— Comment ça va, ma puce ?

— Bien. Beaucoup de pain sur la planche, aujourd'hui ?

Il secoua la tête.

— Non, mais il y a une chose dont je veux te parler. Viens dans mon bureau.

Il me tendit une tasse de café brûlant, et je le suivis dans le bureau plein à craquer. Il était seulement assez grand pour un bureau, un fauteuil, et deux chaises. Le reste était encombré de piles de papiers, un vrai aimant à incendie, et je ne me souvenais pas de la dernière fois où la pièce avait été nettoyée. J'étais certaine que quelque part parmi les piles de feuilles, il y avait des factures qui dataient d'avant ma naissance.

— Assieds-toi, dit-il.

Je m'assis devant lui sur l'une des chaises et le regardai s'installer avec un soupir. Il semblait un peu perturbé, comme si quelque chose le tracassait, et ça ne lui ressemblait pas du tout. Nous étions proches, mais nous n'étions pas du genre à nous confier nos émotions les plus profondes, ni rien de tout ça. Mon père était quelqu'un de bien, un peu vieux jeu et coincé. Il n'aimait pas que l'on voie ses faiblesses, et surtout pas moi.

— Quoi de neuf ? demandai-je d'un ton léger pour ne pas lui montrer que j'avais remarqué que quelque chose clochait.

— Bon, je vais aller droit au but. L'argent ne coule pas à flots, au garage, et vu qu'on a un peu moins de clients que d'habitude, j'ai dû faire des comptes. Je ne pense pas pouvoir me permettre de garder le même nombre d'employés.

Je clignai des yeux, essayant de comprendre où il voulait en venir. Bien sûr, j'avais remarqué que l'on recevait moins de clients qu'avant, mais ça suffisait quand même à nous occuper toute la semaine. Les week-ends n'étaient plus aussi pleins, mais cela ne m'avait pas semblé inquiétant.

— Tu n'as que moi, Rodrigo et George. Ça ne fait pas beaucoup d'employés.

Il hocha la tête et poussa un soupir.

— Je sais. Ça ne fait pas beaucoup du tout. Et je regrette de ne pas pouvoir me permettre de garder tout le monde. Mais c'est impossible, Tay. Je vois toutes les factures qui s'empilent, et il faut que je fasse le nécessaire.

C'est là que ça me frappa : mon père était-il en train de me virer ?

— Attends, moi ? Tu me renvoies ?

Il sembla surpris, et secoua la tête.

— Toi ? Non, bien sûr que non. Tu es ma meilleure employée. Tu es jeune, mais tu es la meilleure. Je ne peux pas non plus virer le plus vieux et renvoyer George. Il est plus jeune que moi. Je me dis que le plus juste, ce serait de renvoyer de la dernière personne à être arrivée dans l'entreprise.

Et cela signifiait que ça allait tomber sur Rodrigo. Je me tournai vers la fenêtre du bureau, qui donnait sur le garage. Rodrigo était toujours en train de travailler, comme il le faisait depuis bien longtemps avant mon arrivée ce matin-là.

— Bon sang, papa, ça semble si injuste de lui faire ça à lui. Il travaille ici depuis un moment, quand même, et il est vraiment doué. Je n'ai pas envie qu'on le renvoie aussi brutalement. Il n'y a rien qu'on puisse faire pour éviter ça ?

Mon père haussa les épaules et secoua la tête.

— J'ai fait les comptes dans tous les sens, et j'ai tenté de trouver d'autres financements, mais tant qu'on n'aura pas retrouvé la même charge de travail qu'avant, je ne trouverai rien. Il n'y a pas d'argent. Je n'ai rien pour le payer. Je vais lui donner un préavis de deux semaines, et ensuite, ce sera fini. J'ai l'impression que je ne peux pas faire mieux, même si j'aurais préféré pouvoir éviter ça. Il a toujours été correct avec nous.

Je hochai lentement la tête et sirotai mon café. Maintenant que mon père m'avait annoncé la vérité, je n'avais plus aucune envie de regagner le garage et d'affronter Rodrigo.

— Quand est-ce que tu vas lui dire ? demandai-je d'un ton solennel.

— Je me dis que le plus tôt sera le mieux. Je voulais simplement te prévenir, pour ne pas te prendre par surprise. C'est un gars calme. Je ne pense pas qu'il pétera les plombs, ni quoi que ce soit.

— Non, sans doute pas, confirmai-je.

Rodrigo s'en remettrait sans doute, mais apprendre que l'on était viré n'était jamais une nouvelle facile à digérer. J'espérais qu'il finirait par l'accepter. Mais les deux semaines suivantes allaient être compliquées.

— Ça va, Tay ? me demanda mon père avec un air inquiet.

Je hochai la tête et fis un geste nonchalant alors que je me levais pour quitter son bureau.

— Oui, ce n'est rien. Je m'inquiète pour lui, c'est tout. Et pour nous. Est-ce que je peux faire quelque chose pour améliorer la situation ?

Il secoua la tête.

— Continue d'être toi-même. Tu travailles dur, tu es douée, et je ne sais pas ce que je ferais sans toi. Merci, Tay.

Je lui souris et je quittai son bureau, en laissant la porte ouverte. J'allai travailler sur l'une des voitures qui étaient garées devant le garage, assez près pour entendre ce que les deux hommes se disaient, mais assez loin pour leur laisser assez d'intimité. J'étais certaine qu'à la place de Rodrigo, je ne voudrais pas que qui que ce soit assiste à la scène, et je ne voulais pas blesser la fierté de mon ami.

La conversation avait dû se passer mieux que prévu, car je ne remarquai pas de changement dans l'expression de Rodrigo ce jour-là, jusqu'à la fermeture de la boutique. Il m'approcha alors que je travaillais, et il n'avait qu'un demi-sourire au visage au lieu de montrer toutes ses dents étincelantes.

— Salut, Tay, me dit-il d'une voix un peu triste.

— Salut, Rodrigo, répondis-je en lui adressant un sourire.

— J'imagine que tu es au courant ? me demanda-t-il d'un air un peu incertain.

— Mon père me l'a dit. Je suis vraiment désolée, Rodrigo.

Je regrette de ne pas avoir d'autre perspective d'embauche pour pouvoir te laisser ma place.

Il secoua la tête.

— Tu rigoles ? C'est ta place. C'est l'entreprise de ton père ; évidemment que tu dois rester. Cet endroit t'appartiendra un jour. Il faut que tu continues à y travailler pour apprendre deux ou trois trucs sur les voitures. Peut-être qu'un jour, tu finiras par devenir une bonne mécanicienne.

Ses sarcasmes me firent sourire. J'étais contente qu'il puisse en plaisanter. Je m'essuyai les mains et me penchai en avant pour le serrer dans mes bras.

— Tu vas me manquer, dis-je, surprise par la force de ce que je ressentais.

— Toi aussi, tu vas me manquer, dit-il en reculant et en regardant mon visage avec une intensité à laquelle je ne m'étais pas attendue. Mais bon, maintenant que je ne travaille plus pour ton père...

Je secouai la tête.

— Tu dis n'importe quoi. Et il te reste deux semaines.

C'était à son tour de secouer la tête.

— Nan, je lui ai dit qu'aujourd'hui serait mon dernier jour. Il faut que je cherche autre chose le plus tôt possible.

— Je comprends, dis-je en haussant la tête. Mais ne nous perdons pas de vue, d'accord ?

Il sourit.

— C'est promis. À bientôt, Tay.

J'agitai la main alors que je le regardais monter dans son pick-up, puis je rentrai dans le garage pour aller voir mon père dans son bureau.

— C'était plus simple que je l'aurais cru, dis-je en entrant dans la pièce, et je surpris mon père alors qu'il passait des papiers en revue.

Il avait toujours l'air inquiet, mais je me dis que c'était à cause du stress que lui avait causé le fait de renvoyer l'un de ses meilleurs employés.

— Quoi ? dit-il. Ah, oui. Il l'a très bien pris. Je suis content. J'espère qu'il trouvera vite autre chose.

Je regardai mon père parcourir des documents posés sur son bureau d'un air distrait.

— Tu cherches quelque chose, papa ?

Il leva les yeux vers moi et tenta de sourire.

— Oh, non. C'est juste que... cet endroit est un vrai dépotoir, hein ? Je devrais peut-être faire un peu de rangement, un jour.

— Tu veux que j'appelle un médecin ? Je ne te reconnais plus.

Il rit.

— Oui, bon, les gens changent, des fois.

Je hochai la tête. Parfois, les gens changeaient, mais c'était plutôt rare.

— Je vais aller chercher Sam, annonçai-je. À demain.

— À plus tard, Tay.

Comme la veille au soir, je fis quelques efforts sur ma tenue et mon maquillage avant de me rendre dans le centre ville pour chercher Samantha au travail - sauf que cette fois, je le fis en ayant Jake Mesa en tête, même si je détestais l'admettre. Ce mec m'avait tapé dans l'œil, et même si j'étais sûre qu'il n'y avait aucune chance pour qu'il se passe quelque chose là-bas, je voulais être sur mon trente-et-un. Je pourrais le faire baver, tout en lui signifiant qu'il n'avait aucune chance avec moi, une chose qu'à mon avis, Jake Mesa n'entendait pas souvent.

Je pénétrai de nouveau dans le bar par l'entrée du personnel, cette fois dans une robe rouge courte et moulante qui épousait la moindre de mes formes et ne laissait pas beaucoup de place à l'imagination. J'allais vraiment devoir être vigilante et accepter l'aide de Céleste pour empêcher les hommes de trop m'approcher ce soir-là.

— Bonsoir, dis-je en m'asseyant au bar.

Céleste me regarda d'un air surpris.

— La vache, tu n'étais déjà pas mal du tout hier soir, mais bon sang, meuf. Dis que tu es en couple, sinon le groupe de clients de ce soir ne va pas te laisser tranquille.

Je lui souris.

— Je peux avoir un verre de vin ? Du Pinot grigio, si tu en as.

Elle hocha la tête.

— Pas de problème.

Je jetai un regard autour de la salle principale du Club V. Le fait qu'il s'agisse d'un jour de semaine n'empêchait généralement pas le club d'être plein, mais cette soirée était particulièrement calme. Et par calme, je voulais dire que personne ne baisait ouvertement en plein milieu de la pièce.

— Voilà ton vin, me dit Céleste en plaçant le verre devant moi. C'est le meilleur qu'on ait. J'espère qu'il te plaira.

Je fis tourner le vin dans mon verre et en pris une gorgée.

— Tu sais, je n'y connais pas grand-chose en vin, mais j'adore le goût qu'il a, c'est phénoménal. Merci.

— De rien. Sérieusement, tu es superbe, ce soir. Une raison particulière à ça ? Cette robe va attirer tous les regards.

Je haussai les épaules.

— Pas de raison particulière. J'avais envie d'être féminine, pour une fois. Je passe mes journées en jean sale, couverte de graisse. Des fois, j'oublie ce que ça fait d'être propre et de porter une robe avec du maquillage et une coiffure autre que la queue de cheval ou le chignon.

— Je ne peux pas dire que je sais ce que ça fait, mais je compatis. Mais tes journées ressemblent au rêve de beaucoup de lesbiennes, dit-elle en ponctuant ses propos d'un rire. J'ai le droit de dire ça.

Je lui souris et levai les yeux au ciel.

— Comment va Amber ?

Céleste se mit à rayonner en pensant à sa femme.

— Très bien. Enfin, je ne pensais pas pouvoir l'aimer davantage, mais elle est de plus en plus belle chaque jour. Et le fait que cet enfant grandisse en elle... C'est impressionnant, tu vois ?

Je hochai la tête. Je n'avais jamais vraiment pensé aux enfants, me disant que j'étais trop jeune pour réfléchir à cette perspective. L'idée qu'un être humain grandisse en moi était stupéfiante.

— Elle accouche quand ?

— Dans deux mois, dit-elle en sortant son téléphone de sa poche pour me montrer des photos. Là, c'est elle avec son ventre tel qu'il est maintenant. Tu sais, avant ça me dégoûtait quand les gens partageaient ce genre de photos sur les réseaux sociaux, mais maintenant que c'est mon bébé, ça n'a rien à voir.

Elle passa à la photo suivante et reprit :

— Et là, c'est la dernière échographie. On va avoir une petite fille !

Je souris en regardant l'image en 3D. C'était un bébé, c'était certain, mais mon œil non expert n'aurait pas pu en plus d'informations.

— Je suis contente pour toi. Vous avez déjà choisi un prénom ?

Elle poussa un soupir.

— Eh bien, on a quelques idées. Le prénom de ma mère était Anita, et j'aimerais beaucoup honorer sa mémoire. Amber aime beaucoup le prénom Bryn. On fera un compromis, mais je n'ai aucune idée de ce qu'on finira par choisir.

À cet instant, un home vêtu d'un costume fait sur mesure

s'assit à deux tabourets de moi et sourit dans ma direction, sans tenir compte du fait que j'étais en pleine conversation avec Céleste.

— la jeune femme voudrait-elle un autre verre ? demanda-t-il.

— Et voilà le prétendant numéro un, Mesdames et Messieurs, murmura Céleste avec un sourire en se déplaçant derrière le bar pour prendre la commande du client.

CHAPITRE 6

— Alors, dites-m'en un peu sur vous.

Le type du bar était venu s'asseoir à côté de moi dès qu'il avait réalisé que personne ne venait me rejoindre, en dépit de mes protestations. Et il ne s'agissait plus seulement d'un inconnu assis près de moi au bar, c'était Chadwick Fontaine, héritier d'un empire du savon. J'étais peut-être jeune, mais j'avais assez vécu pour savoir que quand un mec se vante de sa fortune, c'est qu'il n'a pas beaucoup d'autres qualités pour lui.

— Eh bien, je travaille pour mon père, et je devrais hériter de l'entreprise familiale un jour. Enfant unique, vous voyez, répondis-je avec un sourire en engloutissant le reste de mon vin avant de faire signe à Céleste de me remplir mon verre. Ça allait être ce genre de soirée. J'avais décidé que quitte à être coincée au bar à parler avec ce type, je pouvais au moins m'amuser un peu.

— Ah, vraiment ? Dans quel secteur ? demanda-t-il avec un intérêt sincère.

Ce genre de mec voulait toujours épouser des bons partis. Mieux valait regarder les dents du cheval avant de l'acheter.

— L'automobile, dis-je en prenant un léger accent chic.
— Importation ?

Je hochai la tête et repris une gorgée de mon nouveau verre de vin.

— La majorité de notre travail se fait sur des importations, oui.

— Fascinant. C'est vraiment merveilleux, que vous ayez pu apprendre auprès de votre père pendant toutes ces années. Vous savez quand vous allez reprendre l'entreprise ?

Je le regardai droit dans les yeux avec un sourire.

— Eh bien, étant donné que je viens d'avoir vingt et un ans, et que mon père vient seulement d'entrer dans la cinquantaine, je dirais que ça n'arrivera pas de sitôt.

L'homme sembla surpris que je n'aie que vingt et un ans. C'était un mensonge, bien sûr. J'avais dix-neuf ans, mais je ne voulais pas que ce type l'apprenne et que Céleste ait des problèmes pour avoir servi une mineure. Cela pouvait suffire à faire fermer un club, si la mauvaise personne l'apprenait. Je savais que je faisais plus vieille que mon âge. C'était à cause de mon corps, et du fait que je me comportais avec un peu plus d'assurance que les filles de mon âge.

La surprise disparut rapidement de son visage lorsqu'il pensa aux autres avantages qu'il y avait à parler à une jeune fille de vingt et un ans dans un bar. Soudain plein d'audace, il me passa un bras autour des épaules et me caressa le bras. Je tentai de me dégager, mais il me serra davantage contre lui.

— Qu'est-ce que vous faites ?
— Je me rapproche de toi, ma belle.

Il se pencha et me murmura à l'oreille :

— Je suis là pour faire ce que tous les autres gens sont venus faire ici - et je vais le faire avec toi. Mais je ne savais pas que j'aurais la chance de baiser une étudiante. Et si on allait dans une pièce privée ? Tu voudrais qu'on demande à une autre fille de nous rejoindre ? Ou à un autre homme ? Peut-être quelqu'un qui voudrait mater ?

Je me dégageai de son emprise et bondis de mon tabouret.

— Vous avisez pas de me toucher.

— Hé, qu'est-ce qui se passe ? demanda-t-il en levant les mains comme s'il se rendait.

Je jetai un regard à Céleste pour qu'elle me soutienne, mais elle était coincée à l'autre bout du bar, en train d'agiter un blender, et elle ne pouvait pas m'entendre à cause du bruit de l'appareil et de la musique.

Chadwick tendit de nouveau les bras vers moi, et je reculai, tournant les talons pour aller me mettre dans un coin, lorsque je rentrai brutalement dans le torse musclé d'un certain Jake Mesa.

— Un problème ? demanda-t-il.

Son ton était si calme, mesuré et plein d'assurance, que je fus certaine que s'il y avait eu un problème, ce n'était plus le cas.

Il me mena de nouveau vers le bar et Chadwick, qui regardait Jake avec dédain. Toujours les mains en l'air, il tenta d'en rire.

— Hé, mon pote, y a aucun problème ici. Moi et mon amie, on faisait que parler.

Jake baissa les yeux vers moi.

— C'est votre ami, Taylor ?

— Non, pas du tout, dis-je en jetant un regard noir à Chadwick.

— Monsieur, je pourrais voir votre carte ? lui demanda Jake.

Chadwick fouilla maladroitement dans son portefeuille. Lorsqu'il tendit sa carte à Jake, ce dernier s'en saisit sans la regarder.

— Vous comprenez qu'en signant le contrat pour

rejoindre le club, vous acceptez un certain nombre de règles, n'est-ce pas ?

L'homme hocha la tête.

— Vous semblez avoir du mal avec l'une d'entre elles, poursuivit Jake. Une règle qui, selon moi, est la plus importante de toutes. Cette règle concerne le consentement, le fait de s'assurer que votre partenaire soit aussi intéressé que vous par ce que vous lui proposez. Cette jeune femme ne semble pas souhaiter votre compagnie, et pourtant, vous insistez.

Jake saisit la carte entre deux doigts et l'examina.

— C'est un avertissement. On en donne rarement, mais je suis de bonne humeur, ce soir. Si je vous vois dépasser les bornes à nouveau dans cet établissement, vous regretterez d'avoir mis les pieds ici. C'est compris ?

Chadwick semblait terrorisé alors qu'il hochait la tête. Jake lui jeta la carte, et l'homme d'affaires dut la récupérer par terre.

— Je crois que vous feriez mieux de partir ce soir. Revenez une autre fois, quand vous serez d'humeur plus sympathique.

D'un simple hochement de tête, Jake fit venir deux vigiles, qui escortèrent Chadwick Fontaine hors du bâtiment.

Je levai les yeux vers lui, réalisant comme les avances de cet homme m'avaient perturbée, sans vouloir l'admettre.

— Si vous voulez bien m'excuser, dit Jake, je vais m'assurer que M. Fontaine comprenne parfaitement ce qui est ou n'est pas autorisé dans ce club.

Jake sortit derrière les vigiles, et je me tournai vers Céleste, qui avait fini de préparer sa boisson et qui se tenait en bout de bar.

— Je n'aimerais pas être à la place de ce type, marmonna-t-elle.

— Tu le connais ?

Elle secoua la tête.

— Sa carte de membre indiquait qu'il n'était pas d'ici. Il est sans doute à New York pour affaires. Mais je serais lui, je ne froisserais pas Jake. Il prend les règles très au sérieux, comme tu l'as entendu. Et cette histoire de consentement... eh bien, c'est la pierre angulaire de cet établissement. Si les gens ne traitent pas les autres avec respect, tout s'écroule. Aucun des propriétaires ne peut tolérer ce genre de comportement. C'est le plus sûr moyen de se faire virer. Et pas seulement d'un club, mais de tous les Clubs V. Il risque de ne plus revenir ici.

Je m'assis au bar, un peu secouée. Je ne savais pas quand Samantha finirait le travail, mais j'espérais que ce serait pour bientôt. Tout ce que je voulais, c'était rentrer chez moi, dans mon lit confortable, très loin d'ici.

Quelques minutes plus tard, je perçus un mouvement du coin de l'œil, et je vis que Jake était revenu. Il lissa sa veste et jeta un regard dans la pièce, avant de poser les yeux sur moi.

— Vous êtes toujours là, dit-il, l'air un peu surpris.

Je hochai la tête.

— J'attends mon amie.

Il m'adressa un sourire plein de gentillesse.

— Je voulais vous dire que je suis navré que vous ayez été traitée ainsi au Club V. Ce n'est pas le genre de la maison, et j'espère que vous ne laisserez pas le comportement d'une seule personne ternir l'opinion que vous vous faites de cet endroit.

Je secouai la tête.

— Non, bien sûr que non.

Seigneur, comment ce type pouvait-il être aussi sexy, même dans une situation pareille ?

— Je peux vous inviter à venir boire un verre dans mon bureau ? demanda-t-il. Voyez ça comme un moyen de vous faire oublier le comportement déplorable de cet homme.

Je ne sais pas ce qui m'a pris à ce moment-là. Je savais que si Samantha était là, elle me déconseillerait d'accepter, mais je me surpris à hocher la tête et à quitter mon tabouret.

— Avec plaisir, dis-je avec un sourire en le suivant hors du bar et dans le couloir - le couloir que j'avais emprunté la veille avant de tomber sur son bureau par erreur.

Il ouvrit la porte de son bureau et me fit entrer. La lumière était différente, cette fois. Moins tamisée, mais toujours plus proche d'une lumière d'ambiance que d'une lampe destinée à travailler à son bureau.

— Un bourbon ? me demanda-t-il en se dirigeant vers le bar situé dans un coin de la pièce.

— Très bien, dis-je. Avec des glaçons.

— Ça arrive tout de suite.

Ses gestes étaient assurés derrière le bar, et je me demandai s'il avait déjà fait ce genre de travail.

— Merci, dis-je alors qu'il me tendait mon verre et se dirigeait vers son bureau sans boisson pour lui. Vous ne buvez rien ?

Il secoua la tête.

— Pas ce soir. Je me rends à la salle de sport tout à l'heure.

Je sirotai le bourbon. Il était bon, mais je n'étais pas sûre de m'y connaître assez pour l'apprécier à sa juste valeur.

— Il n'est pas un peu tard pour ça ? demandai-je.

— Vous n'avez jamais entendu parler des salles de sport ouvertes vingt-quatre heures sur vingt-quatre, Taylor ?

— Si... mais, enfin, j'aurais pensé qu'après une longue soirée de travail ici, vous rentreriez chez vous pour vous détendre un peu.

Il hocha la tête.

— Oui, c'est ce que je fais, des fois. Mais pas ce soir. Comment est votre bourbon ?

— Bon, répondis-je avec un sourire en reprenant une gorgée.

— Pardonnez-moi de ne pas vous en avoir proposé hier soir. Si j'avais su que vous étiez dans mon bureau, je vous en aurais volontiers servi un verre, dit-il de sa voix rauque.

Je faillis recracher mon bourbon, mais je choisis plutôt de me retenir, m'étouffant au passage.

— Pardon ? demandai-je quand je pus de nouveau parler.

— Vous savez, quand vous étiez dans mon bureau, hier soir, alors que je recevais une invitée.

— Je... je ne sais pas quoi dire.

J'étais sous le choc. Je ne savais pas quoi dire, ni par où commencer, ni comment convaincre cet homme que je n'avais pas volontairement tenté de l'espionner pendant qu'il couchait avec une femme dans son bureau.

— Eh bien, je ne m'attends pas vraiment à ce que vous vous excusiez. Enfin, ce ne serait pas dans l'esprit du Club V, n'est-ce pas ? Des gens viennent ici pour mater. Vous le saviez ? Certains membres réguliers n'ont jamais touché une autre personne dans cet établissement. Je trouve que c'est un choix étrange, un choix que je ne ferais pas, mais qui suis-je pour juger les désirs des autres ?

Il sourit et s'enfonça dans son fauteuil.

— Vous voulez me parler de vos désirs à vous ? reprit-il.

Je plissai les yeux et posai mon verre sur son bureau. Le bourbon, c'était terminé pour ce soir.

— Déjà, dites-moi comment vous avez su que j'étais là. Si vous étiez au courant, alors pourquoi n'avoir rien dit ?

Il haussa les épaules.

— Je ne l'ai réalisé que plus tard, en vérifiant les caméras de surveillance. Vous voyez, la fille qui était là avec moi... Eh bien, je ne voulais pas que qui que ce soit d'autre apprenne qu'elle était ici, alors j'effaçais les preuves. Je vous le dis, parce que vous ne pourriez pas le répéter à qui que ce soit sans révéler que vous étiez ici, dans mon bureau, sans autorisation. J'ai une vidéo de vous en train d'entrer dans mon bureau, puis en train d'en sortir, cinq minutes plus tard. Ça fait beaucoup de temps dans le bureau d'un inconnu, vous ne trouvez pas ? Surtout quand on sait que vous n'aviez rien à y faire.

— Qu'est-ce que vous allez faire ? demandai-je en tentant de garder un ton neutre et de ne pas laisser transparaître ma surprise. Je ne me sentais pas très en sécurité. Personne, à l'exception de Céleste, ne savait que j'étais là. Le bureau de ce type se trouvait loin de tout le reste du club, et c'était l'un des propriétaires. Jake avait clairement l'avantage.

— Vous comptez me faire chanter ? demandai-je. Ça ne vous rapporterait pas grand-chose. Je n'ai pas d'argent.

Cela le fit rire à gorge déployée.

— Vous croyez que je veux de l'argent ? Non, j'ai plus d'argent que je ne pourrais dépenser en une vie. Non, Taylor Dawson, je veux savoir ce qui vous plaît. Je veux savoir ce que vous avez pensé de ce que vous avez vu ici hier soir. Dites-moi, honnêtement. Comment avez-vous réagi ? Vous êtes restée regarder un bon moment. Qu'est-ce qui se passait pendant que vous étiez là, exactement ? Toutes mes excuses, j'étais occupé, à ce moment-là.

Je déglutis avec difficulté en réalisant qu'il était sérieux. J'étais déterminée à relever son drôle de défi.

— Vous l'aviez attachée à une chaise. Vous la léchiez, et ensuite, vous l'avez punie quand elle vous a appelé par votre prénom.

Il hocha la tête.

— Ah, oui. Elle avait été vilaine, hein ? Dites-moi, Taylor...

Il se pencha davantage et poursuivit :

— Vous êtes une vilaine fille, vous aussi ? Très vilaine, je pense. Si vilaine, que quand vous vous teniez ici hier soir et que vous nous regardiez, vous étiez toute mouillée. Je parie que vous n'en pouviez plus. Je me trompe ?

J'étais furieuse. Le fait qu'il prenne le sujet à la légère ne me facilitait pas les choses. La situation avait beau me déconcerter et me mettre en colère, je restais quand même excitée par sa présence. Ça, plus la façon dont il parlait des événements de la veille, c'était enivrant.

— C'est une réaction plutôt naturelle, quand on voit des gens baiser, rétorquai-je. J'étais justement en train de dire à Céleste que je ne comprenais pas comment vous faisiez pour travailler ici toute la journée, alors que c'est une orgie permanente.

— Pourquoi ? Parce que vous auriez tout le temps envie de vous joindre à la fête ? demanda-t-il. Moi aussi. C'est l'un des avantages du métier.

Je n'avais pas envie d'admettre qu'il avait raison, et je ne voulais pas non plus révéler plus de choses sur moi que je l'avais déjà fait. Il en savait trop. D'une certaine manière, ce n'était pas grand-chose du tout, mais j'avais l'impression que ce type savait lire en moi comme peu de gens savaient le faire, et pourtant, voilà qu'il creusait, qu'il me faisait avouer la vérité.

— Qu'est-ce que vous cherchez chez un homme ? Me demanda en me regardant depuis l'autre côté de son bureau. Qu'est-ce que vous attendez d'un homme ? Parlez-moi de vos précédents partenaires.

J'étais prise au dépourvu. Et comme un chat, il sauta sur l'occasion. Je ne savais s'il lisait dans mes yeux, ou s'il parvenait à deviner ce genre de chose d'une façon ou d'une autre. Je ne pensais pas que Céleste le lui aurait dit, mais après tout, je ne la connaissais pas très bien. Peut-être qu'elle effectuait des repérages pour lui. Les vierges avaient beaucoup de valeur, par ici, mais je doutais très sérieusement qu'elle partage ce genre d'informations avec son employeur.

— Vous n'avez eu aucun partenaire, n'est-ce pas ?

Ses mots étaient prononcés avec lenteur, comme du caramel fondu autour d'une pomme juteuse et bien rouge.

— Ça alors, quelle surprise, reprit-il. D'habitude, je les repère plus facilement. Ce n'est pas que vous avez l'air de vous taper tout ce qui passe - même s'il n'y aurait aucun mal à ça -, mais vous avez une certaine assurance, un air déterminé. On dirait que vous êtes prête à prendre ce que vous voulez, je me trompe ?

Je choisis mes mots avec attention :

— J'ai remarqué que de manière générale, j'obtiens ce que je veux, du moment que je joue mes cartes comme il faut.

Ma réponse sembla lui plaire. Il me sourit et hocha la tête.

— Vous êtes une sacrée, Taylor Dawson.

Je levai les yeux au ciel et regrettai de ne pas pouvoir me lever et partir.

Jake se leva brusquement, et se retourna pour attraper un sac dans un coin.

— J'espère que ça ne vous dérange pas, commença-t-il en ouvrant le sac. Je déteste être en retard à la gym, alors il va falloir que je me prépare pendant qu'on termine notre discussion.

— Je crois que nous n'avons plus rien à nous dire.

Il rit.

— Qu'est-ce que vous avez pensé d'elle ?

— Qui ?

— La fille avec qui j'étais hier soir, dit-il en retirant sa veste.

Dessous, il portait un tee-shirt noir, et je pouvais voir à quel point il était musclé. J'avais du mal à me concentrer sur ses questions dès que j'étais obligée de le regarder.

— Elle était très belle.

Il plissa les yeux et me jeta un regard suspicieux.

— C'est tout ?

Je repensai à l'apparence de la fille. Peu de détails m'avaient marquée.

— Elle était grande.

Il hocha la tête.

— Vous, vous n'êtes pas très grande. Vous faites quoi... Un mètre soixante... huit ?

— Oui.

— Je suis doué pour deviner. Quand au reste... je n'ai pas bien regardé, hier soir, mais maintenant que vous êtes dans cette robe...

Il poussa un sifflement, et reprit :

— Cette robe semble être une taille 38, et je dirais que vous faites un bonnet C.

— Vous êtes répugnant, dis-je sans réfléchir.

Il me regarda en passant son tee-shirt au-dessus de sa tête, révélant les muscles de son ventre et de sa poitrine. Je tentai de ne pas laisser transparaître à quel point j'étais impressionnée par son corps. Mais il ne me laisserait pas m'en sortir aussi facilement. Il déboutonna et dézippa son jean d'un mouvement fluide, et l'enleva.

J'eus le souffle coupé en voyant le corps nu de Jake pour la première fois. Taillé comme un dieu grec, je n'étais pas surprise qu'il soit tout aussi beau sans son jean et son blazer qu'il l'était habillé. En fait, il était beaucoup, beaucoup plus beau comme ça. Bon sang ! Ce qui attirait mon attention, c'était son tatouage. Sur le côté droit de son corps, il y avait un dragon, qui lui grimpait le long du torse et de la cuisse. C'était impressionnant. Je savais le temps et les efforts que demandait un tatouage pareil. Ce type était quelqu'un d'exceptionnel.

Si ses questions ne m'avaient pas déjà fait mouiller, j'aurais trempé ma culotte en le voyant là devant moi, sa silhouette révélée dans toute sa gloire.

Ses muscles gonflèrent alors qu'il redressait les épaules, se retenant visiblement de... de quoi ? De me sauter dessus et de me déchirer mes vêtements ? Cette pensée suffit à me faire perdre la tête, mais je voulais rester impassible. Il était hors de question que je le laisse avoir le dessus, même si j'étais plus excitée que jamais.

— Vous me trouvez toujours répugnant ?

Je me mordis la lèvre avec force pour m'empêcher de dévoiler l'excitation brûlante qui me dévorait. Eh merde, j'avais tellement envie de Jake. C'était comme si je pouvais enfin me l'admettre à moi-même, même si j'avais essayé de croire le contraire. Je savais qu'il serait partant. Je le voyais dans ses yeux. Et si je m'offrais à lui, je savais qu'il n'oserait jamais me refuser ce plaisir. Il était clair qu'il adorait être aux commandes et contrôler la situation. Cela me perturbait légèrement, car je voulais avoir le contrôle. L'idée de le jeter sur le bureau et de le chevaucher jusqu'à l'orgasme me fit presque convulser et tomber de ma chaise sous ses yeux. Bon sang, je me demandais ce que ça lui ferait - me donner un orgasme rien que parce que j'imaginais son membre enflé en moi. Serait-ce vraiment déplacé de lui demander de me prendre ma virginité ici et maintenant ?

Très déplacé, songeai-je en prenant une grande inspiration et en m'étirant la nuque. J'ignorais s'il devinait à quoi je pensais. Pouvoir lire dans les pensées changerait tout. Une partie de moi espérait qu'il en était capable, et qu'il chasserait toute autre pensée pour me prendre là, tout de suite. Une autre part de moi luttait contre le diable sur mon épaule et se battait ardemment pour ne pas capituler trop tôt. C'était peut-être ce que je voulais, mais Jake Mesa n'était certainement pas ce dont j'avais besoin.

Après ce qui me sembla être une éternité, Jake enfila enfin sa tenue de sport. Je me levai pour partir et me dirigeai vers la porte. Il tendit le bras et me posa doucement une main sur l'épaule, chose qui me surprit complètement.

— N'ayez pas peur de vous lâcher, Taylor. Beaucoup de choses vous attendent, là dehors.

Je me dégageai et allai ouvrir la porte. Jake croyait peut-être savoir des choses sur moi, mais il se trompait.

CHAPITRE 7

En rentrant ce soir-là, un message de mon père m'attendait, me disant qu'il n'était pas la peine que je vienne le lendemain, car plusieurs rendez-vous avaient été annulés et il allait simplement faire de la paperasse. Je trouvai ça un peu bizarre, mais j'étais contente de pouvoir faire la grasse matinée. Le bourbon m'était monté à la tête, et après que Sam nous avait ramenées à la maison ce soir-là, je m'étais écroulée dans mon lit, contente d'être chez moi. Chadwick Fontaine avait complètement disparu de mon esprit, désormais, même si ma rencontre avec lui au bar avait été très désagréable. Tout ce que je pouvais voir, c'était le corps nu de Jake Mesa.

Ce n'était pas du tout une vision désagréable - personne ne pourrait prétendre une chose pareille. Mais c'était quelque chose que j'aurais préféré chasser de mon esprit. Désormais, cette image y était gravée à jamais, et elle avait beau être sympathique à regarder, je ne voulais plus jamais la voir.

Comme je l'avais soupçonné, cet homme était arrogant comme tout, et il arrivait toujours à ses fins. Ça l'excitait sans doute de me dire tous ces trucs, d'essayer de me faire admettre que ça m'avait excitée de le voir avec cette fille dans son bureau. Bien sûr que ça m'avait excitée. Qui ne le serait pas, après avoir assisté à une telle scène ? C'était comme tomber par erreur sur un porno torride. Je voyais bien que Jake aurait aimé que je me joigne à eux, mais j'avais le sentiment que ce n'était pas quelque chose que j'aurais beaucoup apprécié.

Cette nuit-là, je tentai de dormir, reconnaissante de ne pas voir à me lever tôt pour aller au travail, mais tout ce qui s'était produit pendant la soirée tournait en boucle dans ma tête, et j'eus du mal à trouver le sommeil tant désiré. Lorsque je m'assoupis enfin, je fus assaillie par des rêves agités. Cela n'avait rien de reposant, et je me réveillai le lendemain matin avec un mal de tête abominable. C'était la dernière fois que je buvais du bourbon.

Samantha commençait le travail bien plus tard, alors lorsqu'elle me trouva roulée en boule sur le canapé, enveloppée dans une couverture, à onze heures, elle parut un légèrement inquiète.

— Tu es malade ? Tu couves quelque chose ?

Je secouai la tête.

— Mon père m'a dit qu'il n'avait pas besoin de moi ce matin. J'ai reçu un message de sa part hier soir. Un vrai coup de chance. J'ai très mal dormi, et j'ai un mal de tête épouvantable.

Sans que j'aie à lui demander, Samantha me prépara une tasse de thé et m'apporta la tasse fumante sur le canapé.

— Merci, Sam. Désolée, je suis vraiment au bout du rouleau.

— Tu veux en parler ?

Je haussai les épaules.

— Je ne saurais pas quoi dire.

— Eh bien, tu n'étais pas très bavarde sur le chemin du

retour, hier, et Céleste et les autres barmaids m'ont dit qu'il y avait eu un incident au bar.

Je hochai la tête.

— Il y avait un type - vraiment, le plus gros con que j'aie vu depuis un bon moment -, et il me faisait du rentre-dedans. Sauf qu'il était très insistant. Et, enfin... il devenait vraiment explicite. Il voulait qu'on aille dans une pièce privée, il me tripotait. Je m'en suis tirée toute seule, dans l'ensemble, mais Jake Mesa a débarqué et a pris les choses en mains. Il a fait sortir ce type et m'a demandé de venir boire un verre dans son bureau.

— Dis-moi que tu as refusé.

— Non, dis-je en poussant un soupir.

— Et ?

— Et je crois que tout ce que tu m'as dit sur lui était vrai. Ne t'inquiète pas, je ne perdrai pas mon temps avec lui. Déjà, ce n'est pas mon genre... et en plus, eh bien, je crois qu'ensemble, on ferait des étincelles. Et pas dans le bon sens du terme.

— Eh bien, dit-elle. Je ne peux pas dire que je sois contente de l'entendre. Je suis désolée que tu aies eu une mauvaise expérience, mais je suis contente que tu aies vu ce côté de lui, si ça te permet de te tenir à l'écart. Je ne voudrais pas que tu souffres.

— Ce n'est pas tout, dis-je en soufflant sur mon thé pour tenter de le faire refroidir.

— Quoi ?

— Il sait que j'étais dans son bureau. Il m'a vue sur les vidéos de sécurité.

Samantha pâlit.

— Tu plaisantes ? Il t'a vue ? Qu'est-ce qu'il a dit ? Il était énervé ?

— Je ne crois pas qu'énervé soit le bon mot. Je crois qu'il était intrigué. Je pense qu'il est un peu pervers sur les bords...

comme si on ne le savait pas déjà. Il me demandait ce que ça m'avait fait de le voir. Il cherchait vraiment des réponses à ce genre de questions, mais je ne lui ai pas dit grand-chose. Je voulais simplement m'en aller, te récupérer, et rentrer à la maison. Je ne suis pas sûre d'y retourner un jour. Je ne veux pas le voir. Pas après ce qui s'est passé hier soir.

— C'est tout ? Il ne t'a rien fait, si ?

— Non, dis-je en secouant la tête. Il s'est quand même déshabillé entièrement pour enfiler sa tenue de sport devant moi, mais il n'a rien fait.

Je ne mentionnai pas l'expression que j'avais vue dans ses yeux, celle qui m'avait indiqué qu'il avait eu envie de me faire des choses. Pas simplement des choses - tout. Et je n'allais certainement pas mentionner qu'à cet instant, j'en avais vraiment eu envie.

Elle grimaça.

— C'est... dingue. Tu devrais te tenir à l'écart un moment. Je trouverai quelqu'un d'autre pour me ramener, ce n'est pas grave. Tu faisais déjà un détour pour venir me chercher, en plus. Peut-être que si tu ne viens pas pendant un moment, il pensera à autre chose et il t'oubliera. Il n'a aucun moyen de te contacter, si ?

Je secouai la tête.

— Non, je ne pense pas. Mais Sam, ce type est milliardaire. Il pourrait sûrement me retrouver, s'il voulait vraiment me parler.

Elle haussa les épaules.

— Oui, je suppose. Mais je peux dire une chose : ils veillent scrupuleusement à ce que les clients respectent les règles là-bas. Il a vu quelqu'un s'approcher de trop près de toi alors que tu n'en avais pas envie, et il est intervenu. Je suis contente qu'il ait été présent pour virer ce type du club. Je ne dis pas que tout ce qu'il a fait ou dit ensuite était approprié, mais je pense que pour ce qui a précédé, il a bien agi.

— Oui, je crois que tu as raison.
— Et ton mal de tête ?
Je réfléchis.
— Ça va mieux. Je crois que je pourrai aller travailler cette après-midi. Je sais que mon père a dit que ce n'était pas la peine que je vienne, mais comme il a renvoyé Rodrigo hier, je pense qu'il aura peut-être besoin d'aide. Au moins, ça me changera les idées.

Sam sourit.
— Fais ce qui te fait envie. Dis-moi, si tu as besoin de quoi que ce soit. Et ne t'en fais pas pour ce soir. Je trouverai un autre moyen de rentrer. Tu ne serais plus jamais obligée de voir Jake Mesa.

Lorsque je me rangeai devant le garage, il était presque dix-sept heures. J'ignorais si mon père serait toujours là, mais je fus surprise de voir deux Cadillacs noires garées à l'extérieur. Elles ne semblaient pas avoir quoi que ce soit à réparer, et le fait qu'elles soient exactement du même modèle me semblait bizarre. Au lieu d'entrer par l'avant du garage comme je l'aurais fait en temps normal, je fis le tour par l'arrière, dans le but de passer d'abord dans l'appartement de mon père afin de vérifier s'il s'y trouvait.

J'entendis les cris dès que j'entrai dans le garage. Je marquai une pause, tous les sens en alerte. Je savais qu'il ne valait mieux pas me précipiter dans une situation inconnue. S'il s'agissait d'un cambriolage, il ne valait mieux pas que je me mette dans une position où je risquerais de me faire tirer dessus. Je sortis mon téléphone et me préparai à appeler le 911 au besoin. Avec le recul, je regrettais de ne pas avoir appelé la police immédiatement.

J'entendis des bribes de conversation. Des choses comme « Écoutez-moi, mon vieux » et « On est sérieux, cette fois ».

Mon père. Mon père était là. Surprise, je rentrai dans une

pile de pneus et les envoyai valser aux quatre coins du garage. Le bruit fut si fort que les hommes qui se trouvaient dans le bureau sursautèrent et qu'ils partirent en courant. Six d'entre eux fuirent le garage, sautèrent dans les voitures que j'avais vues dehors, et quittèrent rapidement les lieux. Contente de leur avoir fait peur et qu'ils soient partis, mais toujours inquiète pour mon père, je me précipitai dans son bureau.

Je ne le vis pas tout de suite, puis je réalisai qu'il était par terre, roulé en boule derrière son bureau.

— Papa ! m'écriai-je. Qu'est-ce qui s'est passé ? Tout va bien ? Tu veux que j'appelle la police ? Ces types t'ont cambriolé ?

Je savais que je posais trop de questions ; et qu'il n'était pas en état d'y répondre. Mon souci principal était de m'assurer qu'il n'était pas terriblement blessé. Après un rapide examen, il ne semblait souffrir de rien de trop grave. Ils ne lui avaient pas donné de coup de pied, ni rien qui pourrait causer une hémorragie interne. Je l'aidai à s'asseoir dans son fauteuil et approchai une chaise.

— Papa, tu veux que j'appelle la police ?

Il secoua la tête.

— Non, ne les appelle pas, s'il te plaît. On ne peut pas les impliquer. Ça empirerait les choses. Il ne faut pas que ça empire.

— Ça me semble déjà assez grave comme ça, dis-je. Qu'est-ce qu'ils voulaient ?

Je voyais bien qu'il me cachait quelque chose, quelque chose qu'il gardait pour lui depuis un bon moment. Soudain, son étrange comportement au sujet des comptes commençait à prendre tout son sens.

— Allez, papa, tu peux me le dire.

Il secoua la tête.

— J'ai tellement honte, Tay.

— Dis-moi. Et ensuite, on pourra régler ça ensemble.

— Je crains qu'il ne soit trop tard. J'avais du retard dans les paiements de la maison, et j'essayais de trouver un moyen d'arranger ça. L'un des types avec qui je joue aux cartes m'a parlé de mecs avec qui il faisait des paris. Je ne savais pas qui c'était. Je ne savais pas à quel point ils étaient puissants. J'ai fait de mauvais paris, j'ai engrangé des dettes. Et maintenant, je leur dois plus d'argent que je ne pourrais jamais rembourser. Je me suis dit que renvoyer Rodrigo me permettrait de trouver un peu d'argent, mais c'est loin d'être suffisant. Ils sont venus aujourd'hui pour me rappeler qu'ils voulaient récupérer leur dû. S'ils m'ont frappé, c'est parce que j'ai raté des paiements.

— Merde ! m'exclamai-je.

Mon père détestait que je pousse des jurons, mais il ne sembla pas le remarquer.

— On ne fait pas le poids face à eux, Tay. Je suis vraiment désolé. On va perdre le garage, à cause de cette histoire. Ils vont nous le prendre, parce que je ne pourrai jamais trouver l'argent que je leur dois. C'est beaucoup trop. C'était déjà trop au début, avant que j'aie des paiements en retard, et maintenant, c'est encore pire. Je ne pourrai jamais rassembler une telle somme. Ils sont dangereux, Taylor. Ils ne plaisantent pas. La prochaine fois, ils s'en prendront à moi, et il ne faut pas que tu sois là quand ils le feront.

— Papa, c'est de l'extorsion. Ils ne peuvent pas se pointer ici et nous prendre le garage comme ça. Il m'appartient aussi. On est une famille, et on va s'occuper de ça ensemble.

— Il n'y a pas que ça, dit-il en poussant un soupir qui me donna l'impression qu'il avait perdu tout espoir.

— Quoi ? Qu'est-ce qu'il y a ?

— Ils ne vont pas se contenter de prendre le garage. Si je ne trouve pas l'argent, ils me tueront. Ils m'enterreront, Tay. Je ne veux plus que tu t'approches d'ici. S'ils savent que tu as un lien avec le garage, ils risqueraient de s'en prendre à toi aussi.

Il me prit dans ses bras, et poursuivit :

— Je ne peux pas te perdre. Je ne peux pas les laisser te faire du mal. Ils feront tout ce qu'ils peuvent pour m'atteindre, et s'ils apprennent ton existence, tu seras en danger. S'il te plaît, quoi que tu fasses, ne t'approche pas du garage. Tu dois pas être impliquée.

Je pris une grande inspiration et lâchai mon père. Je ne savais pas qui étaient ces voyous, mais ils s'en étaient pris à la mauvaise personne ; ils n'avaient pas le droit de se pointer ici, de faire du mal à mon père, de le menacer de mort et de s'emparer de notre entreprise comme ça.

— Combien tu leur dois ?

— Cent mille dollars.

Je poussai un grand soupir.

— Bon, d'accord. C'est beaucoup, mais on peut trouver une solution. Un accord, peut-être, avec des échéances.

Mon père m'attrapa la main et la serra.

— Tay, on n'en est plus là. C'est cent mille dollars dans deux semaines, sinon c'est fini.

Après m'être assurée que mon père allait bien, physiquement, du moins, je le laissai bien au chaud au lit dans son appartement, en m'assurant que la porte était bien fermée à clé derrière moi. Il avait raison, nous ne pouvions pas appeler la police si nous ne voulions pas risquer d'avoir encore plus de problèmes avec la mafia, ou les voyous qui s'en prenaient à lui, quels qu'ils soient.

J'étais sous le choc, et je ne savais pas vraiment quoi faire, mais je sautai dans ma voiture et je pris la route. Je pensai à ma mère, qui était morte en me mettant au monde. Je ne l'avais jamais connue, mais en cet instant, je me demandais ce qu'elle aurait voulu que je fasse pour aider mon père. Elle m'aurait peut-être dit de le laisser s'en occuper. C'était vraiment stupide, de passer ce genre de marché avec des criminels. Il ne le savait peut-être pas au début, mais en général, dans notre coin du pays, on pouvait être sûr que tous les gros paris sportifs étaient gérés par des gens peu recommandables. Qui sème le vent récolte la tempête.

Mais c'était mon père. Je ne pouvais pas laisser une telle chose lui arriver. Il avait travaillé dur pour le garage, l'avait bâti à partir de rien. C'était son deuxième enfant. C'était tout ce qu'il pouvait me transmettre. Je me fichais d'en hériter ou non, même si ça m'aurait plu. Je ferais n'importe quoi pour que mon père soit en sécurité. Menacer l'entreprise était une chose, mais menacer mon père de mort et penser qu'ils s'en tireraient comme ça n'avait rien à voir.

Je me ruai vers le Club V. Je ne savais pas vraiment ce que j'allais y faire, à part tout raconter à Samantha. C'était mon amie la plus proche et ma confidente, et même si je détestais traîner les problèmes sur son lieu de travail, j'avais besoin d'elle. J'avais besoin de son soutien, de son calme, de son bon sens. Elle aurait une idée des solutions possibles, ou alors elle pourrait me donner des tapes dans le dos et me convaincre que tout s'arrangerait. S'il le fallait, je finirais par aller voir la police. Si c'était ce qu'il fallait faire pour sauver la vie de mon père, alors je le ferais. Je ne pouvais pas être certaine qu'il n'irait pas en prison ou qu'il ne perdrait pas le garage, mais au moins, il ne se ferait pas assassiner par ces types.

Je me précipitai vers l'entrée de derrière, mais je ralentis le pas en m'approchant du bar. J'avais envoyé un message à Samantha pour la prévenir de mon arrivée, et elle m'attendait. Elle me fit signe de m'asseoir à côté d'elle.

— J'ai un peu de temps devant moi, dit-elle. Il n'y a pas trop de monde, ce soir, et ils n'ont pas vraiment besoin de moi pour l'instant. Qu'est-ce qui se passe ?

Je lui révélai tout, de A à Z. Samantha était aussi choquée

que je m'y étais attendue, mais elle tenta de prendre un air impassible pour que je ne perde pas encore plus mon sang froid. Céleste nous jetait des coups d'œil de l'autre côté du bar, mais elle me laissait un peu d'intimité avec ma meilleure amie.

— Bon, réfléchissons, dit Samantha. Quelles sont les options qui s'offrent à toi ?

Je haussai les épaules, incapable de savoir ce que je pouvais faire pour rectifier la situation.

— Eh bien, tu pourrais appeler la police, dit Samantha, ce qui ne semble pas être une solution appropriée, alors on va mettre ça à la fin de la liste. Je ne pense pas qu'on puisse se débarrasser de ces types nous même. J'imagine que la seule solution viable, ce serait de trouver cet argent.

Je la regardai avec des yeux cernés de rouge, exaspérée.

— Il nous faut cent mille dollars en deux semaines. Où est-ce que je suis censée trouver autant d'argent en si peu de temps ?

J'ignorais depuis combien de temps il se tenait là. Je ne l'avais pas entendu arriver, mais visiblement, il était là depuis assez longtemps pour comprendre l'essentiel de la conversation.

— Taylor.

Jake Mesa avait prononcé mon nom avec douceur juste derrière nous.

Je me tournai pour lui faire face, surprise de le voir debout là. Ce n'était pas la dernière personne que j'avais envie de voir - non, les voyous qui avaient tabassé mon père occupaient désormais cette place de choix sur ma liste, mais je n'étais pas non plus ravie de le voir.

— Quoi ? demandai-je d'un ton brusque.

— Je crois pouvoir vous aider.

CHAPITRE 8

Je m'assis face au bureau de Jake, au même endroit que j'avais occupé la veille. Ça faisait trois soirs de suite que je pénétrais dans son bureau, maintenant, et je n'avais pas du tout hâte d'avoir cette conversation avec lui.

— Je peux vous offrir à boire ?
— Non merci.

Je n'avais aucune envie de répéter mon expérience de la veille avec le bourbon.

— Je préfère garder les idées claires pour découvrir ce que vous voulez me dire exactement. Pourquoi pensez-vous pouvoir m'aider ?

— Je ne voulais pas écouter votre conversation. En fait, je ne m'attendais pas à vous revoir un jour, après hier soir. J'ai été agréablement surpris de vous voir ici. Mais bon, j'ai entendu ce que vous disiez à votre amie. Et si vous me racontiez tout ?

Je poussai un soupir.

— Je travaille pour mon père, dans son garage. Je suis mécanicienne.

Je crus voir sa mâchoire se contracter lorsque je dis cela, mais je continuai de parler :

— Aujourd'hui, quand je suis allée au garage, j'y ai trouvé mon père. Il venait de se faire tabasser par des voyous qui se sont enfuis à mon arrivée. Mon père avait des retards de paiement sur le prêt de la maison, et il a fait des paris pas très clairs. Ces types venaient récupérer leur dû, ou celui de leur employeur. Enfin, j'imagine que techniquement, ils n'ont rien récupéré aujourd'hui. C'était seulement un avertissement, pour lui rappeler ce qu'il devait leur donner dans deux semaines.

— Quelle somme ?

— Cent mille dollars.

Jake écrivit quelque chose sur un calepin et l'examina. Il sembla faire des calculs, puis il ferma le petit bloc-notes et le glissa dans la poche intérieure de son blazer.

— D'accord, je pense qu'on peut s'arranger.

— Comment ça ? Je ne viendrai pas travailler ici pour vous. Céleste m'en a déjà parlé, et ce n'est vraiment pas pour moi, surtout après le type de l'autre soir. Je peux prendre soin de moi et je sais me défendre, mais je ne veux pas me retrouver entre les pattes de types comme lui.

Jake secoua la tête.

— Nan, je ne veux pas que vous veniez travailler ici. Et pour ce que ça vaut, je suis complètement d'accord. Non pas que je ne respecte pas les gens qui travaillent ici, mais je ne pense pas que ce soit un travail pour vous. Vous êtes spéciale, Taylor. Vous me croyez ?

Je le regardai d'un air méfiant.

— Je ne sais pas où vous voulez en venir. S'il vous plaît, venez-en au fait, ou laissez-moi partir, il va falloir que je réfléchisse à certaines choses, et si vous ne comptez pas vraiment m'aider - ce que je trouverais bizarre, de toute façon -, alors j'aimerais mieux partir pour réfléchir à ce que je vais faire.

Il hocha la tête.

— Vous êtes une femme d'affaires. C'est quelque chose que je respecte. Vous voulez jouer cartes sur table, alors allons droit au but.

Il sortit un chéquier du tiroir de son bureau.

— Je suis prêt à vous faire un chèque du montant qu'il vous faut. Sans rien en échange. Vous m'en avez dit assez, et je vous crois. Je ne pense pas que vous seriez dans cet état si c'était faux.

Pour la première fois ce soir-là, je réalisai ce que je portais. Je m'étais montrée au club habillée pour aller au travail, et même si pour une tenue de mécanicienne, ce n'était pas trop mal... j'étais quand même au Club V en bleu de travail.

— C'est quoi le piège ? demandai-je.

Je ne pouvais pas croire qu'il me donnait cet argent par bonté de cœur.

— Il n'y a pas de piège. Seulement un marché. Je veux passer un marché avec vous, Taylor. Je vous propose cent mille dollars, en échange de vous.

— De moi ? répétai-je en portant la main à ma poitrine. Qu'est-ce que vous...

Puis je réalisai ce qu'il voulait. Il me voulait moi. Il voulait m'avoir. Même si quelques jours plus tôt, cela m'avait paru alléchant, alors que je me tenais dans son bureau et que je le regardais donner du plaisir à une autre fille, mais en cet instant, cela me semblait moins attrayant.

— Avant de me dire non, écoutez-moi. Je ne sais pas si vous avez entendu parler de moi au club. Je suis certain que des tas de rumeurs courent au sujet de ce que j'aime, mais je vous assure que ce n'est pas très différent des goûts des hommes lambda que vous croisez dans la rue.

— Je ne croise pas beaucoup d'hommes dans la rue.

Il sourit.

— C'est pour ça que vous avez tant de valeur. Je n'ai pas souvent l'occasion d'être avec des vierges. Je ne dirais pas que c'est ce que je préfère, mais j'aime leur compagnie une fois de temps en temps. Et je pense qu'avec vous, je pourrais m'amuser. Comprenez-moi bien : je vous désire pour plus que votre corps. Votre esprit m'intrigue. Je veux rentrer dans votre tête, apprendre à vous connaître. Mais je veux que vous vous donniez à moi librement. Je veux que vous décidiez que c'est ce que vous voulez. Ce n'est pas une sorte de truc d'esclavage, vous ne vous vendez pas. Je veux que vous décidiez que c'est ce que vous voulez. Je mettrai bien les choses au clair dans les documents que vous signerez. Vous saurez exactement dans quoi vous vous engagez. Faites ça, et vous sauverez la vie de votre père, ainsi que son entreprise, et vous assurerez votre avenir.

Mes pensées partaient dans tous les sens, et je tentai d'y mettre de l'ordre, de les capturer et de les mettre en cage dans mon esprit, mais c'était trop intense.

— Vous parlez de prostitution.

Il secoua la tête.

— Pas du tout. Je vous parle d'un échange de cadeaux entre deux personnes. Je vous offre cet argent. Vous m'offrez votre présence chez moi pendant deux mois.

— Deux mois ? Vous plaisantez. Je ne veux déjà pas passer deux minutes avec vous, alors deux mois...

C'était un mensonge, et je le sus au moment où ces mots quittèrent ma bouche. Il le savait aussi, mais il ne laissa rien paraître. Comment pouvait-il savoir l'effet qu'il me faisait ? Était-il simplement habitué à affecter les femmes de cette manière ?

— Je ne plaisante pas, dit-il. Je pense vraiment que la situation finirait par vous convenir - non, je peux le garantir.

C'est l'un de mes objectifs majeurs pour ces deux prochains mois, que vous connaissiez un plaisir que vous n'aviez jamais connu auparavant. Il n'y a qu'une condition.

— Laquelle ?

Jake prit un air sérieux.

— Vous devrez vous soumettre à moi complètement. Tout ce que je vous demanderai, vous le ferez. Vous donnerez votre accord pour tout ça à l'avance, alors rien ne sera une surprise. Mais je veux dire que sur le moment, quand je vous ordonnerai de faire quelque chose, vous devrez le faire. Je veux vous apprendre à devenir une vraie soumise - que vous sachiez ce que ça fait, de s'en remettre corps et âme à quelqu'un. De laisser quelqu'un d'autre être aux commandes, pour une fois.

C'était étrange, le sentiment qui grandissait en moi. Je ressentais à la fois de la colère et de l'excitation, du dégoût et de la curiosité. Mais étrangement, par-dessus tout, ce que je ressentais en regardant Jake Mesa, c'était... de la confiance. Il était peut-être plein de choses, mais ce n'était pas un menteur. Je voyais la vérité dans ses yeux, et je savais que je pouvais lui faire confiance. C'était presque tentant, d'envisager de m'offrir à quelqu'un pour qu'il m'utilise pour son propre plaisir. Et pour deux mois ? Je ne savais pas comment je ferais pour y survivre. Mais il ne me ferait pas de mal. Il me donnerait des ordres et s'occuperait de moi ; il me prendrait encore et encore jusqu'à ce que je ne sache plus où j'étais. Tout ça, je le voyais dans ses yeux, et avant de pouvoir changer d'avis, je lui demandai où il fallait que je signe.

Jake Mesa réunit la somme d'argent nécessaire et la fit livrer à mon père. Je lui dis de ne pas poser de questions, que je connaissais quelqu'un capable de tirer des ficelles, et que j'allais devoir prendre deux mois de congé. Mon père, l'homme qui me faisait confiance plus que n'importe qui au monde, avait hoché la tête et m'avait laissée partir. Maintenant que l'argent avait été livré et que sa dette était effacée, il était tranquille pour l'instant. Je savais que nous allions toujours devoir nous occuper du prêt de la maison, mais au moins, nous étions sortis de ce pétrin. Il ne me restait plus qu'à respecter ma part du marché.

Je racontai à Samantha ce qui se passait en lui faisant jurer de ne le répéter à personne. Elle avait peur pour moi, à cause de ce qu'elle avait entendu sur Jake, mais je tentai de la rassurer :

— Ce n'est pas que je crois qu'il m'aime, ni rien de tout ça. Je ne me fais pas d'illusions, mais je pense vraiment qu'il veut me montrer à quel point la vie de soumise peut être agréable. Je sais que ce n'est pas fait pour moi, mais ce n'est que pour deux mois. Je peux supporter n'importe quoi pendant deux mois, non ?

Samantha haussa les épaules et m'aida à préparer mes affaires. Jake m'avait donné une liste de choses à apporter, mais m'avait dit de ne pas trop m'en faire, que presque tout ce dont j'aurais besoin se trouverait dans sa maison de ville à mon arrivée.

— Souviens-toi que je ne suis qu'à un coup de fil. S'il y a quoi que ce soit de bizarre, je veux que tu m'appelles.

Je hochai la tête et tentai de calmer ses craintes :

— Du moment que tu ne dis pas à mon père où je suis. Il ne pose pas de question, sans doute parce qu'il a peur d'apprendre qui m'a donné cet argent. Il doit sans doute penser que je bosse pour la mafia, maintenant.

Samantha rit, l'air pas très à l'aise, et elle finit de m'aider à préparer mes affaires. Quelque temps plus tard, la voiture arriva, et je dis au revoir à mon amie alors que le conducteur m'emmenait dans le quartier de Jake.

La maison de ville se situait dans une rue bordée d'arbres, le genre de rues new-yorkaise que l'on voit souvent dans les films. Elle était pittoresque, le genre de rue dans laquelle vous pouviez élever une famille, si vous aviez des tonnes d'argent. Et Jake en avait, ça, je le savais. Mais à part ça, je ne savais pas grand-chose de lui.

Je fus surprise qu'il m'ouvre la porte et qu'il me fasse entrer dans la maison. Cela me surprit et me troubla. Pour une raison ou pour une autre, je m'étais attendue à ce qu'un majordome m'accueille à l'entrée, et je ne pensais pas le voir avant qu'il ait fini le travail, plus tard dans la journée.

— Il fallait que je prenne des vacances, me dit-il, comme s'il lisait dans mes pensées.

Il ferma la porte derrière moi, et je remarquai à quel point la pièce était sombre. Les rideaux étaient tirés, mais je voyais que le rez-de-chaussée était peint dans des teintes très foncées.

Je le regardai. Sa tenue ressemblait beaucoup à celles qu'il avait portées quand je l'avais vu au club, sauf que cette fois, il ne portait pas de veste.

Il était vêtu d'un jean qui moulait ses fesses parfaites, et un tee-shirt blanc serré. Il ressemblait au genre de mec avec qui j'aurais voulu sortir quand j'étais au lycée.

— Commençons par le commencement, dit-il. Tu vas te déshabiller.

Je le regardai, bouche bée ; puis je me souvins de tout ce pour quoi j'avais donné mon accord lorsque j'avais signé les contrats. Je commençai à me déshabiller, et je le regardai m'observer, sans jamais le quitter des yeux. Alors que j'enlevais couche après couche de vêtements, me révélant de plus en plus à lui, je vis sa mâchoire se serrer. Il avait envie de moi. Évidemment qu'il avait envie de moi. J'étais une vierge de dix-neuf ans, qui se mettait toute nue dans son salon. Quand je me fus enfin débarrassée de ma culotte et que je me tins complètement nue devant lui, il sourit et hocha la tête.

— Tu es magnifique, dit-il en me regardant dans les yeux.

J'avais la certitude qu'il était sincère, et entendre ces mots sortir de sa bouche me fit tout drôle. Pour la première fois, je remarquai ses lèvres. Elles étaient pleines, mais souvent serrées pensivement. Et voilà que je me tenais toute nue devant un homme qui ne m'avait encore jamais embrassée. Je devins légèrement nerveuse alors que je me demandais quand ça arriverait, et je m'interrogeai sur mes émotions : pourquoi ce type me rendait-il toute chose ?

Il s'approcha, assez près pour pouvoir me toucher, mais il n'en fit rien. Je sentais son souffle sur ma joue, et sa proximité me poussa à me tendre vers lui, tant j'avais envie d'être touchée et prise. Je sentis mes tétons durcir et pointer dans sa direction. Il le remarqua également, et je l'entendis prendre une inspiration soudaine.

— Je te le dirai tous les jours, dit-il avec douceur à mon oreille, toujours sans me toucher. Je veux que tu saches à quel point tu es jolie. Tu es absolument sublime, Taylor, et pendant ces deux prochains mois, tu seras à moi.

Le bandeau sur les yeux arriva en premier. Il m'attacha le morceau de soie derrière la tête, et le monde s'obscurcit.

— C'est la première étape, dit-il. Tes sens seront bloqués. Pendant un jour. Peut-être deux. Ça va dépendre de ton comportement. Tu devras t'en remettre à moi pour tout, mais au début, nous ne nous toucherons presque jamais.

Ensuite, après m'avoir conduite aux toilettes pour que je me soulage, il me guida jusqu'au lit, où il m'attacha à quatre colonnes.

— Je veux que tu sois à l'aise, parce que tu vas rester là un moment, dit-il avant de me laisser là.

J'attendis qu'il revienne, et lorsqu'il pénétra de nouveau dans la pièce, j'ignorais combien de temps s'était écoulé. Il m'avait apporté de la nourriture, et il me la fit manger. Au début, je trouvai cela étrange, mais étonnamment excitant.

D'une certaine façon, j'étais simplement contente qu'il soit là avec moi dans la pièce, de ne pas être seule. J'étais nue, allongée sur le ventre, complètement exposée, mais avec le bandeau sur les yeux, je n'avais aucune idée de sa réaction face à tout ça. Peut-être que ça ne lui faisait rien du tout. C'était une toute nouvelle expérience pour moi, mais pour Jake, c'était peut-être quelque chose qu'il faisait souvent. Nous n'en parlions pas. Je gardais le silence, sauf lorsque je répondais aux questions qu'il me posait.

— À qui tu te soumets, Taylor ?
— À vous.
— Et qui suis-je ?
— Jake ?
— Ça conviendra pour l'instant. On reviendra peut-être là-dessus plus tard.

Je crus détecter une pointe de sourire dans sa voix.

Il sortit une plume, ou quelque chose du même genre, et me la passa des pieds jusqu'aux cuisses, puis du bout des doigts jusqu'aux épaules. Il fit des cercles autour de mes seins avec son instrument tout doux, mais évita mes tétons. Il alla jusqu'à mon pubis, mais n'alla pas plus loin.

J'étais mouillée. Je me sentais devenir de plus en plus humide, et l'air frais contre mon entrejambe me donna un frisson, et je frémis.

— Je sais ce que tu veux, dit Jake. Mais ça va devoir attendre.

Toujours avec mon bandeau sur les yeux, il m'amena de nouveau dans la salle de bains. Puis il me fit couler un bain, et en ne me touchant que la main, il m'aida à entrer dans l'eau.

— Je vais te regarder prendre ton bain, dit-il en me tendant du savon et un gant de toilette. Ne pense même pas à te toucher. Tu vas te laver, et rien d'autre.

Je fis ce que l'on m'ordonnait, et quand j'eus fini, il m'aida à sortir et me laissa me sécher, avant de me conduire à nouveau dans le lit. Il me rattacha, et cette fois, il s'assit à côté de moi sur le matelas et commença à me parler à voix basse et rauque :

— Combien de temps tu crois que tu vas rester vierge, Taylor ?

— Aussi longtemps que vous le voudrez, répondis-je. J'avais le sentiment que je jouais bien mon rôle. Être complètement aveuglée, privée de mes sens, était une expérience exaltante, mais je savais quelles étaient ses intentions. Il tentait de m'amener à le désirer. Je me demandais s'il savait qu'il n'avait pas besoin de faire beaucoup d'efforts. J'avais déjà envie de lui, mais il allait faire en sorte que je le supplie. Je dépendais complètement de lui, et quand il me toucherait enfin, je lui appartiendrais. Eh bien, il se mettait le doigt dans l'œil. C'était peut-être agréable, mais personne ne me posséderait jamais.

— Peut-être demain... peut-être après-demain. Tu sais à quel point il m'est difficile de te résister ?

Je gémis d'un air absent.

— Oui, je sais ce que tu veux, reprit-il en me passant un doigt sur le flanc avant de se pencher et de murmurer. Attends.

CHAPITRE 9

Jake s'agenouilla sur le lit. Je ne le voyais pas, mais je le sentais, et enfin, il se mit à me toucher.
Il était passé de la plume aux doigts, puis à la bouche, parcourant chaque centimètre de mon corps, à l'exception des zones que je voulais désespérément qu'il touche.

Durant des jours, il poursuivit ce manège, jusqu'à ce qu'enfin, un soir, il annonce que le moment était venu. Il allait me retirer mon bandeau et allait m'emmener dans son lit. Il n'y avait aucune attente, à part une soumission totale de ma part. Je fus surprise de constater qu'après que mes yeux s'étaient ajustés à la lumière, tout ce que je voulais faire, c'était me glisser au lit avec lui et que ma peau touche la sienne.

— Les choses vont se corser un peu, dit-il en m'attirant contre lui. Je vais exiger des choses de toi, et tu vas me les donner, parce que tu es ma soumise, et que tu veux me contenter. Et parce que je te donne tant en retour.

Je me pelotonnai contre lui, savourant chaque parcelle de sa peau bien chaude. Les jours que j'avais passé attachée au lit avaient été tortueux, mais agréables. Je savais que je ne pouvais toujours pas me caresser, et l'idée de me donner un orgasme me rendait dingue. J'avais beau en avoir envie, je savais que je n'oserais pas le faire. Lui seul était autorisé à le faire, sauf s'il me donnait des ordres contraires.

Il me serra fort contre son torse large. Il était athlétique, comme un sprinter, et ses muscles étaient tendus sous sa peau.

— Mais ta première fois, poursuivit-il, je veux qu'elle soit douce. Pas de fouet, pas de corde. Rien que toi et moi. Je suis honoré d'être ton premier, et je sais à quel point c'est spécial, alors que tu deviens ma soumise. Dis-moi comment tu aimerais que ça se passe.

Mon cerveau se mit à tourner à plein régime. Je n'arrivais pas à croire qu'il me demandait ce que je voulais. Je n'avais pas pensé qu'il m'aurait prise comme ça un soir, mais je n'avais certainement pas imaginé qu'il me demanderait mon opinion.

— J'ai eu envie que tu me baises depuis le premier soir où je t'ai vu. Tu n'as pas besoin d'être doux. Je veux que ce soit comme tu le veux. Je veux que ce soit bon. Je veux avoir orgasme après orgasme, et je ne veux pas que tu t'arrêtes, pas même pour me demander si ça me convient. Je te fais confiance.

Il sourit. Je le percevais malgré l'obscurité dans la chambre.

— Embrasse-moi, m'ordonna-t-il.

Je me penchai en avant et posai mes lèvres contre les siennes. Il approfondit notre baiser et m'enlaça pour me placer sous lui. Quand il fut allongé sur moi, je lui passai les jambes autour de la taille pour le serrer. Je sentais son érection contre ma cuisse, mais il n'était pas encore prêt. Il descendit le long de mon corps, puis il m'embrassa les seins et me suça les tétons tour à tour, les prenant dans sa bouche pour en faire des petites pointes, avant de descendre sur mon ventre et d'embrasser le sommet de mon pubis.

— Tu es magnifique, dit-il en se servant de ses doigts pour écarter mes petites lèvres et pour passer sa langue sur ma peau. Il ne passa pas beaucoup de temps à me titiller, et choisit plutôt de prendre mon clitoris entre ses lèvres et de le sucer comme il l'avait fait avec mes tétons. Je cambrai les hanches contre son visage alors qu'il me pénétrait avec deux doigts, les pliant légèrement pour atteindre l'endroit parfait. Je poussai une exclamation, et il agita la langue contre mon clitoris. Des vagues de plaisir me submergèrent, et je m'agrippai à son corps. Je ne voulais pas que cela prenne fin.

Jake marqua une pause, mais seulement pour me laisser récupérer avant de recommencer. Enfin, quand il m'eut donné deux orgasmes de plus, il me demanda si j'étais prête. Je hochai la tête, et sans préambule, je sentis son sexe se placer devant mon entrée et se glisser à l'intérieur, comme si nos corps étaient parfaitement compatibles.

Il s'enfonça plus profondément, plus fort à chaque coup de reins. La sensation de son sexe qui glissait contre mes parois me donnait un plaisir pur, et je mourais d'envie de le garder là et de ne jamais le lâcher. Je savais qu'il fallait que j'en profite, parce que je ne pouvais pas savoir quand j'y aurais le droit à nouveau. Je ne savais pas du tout quels étaient ses projets à mon sujet en tant que soumise, mais je ne pensais pas que nous ferions à nouveau l'amour de façon classique pendant ces deux prochains mois.

— Baise-moi. Ne t'arrête pas, Jake, lui lançai-je.

Il m'écouta et accéléra le rythme. Je voyais qu'il approchait de la jouissance, et je serrai les jambes autour de lui pour l'encourager. Il poussa un grognement sonore en atteignant l'orgasme, et il jouit en moi, à moitié essoufflé à cause de l'effort.

— Bon sang, c'était bon, dit-il quand il eut repris son souffle.

Ensuite, il me serra contre lui et m'embrassa le visage en me disant à quel point j'étais belle et à quel point ce moment avait été merveilleux. C'était un côté de Jake Mesa que je ne connaissais pas. Il était doux, sensible, et, oserais-je le dire... aimant.

Alors qu'il s'endormait, ses bras toujours autour de moi, il dit d'un ton rêveur :

— Si seulement c'était toujours comme ça.

Je ne savais pas de quoi il voulait parler. Enfin, je croyais savoir ce qu'il voulait dire, mais je n'osais pas croire que Jake Mesa commençait à avoir des sentiments pour moi.

Le lendemain marqua le retour de la privation des sens. Je crois que Jake estimait qu'il m'avait un peu trop ménagé la veille en me faisant l'amour, alors il me priva de nouveau de sexe pendant plusieurs jours. C'était la chose la plus cruelle et la plus délicieuse que l'on pouvait faire à quelqu'un. Il me titilla pendant des heures, apprenant mes limites et les repoussant chaque fois plus. Tout ce que je voulais, la seule chose sur laquelle je pouvais me concentrer, c'était la façon d'atteindre l'orgasme que je désirais si désespérément. Mais à chaque fois, il me posait la même question, et j'y répondais.

— Quand est-ce que tu pourras jouir ?

— Quand tu me laisseras faire.

C'était une torture, mais une torture qui me faisait le désirer encore plus. Je ne savais pas ce qui m'arrivait. Peut-être que je devenais soumise. Je n'avais aucun contrôle sur la situation, et pourtant, j'avais une certaine autonomie. Autant d'autonomie que l'on pouvait en avoir en étant attaché à un lit.

Ensuite, il m'initia au fouet. Il me montra tous les instruments qu'il avait, tous ses fouets et ses cravaches. Il en avait une sacrée collection dans cette maison, bien plus que je n'en avais vu dans son bureau.

Il me massa doucement les fesses avant de tester le premier fouet sur moi. Il ne me frappa pas fort, mais chaque coup gagna en intensité. Je me mis à anticiper ses assauts, et j'appris que cela faisait partie du jeu. Même si ce n'était pas la chose la plus excitante que j'avais connue, je comprenais pourquoi ça plaisait à certaines personnes. Quoi qu'il en soit, après cette séance, j'étais mouillée et prête pour lui, et il le savait. Après avoir plongé en moi avec sa langue, il me pencha et se glissa en moi, me prenant par-derrière.

C'était un nouvel angle, et il me plaisait beaucoup. Je me surpris à crier à chaque coup de reins, son membre s'enfonçant profondément en moi, atteignant des zones qui me donnaient envie de hurler. Alors qu'il me baisait cette fois-ci, il ne se retint pas, pas comme la première fois. Je lui dis que je voulais qu'il y aille plus franchement, et il m'écouta, s'agrippant à mes hanches et plongeant en moi à une vitesse telle que je dus m'accrocher au banc de toutes mes forces pour que nous ne basculions pas par-dessus.

Pendant l'orgasme, il resta en moi et me serra contre son corps, passant les bras devant moi pour me caresser les seins et le clitoris.

Je commençais à croire que je pourrais m'habituer à tout ça.

Mais le lendemain, quelque chose changea. Il me dit que les choses allaient être un peu différentes, qu'il allait m'attacher, me bâillonner et me laisser seule un moment. Cette idée m'effrayait, et je n'étais pas sûre d'en avoir envie.

Il noua la corde avec précision, m'attachant comme j'avais vu les fermiers le faire avec le bétail. Je ne trouvais rien de tout ça érotique, et la seule chose à laquelle je pouvais penser, c'était que j'avais envie qu'il arrête. Je le lui aurais dit, si je n'étais pas déjà bâillonnée.

Je respirai, concentrée sur les sensations dont je faisais l'expérience. Je ne détestais pas, c'était simplement quelque chose de nouveau. Jake essayait de nouvelles choses pour voir comment je réagissais et si ça lui plaisait. Même s'il essayait de faire de moi sa soumise, il voulait également découvrir ce qui m'excitait. C'était comme s'il ne pouvait pas croire que quelque chose d'aussi simple que son sexe en moi pouvait suffire à me faire perdre la tête, mais j'étais partante pour en apprendre plus et apprendre à aimer ces jeux.

Au bout de trois semaines, il me passa un collier autour du cou.

— Tu m'appartiens, désormais. Tu comprends ce que ça signifie ? me demanda-t-il.

— Ça signifie que je me soumets complètement à toit. Je te fais confiance pour que tu prennes soin de moi et que tu me donnes du plaisir.

— Et tant que tu porteras ce collier, sauf si je t'en donne la permission, je serai la seule personne autorisée à te toucher. La seule personne autorisée à te faire jouir. Tu n'as pas le droit de te donner des orgasmes toute seule, sauf si je t'en donne la permission, c'est compris ?

— Oui, dis-je en hochant la tête.

Il me passa le collier autour du cou. C'était un peu trop pour moi. Je n'étais toujours pas certaine de ce que je pensais de tout ça. Porter un collier ne me plaisait pas, même si j'aimais presque tout ce que Jake me faisait. Je n'étais pas sûre de vraiment être une soumise. Mais je jouais mon rôle, et ça semblait plaire à Jake.

Tous mes rêves d'âtre aux commandes s'étaient éloignés. Alors que je le regardais et que je voyais ce qu'il aimait me faire, et même si je ne pensais pas être aussi extrême que lui, je commençais à réaliser que j'étais très dominatrice. Je ne savais pas si je pourrais en faire un mode de vie et être aussi dévouée que Jake, mais peut-être que je pourrais faire un essai, une autre fois, avec quelqu'un d'autre.

Les semaines passèrent plus vite, après cela. J'ignorais si c'était parce que nous avions trouvé une routine, ou parce que nous nous étions habitués l'un à l'autre. Quoi qu'il en soit, je continuai d'apprendre la vie de soumise, et je commençais à l'apprécier, d'une certaine façon. J'aimais le fait que cela m'ouvre à Jake comme jamais je ne l'avais été auparavant. Cela me permettait de lui accorder une confiance aveugle. Il y avait de la liberté et de la sécurité dans le fait de me lâcher et de m'en remettre totalement à lui. Ne plus avoir aucun pouvoir avait quelque chose de presque apaisant. Pour quelqu'un comme moi, qui m'étais battue toute sa vie pour être indépendante, prendre soin de moi et découvrir ce dont j'avais besoin par moi-même, cette expérience avec Jake m'avait ouvert les yeux.

Mais tout de même, après tout le temps qui s'était écoulé, je ne savais toujours pas ce qu'il y avait gagné.

— Il a pris ta virginité, déjà, dis-je à mon reflet du miroir le matin de mon départ.

Ce matin-là, nous couchâmes ensemble une dernière fois. C'était différent de d'habitude. C'était moi qui étais aux commandes. Il ne résista pas, et il sembla apprécier le fait qu'après toute cette soumission, j'avais toujours assez envie de lui pour lui sauter dessus à la moindre occasion.

Je léchai son sexe de la base jusqu'au gland, le titillant avec ma langue durant plusieurs minutes avant de me glisser sur lui. Je me balançai d'avant en arrière, portant sa main à mon clitoris et le laissant me caresser alors que je le baisais lentement, sans jamais le quitter des yeux.

Je ne savais pas ce que j'y voyais. Ils étaient d'un vert

lumineux, et je m'étais mise à aimer les voir tous les jours. Ils contrastaient tellement avec sa peau et ses cheveux noirs, qu'il portait toujours en courte queue de cheval.

J'ondulai sur ses hanches, de plus en plus fort, jusqu'à ce que je le sente se tortiller sous mon corps. Il caressa mon clitoris et me mena vers l'orgasme tandis que les parois de mon vagin l'aspiraient jusqu'à la dernière goutte.

— Ça va me manquer, dit-il alors que je me laissais tomber contre son torse et que je restais allongée là.

Je n'aurais voulu me trouver nulle part ailleurs, mais je n'osais pas le dire. Rien de ce que disait Jake n'avait jamais suggéré qu'il avait des sentiments pour moi, et je ne voulais pas être la première à dire une chose aussi importante.

Je descendis au rez-de-chaussée, tout habillée après avoir fait mon sac et pris ma douche. Ce simple fait était étrange. Chez Jake, j'avais passé la majorité de mon temps nue. Porter des vêtements était presque inconfortable, mais c'était un peu plus chaud.

Jake était au rez-de-chaussée, le petit-déjeuner prêt dans la cuisine. Nous mangeâmes ensemble en silence. Je ne savais pas du tout quoi dire. Il s'était passé beaucoup de choses pendant le temps que j'avais passé chez lui, mais je ne savais pas encore vraiment quoi en penser. J'avais besoin de passer un moment seule pour y réfléchir et me remettre de cette drôle d'exaltation.

Jake porta mes sacs jusqu'au salon et resta debout là avec moi pendant que nous attendions le chauffeur.

— J'espère que tu as passé un bon moment ici, dit-il.

Je hochai la tête.

— Oui, merci.

Il semblait presque nerveux, ce qui n'était pas habituel chez Jake Mesa.

— J'aurais voulu que nous ayons un peu plus de temps pour faire des choses... Enfin, j'avais prévu de t'emmener à

Las Vegas pour que tu voies le club de là-bas. Tu ne l'avais peut-être pas deviné, mais je suis un vrai fêtard.

Il me fit un clin d'œil et me sourit.

— Ça ne m'étonne pas, dis-je.

— Je voulais te montrer tant d'autres choses, mais je pensais que tu apprendrais plus en restant ici, au même endroit, en voyant en quoi consiste ce mode de vie.

J'avais du mal à savoir quoi lui dire en cet instant. Merci d'avoir pris ma virginité ? J'espère ne pas t'avoir déçu ? Je savais très bien que je ne l'avais pas déçu, mais je n'étais pas sûre de ce que j'avais accompli au cours des deux derniers mois... si j'avais accompli quoi que ce soit.

— Tu voudrais qu'on se revoie, pour boire un café, ou un truc comme ça ? demanda-t-il.

— Pour boire un café ?

— Ou... tout ce que tu voudras.

J'étais perplexe. J'avais passé ces deux derniers mois complètement nue avec cet homme, et voilà qu'il me demandait si je voulais boire un café un de ces quatre, comme si nous venions de nous rencontrer dans la rue et que nous nous connaissions à peine.

Je haussai les épaules.

— Pourquoi pas, si tu passes dans le quartier, ou quelque chose comme ça.

— Où est ton quartier ?

Je sortis l'une des cartes de visite du garage de mon sac à main, et je la lui tendis.

— Je suis plus souvent là-bas que chez moi, alors c'est plus pratique. Ou peut-être que je te verrai quand je viendrai chercher Samantha au travail.

Il hocha la tête.

— Oui, peut-être.

Je poussai un soupir et secouai la tête. Cette discussion était l'une des plus bizarres que j'aie jamais eues.

— Merci encore pour ce que tu as fait pour mon père. Tu ne peux pas savoir à quel point c'est important pour moi, que tu aies proposé de m'aider. Sans toi et ton argent, quelque chose de terrible aurait pu lui arriver. Et je te suis reconnaissante pour ta gentillesse.

Jake me prit la main, et cela me fit sursauter, mais il m'attira contre lui, et ça, ça n'avait rien d'étrange. En fat, c'était le moment le plus naturel de toute cette conversation.

— Je veux que tu saches que si tu as besoin de quelque chose, n'importe quoi, tu peux me le demander. Je serai toujours disponible, pour quelque raison que ce soit. Quelque chose d'important, de pas important... je ne sais pas - peut-être si tu veux qu'on passe la nuit ensemble un jour. Je ne suis qu'à un coup de fil.

Cela me fit rire. Il savait toujours comment me détendre.

— Merci, Jake. Et c'est pareil pour moi, même si...

Je repensai à toutes les filles qu'il y avait au club, toutes ces femmes sublimes auxquelles il avait accès. Je doutais que Jake m'appelle un jour pour que nous passions la nuit ensemble.

— Non, rien, ajoutai-je.

Je regardai par la fenêtre juste à temps pour voir la voiture se garer et le chauffeur en sortir pur venir chercher mes sacs. Je me mis sur la pointe des pieds pour embrasser Jake sur la joue, mais il tourna la tête et posa ses lèvres contre les miennes.

— Contente de t'avoir connue, Jake.

Je me dégageai et sortis de la maison sans me retourner.

CHAPITRE 10

Mon premier jour chez moi fut solitaire. Samantha travaillait toute la journée, et j'étais seule. J'aurais pu aller travailler au garage, mais je n'en avais pas envie. Mon père n'avait pas besoin de moi, de toute façon, et il avait réembauché Rodrigo pour l'assister. Ils pourraient se passer de moi une journée de plus.

J'allai dans ma chambre et je commençai à déballer mes affaires. Seuls quelques objets étaient nouveaux. Jake m'avait dit de garder le collier, même si je savais que je ne m'en servirais pas. C'était une chose qui ne nous concernait que tous les deux. Je ne pouvais pas m'imaginer dans une relation avec un autre homme qui voudrait que je porte un collier.

Je m'interrompis brusquement. Une relation ? Qu'est-ce que je racontais ? Ce qu'il y avait entre Jake et moi n'avait rien à voir avec une relation. C'était un arrangement, sur lequel deux adultes consentants s'étaient mis d'accord. Nous n'étions pas ensemble, et en principe, nous ne le serions jamais. Si Jake avait dû me révéler ses sentiments, il l'aurait déjà fait.

Il était clair que ce n'était pas ce qu'il voulait, quoi que je ressente à propos du temps que nous avions passé ensemble. J'ignorais pourquoi un homme de son âge n'était pas prêt pour une relation. Mais pourquoi pensais-je à cela ? Ce n'était pas ce que je voulais avec lui, si ?

— Taylor Dawson, il faut que tu découvres quels sont tes propres sentiments, avant de te soucier de ceux de quelqu'un d'autre, dis-je tout fort en me regardant dans le miroir de la salle de bains. J'avais la même apparence qu'avant mon départ, mais je me sentais très différente. Que m'était-il arrivé là-bas ? Je me sentais un peu plus ouverte et libre, libérée, en quelque sorte. Mais à la fois, je me sentais vulnérable - comme si j'attendais que quelque chose me tombe dessus. C'était un sentiment qui m'était inconnu, et quelque chose que j'avais du mal à associer à la personne que j'étais avant mon marché avec Jake.

Il valait peut-être mieux que je sorte de chez moi. Retourner travailler me ferait du bien, mais ma voiture était au garage, alors il faudrait que je parcoure les cinq kilomètres qui m'en séparaient à pied. Tant mieux. J'aimais bien marcher, et un peu d'exercice ne me ferait pas de mal. Mon corps s'était habitué à brûler un certain nombre de calories par jour, et il fallait que je garde le rythme.

Le trajet fut lent, mais agréable, et je tentai de m'imprégner de la beauté du chemin qui menait au garage. C'était une jolie rue qui conduisait jusqu'à l'endroit où j'avais vécu, avec beaucoup d'arbres et de vieilles maisons. Mon père avait choisi un très bon emplacement pour ouvrir son entreprise, et j'espérais pouvoir continuer d'y travailler et la garder en vie pendant les années à venir.

Lorsque j'arrivai au garage, je fus surprise d'y trouver la voiture de Jake. Il y était adossé et regardait au loin.

— Qu'est-ce que tu fais ici ? lançai-je, le faisant sursauter.

Il se tourna vers moi et m'adressa un sourire.

— Je me sentais un peu seul chez moi, dit-il en haussant les épaules.

Je hochai la tête.

— Oui, moi aussi. Samantha travailla aujourd'hui, et je comptais prendre ma journée, mais je me suis dit que je ferais mieux de me replonger dans le travail tout de site.

Je lui jetai un regard suspicieux, et ajoutai :

— Mais attends, tu es vraiment venu parce que tu te sentais seul ?

— Oui, je me sentais seul, mais ce n'est pas tout à fait pour ça que je suis là.

Je sentis une gouttelette de pluie me tomber sur le nez, et je levai les yeux vers le ciel. Une averse approchait, et nous allions nous retrouver juste en dessous.

— Je voulais te donner quelque chose avant ton départ... Enfin, je ne savais pas quel serait le bon moment pour te le donner, mais c'est quelque chose que j'avais vraiment envie de t'offrir. Sincèrement, du fond du cœur. C'est à toi.

Il me tendit une enveloppe, et je l'ouvris pour y trouver un chèque.

— Non, c'est une erreur, dis-je en sortant le chèque de l'enveloppe.

La pluie se mit à tomber pour de bon, doucement d'abord, puis plus fort.

— Non, ce n'est pas une erreur. Promis. Je veux que tu l'encaisses et que tu fasses quelque chose qui te rendra heureuse avec.

— Attends, c'est pour quoi ? demandai-je, sans être sûre de ce que je regardais exactement. Mon cerveau arrivait à comprendre de quoi il s'agissait - un chèque de cent mille dollars -, mais je ne comprenais pas pourquoi il me donnait un deuxième chèque. Il avait déjà payé pour l'erreur de mon père, tout comme moi. Je lui avais donné deux mois de ma vie, et je les avais passés avec cet homme. J'ignorais toujours ce que Jake avait tiré de cette expérience, à part me faire me soumettre à lui et en tirer du plaisir.

— C'est pour toi, dit-il. Je ne t'ai rien dit parce que je ne voulais pas que tu te sentes obligée de rester plus longtemps, ou que tu t'imagines que j'essayais d'acheter ton affection, mais j'avais prévu de te donner cet argent depuis le début. Écoute, je ne t'en ai pas parlé parce que je savais que c'était un sujet sensible pour toi, vu ce que toi et ton père étiez en train de traverser à ce moment-là, mais tu vois... ma famille est riche. Très riche. J'ai toujours pu m'offrir tout ce que je voulais. J'ai plus d'argent que je ne pourrais utiliser. Même en en donnant tous les jours, j'en aurais quand même trop. Je ne dis pas que ce n'est rien pour mi, je dis qu'il est important à mes yeux qu'il te revienne. Parc que je veux que tu aies les choses que tu désires et dont tu as besoin. Je veux que tu aies le genre de vie que tu mérites, mais que tu n'as peut-être pas encore les moyens de t'offrir.

Je secouai la tête.

— Je ne sais vraiment pas quoi te dire, Jake. C'est beaucoup trop généreux. Enfin... Est-ce que c'est pour le temps que j'ai passé avec toi ?

Jake secoua la tête, et de la pluie tomba de ses cheveux noirs, qui lui tombaient jusqu'aux épaules.

— Ce n'est pas que tu l'as gagnée, Tay. Tu le mérites, tout simplement. Je veux que tu l'acceptes et que tu t'en serves pour faire quelque chose d'exceptionnel. Tout ce que tu voudras - aller à la fac, développer l'entreprise familiale. Tout ce que tu veux - quel que soit ton rêve, je veux que tu le réalises. Je sais que l'idée de te soumettre à moi ne t'enchantait pas, mais le fait que tu l'aies fait - que tu aies mis tes émotions de côté et que tu aies fait un saut dans l'inconnu en me laissant te guider. Ça, Tay... c'est ça qui est tellement sexy chez toi.

Je ravalai des larmes. Nous nous tenions sous la pluie

comme dans une comédie romantique ridicule, sauf qu'il n'y avait rien de comique dans tout ça. Il se tenait face à moi en essayant de me dire ce qu'il ressentait, et je ne savais toujours pas ce que je ressentais pour lui, si ? Toutes ces émotions lorsque j'avais quitté sa maison, alors qu'il m'avait renvoyée sans à peine un au revoir... j'avais eu l'impression d'avoir le cœur brisé, mais pourquoi ?

— Tay, je n'essaye pas de te dire ce que tu dois ressentir, dit Jake en parlant plus fort pour que je l'entende malgré la pluie battante. Mais je crois que tu n'es peut-être pas aussi en phase avec ton cœur que tu le penses. Je ne sais pas ce qui est le mieux pour toi. Mais je peux te dire ce qui est le mieux pour moi, et c'est toi.

— Moi ? lançai-je à travers la pluie avant d'attraper Jake et de le traîner dans le garage. Je sais qu'on est trempés comme des soupes, mais a moins ici, la pluie ne nous martèle pas le visage.

— Je te veux ! s'exclama Jake. C'est ça que j'ai appris pendant ces deux mois. Que je veux quelqu'un qui soit capable de prendre des risques avec moi, quelqu'un qui soit prêt à me faire confiance pour que je prenne des décisions. Je ne le savais pas, Tay. Pas avant toi. Tu m'as révélé tellement de choses sur qui je suis. Tu m'as montré ce que je voulais à un moment où je l'ignorais complètement.

— Mais tu as cette vie de dingue avec le club, et je ne sais pas quelle serait ma place dans tout ça. Est-ce que c'est une chose à laquelle tu es prêt à renoncer ? Parce que je ne veux pas me lancer dans quelque chose, tout ça pour découvrir que tu as changé d'avis. Je suis jeune, et j'ai toute la vie devant moi, alors je ne veux pas m'engager dans quelque chose qui pourrait s'envoler en un instant.

Jake m'attrapa et m'attira vers lui.

— Écoute. Tout ça pourrait s'envoler en un instant. Tu le sais aussi bien que moi. Regarde comment les choses ont tourné pour ton père. Ça aurait pu se passer d'une manière totalement différente, mais finalement non. Je ne veux pas que tu continues à vivre dans la peur, à attendre le prochain coup du sort. Je cherchais la bonne personne avec qui me poser, mais pas à me poser tout court. Ce que je veux, c'est quelqu'un avec qui m'envoler - quelqu'un avec de grands rêves, et qui ne renonce pas. Je veux être avec quelqu'un qui sait qu'elle est le capitaine de son propre destin.

Je ris en pleurant des larmes de joie, quelque chose qui ne m'était encore jamais arrivé.

— Je pleure, Jake. Je pleure parce que je suis heureuse. Qu'est-ce que c'est que tout ça ?

— Je ne sais pas. C'est nouveau pour toi ?

Je hochai la tête et l'enlaçai.

— Je ne savais pas quoi penser en partant de chez toi ce matin. Je croyais que tu ne voulais pas de moi, ou que les moments qu'on avait passés ensemble ne représentaient rien à tes yeux, ou...

Il recula pour me regarder dans les yeux. Les siens étaient d'un vert brillant que j'avais appris à aimer durant ces deux mois, les yeux verts qui m'avaient accueillie chaque matin lorsque je me réveillais sans bandeau sur le visage.

— les moments qu'on a passés ensemble sont tout pour moi, dit-il. Je ne voulais pas que ça prenne fin. Je ne te demande pas de me promettre quoi que ce soit pour l'instant, mais j'aimerais qu'on avance ensemble dans la vie. C'est quelque chose qui t'intéresserait ?

Je hochai la tête d'un air décidé.

— Et encore une chose.

— Quoi ?

— Je t'aime, Jake Mesa, dis-je en l'embrassant sur la bouche.

Six mois plus tard, nous ajoutions une extension au

garage. Nous avions une nouvelle pancarte, une nouvelle couche de peinture, et assez de nouveaux clients pour engager six nouveaux employés. Mon père était ravi, et avait rebondi comme si de rien n'était après sa période sombre de quelques mois. Il avait appris de ses erreurs, comme nous tous, et nous en étions tous sortis plus forts.

Jake était toujours propriétaire du Club V, et il le resterait, travaillant tout autant que ses copropriétaires. Je m'y arrêtais toujours de temps en temps, moins souvent pour chercher Samantha au travail, et plus souvent en tant que fiancée de l'un des propriétaires. Cela m'apportait tout un tas de privilèges, et je comprenais pourquoi Jake aimait tant cette vie-là. Ce n'était pas ce que j'avais imaginé pour moi, mais j'apprenais à adorer ça.

— Qu'est-ce que tu penses de tout ça ? me demanda Jake en se plaçant derrière moi et en me glissant un bras autour de la taille pour me serrer contre lui.

Je levai les yeux vers le garage et tous les changements qui se produisaient autour de moi.

— Tu sais, je crois que je commence à m'habituer à ne pas être aux commandes.

— Ça, c'est sûr, dit-il en me calant contre son pelvis avant de se frotter à moi.

Je sentis son érection grandir dans son jean, et cela me donna douloureusement envie. Je n'étais jamais rassasiée de lui, et le fait que cela soit réciproque me comblait de bonheur.

— Tu sais, dis-je alors qu'il commençait à m'embrasser la base de la nuque, me faisant rire. Même si j'adorerais que tu me baises devant tous ces nouveaux mécaniciens que mon père a embauchés, je me disais qu'on pourrait peut-être essayer un autre endroit.

Jake recula et me regarda.

— Ah bon ? Montre-moi.

Je souris et le pris par la main pour le guider vers l'appartement au-dessus du garage.

— Je sais qu'on n'a pas fait beaucoup de jeux de rôle, mais je crois que je dois toujours avoir mon uniforme scolaire dans mon placard. Ça te dirait que je le mette et qu'on le fasse dans mon ancienne chambre ?

Je vis le désir grandir dans ses yeux, et il me souleva pour me porter dans ma chambre, avant de refermer la porte d'un coup de pied.

— On pourra sortir l'uniforme plus tard, dit-il en me jetant sur le lit. Pour l'instant, j'ai des choses à faire.

Dix minutes plus tard, nous étions allongés sur mon lit, étalés sur les couvertures, en sueur et rassasiés... pour l'instant.

— T'es contente d'être tombée sur mon bureau par erreur, ce soir-là ?

Je hochai la tête et lui adressai un sourire ensommeillé.

— Même si j'ai dû te regarder baiser une autre fille. Enfin non, justement parce que j'ai dû te regarder baiser une autre fille. Je voulais savoir dans quoi je m'engageais.

Jake poussa un grognement rauque, et dit :

— Je vais te montrer.

CHAPITRE 11

Kayla

Le moment était venu de rendre visite à Daniel, mon beau-père. Il m'envoyait des messages depuis deux semaines, à présent, en me disant qu'il voulait me donner des nouvelles de ma mère. J'avais remis ma visite à plus tard en disant que je devais poser des congés à Greens, l'agence immobilière pour laquelle je travaillais. Il savait forcément que je me foutais de lui, il n'avait jamais été stupide. Alors que je jetais des vêtements dans ma valise, Haley, ma colocataire, se plaça dans l'encadrement de la porte.

— Tu vas me manquer, Kay. Ça va être tellement bizarre, d'être toute seule dans l'appartement.

— Hé, ce n'est que pour deux semaines, Haley. Tu pourras passer tout ton temps à te masturber, comme je ne serai pas là pour entendre tous les bruits. Tu pourras crier à pleins poumons.

Elle leva les yeux au ciel. Haley était habituée à mon caractère, vu que nous vivions ensemble depuis un bon moment, désormais. Jusqu'à il y a un an, nous avions été trois, mais notre autre amie, Tiff, vivait désormais dans l'appartement voisin avec son mari, Brandon. J'avais repris sa part de l'appartement, ce qui signifiait que j'avais deux grandes chambres et ma propre salle de bains. Nous voyions toujours Tiff tous les lundis pendant notre soirée filles, lors de laquelle nous mangions de bons petits plats en regardant un film et en bavardant.

Mais je ne leur avais jamais beaucoup parlé de mon beau-père. Ni de ma mère. Elles savaient qu'elle avait fait défiler les beaux-pères alors qu'elle courait après leur argent. Ma mère ne pouvait pas vivre sans argent, et j'avais été un malencontreux accident. Sa relation - si l'on pouvait l'appeler ainsi - avec mon père avait été le catalyseur de tous les drames qui avaient suivi. Il l'avait laissée sans le sou et elle avait juré que cela ne se reproduirait plus.

De tous mes beaux-pères, Daniel, que j'avais rencontré lorsque j'avais dix-sept ans, avait été le seul à être correct. Le seul qui réalisait que j'existais, que je n'étais pas seulement un fardeau. Il m'avait dit que j'aurais toujours une place chez lui, et même après que ma mère avait dilapidé tout son argent et s'était enfuie avec Chuck, le beau-père suivant, il m'avait quand même rappelé que je pouvais venir quand je le souhaitais. Je n'avais jamais vraiment compris la relation de ma mère avec Daniel. Ils n'avaient jamais semblé être accros l'un à l'autre comme elle l'avait été avec d'autres. Ses marques d'affection avec certains d'entre eux m'avaient filé la nausée. La plupart du temps, j'avais gardé la tête baissée et j'avais fait de mon mieux à l'école, en dépit du fait que je n'étais jamais restée dans la même école très longtemps avant que ma mère nous fasse déménager à nouveau. Quand j'avais eu dix-huit ans, elle avait déménagé une fois de plus, et cette fois, elle avait dit qu'elle en avait assez de m'élever, et que je devais me débrouiller toute seule.

Cela ne m'avait pas choquée autant que ça aurait dû. Comme je l'ai dit, elle avait été absente durant la majorité de ma vie, de toute façon. J'avais obtenu mon diplôme, et j'avais commencé à travailler chez Greens, où je m'étais fait de très bonnes amies, et je n'avais plus jamais regardé en arrière. J'avais eu quelques petits amis, mais rien de très sérieux. Mes copines étaient habituées à mon ton cru lorsque je parlais des hommes, mais pour être honnête, je parlais beaucoup, mais je n'agissais pas tant que ça, si vous voyez ce que je veux dire. Je n'avais pas beaucoup d'expérience, bien que je ne sois pas vierge. J'étais un peu jalouse de mon amie Tiff. Elle était en ménage depuis un an. Elle avait toujours l'air d'être en train de se faire pénétrer. J'aurai juré qu'elle avait un sourire narquois permanent. Jalouse, moi ? Carrément !

Enfin bref, je ne pouvais pas repousser ma visite chez Daniel plus longtemps, car il m'avait dit que ma mère s'était remise à faire des siennes, et qu'il devait me mettre au courant. J'espérais qu'elle n'essayait pas de s'en prendre de nouveau à son argent, car il avait récemment refait fortune, après qu'une galerie prestigieuse avait acquis ses œuvres d'art. Lorsque je l'avais rencontré pour la première fois, lorsque ma mère et lui s'étaient mis ensemble, il était propriétaire d'une chaîne de salons de tatouage. Il peignait secrètement des toiles, se servant de son talent pour le dessin, avant d'enfin avoir le courage de les montrer à quelqu'un. Ces personnes avaient adoré ses toiles et en avaient pris quelques photos pour les montrer dans une galerie, où elles avaient été achetées par un collectionneur le jour même. Il avait désormais une nouvelle profession, ce qui était une très bonne chose, car ma mère avait presque causé la faillite de son entreprise de tatouage.

Je n'avais pas vécu longtemps chez Daniel. La mère d'une amie m'avait pratiquement laissé emménager chez elle, car elle connaissait mon passé avec ma propre mère. Non, je n'avais pas vécu longtemps chez Daniel pour une très bonne raison.

J'avais toujours craqué sur mon beau-père. Je n'aurais jamais pu vivre avec lui et ma mère. S'ils s'étaient embrassés devant moi, j'aurais eu envie de donner un coup de poing dans le mur. Je savais que c'était stupide. Avoir un coup de cœur pour quelqu'un, ça arrivait sans arrêt. Mais Daniel, c'était autre chose. Il avait dix ans de moins que ma mère, et la première fois que je l'avais rencontré, il avait vingt-huit ans - onze ans de plus que moi. Il avait des cheveux noirs ébouriffés, à l'époque, et des yeux très foncés. Lorsqu'il souriait, il était sexy et attendrissant à la fois. Son visage se fendait de tout un tas de rides. Lorsqu'il souriait, ses joues étaient rebondies. J'avais toujours eu envie de les toucher. J'étais certaine qu'à chaque fois que je lui parlais, le rouge me montait aux joues. Je crois que c'est à ce moment-là que j'avais commencé à me la raconter, parce que je n'avais pas envie de sembler toute jeune et innocente devant lui. J'avais toujours eu l'impression qu'il essayait de me sauver, vous voyez ? Toujours à me dire que chez lui, c'était aussi chez moi, même après que ma mère l'avait presque ruiné. Il avait eu ce regard dans les yeux, comme s'il n'avait pas envie que je coupe les ponts, et même si j'avais essayé de couper tous contacts avec lui durant les années qui avaient suivi, il n'avait jamais baissé les bras. Il continuait de m'envoyer des messages, de m'appeler, de m'envoyer des cartes d'anniversaire et de Noël et des chèques que je n'encaissais jamais. Lorsque je lui rendais visite, c'était en coup de vent, alors que je me rendais ailleurs et que je ne pouvais pas rester longtemps. Être trop proche de lui me tuait. Mais à présent, il fallait que j'aille le voir, et il m'avait dit qu'il allait falloir que je reste un moment - au moins quelques jours, alors d'une manière ou d'une autre, il allait falloir que je dépasse l'attirance que j'avais pour lui. J'avais vingt-quatre ans, à présent.

Ça faisait six ans que ma mère était passée à sa victime suivante. Je n'avais plus jamais entendu parler d'elle ensuite, et pourtant, elle trouvait toujours le moyen de faire quelque chose pour nous affecter, Daniel et moi.

Je remontai la fermeture éclair de ma valise et je me tournai vers la porte d'entrée. J'étais tellement perdue dans les pensées que Haley était partie. J'étais sortie pour passer un peu de temps avec elle avant de me rendre chez Daniel. C'était ma meilleure amie, et elle allait me manquer pendant mon absence.

Le trajet jusqu'à Port Jeff prit moins de deux heures, ce qui rendait mon manque de visites encore plus inexcusable. Je me rangeai dans la grande allée qui menait à la bâtisse coloniale de Daniel. Il avait tellement de chance de ne pas avoir perdu cette propriété incroyable. Sa maison de quatre chambres et de quatre salles de bains située à Harbor Hills donnait sur la côte, et elle possédait une plage privée. Je sortis de ma voiture, la laissant devant le double garage, et je me rendis devant la porte d'entrée, où j'appuyai sur la sonnette. Au bout de quelques minutes, la porte s'ouvrit sur Daniel.

Il était aussi canon que d'habitude, et je sentis mes joues s'empourprer à nouveau. Pourquoi étais-je si sensible en sa présence ? Son visage se fendit de son fameux sourire, et il s'avança pour me prendre dans ses bras. La chaleur de son corps m'enveloppa. Je n'avais pas envie de bouger, mais il tendit ses longs bras et me regarda de la tête aux pieds.

— Salut, Kayla. Je suis content de te voir. Tu as l'air en forme.

Je lui adressai un demi-sourire, mal à l'aise.

— Mince, ne fais pas attention à mes mauvaises manières, à te laisser comme ça sur le porche. Entre donc. Tu as besoin d'aide avec tes bagages ?

— Oui, je veux bien. Il y a une valise dans le coffre.

— Je vais la chercher, et ensuite, je garerai ta voiture dans le garage. On va mettre tes bagages dans ta chambre, et puis on boira quelque chose, d'accord ?

— D'accord, répondis-je.

Je restai dans l'entrée en l'attendant, admirant la pièce spacieuse. Chaque fois que je venais ici, sa maison me coupait le souffle. Daniel n'avait pas décoré les lieux, et l'agente immobilière en moi voyait le potentiel que sa propriété pouvait encore révéler. L'entrée possédait un grand escalier qui menait à un palier à partir duquel toutes les pièces se succédaient. Il était un peu trop vieillot à mon goût, avec ses moulures en bois. Il fallait vraiment tout remettre au goût du jour. Si c'était chez moi, ce serait fabuleux.

— Bon, allons mettre tes affaires dans ta chambre.

Daniel avait réapparu avec ma valise. Je récupérai mon fourre-tout sur le sol et je le suivis dans les escaliers.

Mauvaise idée. Il portait un jean qui lui moulait les fesses alors qu'il montait les marches. J'avais envie de tendre les bras et de les toucher, pour voir si elles étaient aussi juteuses qu'elles en avaient l'air. Ses biceps étaient gonflés alors qu'il portait ma valise. Je sentis mon entrejambe devenir mouillé. Nom de Dieu, il ne faisait que marcher !

Nous longeâmes le couloir jusqu'à mon ancienne chambre. Il ouvrit la porte. La pièce était exactement comme je l'avais laissée, ou plutôt, comme ma mère l'avait décorée. Il y avait du bleu océan partout. Avec les rideaux et les draps à froufrous, ça me piquait les yeux. Daniel aperçut ma grimace.

— On devrait peut-être la redécorer pendant ton séjour ? La rendre plus à ton goût ?

— Peut-être. Mais je ne compte pas rester trop longtemps, tu sais. J'ai ma vie à Brooklyn, et il faut que j'y retourne le plus vite possible.

Daniel hocha la tête. Il semblait légèrement déçu, et je me sentis coupable.

— Mais bon, un peu de changement ne ferait pas de mal, vu cette affreuse teinte de peinture.

— Super, dit-il avec un nouveau sourire. Ce serait bien de moderniser un peu la maison. Il faut que je profite d'avoir une agente immobilière super bonne chez moi.

À ces mots, mon visage se mit à me brûler tellement fort qu'il m'aurait un extincteur.

Daniel passa une main dans ses cheveux ébouriffés.

— Bon sang, Kayla, je voulais dire bonne dans le sens, bonne dans ton travail. Seigneur, je suis un idiot.

— Ce n'est pas grave, dis-je en agitant une main devant mon visage. Je savais ce que tu voulais dire, et c'est vrai que je suis bonne dans mon travail.

Il fallait que je retrouve la Kayla avec du répondant le plus vite possible. J'étais comme ça. J'avais confiance en moi, et je disais ce que je pensais.

— J'ai assez vu cette chambre pour l'instant, déclarai-je. Et si tu me préparais à boire, et qu'on s'asseyait sur la terrasse ?

— D'accord, dit Daniel.

Il fallait absolument qu'il sorte de ma chambre.

Nous redescendîmes les escaliers et prîmes un couloir, avant de tourner à droite et de traverser son gigantesque salon, avec ses fauteuils en cuir noir et son énorme télé, puis nous sortîmes dans le jardin de derrière. Le terrain faisait quatre mille mètres carrés, avec une piscine chauffée tout au fond et un petit chalet. J'avais passé beaucoup de temps dans ce chalet lorsque ma mère vivait ici et que je venais en visite. Ça avait été un endroit où m'échapper, avec ses canapés confortables et ses deux pièces séparées, l'une avec un grand lit, et l'autre une salle de bains. Je voyais que tout était ouvert. À gauche se trouvait le salon, avec son grand écran plat sur le mur. À droite se trouvait une cuisine avec tous les équipements dernier cri. C'était parfait pour les chaudes soirées d'été, pour se prélasser au bord de la piscine en faisant un barbecue. Nous n'avions jamais fait ça ici. Nous n'avions jamais suffisamment formé une famille pour manger ensemble, et encore moins pour nous détendre ensemble.

— Je sais qu'à l'époque, tu aimais bien rester là-bas, dit Daniel en montrant le chalet d'un signe de tête. Mais pour ce séjour ici, il vaut mieux que tu restes dans la maison.

Il s'excusa et alla préparer du café pendant que je m'asseyais sur la balancelle située sur la terrasse. Elle comptait deux places, alors je ne serais pas obligé de m'asseoir trop près de Daniel. Il sortit avec deux tasses fumantes de café et les plaça sur une petite table à côté de la balancelle avant de s'asseoir à son tour.

— Alors, qu'est-ce qu'elle a fait, cette fois ? demandai-je.

J'allais droit au but. Inutile de tourner autour du pot avant de découvrir ce qu'avait encore fabriqué ma mère.

Daniel se tourna vers moi.

— Elle s'est mise avec un producteur de cinéma, cette fois. Ils se sont mariés il y a un mois.

C'était agréable, de voir que ma mère n'avait pas changé. Elle courait toujours après les hommes riches et excluait sa fille unique de sa vie. Non que j'aurais voulu assister à la cérémonie, mais quand même, ça aurait été sympa d'être tenue au courant du nouveau mariage de ma mère.

— Alors, quel impact ça a sur nous ? demandai-je. Ils comptent faire un film sur sa vie, et ils veulent qu'on joue dedans ?

Daniel poussa un soupir.

— Ah, rien d'aussi amusant, alors, dis-je.

— Son mari a un fils. Apparemment, il a toujours été un peu rebelle. Renvoyé de l'école. Ce genre de choses. Sa mère est morte quand il avait huit ans. Son père excusait son comportement, jusqu'à sa rencontre avec ta mère.

— Pas étonnant.

— Il a jeté son fils dehors il y a un peu plus de deux semaines. Parker - c'est comme ça qu'il s'appelle - a fouillé dans les affaires de ta mère et a trouvé mon adresse, alors il est venu ici pour te trouver. Il pense que tu pourrais raisonner ta mère. J'ai tenté de lui expliquer la situation, mais il ne voulait rien entendre. Je lui ai dit que je t'inviterais ici et qu'on pourrait parler tous ensemble. Voir si on peut faire quelque chose. Je lui ai dit qu'il fallait qu'il te laisse lui expliquer la relation que tu avais avec ta mère et que tu n'avais pas non plus eu la vie facile.

— Alors, où est ce sale gamin, que je puisse mettre les pendules à l'heure ?

Ses lèvres se soulevèrent légèrement aux commissures, comme s'il savait quelque chose que j'ignorais, ce qui serait évidemment le cas, vu qu'il avait déjà rencontré ce fils qui avait été exclu de l'école.

— Je lui ai dit d'attendre dans sa chambre. Je vais le chercher.

— Attends ! Dans sa chambre ? Il vit ici ?

— Ouais. J'avais de la peine pour lui. Il n'a personne. Alors je lui ai dit qu'il pouvait rester ici en attendant de retomber sur ses pieds. Je crois qu'il a un peu besoin d'une figure paternelle ?

Je secouai la tête.

— Le refuge pour enfants Daniel Scott. Tu ne peux pas tous nous sauver, tu sais ? Parfois, certains parents sont irrécupérables.

— Oui, les miens étaient comme ça, alors j'imagine que ça me touche quand je vois ça ailleurs. Enfin bref, j'ai trente-cinq ans. Je suis trop jeune pour être ton père, ou le sien. Je sais que tu m'as toujours considéré comme ton beau-père, Kayla, mais ta mère et moi n'avons jamais été mariés, alors ce n'était pas vraiment le cas.

La porte claqua alors que Tom Hardy faisait son entrée.

Enfin, il ressemblait à Tom Hardy, avec ses cheveux bruns rasés de près, ses yeux de biche et sa moue boudeuse. À l'évidence, il s'agissait d'un des employés de Daniel. Il fallait qu'il apprenne les bonnes manières. Il se comportait comme s'il était chez lui.

— C'était tellement mignon, cette petite réunion de famille, que je me suis dit que j'allais me joindre à vous.

Il me tendit un bras musclé. Ce type était super bien foutu, il devait faire de la muscu. Il aurait sans doute pu me porter d'un seul bras.

Je me levai et lui pris la main, en jetant un coup d'œil à Daniel pour avoir une idée de qui était ce sosie de Tom Hardy.

— Je m'appelle Kayla, dis-je.

— Ohhh, tu es bien formelle, petite... Euh, comment est-ce que je devrais t'appeler ? Ta mère a épousé mon père, alors... demi-sœur ?

Je fis un pas en arrière.

— C'est quoi ce bordel ? dis-je en me tournant vers Daniel. C'est lui Parker ?

Je m'attendais à un garçon fraîchement exclu de l'école. Ce type n'était pas si jeune que ça.

— Oui. Parker, je te présente Kayla. Kayla, voici Parker.

Parker me prit la main et la serra. Un peu trop fermement. Je me sentis mal à l'aise alors que la première chose à laquelle j'avais pensé, c'était que l'employé de Daniel était sexy. Et voilà que je découvrais que c'était mon demi-frère.

— Je suis désolée, dis-je, troublée. Je m'attendais à quelqu'un d'un peu plus jeune.

— J'ai vingt et un ans, alors je ne suis pas si vieux que ça, répondit-il. Et toi ?

— Vingt-quatre ans.

— Bon, maintenant que les présentations sont faites, il faut que tu reviennes à Los Angeles avec moi pour convaincre ta salope de mère de laisser mon père tranquille, dit-il en ricanant.

Je poussai un soupir.

— Si seulement c'était aussi simple.

— Tu plaisantes ? C'est très simple. On rentre à la maison. Tu racontes à mon vieux son passé avec les mecs. Il la jette dehors. Mission accomplie.

— Ma mère ne m'a pas contactée depuis six ans, alors si tu crois que je vais m'approcher d'elle, tu te trompes.

— Eh bien, il faut que tu essayes. Je suis à court d'options, là. Elle le saigne aux quatre veines. C'est de mon héritage qu'on parle.

— Oh, contente de voir que c'est ton père qui te manque le plus, dis-je d'un ton sarcastique. J'en ai ma claque des gens obsédés par le fric comme toi.

— Tu ne dois pas être très fauchée, rétorqua-t-il. Dan dit que tu vis à New York.

— Je vis à Brooklyn. En collocation. Je travaille comme une dingue pour payer mon loyer. Ne joue pas les martyrs avec moi, parce que ça ne marchera pas. Tu veux avoir une belle vie ? Va travailler et mérite-la. Je ne t'aiderai pas avec tes histoires.

Je me tournai vers Daniel et dis :

— Merci pour le café. Je vais retourner dans ma chambre pour défaire ma valise. M'allonger un moment, peut-être. Je sens la migraine qui monte.

— D'accord Kayla.

Je voyais dans le regard de Daniel qu'il voulait en dire plus, mais qu'il ne pouvait pas.

— Moi je vais aller dans la piscine. J'ai un peu chaud, déclara Parker en quittant la terrasse.

— Je suis désolé, Kayla, dit Daniel, les coins des lèvres baissés, les épaules voûtées.

— Tu n'as pas à être désolé, lui rappelai-je. Je suis désolée que ta relation avec ma mère t'ait mêlée à ces problèmes.

— On devrait en parler, un jour, dit-il. De ma relation avec ta mère.

— Pas besoin.

— Je crois que si, Kayla, parce que je doute que ce soit ce que tu crois.

Je hochai la tête et regagnai la maison. Mon esprit était déjà embrumé par ma rencontre avec Parker, et le fait que l'on m'ait rappelé les frasques de ma mère. Je n'avais pas besoin que Daniel en rajoute avec des énigmes.

CHAPITRE 12

Daniel

Je ne savais pas du tout comment gérer la situation. Kayla était entrée dans ma vie quand elle avait dix-sept ans, prétendument en tant que belle-fille, mais je ne l'avais jamais vue comme ça. J'avais tout de suite remarqué que sa mère en voulait à mon argent, et je ne serais pas resté s'il n'y avait pas eu cette jeune fille, grande et mince avec de longs cheveux roux qui lui tombaient dans le dos. Elle était sublime, mais un peu déprimée. Je m'étais dit qu'elle avait besoin que l'on s'occupe d'elle, que l'on croie en elle. Alors j'avais continué de donner de l'argent à sa mère pour que Kayla puisse avoir un foyer. À la place, j'avais fini par garder un œil sur elle alors qu'elle décidait qu'elle préférait vivre chez la mère de son amie plutôt qu'ici. J'avais tenté de ne pas le prendre trop personnellement. La relation qu'elle entretenait avec sa mère était compliquée. Mais lorsque je la voyais, elle était toujours mal à l'aise en ma présence. J'avais beau essayer de lui montrer que je n'étais pas comme les autres beaux-pères qu'elle avait eus, elle gardait ses distances. Lorsqu'elle avait eu dix-huit ans, j'avais demandé à sa mère de partir. Elle l'avait fait, et Kayla avait cru que c'était sa mère qui m'avait quitté. Je n'avais aucune raison de garder le contact avec Kayla, mais je n'avais pas pu m'en empêcher.

Lorsque je lui avais ouvert la porte aujourd'hui, j'avais été époustouflé. Ses cheveux roux étaient ébouriffés, et la brise avait fait tomber quelques mèches sur son visage. J'avais envie de les replacer derrière son oreille. J'avais eu une érection lorsque mon regard avait parcouru sa robe vert clair, avec ses fines bretelles posées sur les épaules parsemées de taches de rousseur de Kayla. Le coton ample retombait sur sa silhouette toujours mince, et la lumière derrière elle avait rendu la robe légèrement transparente, de sorte que la forme de ses jambes et l'espace entre ses cuisses étaient apparents alors qu'elle se tenait debout dans l'entrée. Ma première pensée avait été de l'enlacer - elle était enfin là. Puis je m'étais rappelé que Kayla n'était pas très câlins, alors j'avais reculé. J'avais prétexté devoir récupérer ses bagages pour pouvoir placer la valise devant mon entrejambe. La dernière chose que je voulais, c'était la mettre mal à l'aise. Je savais qu'elle aurait déjà assez de choses à penser, car elle allait bientôt rencontrer Parker.

Puis je lui avais montré sa chambre, même si elle savait très bien où elle se trouvait. Cela faisait tellement longtemps qu'elle ne m'avait pas rendu visite qu'elle se comportait comme une étrangère. La pièce était affreuse, avec une peinture qui aurait plus eu sa place dans les années quatre-vingt-dix. J'adorais peindre, mais plutôt sur des toiles que sur des murs, malheureusement. Je lui avais tout de même suggéré de la redécorer. Une nouvelle fois, j'avais parlé parce qu'alors que je me tenais dans la chambre avec elle, je n'avais qu'une seule envie, la jeter sur le lit et soulever sa robe pour voir ses endroits les plus intimes.

Et j'avais dit qu'elle était une agente immobilière super bonne. J'avais eu la honte de ma vie.

Mais le pire, ça avait été lorsqu'elle et Parker avaient été présentés. Je savais que Parker était beau mec, et je ne voulais surtout pas qu'ils se plaisent, alors j'avais bien souligné le fait qu'il s'agissait de son demi-frère. Je me disais que même s'ils n'étaient pas du même sang, si elle le voyait comme un membre de sa famille, elle ne le verrait pas sous cet angle.

C'était également pour cette raison que j'avais recueilli Parker chez moi. C'était plutôt quelqu'un de bien, quoiqu'un peu égocentrique. Mais cela me donnait un prétexte pour inviter Kayla chez moi. Je ne voulais pas qu'elle coure à Los Angeles à la recherche de sa mère. Même si je savais bien qu'elle ne le ferait pour rien au monde. Mais ça avait beau être égoïste, je voulais qu'elle reste ici un moment avec moi. Comme ça, je pourrais la voir rire, écouter ses remarques impertinentes et, il fallait bien l'admettre, m'imaginer faire l'amour à son joli petit corps. Je l'avais toujours désirée, pendant sept longues années, et si ça ne tenait qu'à moi, elle ne me verrait plus du tout comme un beau-père lorsqu'elle rentrerait chez elle - si elle rentrait chez elle.

Parce que si les choses se passaient comme je le voulais, elle serait à moi et enceinte dans quelques semaines.

Je regardai Parker sortir de la piscine. Il attrapa une serviette et se sécha. Je lui avais donné du travail à la galerie que j'avais ouverte sur Chandler Square. Amusant, comme ma carrière avait changé. Lorsque Patty, la mère de Kayla, était entrée dans ma vie, j'étais à la tête d'une chaîne de salons de tatouage. L'on aurait pu penser que ce genre de commerce ne marcherait pas bien dans les quartiers chics de New York, mais au contraire. Toutes les riches femmes au foyer se battaient pour savoir qui avait le plus beau tatouage, et mes dessins étaient reconnus. Tous mes salons employaient les meilleurs artistes du milieu, et le résultat était garanti. Pourtant, après douze mois avec Patty, j'avais dû vendre mon entreprise pour ne pas être ruiné. J'avais failli perdre la maison, mais après le départ de Patty, alors que j'essayais de vendre certains de mes meubles, un collectionneur d'art avait repéré deux de mes toiles - je les avais peintes pour m'amuser -, et à ma grande surprise, il les avait montrées à un galeriste. Celui-ci m'avait contacté pour que je lui vende d'autres de mes œuvres. Bien vite, ce loisir s'était transformé en passion et avait redonné de la vigueur à ma vie. J'avais ouvert ma propre galerie à Port Jeff, un endroit où acheter les toiles de tout nouveaux talents et où exposer mes toiles de manière permanente. J'avais eu beaucoup de chance. Alors je pouvais largement nourrir les deux vingtenaires qui se retrouvaient chez moi jusqu'à ce que je trouve comment faire partir Parker sans qu'il emmène Kayla avec lui. Je voulais qu'elle reste.

J'avais chaud, et je me sentais bien. La chaleur de la journée faisait que mon tee-shirt me collait au corps, et penser à Kayla me donnait envie de me masturber. Je décidai d'aller nager maintenant que Parker était allé dans la salle de bains du chalet. Je ferais quelques longueurs pour me rafraîchir et essayer de me calmer avant le dîner, où je pourrais la revoir.

LIVRES DE JESSA JAMES

Mauvais Mecs Milliardaires

Du Bout des Lèvres

Un Accord Parfait

Touche du bois

Un vrai père

Le Club V

Dévoilée

Défaite

Percée à Jour

Le pacte des vierges

Le Professeur et la vierge

La nounou vierge

Le Cowboy

Comment aimer un cowboy

Livres supplémentaires

Supplie-Moi

À PROPOS DE TOUCHE DU BOIS

Il avait renoncé aux femmes… jusqu'à leur rencontre.

Jack a déménagé en Alaska pour y trouver la paix et le calme. Mais chaque semaine, la tentation arrive sous les traits d'Anna, belle, mais ombrageuse. Rien qu'en pensant à la manière dont elle manie le manche de son hydravion, il se demande comment elle le prendrait en main. Il a besoin de la sortir de son avion et de la mettre dans son lit.

Anna a des objectifs… et se jeter dans le lit d'un milliardaire sexy et mauvais genre au fin fond d'une forêt n'en fait pas partie. Elle ne veut pas tomber amoureuse d'un homme de la montagne. Elle veut s'enfuir. Elle en a marre des nuits froides, sombres et solitaires. Son rêve l'appelle, dans les états centraux des États-Unis. Son seul problème ? Jack. Quand une tempête la force à amerrir en urgence, les passions s'enflamment.

Être isolée dans les bois avec un apprenti bûcheron ne devrait pas être un problème. Ce n'est qu'une nuit. Pas vrai ?

BOOKS IN ENGLISH BY JESSA JAMES

Bad Boy Billionaires

Lip Service

Rock Me

Lumber Jacked

Baby Daddy

The Virgin Pact

The Teacher and the Virgin

His Virgin Nanny

His Dirty Virgin

Club V

Unravel

Undone

Uncover

Additional Titles

Beg Me

How to Love a Cowboy

Valentine Ever After

À PROPOS DE L'AUTEUR

Jessa James a grandi sur la Cote Est des États-Unis, mais a toujours souffert d'une terrible envie de voyager. Elle a vécu dans six états différents, a connu de nombreux métiers, mais est toujours revenue à son premier amour – l'écriture. Jessa travaille à temps plein comme écrivaine, mange beaucoup trop de chocolat noir, à une addiction aux Cheetos et au café frappé, et ne peut jamais se lasser des mâles alpha sexy qui savent exactement ce qu'ils veulent – et qui n'ont pas peur de le dire. Les coups de foudre avec des mâles alpha dominants restent son genre favori de nouvelles à lire (et à écrire).

Inscrivez-vous ICI pour recevoir la Newsletter de Jessa
http://ksapublishers.com/s/jessafrancais

www.jessajamesauthor.com

www.ingramcontent.com/pod-product-compliance
Lightning Source LLC
LaVergne TN
LVHW011840060526
838200LV00054B/4119